W9-BAG-691

Exhausted and overworked, he was called back for overtime on only a few hours' sleep. What else could go wrong...

Deacon watched the three males cautiously approach the vehicle. Sergeant Matthews gave the wire channel play by play over the TAC channel. "Muscles made the intro. Deal's going down. We got good dope talk. More dope talk. Still more dope talk. Damn, this guy won't shut up. What is he, a used car salesmen?"

Deacon snickered, wondering the same thing. A split second later, all humor fled. The marked unit had eased out from the side of Lowe's. "Edward 15, King 93. Stop moving. Do not proceed. Wait for the bust signal!" he snapped.

Deacon released the button on his radio's mic and Matthews barked, "Edward 15, Nora 10. Stand down. Follow orders! Stand down!" Deacon's gut knotted. Ice crept up his spine. He kept his binoculars trained on Bautista, who was scanning the parking lot. *Ah hell*. The gangbanger hadn't stopped his counter-surveillance. *Damn, he is good. Too good.* A second later, Bautista spotted the front end of the black and white Dodge Charger with its light bar. Deacon crushed down on his mic. "Edward 15's made."

Immediately, the wire's channel filled with accusations:

"You're a snitch!"

"Not me," Muscles said.

"Who's wearing a wire?" Bautista demanded.

"Not me. Not me," Muscles and Andrews said simultaneously.

"*Hijo de puta,*" a goon said.

The OP had gone south and was heading to shit—fast. Deacon wasn't waiting for shots fired. He dropped his binoculars.

"You set me up, you piece of shit. You're dead," Bautista snarled.

The radio buzzed. In his ear, Deacon heard, "Move, move! Go, go, go!"

After working a graveyard shift, K9 Officer Daniel Deacon gets an unwelcome call ordering him back to work. Deacon and his K9 partner, a German Shepherd named Justice, return for a long overtime swing shift in the heat of Central Valley, California. When an undercover drug sting goes south and the manager of the local electronics big-box store, Jessica Grady, discovers that she has a serious theft problem, Deacon and Justice are pulled into a dangerous web of deception, betrayal, and murder. Exhausted from the long hours and lack of sleep, Deacon chases and shoots a suspect—who was about to kill Jessica—only to discover he has just shot the wife of the local drug lord. Although he had no choice, his actions have put him, Justice, and Jessica on a deadly assassin's hit list.

KUDOS for *Savage Justice*

In *Savage Justice* by Dustin Dodd, Daniel Deacon is a K9 cop in Cain, California, with his partner, Justice, a German Shepherd. Deacon and Justice are working a lot of overtime due to staff shortages. Low on sleep, exhausted, and not functioning at an optimum level, they take part in an undercover op that goes south. The drug dealer they are targeting makes them before their sting goes down and he gets away, leaving five kilos of coke behind. The gangbanger's supplier is not happy and gives the dealer one mouth to come up with the 200 thousand he owes for the confiscated drugs. The drug lord sends his wife to babysit the dealer until the debt is paid, and thing just go downhill from there. The book is well written with a strong, well-thought-out plot, believable characters, and enough tension to keep you on the edge of your seat. ~ *Taylor Jones, Reviewer*

Savage Justice is the story of Deacon, a K9 cop in California and his German shepherd partner, Justice. Together the two fight drug dealers and other bad guys. But when Deacon shoot and kills a drug lord's wife, he and Justice end up on an assassin's hit list. I love the glimpse we are given of life with a canine partner—the slobber all over the computer, the potty accidents when the dog has to wait in the car too long—because, no matter how well trained the canine partner is, a dog is still a dog. *Savage Justice* will keep you turning pages from beginning to end. Based on Dodd's real life experiences as a K9 cop, the story is a solid, entertaining, and exciting read. ~ *Regan Murphy, Reviewer*

ACKNOWLEDGEMENTS

I wish to personally thank the following people for their contributions and other help in creating this book: Linda Campbell, Lauri Wellington, Faith, and the staff of Black Opal Books. Thank you for giving me a shot.

Savage

Justice

Dustin Dodd

A Black Opal Books Publication

GENRE: MYSTERY-DETECTIVE/THRILLER/ROMANTIC ELEMENTS

SAVAGE JUSTICE
Copyright © 2016 by Dustin Dodd
Cover Design by Jackson Cover Designs
All cover art copyright © 2016
All Rights Reserved
Print ISBN: 978-1-626944-24-4

First Publication: FEBRUARY 2016

Published by Black Opal Books **http://www.blackopalbooks.com**

DEDICATION

To Beautiful, whose patience with my endless projects makes even the angels jealous. I couldn't have done this, or anything else in this world, without you.

To the men who pulled me out of so many jams over the years and helped to inspire this book. Our friendship and exploits will live forever.

To Kota, my partner. Your loyalty and selflessness were unparalleled. You gave me everything you had until the very end. I didn't deserve you. You are missed.

Glossary of Terms

10-15: Suspect in custody

11-44: Deceased party

11-99: Officer in emergency, send all units

AFIS: Automated fingerprint identification system

APC: Armored personnel carrier

CAFIS: California automated fingerprint identification system

CCTV: Closed circuit television

CI: Confidential informant

Code Three: Driving with lights and siren activated

Code Four: Situation is secure

CPR: Cardio pulmonary resuscitation

DA :District attorney

DVR: Digital video recorder

EMS: Emergency medical services

EMT: Emergency medical technician

EOD: Explosive ordnance disposal

ETA: Estimated time of arrival

FLIR: Forward looking infrared radiometer

HMA: Hispanic male adult

K9: Canine

LED: Light-emitting diode

Leg bail: Suspect fleeing on foot

MRAP: Mine resistant ambush protected vehicle

OIS: Officer-involved shooting

OP: Short for operation or mission

Pied: Tactically turn a corner, paying careful attention to all angles rotating on a focal point similar to a slice of pie

SAC: Special agent in charge (FBI)

SOP: Standard operating procedure

SWAT: Special weapons and tactics

TC: Traffic collision

UC: Undercover officer

CHAPTER 1

Alejandro Bautista checked his watch. *Shit, two forty-five.* He was going to be late. He swore at himself again for not leaving sooner. It was always a good idea to be on time when getting multiple kilos of crank from your supplier. It was not only bad for business, but also bad for one's health.

People had died for less, he thought, flooring the accelerator. His white Honda Civic lurched forward. The mighty four-cylinder engine immediately jumped to six thousand RPM as it accelerated from sixty-five to sixty-seven miles per hour.

He was furious at himself for not having stolen something with more horsepower. He inhaled with a shudder. He was screwed. Still, being late was better than a no show. That would really piss Tuefel off.

Teeth gritted, Bautista exited the highway onto Vista de su Muerto road. *View of Your Death. Nice.* Hauling way too much ass as he took the corner, his car went into a skid. The wheels slid, kicking up gravel. Tiny crumbles of granite skipped off the shoulder and down into a one hundred foot ravine. He kept the accelerator smashed against the floor. He fishtailed once, then the tires regained traction.

As he drove up the winding pass, the foothills yielded to

their mountainous big brothers. The towering behemoths of the Sierra Nevada Mountains rose before him, snowcapped from their shoulders to their crests. At this elevation, gnarled oaks began to intermingle with pine and redwood, weaving a dense network of forest with sunlight scattering shadows of the old giants across the Civic.

While the air was fresh, the lack of smog worried him. He didn't trust air he couldn't see.

After several minutes, he came upon the camouflaged access road. Shaking his head, he admitted Tuefel did a helluva job hiding the road. Even looking for it, Bautista had nearly missed it. He slammed his breaks, threw the car into reverse, and pulled over.

He threw open the door and bolted from his smoking excuse of a car. He raced over to a pile of debris and brush, shoving his arm beneath the foliage. Finding the chain link fence gate concealed underneath, he dragged the fence back enough to get his car through.

With a grimace, he eased the car through the newly formed opening on the side of the mountain. After clearing the fence line, he pulled the hidden gate shut, ensuring no unwanted guests crashed the party.

Ten minutes later, he stopped at the top of the embankment that overlooked the lab entrance as an armed man flagged him down. At six feet and two hundred fifty pounds, Bautista had never felt like a small man. But this one made him feel as if he should go back to the farm and finish growing up.

Before getting out of the car, he locked his pistol in the glove compartment. He couldn't risk being found with a gun during the pat down. If he was, he'd receive a bullet in the head for his trouble.

The bookend approached the driver's door. While he had been here over a dozen times and the two of them had met on several occasions, the man was emotionless as rock and seemed to lack a soul.

Bautista froze at the H&K MP5 pointed at his face, the

barrel looking like a cannon. Damn, by now, one would think it was overkill.

Looking past the barrel and at the face of the man, Bautista rolled down his window. The stench of hair spray hit him like a sledge hammer. Someday, someone would strike a match.

His gaze narrowed on the watchdog. The man wore mirrored aviator style sunglasses. He looked like he was straight out of the '80s or a movie, maybe *Top Gun*.

Nice touch, Maverick. Under other circumstances, say those where he wasn't holding a submachine gun, Bautista might have asked if he had permission to do a flyby.

But not today. Today, the man holding an automatic weapon was the one who got the privilege of cracking the jokes and slinging the insults.

"You're late."

"No shit. I'll tell the man I'm sorry myself. Traffic was a bitch and I got a flat."

The toothpick in his mouth rolled to the opposite side. "I don't care. Mr. Tuefel's waiting. Park your shit and get down there, yesterday."

"You mind lowering the heat and getting the hell out of the way so I can get down there?"

The guard returned a look as cold as ice and stepped aside.

Bautista put the car in gear. With Maverick on his tail, he drove down to the entrance and main loading area for the lab.

He parked beside the loading dock. The dock was a slab of granite at the mouth of a natural cave. The cave itself was fairly wide and deep, which made it the perfect location for a methamphetamine lab.

When it came to drug cartels doing business in the Sierras, they adopted the al Queda playbook—get underground. The advantages were plentiful. Random law enforcement fly-overs could not see through solid rock. Bodies were easily dispatched at the end of the cavern. All very convenient.

Slowly, Bautista opened his door. A soft, pine-scented breeze buffeted him. Mountain air always calmed him. He stepped out of his car and took in the view.

Peering into the lab, he saw glass beakers and various cooking supplies hooked up to the gas piping vents. Along the opposite side stood a growing pallet of neatly pilled white bricks. The only man operating the cooker seemed to be taking inventory of the pallet. From his days as a Coyote, Bautista recognized his type—an illegal smuggled across the border to do one thing—cook meth. When the job was completed, the illegal would be rewarded for his services by Tuefel's wife Rachele. He'd join his predecessors in the ravine at the end of the cavern.

Known for a few trademarks, Ubel Tuefel ran his small crew with an iron fist. Whereas, a six-inch knife to the base of the skull was Rachele's trademark. Few people survived the two. It was all about profit and fewer people to sell them out.

It always surprised Bautista that, after she'd disposed of the body, Tuefel would send his goon to the border to get another couple chefs for the next cook and no one asked questions. Bautista thought the whole operation was both brilliant and crazy. He also knew the big man would never turn on the two. The knuckle dragger had neither the brains nor the firepower to pull it off.

A large hand grabbed him by the back of the neck. *Damn dude not so hard.*

"Thank you, Luis, for hurrying Alejandro along. I was growing impatient. In fact, I'd started to think our friend here had backed out of our agreement." Tuefel reached out and grasped the back of Bautista's neck and squeezed.

Bautista's blood ran cold. "No, sir. I had a flat on the way up."

At Tuefel's cold, lifeless laugh, Bautista involuntarily tensed. If he'd been a dog, his hackles would have risen.

Tuefel sneered. "Only you would have that kind of luck."

They walked over to the pallet, his vice grip still on the back of Bautista's neck. "Look at it. Isn't it beautiful? This batch will be finished in a couple of hours."

Bautista spotted Rachele staring at the cook with a look that was part glee, part lust, and all evil.

Tuefel followed Bautista's gaze to his wife. "Too bad for him, he just finished his job."

Swallowing hard, Bautista watched Rachele amble over to the unfortunate man. Smiling, she put left arm around his shoulders as she fingered the ivory handle of the blade on her hip with her right hand.

"Yes, it is." He was willing to agree to anything to get the hell out of there.

Alive.

Tuefel cleared his throat. "Now, how many kilos did we discuss?"

"Five, sir."

"I'm impressed. That's your biggest order to date, Alejandro. Is your man good for it?"

He'd better be. "Yes. He's hooked up and dealing this shit in all the high schools. Plus, I'm going to cut it a bit to milk him for more money."

"That's a good idea. Oh, and I expect my $200,000 immediately."

"I'll have it. I won't let you down."

At the pallets, the grip on Bautista's neck was released. Ignoring the stiffness in his shoulders, he selected five neatly wrapped kilos and headed for his vehicle. A moment later, he struggled to open the door, nearly dropping the merchandise.

Once he popped open the trunk, he stashed the five bricks on its floor.

After he'd secured the product, he glanced behind him. At the entrance to the cave, like Lucifer at the mouth of hell, Tuefel stood motionless, watching Bautista's every move and Bautista realized he'd worn out his welcome.

Time to go!

With a nod, he slid behind the steering wheel. As he punched his screwdriver into the ignition, he jerked at the sound of rocks and the echo of something heavy crashing down the ravine in the canyon.

Fighting the urge to floor the accelerator and haul ass out of there, he focused on the trail and slowly drove his smoking car toward the gate.

CHAPTER 2

Deacon had never been so happy to be off-duty. Heat exhaustion and unrelenting boredom did not a happy camper make. Even Justice was antsy. The most excitement they'd had was at the beginning of his shift, when they had pulled over a car filled with drunken teens. Well, excitement for Justice, not so much for him.

God, he hated when drunks hurled all over his last clean uniform. Damn it! If he didn't go to the dry-cleaners, he'd be forced to wear a well-seasoned one tomorrow. Even he wouldn't do that. He wanted to keep his job and friends. That meant only one thing. He had to get his ass in gear earlier, switch out his dirty uniforms for clean, and be wearing one.

"If don't, I'll probably be written up for not maintaining a professional image," he muttered.

Some days, he questioned why he hadn't gone into another line of work. Ah, hell, he knew why. Because, even at eighteen, he recognized that being a good but not great at sports didn't put you in the money. But on hot, dry days like today, he longed for the surf and the beach.

Turning off the primary road, he entered his subdivision and made an almost immediate left into their cul-de-sac. "We're almost home, buddy."

Cookie-cutter houses lined street. Four different models were sprinkled throughout the neighborhood, along with varying-colored stucco, which provided enough variety to prevent monotony. While some people couldn't stand track homes, he didn't mind them. He found the similarities in design to be oddly comforting.

Half a block in from the main artery leading to his neighborhood, he spun the car along the curb and stopped. He always parked beside the little greenbelt path alongside his house. The first thing he wanted someone to see when they walked into his subdivision was a black and white K9 unit. He'd laughed when his father had told him that it looked like he was marking his territory.

He glanced at the three-bedroom, two-bath building— his first house—and smiled. He'd had it built a little over a two years before the California housing market crashed. And he didn't regret buying it, not with the market now in recovery.

He hit his dash mounted door pop. Justice sprang from the car. Poor guy. After an evening of being in the rear cage, he was more than eager to play or work. Do anything really. He ran circles around the car, as if urging Deacon to hurry up and get the lead out.

The dog ran right up to his master's left knee and sat, whining at the top of his lungs. With eyes piercing Deacon's soul and a tail sweeping the asphalt, he knew he had no choice. *I'll sleep when I'm dead.* "All right. All right. Let's get some quick obedience in. But we go to bed before the sun comes up."

Justice responded with a loud bark as Deacon pulled his six foot lead from his cargo pocket on his left side and clamped the latch onto Justice's D-ring collar.

They spent the next fifteen minutes walking the neighborhood on and off lead. Obedience training at home was a mandatory daily detail. At every official training session, other handlers in the unit complained about it being boring and time consuming. Whereas Deacon enjoyed this time alone with his partner. It was what made them a great team.

And after spending nearly an hour cleaning some drunken asshole's puke off of his pants, it would allow his mind to settle and Justice to burn off his pent-up energy.

Obedience complete, they entered their backyard via the side gate. Justice ran straight into his open kennel. He knew what was coming next in their nightly ritual. A ridiculously large puddle of drool gathered like a lake against a dam. Deacon opened the plastic garbage can, scooped out nearly three cups of high-protein dog food, and poured it into Justice's bowl. The pooch nearly inhaled it. "This stuff's like jet fuel in a Corvette," Deacon muttered, giving his partner one last scratch behind the ears, and was rewarded with a kibble-encrusted kiss. With one last look to ensure Justice's automatic water bowl was turned on, Deacon locked the kennel, walked through his back door, and entered the kitchen.

As he scanned his front room, he sighed. Oblivious to interior design, his house was filled with a hodge-podge of nautical crap, enough to sink a ship. He had spent the better part of the first year buying pieces for each of the rooms. Wherever he went, as long as it related to boats or the ocean, he had bought it.

Some of things, like the old trunk for a coffee table, were great additions. Others, like the handcrafted boat on the entertainment center with its tiny man bent over the railing relieving himself, weren't. It was a total bachelor pad in desperate need of a woman's touch.

Heading into the master bath, he stripped. Years of working out religiously, coupled with his recent stint in hitting the department gym, had sculpted him into the best shape of his life. For the prior three months, he had been at it twice a day to prepare for SWAT and Explosive Ordnance Disposal testing.

It was a good thing, too. He'd need to be able to run the SWAT assault course and wear a hundred plus pound bomb suit for the EOD test. Both tests were coming up in a couple of weeks, and he was determined to prove his worth.

Deacon's eyes widened. Crap. He'd stood before the mirror like some narcissist while thinking about the tests. After a brief moment of vanity and embarrassment, he jumped into the cold shower and washed off the stink of some kid's drunken debauchery. Hot water would only awaken that demon and ruin what was left of his night. After several minutes of freezing torture, he twisted the valve, killing the liquid ice. Then he lathered up and rinsed off in warmth. He quickly dried off and threw his uniform into the washer before crawling, naked, into bed.

ℰↄℰↄ

Unending ringing shattered Deacon's dream. Swimming his way back to consciousness, he peeled his face off his drool-encrusted pillow and glared at the phone on his nightstand. The phone number displayed by the caller ID belonged to the City of Cain. *Great. Just great.*

He glanced at the bedside clock's large digital display. *What the hell?* Shit, the sun had barely cracked the sky and he'd only gotten two hours of sleep. What did they want now?

Eyes burning, he blinked as he rooted for the phone like a drunken monkey. Finally getting it to his ear, he growled, "Someone'd better be dead."

"It's Sergeant Munoz. Today's your lucky day. You've been officially ordered to work the swing shift."

"Thanks."

"Be here by 1130 hours."

"Copy that, 1130 hours for mid-day swing." Scowling, Deacon disconnected the call. Damn, he'd gotten ordered in again. It was past time the city cancelled the freeze on hiring.

Every time he'd asked why he'd been ordered in, he didn't get a straight answer. The bullshit reasons changed but they all had the same result—he went to work. Not that the reason given mattered. He knew the truth and it was crap. Someone near retirement wanted an extra day off or someone in the *Good 'Ol Boy Network* was gone for the day on some bullshit project they hoped would justify a promotion.

No one seemed to care that the frequent orders back to work extra shifts left him and other officers fatigued—that the broken sleep they suffered from had started to take its toll. That they fell ill more frequently. And now, even going to sleep proved more difficult, not to mention he'd become so irritable he could be called on the carpet for being losing this temper. Luckily, it hadn't happened with the public or a supervisor. Yet.

Sighing, he rolled out of bed and stumbled into the utility room. He threw his uniform into the dryer. His feet followed his bloodshot eyes back to his bathroom and into the shower. He opened the valve and liquid ice beat down on his body. With a shiver, he slumped down on the shower floor. The frigid water helped him shake off the last remaining cobwebs of sleep clinging to his eyes and mind. After several minutes of self-inflicted torture, he reached up and shut off the needles spewing from the shower head.

Quickly dressing in his freshly laundered patrol K9 uniform, he made his way to his garage. He unlocked the cabinet where he stored his gear and performed an immediate inventory. Satisfied that all of his equipment was operationally ready, he strapped on his load-bearing vest which contained his ballistic armor within its carrier panels. Then he grabbed a tactical light off the shelf and screwed it onto the undercarriage of his Glock pistol. Performing a press check on the slide of the weapon confirmed a round was chambered. Finally, he locked his pistol into his holster on the thigh rig strapped to his right quadriceps and exited his house.

The heat hit him in the face. *Cold front coming in, my ass.* He glanced skyward and winced. Spread out in a skirmish line, even the clouds looked dehydrated, searching desperately for something to drink. Shaking his head, he checked the forecast on his smart phone. The app's weather forecast called for heavy rain, too. From the way the day was starting to shape up, Deacon doubted it was in the cards, even if the clouds wanted to cry. Even the beading sweat on his brow declared its agreement.

He slid behind the steering wheel. His head dropped back onto the headrest and he released a long sigh. It looked to be a long-ass day. It was definitely too early for a grave-yard dog to be awake. All he needed to burst into flames was sunlight, holy water in the face, or a garlic necklace.

As he started his patrol car, from the side of his house, Justice began barking in protest.

Crap. Smooth move, Deacon. Nothing like leaving your partner behind.

A minute later, he opened the fence gate. The dog clawed at the door of his kennel in a mad attempt to not be left behind. "Sorry, buddy." Walking through the gate, he hurried to open the kennel before the boy destroyed it. The door burst open and slammed into the wall. Justice flew from his den and sprinted to the patrol car.

Deacon quickly hit his door pop and barely managed to avoid a collision as the massive dog bounded into the back. Laughing, he shook his head, remembering the first few times when their timing had been off and Justice had gotten his bell rung by the opening door panel. God, he loved that dog. And the feeling was mutual. Thankfully, the beast loved to work. Given the duty hours they'd been pulling, it was good thing, too, he thought, sliding behind the wheel.

CHAPTER 3

I t was taking Deacon longer than usual to get to work, which given the hour had surprised him. But he'd gotten stuck behind a blue Chevy Cobalt, and the genius operating it had stayed twenty below the speed limit. If he hadn't known better, Deacon would swear she was driving by Braille. She car-danced, bouncing and bee-bopping within her lane of traffic, and over-corrected every time her tires hit the lane makers. Worse, she was a teenager driver.

With its bass thumping through his patrol car, he frowned. Shit. How high had she cranked up the radio? The longer it continued, the more he wondered what she was rocking out to. Most likely the latest bubble gum boy band topping the charts. He rolled his window down and recognized the artist immediately.

Oh, God, not that asshole. That spoiled brat really needed to take a long walk off the map. So did the fad with those emo haircuts. It was as if the entire industry decided to declare that it was no longer about talent, but was now who had the best marketing plan.

Fed up, he closed the gap between them to an unsafe distance. Any closer and he would have lock bumpers. Grimacing, he watched as she sang her heart out, using either a hairbrush or cellphone for a microphone.

Finally, he moved right on top of her, hoping she'd see his car on her ass and either pull over or accelerate to the speed limit.

She did something different, all right. She ditched the microphone, replaced it with a pair of imaginary drumsticks, and started to wail away on her wheel.

Disgusted, Deacon hit his light bar and lit her up. He didn't call in the stop to dispatch. He should've, but this particular warning would only take a second. There was no change from the driver, save for a more vigorous drum solo. Teeth clenched, he hit the siren. No reaction. None, nada, zip. *What's it going to take—a bullhorn?*

Five miles later, the *American-Idol*-wannabe-turned-drummer realized he was behind her and pulled over onto the shoulder.

Dust swirled around their cars as they skidded to a halt. Patience all but gone, Deacon pulled up the car's plates on his computer, got her name from the DMV, and exited his patrol car. Justice violently voiced his opinion at being left.

Heat reflecting off the gravel gave it a soothing crunch beneath Deacon's feet. Taking a deep breath, he attempted to recapture his calm. The last thing he needed was an internal affairs investigation or complaint over saying something stupid. It'd kill any chance of getting into SWAT or EOD where absolute control was critical.

Not wanting to be exposed to passing cars, he approached from the passenger side of her vehicle and saw her staring out her driver's side mirror and looking for him. One look at her face and Deacon smiled. She was terrified. Her hands were shaking so badly the steering wheel quaked.

About time.

Biting back a snicker, he knocked on her passenger side door window.

She jumped.

He knocked again.

She glanced to her right, then hit the power button and lowered the window.

"Good afternoon, Miss Sally Henderson."

"Hello, I—wait, how did you know my name?"

"I know you're scared. Don't be. I'm not asking for your license or citing you. However, I'm begging you to, please, for the love of God, retire your hairbrush microphone and imaginary drumsticks. Quit rocking out to your radio. Pay attention to the road. Drive your car."

"You saw that?"

He ignored her blush. "What do you think initially got my attention?"

"My singing?"

"No. Driving twenty below the speed limit. You're aware that you can get a ticket for going too slow, right?"

She nodded with a sniffle.

"And at that speed, you could've caused an accident, right?" At her teary-eyed nod, he continued, "And yeah, I saw the whole nine yards. The singing and the drum solo are what we call a clue in my line of work."

The shaking intensified. She hung her head. "I—I—"

"What worried me most was when I drove almost right on top of you with lights on and you didn't notice. Not even after I've turned on my siren. Even then, you continued rocking out so hard it took another five miles before you realized I was pulling you over."

"Oh, God."

"No, I'm not Him. But unless you want an express ticket to go see Him, drive safely. If you don't, you might find yourself on a one way trip to see the Almighty Rocker Himself."

"Thank you, thank you. I will, I promise. And I'm so sorry."

"Just remember, drive safe, okay?"

"I will."

Justice continued his protest as Deacon returned to the patrol car. Once in his air-conditioned sanctuary, he saw that dog spit now covered the car's computer screen and keyboard.

"Easy, buddy, easy. Calm down!" No luck. He looked over his right shoulder. "Hey!" The dog stopped mid bark. "Thank you. It was just some kid, okay? Look, I'm back in one piece, buddy. I'm fine."

The dog stared at him for a moment. Then after giving him the once over, just to be sure, he turned to look out the window where, no doubt, the thousand smells outside were more interesting.

With a snort, Deacon got a baby wipe from the container behind the seat. He'd learned long ago to keep them on hand for just such an occasion. After wiping down his computer, he put the car in gear and drove off, the tires chewing gravel and throwing it all over the shoulder.

∽∽∽

Deacon pulled up to the back lot gate of the station and entered his code. The locking mechanism hummed. The light turned green. He heard the familiar beep of his code being accepted.

He always felt relief that his code still worked. A working code meant he still had a job. Everyone was antsy. The city was pressed financially, and the cops all wondered who was going to lose their job next. Just last week, one of his buddies had entered his code only to find it did not work. After several failed attempts, he freaked out, positive he was locked out because he'd been fired. He eventually called in to dispatch and they opened the gate for him.

Later, several of the guys in briefing told him that the code boxes were down. Talk about pissed, yet grateful. Deacon snickered remembering the look on his friend's face when he'd learned the boxes were down. It had been priceless. It was still an ongoing joke at the department. One his buddy would not live down for some time.

Deacon stared at the gate waiting for it to open. The bright crimson gate was made of cast iron bars. Hard to miss, yet somehow several people found ways to hit the damn thing with their patrol cars—repeatedly—over the years.

He didn't get it.

The gate bore a sign on it depicting a stick figure getting smashed in between the gate and the brick pillars that the gate rested against when closed. A sign like that only meant one thing. Some moron had gotten stuck when it closed and sued, claiming that they wouldn't have been caught if the city had put up a warning sign.

Drumming his fingers on the wheel, he waited. At less than a mile per hour to open and close, it took longer than his temper could handle today. Finally, the gate fully opened. Deacon pulled in and parked. Getting out of his car, he hit his belt door pop. No Justice. Deacon rounded the rear of his car and found his partner lying on his back with limp paws up in the air—snoring—still inside the back. Laughing, Deacon shook his head. His partner was funnier than any comedian he had seen. "You're one helluva clown."

Shutting the patrol car pop door, he cracked open a window and headed inside for the shift briefing. Unlike other stations, his had warm, inviting hardwood floors. They were also really easy to clean. Reminders of department training for all sworn personnel next Thursday, with instructions to bring all assigned weapons for qualification, covered the wall. A functional waterfall, that was never turned on, bore a large badge which was polished to a fine shine. At least it gave the department a place for photo-ops when holding award ceremonies and swearing-in new officers.

Their briefing room was state of the art with several forty-two-inch 4K HD TVs mounted to the walls. No one knew where the money came from to buy them. Every time Deacon asked, he was told, "The Building Fund." Yeah, right. Try the personnel budget. That would certainly explain the hiring freeze.

With a mental shake, Deacon examined the call screen

and all relevant calls for service information. It showed calls for service and the patrol units assigned, where the units were presently, and calls pending or on hold. Currently the screen was green. All units were available, no calls holding. No calls meant that the day would likely be slow and long. It'd be a fight to stay awake with nothing to do.

He paused. Damn, the briefing had started on time. Gridding himself, he entered in the room. Being late came with a cost. He was about to be roasted over the coals by the veterans. Before he could even sit down, the cat calls from the assholes began.

"They gave you keys to a car? Are you old enough to drive?"

"What size shirt you wear? Coming in this late, I'll buy your uni off of you when they give you the boot."

"Boy, I've got underwear older than you."

Deacon shot them a half-smile-half-eat-shit-look. Knowing more shots were being readied, he stood, removed a twenty from his wallet, and threw it down in front of the officer who'd made the last comment. "If you've got underwear that's twenty-eight years old, then you're in serious need of some new pairs."

They were the same stupid-ass jokes from same guys who were old enough to be his father. Nothing had changed since he'd started working with these morons seven years prior. That he'd been the youngest guy ever hired, barely twenty-one at that time, didn't help. Talk about being out of his depth. He'd been investigating check fraud at a time when he'd only had a personal checking account for three years. Hell, on occasion, he still wondered how he'd gotten this job.

When the briefing ended, Deacon stood and left to a "Go get 'em tiger" and laughter following him out into the hallway. He paused and rubbed the bridge of his nose. He would have to add that nickname to the long list of stupid nicknames he received over the years. *It'll likely only take a week or two to die out.*

Yawning, he stretched and strode over to the Investigations Division which housed General Investigations and its seven investigators, a corporal, and a sergeant. Gangs had two investigators, a corporal, and a sergeant and Narcotics rounded out the division with three investigators and a sergeant.

Severely understaffed, each division could barely function. All in all, there were too few detectives for a town of over 100,000. He passed the empty narcs desks. It looked like they were still in bed from the previous night's festivities. Lucky them.

An Airsoft pellet bounced off a nearby cubicle and hit him. "What the hell?" Rubbing his ear, he immediately dove behind cover and made himself as small a target as possible. Several more rounds flew over his head.

"Cease fire! What the hell?"

Laughter erupted all over Investigations. Apparently, he'd once again walked into the middle of another friendly Airsoft firefight between the detectives.

"Yo, Deacon!" Detective Jack White stood, gathered his things, and got ready to head out.

Deacon's gaze honed in on White's SWAT ballistic glasses, which he wore to prevent taking a stray Airsoft round in the eyes. Nothing like having to need eye protection when typing reports. Deacon shook his head. Shirt, tie, slacks, and ballistic glasses—damned if White didn't look as if he belonged in an office with a Silicon Valley microchip company.

Running the gauntlet of cubicles, White tried to avoid the incoming hail of bullets. He survived and hooked up with Deacon beside the secretary's desk. "Hey, brother, you got a second?"

"Sure." Deacon grinned at White. They had been in a lot of shit together, including multiple Airsoft wars. The man had grown up at the department with Deacon and was one slot above him in seniority.

Hearing an incoming round, they ducked. It ricocheted off a computer monitor on the desk.

"I'm heading out to do some follow up. Let's get out of here before we're casualties suffering head wounds."

"Not funny."

"Not joking."

Without a backward glance, they bent low and darted out of Investigations. Once clear, they headed for the back parking lot.

"So what's up, big guy?" Deacon asked.

"I'm in Hell."

"What?"

"I've been dealing with another jurisdiction's detective. You remember the home invasions from last week?"

"We're talking about the one where they're tying up some seniors for their gold?" At White's nod, Deacon asked, "You ID the suspects?"

White nodded again. "Yeah. I had our victims look at ten photo lineups. They've positively IDd several of the suspects."

"That's great!"

"You'd think. But they're the same suspects in the other detective's cases of home invasion. Which is why I'm stuck in Hell, working with this asshole. I'm tellin' you, Deacon, the guy's a freaking moron. He couldn't figure out Blue's Clues."

Deacon recognized the name only because White talked about it. As the father of five, he watched it with his youngest kids. Afterward, he'd grouse to anyone who would listen about the ease with which Blue solved puzzles. "Isn't that the kid's show where the blue dog finds clues and solves—"

"Riddles and puzzles, yeah."

Deacon snickered at his look of frustration. "You're kidding, right?"

"I wish. During an interrogation of a suspect, the sonuvabitch interrupted a confession. A freaking confession! Can you believe it? Then he told the suspect he was full of shit. He even demonstrated the level of bullshit with his 'bullshit meter.'"

Deacon howled. "His *what*?" he asked between gasps.

"You heard me. I swear, the dude raised his left arm, parallel to the ground like this." White stretched out his right arm perpendicular to his left.

Deacon's eyes widened. "You're sure this guy's a detective?"

"Unfortunately. He's lucky to be alive."

"Why?"

"I almost killed him. It's a miracle I got a confession out of the suspect. If I hadn't, both cases would've been screwed."

"Unbelievable."

They walked down the hallway, Deacon's boots and White's dress shoes, sounding like a squad of storm troopers on the hardwood. White opened the door to the rear parking lot and, with his palm up, motioned Deacon through. "Ladies first."

"Ass."

"So why're you here? You worked last night."

Deacon grunted. "Got ordered in. My guess is someone put in for a day off and was denied, so they called in sick."

"At least the check will be nice when it shows up."

"As long as it doesn't bounce, my brother."

Grinning, they bumped fists. "Ain't that the truth. But if they stop payin', we stop coming. Hey, if you need anything, call me. I'll see what I can do."

"I'm fatigued, but that's what coffee's for. What's the worst that'll happen? Swings is a quick-paced shift, right? Don't worry, brother. I'm good, and mids'll be out soon enough to cover us."

"Famous last words. All right, man. I gotta go. Call me if there's a problem."

"I'll be sure to call you when I get into a shooting."

"Right. Take care, and have a good one."

"You, too."

"Oh, and, Deacon?"

Deacon pivoted and faced his friend. "Yeah?"

"Don't get into any shootings, okay?"

"No promises. But I'll try."

CHAPTER 4

Deacon grinned at how the day had turned out. It had gone from numbingly dull to him being stationed on the roof of the Lowe's shopping center. He peered through his binoculars and scanned the parking lot below as he listened to two radio channels—the tactical radio channel and a wire radio. His ability to keep the two conversations straight was more than an acquired skill. It was art. He was also grateful that the team used the TAC radio. It kept traffic stops, calls for service, radio ten-code, and the other mundane chatter on another channel, enabling him to focus on the operation and the undercover officer in the car with his CI.

Given his God's-eye view of the lot, Deacon's frustration at being placed atop the roof road him hard. He should've been on the ground with Justice. Had he been positioned anywhere else, they could have assisted in the take down. Instead, Justice sat in his patrol car behind Lowe's, the perfect location to be completely useless. However, if things went to shit, the powers that be worried that the odds of Justice biting the UC cop were high.

Deep down, Deacon knew it was the right call, but it didn't make the pill any easier to swallow. At least he didn't have to cut paper for this. For that he was thankful.

Let the rookies write the reports.

It was always fun to play when the paper belonged to someone else.

The night was clear. Unfortunately, it had also grown unseasonably cool and each exhale was visible as a thick cloud. *Damn weatherman looked to be right after all.* He hoped the weather didn't screw the op. But it might. A cold front was moving in. The latest weather report predicted there would be a major storm. He frowned, realizing he'd become distracted by the clouds forming on the horizon to the west. Suddenly, his partner's wire picked up.

"Mute count in five...four...three...two...one..."

∂∞∂

Narcotics Detective Chad Andrews killed his car radio. He glanced at himself in the rearview mirror of his white Nissan Sentra and shook his head. He almost didn't recognize himself. *What a tool.* He was definitely a long way from his days as the starting quarterback at the local high school. *Toto, I've a feeling we're not in Kansas anymore.*

Putting on his game-face, he did his best to match the facade reflected back at him. In his black Fresno State beanie, dark red Bulldog's jersey, and looking oddly similar to the lead singer from the Foo Fighters, no one would take him for a cop. No way, not when he looked like some of his former friends who had given up having a football career and had gone pro on pain killers.

Seated beside him was his confidential informant whom they had recently busted for possession of meth for sale. The CI was here because he'd sworn he could work off his sales charge. Andrews slanted a gaze at his CI. He referred to him as "Muscles" because of his new-found desire to lift weights and "get clean." And here he sat, dressed like a thug in a piece of shit car, all because Muscles had arranged for them to buy a large quantity of meth from his supplier, one Alejandro Bautista.

According to Andrews's solid intelligence, Bautista was a middle-sized fish in a big pond. He had also been the thorn in the side of the narcotics division for quite a while. Several CIs described Bautista as a connected dealer who had done a stint in prison and was likely the main player in the area, dealing all over town. Yet none of them had been able to buy any major quantity of meth from him until now. Most of them only knew him as Bautista or by some other stupid-ass street name.

That was a constant problem when forced to use CIs, which meant cops dealt with crooks, knowing the clowns wouldn't give you a straight answer. It was always "some guy" they knew or "Little Big Mac," "Pokey," or "Ray, Ray." No one knew anyone by their given name. But Muscles had promised to deliver and, by deliver, he meant kilos of the stuff. "I'll get you the good shit, Andrews. Bricks of that shit, man."

Andrews had told him it was either that or prison. It really didn't prove a tough decision for Muscles.

To his credit, Bautista's style was another reason why he hadn't been caught. He never did any of the deals himself. Through arms-length deals, the drugs were delivered to the dealers who handle the customer sales. Yet when Muscles guaranteed he could arrange for Bautista to show in the flesh, Andrews snapped at it, refusing to lose this golden opportunity.

It was his, and the Department's, best shot to get this sonuvabitch off the street. Not that it would stop the meth trade, as another "Bautista" would eventually rise up and take his place. Nonetheless, a lot rode on the word of his teenage punk-kid-CI-turned-poser-jock.

"You're sure he will be here, right? I'll be royally pissed if we did all this for a no-show."

"He'll be here, Andrews. I swear. Bautista's always late, but he's good for it." With that, Muscles's cell phone beeped. He checked his text message. "He'll be here in five minutes. He is bringin' five kilos of the shit."

Tucking his chin to his chest, Andrews spoke into his wire mic. "We got the good wire. Here's hoping you guys copy everything."

Another detective, Kirk Williams sat in an unmarked car a few cars away. "Confirm he said five kilos?"

"Affirm."

"Copy that."

⁙⁙⁙

Hearing the exchange between Williams and Andrews, Deacon's gaze skittered over the lot as he examined it. A small smile played at the corners of his lips. There was enough holiday traffic that the four undercover cars blended in. Each contained two-man teams primed for the high-risk take down. They were parked a couple of stalls from Andrews' car, yet able to maintain a visual on him and ready to bring the rain if things went to shit. The takedown should be a simple vehicle assault with overwhelming force. Surprise. Speed. Aggression. Tactically rush the car, arrest Bautista and whoever had come with him. They'd also arrest both Andrews and Muscles, though those arrests would be only for show, to prevent blowing their covers.

On the upside, with everyone handcuffed and thrown in the back of a police cruiser, it was unlikely Bautista would make Muscles as the guy who had sold them out. On the downside, he could blame the nameless guy in that Fresno State beanie. On paper, it was a good plan. So why was acid crawling up Deacon's throat? That was easy. Bautista hadn't risen to his level by being stupid. Deacon knew he would figure it out. Eventually.

For now, Deacon would rely on The "Powell Doctrine." As long as they maintained cover and utilized sound tactics, they could minimize the threats and force the suspects to surrender. It also fit with his view of diplomacy—at the end of a gun. But today, it looked like he wouldn't get any the action. Sighing, Deacon scanned the parking lot again. The only snag he saw was the marked unit assisting with the take down. A rookie fresh out of training might be a good choice in transporting arrestees, but in a takedown of a senior dealer in a major op, it could prove tragic.

However with the department at minimum staffing, due to massive budget cuts, injuries, and retirements, they were lucky to have a transport unit at all. "Just do what you're told and not a second sooner, kid," Deacon muttered.

He glanced west and noticed three male's approaching the shopping center on foot. They appeared to be Hispanic and were wearing identical red jerseys—Eastside Bulldog gang members. "I've got visual on three Hispanic male adults heading toward the lot. They're wearing Bulldog jerseys. One's carrying a large duffel bag. Another has a tattoo of "Eastside" on his forehead. HMAs are moving toward Nora 11."

Using the TAC channel, Sergeant Dane Matthews, the supervisor of the Narcotics Division and of this operation, said, "Copy that. Have a visual on them. That's a positive ID on Bautista. All units sit tight. We don't move until buy signal."

Deacon watched the three males cautiously approach the vehicle. Andrews, along with Muscles, exited the car.

Sergeant Matthews gave the wire channel play by play over the TAC channel. "Muscles made the intro. Deal's going down. We got good dope talk. More dope talk. Still more dope talk. Damn, this guy won't shut up. What is he, a used car salesmen?"

Deacon snickered, wondering the same thing. A split second later, all humor fled.

The marked unit had eased out from the side of Lowe's.

"Edward 15, King 93. Stop moving. Do not proceed. Wait for the bust signal!" Deacon snapped.

Deacon released the button on his radio's mic and Matthews barked, "Edward 15, Nora 10. Stand down. Follow orders! Stand down!"

Deacon's gut knotted. Ice crept up his spine. He kept his binoculars trained on Bautista, who was not looking toward Andrew's car but was scanning the parking lot. *Shit!* The fucker hadn't stopped his counter-surveillance. *Damn, he's good. Too good.*

A second later, Bautista spotted the front end of the black and white Dodge Charger with its light bar. Seeing him mouth, "Oh, shit," Deacon crushed down on his mic. "Edward 15's made."

Immediately, the wire's channel filled with accusations:

"You're a snitch!"

"Not me," Muscles said.

"Who's wearing a wire?" Bautista demanded.

"Not me. Not me," Muscles and Andrews said simultaneously.

"*Hijo de puta,*" a goon said.

The OP had gone south and was heading to shit—fast. Deacon wasn't waiting for shots fired. He dropped his binoculars.

"You set me up, you piece of shit. You're dead," Bautista snarled.

The radio buzzed. In his ear, Deacon heard, "Move, move! Go, go, go! Bust it!"

He raced across the roof, slammed his feet against the either side of the ladder and, with his hands, moved down it in a quasi-slide to the sound of car doors banging.

The Powell Doctrine was in full effect. The stink of fear permeated the air. Andrews was at risk. Car doors slammed. Eight detectives raced toward the HMAs, their MP-5s, shotguns, and AR-15 assault rifles at the ready.

"Hit the ground," Williams yelled.

They couldn't put their hands up fast enough. Except for Bautista. He was one step ahead of them. He'd reacted instantly. Darting from the lot, he sprinted due west and disappeared on a nearby bike trail that tunneled beneath the intersection.

Deacon charged after him, knowing he didn't have a

prayer of catching him. The bastard had too great a head start. From reflex, Deacon hollered, "Stop or I'll send my dog!" then winced as he looked down at his side. He'd known he should've stopped and grabbed Justice. "Shit!" His partner was locked in the car over a quarter mile back. Not even the most advanced remote door opener could reach from this distance.

Teeth gritted, he poured all he had into racing down the embankment for the trail. Training kicked in. In between sucking air, he gasped into his radio, "King 93. Leg bail. Headed southbound. Toward bike trail from Lowe's. HMA. Bulldog jersey." As he finished, it hit him. Using his radio was pointless. Dispatch didn't monitor the tactical radio channel. Eyes on Bautista, not the path, Deacon tripped on a tree root. He did his best impression of Superman and failed, face-planting in the middle of the bike trail. With road-rash-covered palms, he pushed up against the asphalt trail in time to see Bautista glance back at him. Their eyes momentarily locked.

With a grin, Bautista vanished out the end of the tunnel.

Bruised but not beaten, Deacon stood and dusted himself off. His nose started to itch, then the coughing began. Bracing himself, he looked down at his duty belt. "Son of a bitch!" When he'd fallen, his can of pepper spray had ruptured. Not having been directly exposed to the spray, the worst he would get was watery eyes, a light cough, an itchy nose, and skin irritation. Plus a hefty dry-cleaning bill. Pissed, he began the trek up the embankment.

Reaching Andrews's vehicle, Deacon was relieved to see Bautista's two compatriots face down on the pavement. The long guns had been slung and eight Glock 22s were aimed at them. The rookie quickly secured them using flex cuffs. At least he did that right. Williams removed large bricks of white crystalline substance wrapped in foil from the dropped bag. Andrews stacked them on the trunk of the pathetic excuse for a car, while other detectives escorted the two HMAs to their new taxi.

Deacon jogged over to join the takedown debrief. Leaning over, he whispered to Andrews, "Nothing like a well-planned OP turning into a cluster fuck."

Andrews pinched the bridge of his nose as if in pain. "Yeah, but no surprise for an undercover OP with an excited rookie."

"At least you got five kilos off the street."

"True. But we didn't get Bautista. Fuck! We've not only lost access to the bastard, but we have to get Muscles to stay under the radar."

"Good luck with that."

"No kidding." Andrews rammed the packages back into the bag. Lifting his head, he narrowed his eyes at the black and white. "Fucking rookie!"

Deacon nodded. "Yeah. You're right. Those two idiots won't change a thing. Within a week, Bautista'll have two new ones to—" He spotted Sergeant Matthews bee-lining for the marked unit. Deacon couldn't decide who was about to have a worse night, the two dealers or the rookie in Matthews's crosshairs. Yes, he did. The rookie.

"God damn it, Brown! I ordered you to hold! We had him! What the fuck were you thinking?"

"I'm sorry, Sarge. I thought if I saw the car and the deal, I could time it better."

"Ah, and there's the problem. Your job's to follow orders, not think. Get your ass back to the station. And if there's ever a next time, you move when I tell you! You stand down when I tell you! And you take a shit when I tell you!"

Deacon did his best to smother his laugh. His best was barely good enough.

With no need to fake his arrest, Andrews got into his vehicle. As Deacon started the long walk to this patrol car, Andrews braked. Rolling down his window, he leaned out. "Hey, Deacon. Thanks again for covering my six."

"No problem."

CHAPTER 5

For his first visit, Bautista would have preferred to arrive in Tuefel's home office under his own power. Luis slammed him down onto his knees before the office's massive desk. Over the past hour, Bautista had tried to get the bookend to understand that the police had gotten the five kilos when they'd almost busted him.

Looking up from the floor, he stared at his boss's back as the man continued to look out the windows at the Sierra Nevada mountains. This was the man who had taken over as the main drug trafficker in town and not the Eastside Bulldogs. Swallowing hard, Bautista fought the urge to escape. His life balanced on a knife's edge. God help him if he pissed himself.

He licked his dry lips, staring at Tuefel's six-foot-two height, and struggled to control his trembling before this man who was known for being as intelligent as he was ruthless. "The Krusnik" had bought out, set up, or simply murdered all the major drug suppliers within a two hundred mile radius. With one eye swollen shut, Bautista lifted his head and tried to focus on Tuefel who was still standing with his back to him.

Luis's boot smashed onto the back of Bautista's head. The Italian tile floor stopped his face. The snap of his nose broke the silence. Blood gushed out. A muffled cry escaped before he could stop it. He couldn't afford to appear weak. He couldn't utter another sound.

"I will no longer tolerate your insolence, *A-le-jan-dro*. Or that of any of your 'home boys,'" Tuefel said in a hard, emotionless voice.

A large fist plunged into Bautista's left kidney. Another small whimper escaped. *Mierda*! He'd pee blood for a couple days, praying he didn't start while on his knees before them. If they smelled *that* hint of weakness, he wouldn't leave this room alive.

"Due to your recent failure, I'll now require seventy percent of your proceeds instead of the previous fifty. It would be most unfortunate if I had to conduct similar negotiations with your mother Isabella or daughter Christina."

At hearing the names of his mother and daughter, shock overwhelmed Bautista's fear. He began to stand. Bookend shoved him back to the floor, kicked him in the kidneys, and, grasping Bautista's hair, jerked his head up.

Terror gripped him. His one working eye blurred. Unable to focus, he didn't see Tuefel until after he had rounded the desk and squatted in front of him.

Tuefel grabbed Bautista's chin and yanked his face upward. He turned his head from side-to-side, examining the multiple tattoos covering his shaved skull. With a scowl, Tuefel uttered something Bautista neither heard nor understood. The man's hot breath brushed against his cheek. He almost gagged at the odor of sausage.

When he faced forward again, their gaze was inches apart. He felt as if the man's eyes pierced him, seeming to swallow his soul. *Dios mio, shark's eyes*.

"Listen very carefully, *A-le-jan-dro*. You still owe me two-hundred-large. I want it within a week." With a flick of his wrist, Tuefel released his face.

Bautista had no spit to wet his parched throat. "Y— you'll have your money, s—soon. Got something going," he croaked between cracked lips.

Bookend punched the side of his face. Blood filled his mouth. Choking, he coughed. Blood spattered onto Tuefel's Italian suit. The man's frigid stare didn't falter.

"Not unloading a bunch of shit. Serious coin. Need time. A few more hits, will have it all. *Lo juro*," Bautista swore.

Tuefel stood, straightened his suit, and, returning to his desk, blotted the blood off his suit jacket with a white, linen handkerchief.

"This is good news. Very good news—for you—and Isabella and Christina. You have a month to get me my money. One month. If you're late, the next time we meet, a piece of you will stay with me—permanently. Now, get the hell out of here," Tuefel said, flicking a piece of lint off his suit.

Bautista inched his battered body off of the floor and limped toward the door that seemed miles away.

"Oh, and, Alejandro, one more thing."

Arm wrapped around his ribs, Bautista slowly turned around only to face his boss's back as the man, once again, stared at the mountain range.

Tuefel pivoted back toward him. "Until you're paid up, Rachele will be at you're side."

Bautista froze. If he could have moved it, his jaw would have dropped.

The boss laughed. "Ah, good, you approve. I'm sure she'll find ways to properly motivate you. If you don't make good, she'll deliver a piece of you or your family to me until you do."

With a nod, Bautista shuffled out of the office.

Luis escorted him to the front door of the estate. "Get your shit together and get the boss his money, or it'll be the last thing you fail at." Grinning, he slammed the door shut.

Bautista made his way over to a newly stolen car. He fumbled opening the door, then eased onto the driver's seat. Lowering his head onto the steering wheel, he rested.

Tuefel was dangerous, but having the man's psychotic wife watching his every move chilled him to the marrow of his bones.

ຕຈຕຈ

Bautista pulled in behind Speaker City, rolled to a stop behind the large Conex storage container, and killed the engine. Reclining against the seat, he waited. It was only a matter of time before his patience would be rewarded.

It took a couple of hours, which was far shorter than the week it had taken to track the snitch rat bastard down. Now that he had him, he'd pay.

His gaze narrowed on the door to the loading dock as it crawled to the roof.

A store clerk emerged carrying four pallets. He strutted his way toward the Conex. *Well, well, look who showed up.* No mistaking it was him. Not with those tattoos.

Dios, he was wearing the same World Class Warrior dry fit shirt that he wore the night of the bust. *I've got you, you son of a bitch. I'm neck deep in this bullshit because of you. And you're going to pay in more than one way, but first you're going to get me my money.*

Bautista sneered as he watched the clerk's muscles bulge throwing the last one onto a growing pile of their wooden brethren. He stepped out of car and drew his pistol from the small of his back.

Dios, the stupid fuck didn't see him, Bautista thought, watching the clerk admire his biceps. Bautista moved behind him, swung the pistol by the barrel, and smashed the buttstock against the clerk's head.

Muscles collapsed like an imploded building.

Bautista flipped him onto his back and slammed the gun barrel into the bastard's jaw, driving his teeth through his tongue.

"It wasn't my fault, man," Muscles croaked, his punctured tongue spurting blood.

Bautista pressed the gun hard against his swelling jaw. "Bullshit. I know it was you. Don't you lie to me, you piece of shit!"

"Don't hurt me, man, I'll do whatever you want!"

Bautista lowered his face to mere inches from Muscles's. Spittle flew from his mouth and gave Muscles a disgusting sheen. "Yes, you will. You cost me two-hundred-K, and I want it."

"I don't have anything," Muscle's whimpered.

"Yeah, you do." Bautista pointed into the store's storage area. "You're going to jack some shit for me."

"I—I can't. I don't have keys. I'm just a clerk. I can't get into the safe."

"Listen, dumbass, I don't want you to steal cash. You're too stupid and you'd get caught. You're going to help me jack some of those new 4K televisions. I'll handle the rest. If you fuck this up, you're dead."

Muscles swallowed hard. "I'll leave the back access door by the dock open. You can enter, take what you want, and leave without notice."

Bautista gripped his throat and squeezed. "*Dios*, you're a major dipshit. They'll know the moment we take those sets. They're tracked with barcodes and shit." He squeezed harder.

"I—I've got an idea. How about I swap them out?"

"Talk fast."

"It—it's like this. A—all I've gotta do is swap them out. I'll cut bottom of the boxes, swap 'em out, and reseal 'em. No one'll ever know. I'll even mark 'em so you get the right boxes. You buy the TVs on the cheap an' sell 'em at a premium."

"*Un idiota*. That won't work."

"Yes, it will! You've gotta believe me," Muscles pleaded. "The customers find they've got the wrong sets and return them. Everybody'll think the factory fucked it up."

The pressure on Muscles's jaw from the barrel of the pistol eased slightly. "Do it. I want all the new 4Ks. Swap them with a cheaper LED. That way it'll look like the factory screwed up a whole shipment."

"Okay. Okay. I'll get it done. I swear. Just don't kill me."

"How will I know which ones you've already hooked up?"

"I'll mark 'em. I'll ink the boxes of the ones I've done. A dot in the 'D' of the LED."

Bautista stood, the pistol aimed at Muscles's forehead. "I'm not buying it."

"It'll work, I swear!"

"Not that, *idiota*. I'm not paying a dime for the sets. No paper trail. Get this done. When they're ready, you're going to make sure I have a way in to come get them."

"Told you, I'll make sure the loading dock's access door is unlocked. I'll let you know when they're switched."

Bautista lowered the gun. "You'd better not fuck this up." He returned the pistol to his waistband.

"I won't. I swear. I'll have the first bunch ready to go Tuesday night. Just remove the tape from the door after you're finished."

"This better work or you're dead."

CHAPTER 6

Standing outside his patrol car, Deacon braced himself for another long, boring day of forced overtime on day shift. Having worked the shift the night before, he knew he'd be a zombie by nightfall. The only blip of excitement he'd had in the last month was the undercover op. And that was two weeks ago.

Whoever had said police work was ninety-nine percent boredom and one percent sheer terror had it right. And for him, that one percent had only reached excitement. Given that he didn't work in the high adrenaline areas, he doubted he would ever experience that one percent.

On a sigh, he unlocked the car and crawled behind the wheel. Out of habit, he flicked a glance at the rearview mirror for his partner. Always good to know what mood Justice was in after being cooped up for an hour.

Not bad. He must have just woken from a nap, because the stare the dog aimed at him was only chastising, as if to say, "What took you so long?"

"Don't worry, buddy. With this overtime check, you'll get a ton of milk bones and maybe even some chili dogs."

The dog chuffed as if saying, "Whatever."

Grinning, Deacon put the car into gear and pulled forward. He glanced into the rear view mirror and met Justice's loving, yet penetrating, eyes in the mirror. He'd always thought Justice's eyes looked like two little solar eclipses. Balls of flame surrounded black cores. It was eerie at times. His fellow handlers in the K9 unit said they looked like balls of fire. He agreed. It was as if the dog's eyes burned right through everyone.

Jerking his gaze from the mirror, Deacon checked his mobile data computer for any calls for service holding. It took a moment for the reply to queue. Disappointment hit him. No calls holding. So much for adrenaline-fueled action keeping him awake.

Two hours later, Deacon gave up and headed for the local quick stop to stretch his legs, get a cold, caffeine-loaded soda, and try to stay awake. Years ago, he'd figured out intense heat plus a healthy dose of exhaustion equaled a patrol car crash. Making a left turn, he aimed for the nearest store.

୧৩୧৩

"Another returned 4K?" For a perfectionist like Jessica Grady, this was unacceptable. She prided herself on ensuring her store only stocked the best, the most state-of-the-art products available. She'd thoroughly researched each item, verified it was reliable to cut down on any returns. This was critical since corporate's return policy included a five percent store credit to the inconvenienced customer. And the corporate bean counters paid close attention to the total of store credits due to returns. Coupled with a spike in the missing inventory of LED televisions, she had a big problem. If she had anymore this quarter it would be catastrophic.

Frowning, she stared at this week's inventory count. "Please, not again."

It didn't take a rocket scientist to realize Speaker City's corporate office would place all the blame on her shoulders. They could justify it, too.

If she didn't stop the shrinkage of LED TVs and the tidal wave of the 4K television returns, she'd find herself on the street. She had to do something. Right now. She'd been stuck here as a manager too long. And because some ass-hole was stealing from her, even if she weren't fired, she'd never move out of this small store in a poor neighborhood and into a leading store on the north end. This thief had made one major mistake. It was now personal. Her career with Speaker City—no, any company in retail—was in jeopardy. So, too—as base as it sounded—was her bonus. The entire thing left her feeling like she'd been mugged.

Her desk phone rang. *What now?* She lifted the handset.

"Jessica?"

"Yes?"

She heard the voice of a man in the background yelling about something being bullshit. "Can you come down, now? We got a customer going ballistic. He's demanding to speak with the manager—that's you," whispered the clerk.

She sighed. "I'll be right there."

A pissed-off customer wouldn't just tell ten potential customers about their lousy experience, but would also drive ten current ones from the store. She threw herself down the stairs and was behind the counter at returns within ninety-seconds.

"What kind of racket are you people running here?"

Jessica inserted herself between the counter and clerk—who measured about half the customer's height and looked terrified out of her mind. "Sir, my name is Jessica and I'm the manager here—"

"Finally, someone with authority. Three hours ago, I spent $3,500 on a 4K TV. I opened the box. Did I find what I bought? No." He laid the 4K box on the counter and flipped it open. "This is a damn LED. What the hell're you trying to pull?"

Jessica started to apologize out of habit. "Sir, I am sorry for the confusion and we'll be happy to replace—wait, what did you say?"

"I said *that* I took this box home—" He waved at the box on the counter. "—opened it, and found an LED television in it, not the 4K I bought."

Teeth gritted, she examined the 4K box. The top was unevenly cut along the seam, probably with a kitchen knife. She moved around the counter and stood beside the irate man. Together, they removed the LED and moved it to the side on the counter. She examined the box, looking for something—anything. She didn't see any signs the box had been opened or altered. Then she lowered the box onto its side and saw it.

"What the hell is going on?"

"Sir, shut up." Her words were so unexpected, everyone around her did. She peered closer. The bottom of the box appeared to be factory sealed—save for enlarged holes where the staples were. Son of a bitch! Someone had pulled them out, switched the sets, and then resealed the box. But how had the thieves known which boxes to take? "We're very sorry, sir. It looks like a factory mistake."

"Just give me what I ordered."

"I wish I could. At the moment, I need to confirm this was an isolated case. Candy, give this man a refund and three hundred fifty dollar gift certificate. I look forward to seeing you again." With a nod to them, the former all-county sprinter and long distance runner bolted for the storeroom, clutching the LED box to her chest.

Ignoring the stares she drew, she charged through the double swinging doors marked employees only. Rounding the corner a little too fast, she nearly face-planted on the cold, concrete floor. Turning onto the isle where the LEDs were shelved, she skidded to a stop in front of the first unit. The box looked pristine and freshly shipped from the factory. Her eyes poured over every inch of it. Her pupils focused on a single, tiny red dot next to the inside curve of the D.

She knelt to examine the remaining sets and her right knee screamed in protest. Her eyes slammed shut and

brimmed with tears—the old, career-ending state champion-
ship injury reminding her to take it easy and that she was
indeed human.

After a moment of controlled breathing, the pain subsided. Jessica quickly confirmed the number of LEDs marked
with the scarlet letter. She turned and counted the number of
4Ks they supposedly had in stock. "Holy shit."

Licking her lips, she scanned the storeroom then returned
to her office. Rubbing her temples, she felt a twelve-pound-
eight-ounce headache building in the front of her skull. She
wasn't looking forward to another restless night due to her
migraine medication, but it beat suffering from blinding
pain. She pushed a binder off of her desk. *I've got to figure
out who is doing this!*

She considered calling the police—again. She thumbed
through the numerous business cards bearing the names of
Cain's finest, each with a sloppy and hastily written police
report number scrawled on the front. Worthless. Every single one of them. So much for protecting and serving.

The cops claimed they'd conducted thorough and complete investigations when prior inventories showed missing
merchandise. Their investigations had ranged from interviewing her employees to examining shipping manifests.
One officer had even spent a few hours examining her
store's video surveillance footage. Another had the balls to
insinuate she couldn't conduct a proper inventory, as if she
didn't know how to count. That one had set her off. Why
hadn't they, or she for that matter, caught the red dot or recognized its significance? Because the product had already
left the store.

God, how many people had bought 4Ks and not realized
they'd gotten an LED?

One or more employees were stealing from her. No way
could she deny it was internal. Jessica rubbed her forehead
with her fingers as she pressed her thumbs against her temples. She had to discover who was ripping-off the store.

Focused on the inventory errors, employee schedules and

the throbbing in her head, which felt like a mushy melon, she didn't hear her office door open.

"Excuse me, Jessica?"

She glanced up. One of her clerks hovered in the doorway of her office. This particular one was a dichotomy—a hard worker and dumb as a brick. Built like a truck and strong as an ox, he was also notorious for attendance issues. And recently, he'd difficulty telling the truth—five grandmothers had died over the past three weeks. *I should've fired his ass two weeks ago. Now, I have to keep him here under a microscope.* "Yes. What is it?"

"I was wondering if I could go home early today? I've got a—"

"Do we have sufficient staffing?"

"I think so."

He thinks so? She leveled a glint-eyed glare on the kid. "Go, get the hell out of here." At her harsh words, the ashen-faced clerk turned and washed from the office.

Much as she hated to admit it, she needed help. *Now!* It was past time she and her lead loss prevention officer Brian Bradford started their own internal surveillance operation and caught the bastard responsible.

She bit her lower lip and stared at her phone, then picked it up and dialed. Busy. Slamming the phone back into the cradle, she stood and headed for the door. Downstairs, she called Brian, this time on her cell. While she waited for him to answer the damned phone, she walked the floor, studying her employees.

One of them was ripping her off.

Not the store, but her.

They were destroying her life.

CHAPTER 7

"King 93."

Standing in line before the checkout, Deacon keyed up the radio microphone. He pushed the button and called back into his dispatch center. "King 93, Go ahead." He began all radio traffic by advising dispatch of his unit identifier, King 93.

The department used his identifier to signify he had a K9—King 90—on board and that he was the third K9 unit on patrol, thus the ninety-three. The number had nothing to do with seniority or number of dogs on the street at any given time. It was simply a number to separate the different K9 units.

"King 93, respond to 1245 Stanford Ave. Contact the Reporting Party regarding a possible vandalism. Information is in the call."

"King 93, ten-four."

"Information is in the call" was the unofficial way of Dispatch advising him there was information available to him via the computer that was either sensitive or inappropriate to say over the radio with so many people listening in on police radio traffic with scanners.

Deacon quickly paid for his wild cherry soda and bag of barbeque sunflower seeds. Walking back to his car, he took a long, slow draw on the icy, cold drink. It bathed his parched throat, soothing him to his core. He snorted. Everyone had their vice. For some guys it was a daily Starbucks. Others still hit Marlboros and Jack. Not him. His Achilles's heel had always been his seeds and soda. Not good for the kidneys, but not too bad for his waistline. Besides, he could afford the extra calories. He was a gym rat, after all.

He paused a moment to enjoy the sugar rush to his tired brain. Pleasant and desperately needed. Unlocking the car with his remote, he slid into the seat. "Well, buddy, let's take a look at the call to see what kinda bullshit we've gotten now."

Behind him, Justice flopped onto his stomach and farted. Deacon laughed. "My sentiments exactly."

The call was for a report of vandalism to a residence. It advised Deacon to contact Shirley Johnson. She requested to speak with an officer because of numerous tennis balls that were in her pool. Equally apparent was that Dispatch couldn't figure out how to title the odd call for service, so they'd slapped vandalism on it for a lack of a more appropriate title.

Deacon took his time driving to the residence in a vain attempt at delaying the inevitable. It wasn't as if the tennis balls were damaging the water. Seemed karma agreed. He'd hit every red light and had never been more grateful for them.

When he finally arrived at the residence, he put on his best game face. This particular repeat customer averaged three calls a week. She'd require all the professionalism he could muster. She'd become a real nuisance and, as the tennis balls proved, had run out of excuses to generate calls. Part of him felt sorry for the old bird, but the other part was irritated. There were better ways to alleviate loneliness. Also, the city had much more important things that he and his partner could be doing.

Deacon stepped out of his car, his gaze examining the area. Given the high school tennis court behind the house was the culprit of the Great Tennis Ball Caper of 2015, pity flooded Deacon at the woman's lonely desperation. Then looking at the house, the emotion quickly died. "I'll be right back, buddy. Don't get too worried about me." Justice, sensing the boredom of his master, and clearly not worried about this particular call, went back to sleep.

Johnson's small residence was an ordinary tract home in a middle class neighborhood. It appeared fairly new. Recently painted, it sat in the center of suburban sprawl—a cookie cutter community governed by the all-powerful Homeowners Association.

Deacon's gaze flicked to the houses flanking the small home, a smile playing at the corners of his mouth. Johnson's wooden, dark-cherry lacquered shutters clashed violently with the canary yellow stucco and emerald green trim. It looked as if someone on a bad acid trip with too many crayon options had had fun. It also told him a lot about the owner—she not only didn't give a rat's ass about the association's rules, but was giving them the proverbial finger.

Yet the Bermuda lawn was meticulously kept, rivaling the best greens of Pebble Beach. Not a blade was out of place. The blue aptos pines in the corner of the property had been painstakingly pruned to remove the bottom five feet of branches off of the twenty-foot trees. It was a shame that they weren't in the back as, here, they were incapable of stopping the onslaught of the sinister tennis balls.

As Deacon stepped from the car, sweat beaded on his forehead. The latest call for rain appeared to be another wrong number. *Only a weatherman could be wrong this often and keep his job.* Unusually high temperatures for this time of year must be what they meant by global warming. He scanned the street and spotted some kids cooking eggs on the asphalt.

While he didn't want to, he had to leave his car running to ensure the air conditioner would blow for Justice. A nasty side effect of leaving the car idling was the lack of airflow through the engine to help cool it. Unlike NASCAR hoods, his patrol car's hood lacked vents to help the heat escape. It would kill the car along, with the AC, years sooner than other patrol cars. But he had no choice. If the AC died, so did Justice. The solution was a bit embarrassing.

He reached in and popped the hood on his patrol car. It made the car look as if it had broken down in front of the house. That was, of course, better than coming back to find a dead dog. He prayed that no one would cut a hose while he was away. At least he had two keys. With a sigh, he locked the car, swallowed his pride, and approached the door.

Deacon quickly realized that he could spend a few minutes on this call now and come back later, or take longer than what would be considered normal for a call of this magnitude and fix the problem. Once he'd realized his fate, he returned to his car, shut the hood, and freed his partner.

ↂↇↂ

Two and a half hours later, Deacon glanced at Justice laying a few feet to his left. The entire time he'd slaved attaching a wooden lattice to the fence behind the house, Justice had drunk his fill of water, preened under the cooing ministrations of Mrs. Johnson, and rested in the shade beneath a bay laurel. If reincarnation existed, Deacon sure hoped he came back and lived the life of a pampered dog.

As he stared at his handy work, he shook his head. Nothing he did would stop the calls. The woman was too lonely and hungry for human interaction. But something had to be done. His watch commander, having been briefed by Dispatch, had phoned him a while ago and ordered him to, "take any and all steps necessary to ensure calls from Johnson's house ceased."

Then when he'd added, "I don't care how long it takes you or if you have to marry her, make it happen," Deacon got pissed. Like that would do anything to stop this woman.

He never should've given the Johnson woman his business card. He could see her call now, "King 93 for suspicious activity. Respond to 1245 Stanford for a report of illegal dumping of tennis balls in the RP's side yard."

He'd solve that problem now, before he left. "Justice, heel." With his partner at his side, he approached the glass sliding door and knocked. As soon as Mrs. Johnson opened it, he canted his head at the fence. "I believe the problem's solved, ma'am."

"Thank you so much, Officer Deacon."

He handed her another business card—a new one. "You're welcome, Mrs. Johnson. Should the lattice come down, don't hesitate to call Royce. He's a retired cop and does honest work. He'll take of you."

"Thank you again for everything. You're a life saver."

Yeah, sure. He didn't feel like much of a lifesaver. Along with his fatigue and frustration, he felt a bit sad. *It must be rough being lonely.* His heart went out to old Mrs. Johnson, along with a bit of shame. Not every call was a foot chase after some crackhead who'd sell his own child for a quick fix. He'd been so focused on how this wasn't a police matter he'd forgotten it was his duty to help those who couldn't help themselves. That was the reason he'd signed up in the first place. Embarrassment flooded him.

Out front, he paused, stared back at the residence, and snorted again at his handiwork. His cheap, hasty construction had added yet another color to the cornucopia of crap. At least the bright red/orange painted lattice kind of went with the brown of the fence. *Nice.* And while at first glance it seemingly clashed like everything else, it worked.

Once he'd secured Justice, Deacon got behind the steering wheel, drank a half of a liter of water, and then threw the face page of his report on his makeshift desk—his dash. Damn, he was in rough shape.

He'd been too focused on completing the job, and had ignored the blistering heat, lack of direct shade, his ballistic body armor, along with the thirty pounds of gear on his chest, all of which explained how he'd become dehydrated.

Finishing the water, he drained what was left of his warm, flat soda.

"Maybe she isn't so crazy, buddy."

Justice sat and, staring at Deacon's reflection in the rearview mirror, cocked his head at a forty-five-degree angle, as if saying, "What the hell you are talking about?"

"Maybe, maybe she's a genius. She just got the city to do two and half hours of work for her and it didn't cost her a dime." Justice gave a quick woof and returned to staring out the window. "I know. I know. I'm the crazy one. The joke's on me."

Putting the car in gear, Deacon headed toward the mall. As he stopped for a red light, he glanced at the sky. The clouds on the horizon had clearly hit the juice. "And I sit corrected, buddy. It looks like the weatherman's right. We'll, finally, get rain tonight, after all."

Less than ten minutes later, Deacon heard panicked scratching from the back seat and recognized it immediately. It was the, "Open this door, now, you moron, or I'm gonna crap all over the back of this car," pawing. Deacon broke another sweat, fearing they wouldn't be able to pull over in time. Thick traffic ignored his turn signal and escalated his worry.

As Justice's clawing and running circles increased, Deacon activated his "excuse me" lights and, making a hole in traffic and using the shoulder and bike lane, raced for the nearest convenient spot—the parking lot of Jefferson Elementary School.

He screeched to a stop, hit his door pop, and the right rear door of his patrol car sprang open. Justice paused at the sight of a bunch of kindergartners at recess. The dog hated doing his business with anyone watching. "Don't look a gift flower bed in the mouth. Go."

With a woof, Justice erupted from the car and bolted for the end of the lot, barely reaching the bushes in time. "Damn, buddy, that was close."

Standing beside the back door, Deacon shook his head as Justice, clearly relieved, loped back to the cool safety of his cage. "You couldn't just use the bushes near me, could you?" At his partner's snort of seeming agreement, Deacon removed a plastic bag from the trunk, reminding himself that he was the master of the dog, not the other way around.

After he'd cleaned up the mess, he pitched the bag in a trashcan and retrieved a heavily insulated five-gallon jug of ice water from the trunk. It kept Justice's water cold during their ten-hour shift.

He poured a small amount into the metal bowl he carried in the trunk then set it on the ground beside the open door. Justice leapt onto the sidewalk and lapped so frantically that half the water hit the pavement, sizzled, and evaporated in seconds. The bowl licked dry, Justice lifted his head and, with a goofy grin, shook his muzzle, spraying the inside of the car with water.

"Your mess, your seat, buddy," Deacon said, shutting the door and placing everything in its proper place. Sticky with sweat, he sat behind the wheel and yanked his uniform, which was pulling tight, off of the back of his neck. *At some point I have to get to the dry cleaner for my uniforms.* When it came to a wool uniform, starch was your friend.

He inhaled and sneezed. "Jesus H—" God, he stank. The longer the day went, the worse his odor and the stench of wet dog got. Hell, dealing with a car-dancing teenager was better than this. "Shit! I really am getting desperate if little Miss Alex Van Halen is the high-point of my shift." And it looked to be a long day.

While he knew better than to call down the thunder, that didn't stop him from wishing something, anything would happen. Right now, his enemy, fatigue, was winning the battle.

CHAPTER 8

When Brain got to the store, Jessica quickly brought him up to speed. It would be all too easy for a shady employee to offload the merchandise out the back dock. To confirm their theory, they checked the store video surveillance tapes. Just as with the cops, they found nothing. She slanted a frustrated glance at him. "Why isn't our surveillance catching the thefts?"

"Either someone's screwing with our cameras—moving them—or they're hacking into our system and inserting a loop while they make-off with the stuff. I'm voting for shifting the cameras because it's easiest."

"Let's go, I want to show you what I've found."

"Lead the way."

Once in the storeroom, he nearly rammed into her back when she stopped as if frozen. "What's wrong?"

"The sets have been moved. When I found the dots earlier they were down at the opposite end of the rack. Now they're down here."

"By the exit door."

"Yeah. It has to have been what's-his-name with the five grandmothers. He must be setting up the next theft before going home early. Let's check the tapes and pray they show something."

"Wait—five what?"

"Never mind. Let's go."

In his command center, Brian checked all the surveillance cameras again and scowled. "Damn it, Jessica, the cameras don't even show us in there. Their focus has been changed."

She slanted a frustrated glance at him. "Pan out onto the loading dock door camera and the one that covers the expensive merchandise please."

"I'm sorry, that's it. It shows nothing."

Jessica ran her fingers through her hair, leaning back in frustration. Then it hit her. She sat up stiff as a board. "Earlier, when I was looking at the shipping manifest, I realized we got all these TVs on the same day. Then I checked back on the previous shipments. Same thing. That one clerk worked each of those days." Jessica watched as he thought about it and, from his expression, he wasn't getting it. "What is today?" Jessica saw the moment the light bulb lit.

"Today's Tuesday, my day off."

"And nutso works on Tuesdays but always leaves early, like today. Today, he left right after the customer raised hell over getting an LED in his 4K box. And I don't think he actually left, just hid. Because, before I called you, all of the red-dotted TVs were at the far end of the storeroom, near the store itself. Now, they're by the rear door waiting to be ripped off."

"I'll get that camera moved right now."

"No, I will. I'm not sure any of the clerks saw you arrive, and I don't want them alerted to what we're doing. We don't know if there's more than one involved."

"Right." Brian handed her a small earbud. As she inserted it, he clipped the cordless mic onto her blouse. "These'll allow us to contact one another. They'll also alert me to any trouble. That way I can call the cops before it gets out of hand—or you're hurt. Who knows? The DA might even find our video and audio useful."

As soon as she headed out, he checked the focusing of

the store's entire surveillance operation. It was state of the art, as long as no one screwed with it. He accessed the cameras in the storeroom and confirmed Jessica had readjusted them so they covered what was needed. Then he refocused the loading dock camera to a medium range wide-angle to maximize clarity for coverage on both the door and the LEDs next to it. Finally, he switched cameras and aimed the exterior rear camera to cover a close up of the loading dock door. *Perfect. Guaranteed I'll get a clear shot of anyone entering or exiting.* He dedicated both camera feeds to a single DVR. That way, they'd be sure to have a copy of the afternoon's events. Then he partitioned the DVR from the main surveillance system to expedite the reproduction of the footage, ensuring that they wouldn't have to fish for it later or worse, have it copied over or lost.

He dedicated one of the store's closed-circuit monitors to the rear dock. To guarantee they cut down on any delays in providing up-to-date information to Jessica when another theft took place, he'd watch the monitors himself. As agreed, he'd also handle calling the police. It should be an easy case for the district attorney and save both their careers at the same time.

He also dedicated a camera specifically on the LEDs available on the floor. He repeated the process on the 4Ks in both locations. Brian suspected their store wasn't the only one hit. Too much money could be had if they had gotten the right merchandise.

They'd had multiple open burglary cases and he wasn't about to have the DA can this case because of lack of video surveillance footage. His plan was to guarantee they had everything the cops and DA needed to not only file the case, but get a conviction.

Once he was confident he had his store covered, he contacted the loss prevention officers of the Speaker stores. After explaining what they'd discovered, each officer said he'd be in touch within the hour.

cᴐcᴐ

"I said hurry up, damn it!" Rachele growled.

Bautista shut the door to his apartment and jogged to his newly acquired Chevy Blazer. He'd had enough of yet another gutless Honda and had finally stolen something worth stealing. This ride had it all—four-wheel drive, power windows. It even had heated front seats.

He opened the driver's door and glanced at his passenger. *Damn it.* The look on Rachele's face said he was running out of time in more ways than one. But, for now, they risked being late. Immediately, sweat dampened his pits as his throat went dry. He flopped into the driver's seat and bumped her left elbow with his right arm. "Sorry."

"Just get your shit together already. I'm sick of following your stupid ass around."

He shut the driver's door, picked up a screwdriver, jammed it into the damaged ignition, and started the vehicle.

Rachele held her hand out in front of her, examining if her nails were in need of trimming. "So where the hell are we going today?"

"The same store as before."

"Again? Are you kidding?"

He swallowed hard. The arid desert he called a mouth was not cooperating. He glanced at her. "They have no clue what we're doing and—"

"What you're doing," she interrupted.

"Getting product I can move to pay your husband. Right now, I'm golden. I can stick my hands back in the cookie jar a few more times." He backed out of the driveway and, pulling out into the street, headed toward the mall. "I figure I can boost a few more HD's before I've gotta switch stores. With this trip, I'll have almost the entire two-hundred-K."

At the sound of her ivory-handled blade being unsheathed, Bautista stole a glance in her direction and wondered how long he could keep it together. She ran her finger along the edge. The tip of her tongue slipped between her lips and, raising her weapon to her cheek, she rubbed against it as if she were nuzzling a lover. "You're running out of time."

Why do you think I'm taking these chances, you crazy-assed bitch? Not wanting to go there, he cleared his throat and tried to steer the conversation onto safer grounds. "Which reminds me, when we get back, I'll give you what I have so far. You can take it to him. Just tell him I've almost got all of it. I'll pay him the rest as soon as I have it."

Rachele balanced the blade by its tip on her finger. The sunlight reflected off the metal, matching the gleam in her eye. Like a lover, she gently returned the knife to its sheath. "I hope you don't."

They remained silent for the duration of the drive. Rachele's knife remained securely tucked away, much to Bautista's relief. He pulled into the parking lot, the radio's bass announcing its presence to the world. He circled the lot, conducting counter-surveillance. He didn't see any cars with exempt license plates in the lot and he didn't see anyone give them a second glance. Satisfied there were no unmarked police cars there, he drove behind the business and parked in a space near the Conex container.

As he put the Blazer in park, it erupted with a backfire. He took a deep breath and turned down the radio. *So much for style. Malverde, help me.* He twisted in the seat and faced Rachele. "You remember how this goes, right?"

"Do I look like a dumbass?"

Better not answer that. "I just wanted to make sure nothing goes sideways." One look at her wild-eyed glare and he almost rolled out of the car and ran for cover. Under the best of circumstances, she barely controlled herself. This wasn't one of those moments. *Be careful, she's on the edge of losing it. One wrong word or look and you're dead.*

"This shit had better work."

"It will. My guy hasn't failed yet. Remember, we take

the units by the door with the red dot in the D."

"*No soy estúpido. Pero*—" At his arched eyebrow, she switched to English. "You fail, I'll do you in the parking lot and dump your carcass in the dumpster."

Why do you think I have a hidden Glock, you crazy bitch? "It'll be fine."

"Let's go."

He didn't move, just arched his eyebrow again. He'd learned that got her attention without inciting explosive rage. "Unless you want the cops on your ass, you'd better leave that machete under the seat. I'd like to avoid unwanted attention."

She slid it under the seat. "Satisfied?" she hissed.

"Yeah."

Ten minutes later, Rachele sighed. "How much longer is this gonna take?"

Bautista slanted a glare at Rachele, who was pressed against the Conex. *If it weren't for your husband, I'd*—For a split-second, he fantasized gutting the bitch. Prison sounded a hell of a lot better than listening to her bullshit. *Who am I kidding? The Krusnik will have me stuck before I've made it to my cell*. He inhaled deeply. "It'll take as long as it takes. I don't want the cops called. Do you want them here jacking you up?"

"No. Just get it done already. I'm sick of babysitting your sorry ass," she said, turning her back to him.

⌁⌁⌁

Brian's gaze locked on the car that had parked near the Conex. "My, my," he murmured as a couple exited their car and approached the loading dock. Pressing the talk button on the portable radio, he said, "Heads up, Jess. A couple's on the loading dock. They've just entered the store room." He zoomed in on the open door. "Looks like the bastard used duct tape to prevent it from locking."

"On it," she said.

Brian watched via the camera as she flew out of her office and down the stairs, like a Peregrine Falcon in a dive, and headed for the storeroom. With a grin, he trained the hidden overhead cameras on the action and recorded every move the two made.

"Damn, I'm good," he said with a smirk, watching the man peer at the LED boxes next to the door then, grinning, nod to the woman.

CHAPTER 9

Secure in Brian working his magic, Jessica felt like a stalking lioness, ready to attack. If only she knew who she'd be ensnaring in their trap. "Jess, they've removed six of the sets. They're setting them on the loading dock. Looks like they'll move them to their vehicle, once they've gotten them all."

"Copy that. Call the cops. Get them here yesterday. Make sure you track everyone on the monitors. Move the cameras as needed."

"You know it."

Running at Mach three with her hair on fire, she skidded to a stop and paused just prior to hitting the double doors to the storeroom. *Stop, deep breaths. Calm. Okay, go.* She eased one open, inched inside, then edged to the corner just in time to see the male approaching the mislabeled sets stacked next to the access door.

She kept the man to her left as she walked down a nearby aisle. Believing the best way to blend in was to act normal, she pretended that she hadn't seen them. Yet, she feared she stuck out like a sore thumb.

A second later, Jessica's eyes widened. The two crooks each held a set and were headed toward her. *Dumb. Dumb. Dumb.* She was not only horribly exposed, but stupidly so.

She hadn't planned for this situation. As such, she'd inadvertently planned to fail. Shit. With the distance between them shrinking, her heart thumped like that of a terrified jackrabbit.

Hoping to buy herself some time, she hid behind several larger items. She knelt and pawed through a stack car stereos. Her knee disagreed with her chosen tactic, but the pain quickly faded.

As they passed her, Jessica got a good look at them. At first glance, the female didn't look like a criminal. She was pretty, with long, beautifully highlighted hair. At about five feet, four inches tall she was slender, maybe a buck-ten soaking wet. Even wearing a ratty, green shirt with tattered jeans, she was noticeable. But what made her memorable was the crazed look in her eyes. If they'd made eye contact, Jessica would have lowered her gaze. The woman looked bat-shit crazy and two seconds from ripping out someone's throat with her teeth.

When her spidey-sense continued screaming, she spotted the tattoo on the back of the woman's neck—a dagger with a cut down the center of the blade that divided it into a weapon with two blades. A second later, she realized the dagger was stabbing something. What it was, she didn't know. The movement of the woman's ponytail masked the object.

However, the man looked like what she'd expect of a gangbanger. A shaved head with a large tattoo of "Eastside" on his forehead. Another tattoo—a tear drop at the corner of his left eye—declared he'd killed at least one person.

Beneath his badly broken nose, his mustache and the "soul patch" of hair on his lower lip were neatly groomed. The hair looked to be growing out, making the skull tattoo blurry, but not enough to hide a bulldog face on the back of his head.

The number of tattoos repulsed her. Why anyone would do that to themselves confused her. Sure, it warned everyone that he was in a gang but so did the Bulldog jersey with matching mesh shorts sagging so low she doubted he could run. She'd swear his waistband rested just under his ass.

She ducked her head again. A former Criminology student at Fresno State, she had written a number of papers on street gangs. She had learned that the Bulldog street gang had supposedly broken away from its parent, a California prison gang, the Mexican Mafia. The Mafia called themselves "Nortenos" or northerners.

At that time, they had used the moniker F-14 or just "N" because "N" was the fourteenth letter of the alphabet. After a major clash over the division of profits from drug trafficking and multiple disputes over prison hits and assassinations, the F-14 members broke-off from the Mexican Mafia. Once on their own, they claimed the local college mascot as their own and now declared themselves to be enemies of the Nortenos, and Surenos—the Southern Mexican gangs. The Bulldogs' reputation of resorting to extreme violence was well earned. And this particular Bulldog was not only a huge man but he was carrying her last 4K out under his left arm.

Cripes, they needed a lot more help.

Jessica lifted two laptops and using her reader, scanned their skew numbers as they walked off with her televisions. She slanted a glance over her left shoulder. On the back of each shoulder, "ES" tattoos peeked out from beneath his T-shirt.

Jessica knew what they needed to do but was afraid of how the plan would unfold. Rage merged with terror. She wanted to break his freaking neck. If she attacked the man outright, she would be lucky if all that happened was getting her ass handed to her. As much as she wanted to stop them, she swallowed the bitter taste of her anger and ordered herself to say alive so she could be a good witness. She'd watch them like a hawk and wait for the cops. *Damn, Brian, you'd better have called them already.*

❦❦

Bautista shouldered a marked box. The corner collided with another set. It crashed onto the concrete floor sounding like an exploding bomb.

Rachele spun, stared down at the mess, and looked up at him. "What the hell are you doing?"

Bautista's gaze widened at the accumulating spittle at the corners of her mouth. Shit, she looked like a rabid dog. A really pissed-off rabid dog. Focusing death on him, she used the back of her hand and wiped her mouth.

"Sorry."

"Shut up and let's just get the hell out of here."

Yeah, let's. The sooner I can get the hell away from you, the better.

☙❧☙

Anger mixed with desperation as Jessica waited for someone, anyone, to help. Where the hell were the damn cops? The window for catching these two was closing fast. She knew they'd get away unless she did something.

As they moved toward the exit, Jessica followed. She'd just scrambled past a stack of speakers when tragedy struck. She tripped over a loose speaker lying in the aisle and fell face first and arms flailing.

She hit the ground hard.

Her chin struck the concrete, the sound of her groan re-verberating throughout the storage area. Blood poured through her slashed lips. Coughing, she saw a piece of a tooth land in a growing red puddle. Thank the Lord her tongue hadn't between her teeth. If it had been, she'd be staring at half of it, not just a chipped corner of her front tooth. A white lance of pain shot through her head, evaporating all trace of the migraine. She touched her chin and winced. Blood dripped from it like a leaking faucet.

Her gaze latched onto the stereo. Oh, my God, she thought, watching it slide along the tile floor like a hockey puck on smooth ice. Horror assaulted her as it hit the left heel of the man. He stopped. His eyes glanced down at the stereo and then at her.

She crawled to her feet. Her blood looked like a growing rising sun on the floor.

Instinctively, Bautista started to lower the television to confront the woman. *Oh shit!* She was a bloodied, hair-matted, teeth-bared reptilian savage who was in full fury.

She charged.

Clutching the box to him, Bautista grabbed Rachele by her upper arm. "Hang onto your set and move it!" He jerked her toward the door.

They fled with a bloodied maniac closing in on them.

"Brian! Help!" Jessica screamed into her radio and sprinted after the thieves.

CHAPTER 10

Bautista dragged Rachele behind him as they spilled out onto the hot asphalt. "Hold onto that box," he snarled, dropping her arm. "Move it!" They sprinted for the Blazer, two spots away.

A second later, he spotted a teenage-driven bomb hurtling for them.

Before he could move, the fender and grill smashed into his legs. The grill buckled. The box flew out of his arms and into the air. Bautista landed against the windshield, rolled off the hood, and kissed the pavement.

The female driver screamed.

Bleary-eyed, he looked up from the ground, trying to figure out what had happened. *That's right. Some crazy-assed teenager ran me over.* He couldn't see her. The windshield was now an abstract spider web that his back had created.

Then he heard a gut-wrenching crunch. The passenger door had hit Rachele with a glancing blow. Too bad. She would've looked great as a hood ornament.

A split-second later, the car halted just short of a pole, coming to a stop with an ear-piercing screech.

A teenage girl jumped out of the driver's side. "I'm so sorry. I'm so sorry. Please don't be dead," she sobbed.

Bautista didn't want to hear, "I'm sorry." He wanted his fucking 4K TVs. He had to have them if he wanted to live. Forget that, his life wasn't worth spit. All he really cared about were his *mamacita* and his little, girl. She was all he had left of his late girlfriend. If she survived, at least a piece of his lover would endure.

But if he wanted to save them, he had to move. Still feeling like a human crash-test dummy, Bautista struggled to stand. Miraculously, he remained upright. With hands clasping his aching head, he tried to sort out what had happened and if the cops had arrived. They weren't here yet, but he knew they were on the way.

He quickly took in the scene and stumbled, limping to his car with Rachele hard on his heels. They jumped into their Blazer. He reached out to start the car and grasped only air. "Where the hell's the damned screwdriver?"

"How the hell would I know? You're the one who's driving this bucket."

He rubbed his head again and forced himself to think. Then he remembered. Grimacing, he reached under the seat and fumbled around on the floorboard. His fingers curled around the screwdriver, and he jammed it into the ignition.

***

The dispatcher's voice pierced the quiet of Deacon's patrol car, "King 93."

"King 93, go ahead."

"King 93, for a burglary in progress and possible pending disturbance. Speaker City at 903 Marathon Avenue."

"King 93, copy. I'm two out. Almost ten ninety-seven."

Possible pending disturbance? Isn't that a bit redundant? Like a possible, possible fight?

"Cain One copies. King 93 is ten ninety-seven. Two suspects. Suspect number one is male. Six-feet-two. Approximately two hundred twenty-five pounds. Shaved head. Has an 'Eastside' tattoo on forehead. Wearing a Fresno State Bulldogs jersey. Suspect number two is female. Five feet four. Approximately one hundred ten pounds, wearing a green shirt and jeans. Store loss prevention officer and store manager following suspects. They're approaching the store exit, 903 Marathon, for a burglary in progress."

"King 93, copy. Confirming male's wearing a jersey and has a tattoo on his forehead."

"Affirm."

That sounds like Bautista. "I'll take a fill unit."

Dispatch put out a broadcast. "Cain One broadcasting for any units in the area that can fill with King 93." There were several silent moments as Deacon accessed his computer's unit status screen. All officers were tied up on other priority calls. "King 93, I'll have eyes on the back exit in about two. Advise when fill is available. I'll take one when you can find one."

"Ten-four," Dispatch said.

"Confirm which exit their headed to?"

"We're awaiting further info."

Which means I'll get on scene and figure it out before the dispatcher can get it out of the caller. Deacon whispered a prayer of thanks to God for his immediate backup located right behind his seat. He glanced into his review mirror. "Here we go, buddy. Looks like we might get another crack at this fool. Hold on to your butt."

Justice stared back at him. It might have been Deacon's imagination, but he would have sworn Justice had just licked his chops and was grinning in anticipation. Seemed they both wanted—make that needed—some action. "King 93, I am pulling into the lot now. Do we have any updates?"

"Affirmative, King 93. Loss prevention is advising that the suspects got into a brown Chevy Blazer and are currently on Marathon headed north. Also, the male suspect was involved in a T/C in the parking lot. He was struck by a motorist who is still on scene. The store manager is following in a ninety-eight, white Nissan coupe."

"Copy that, any luck with my fill?"

"Negative 93, you are my only unit."

Deacon took a corner on two wheels. "Copy that. Get me that fill and get me another unit to check on that motorist."

⌘⌘⌘

Racing a slalom course of the flattened LED boxes, Jessica dodged them like an NFL running back and sprinted into the parking lot.

A Blazer roared to life. She recognized the dagger tattoo on the back of the woman's neck, released her reserves, and charged toward their vehicle. She had closed the gap enough to read the license plate. Heck, she could almost touch it.

Then, its tires burning a mark into the asphalt, it backed out of its space and rocketed toward Marathon Avenue.

Blind fury controlled her. No one stole from her.

She yelled the plate number into her blue tooth, knowing Brian would relay it to the cops, and dashed to her car. Starting her car, she had one thought in her mind—*you bastards aren't getting away with this.*

First a red light sidelined Jessica, then the heavy traffic. *This is not happening!* Punching her steering wheel, she set off the horn. Desperate, she called the store on her radio, thankful she wasn't out of range. Brian answered, but she could barely hear him over the static. "Tell me you got the whole thing! Tell me you got PD responding!"

"Yes and yes, Jess. You know—"

"Tell the 9-1-1 that a marked unit just passed me with its lights and siren going and the Blazer's turning onto Shaw!"

⌘⌘⌘

"King 93, I'm ten ninety-seven. Confirm the description of the suspect vehicle?"

"Ten-four. Suspect vehicle is a brown Chevy Blazer, now headed east on Shaw Avenue."

He yanked the wheel. The K9 unit's tires screamed. The car whipped around and Deacon slammed the accelerator, launching the unit out of the parking lot onto Shaw Ave.

"Copy. King 93, I've got the suspect fleeing eastbound on Shaw Avenue from Marathon Avenue. I'm initiating traffic." He positioned his vehicle to block as much traffic as possible and pull the suspect vehicle over. "King 93, traffic."

"King 93, go ahead," Dispatch responded.

"King 93, I have traffic on three Boy Henry Robert four seven six, I'm—standby."

A raised H2 abruptly changed lanes and nearly collided with his patrol car. He released his mic and dropped it into his lap. Damned asshole thought he was too cool to use his damn blinker or check his blind spot. *If I weren't chasing some dirt bag, I'd write you a boat load of tickets. Too bad I can't arrest someone for general stupidity.*

Deacon yanked the wheel and quickly charged into the open lane to his left. As he blew past her, he saw that the driver talking on her cell phone. She'd slowed to thirty miles per hour in a fifty mile an hour zone but hadn't stopped yakking.

With a flick of his wrist, he was back behind the Blazer, completing the evasive maneuver, and narrowly avoided hitting the moron who was getting four gallons per mile. "Freaking dumbass." Luckily, he hadn't accidentally keyed the microphone in his lap while venting. The last thing he needed to do was say something stupid over the air.

The Blazer changed lanes, and Deacon followed suit, returning to the number three or right most lane of the three-lane road. "King 93, continuing, three Boy Henry Robert four seven six, I'm eastbound on Shaw Avenue now at Cole Avenue. It's a brown Chevy Blazer with two onboard."

"Copy that, King 93, with two at Shaw and Cole."

Deacon initiated his overhead lights and siren, hoping

that the suspect driver would pull the vehicle to the side of the road. The motors whirred to life under the lights, making them spin inside their little colored worlds. Behind him, Justice was barking as if his life depended on it. With nothing but adrenaline dumping into his veins, the one-hundred-twenty-five-pound German Shepherd drowned out the siren. In the dog's two plus years of working the street with Deacon, his partner had learned very quickly that Dad-plus-traffic-stop equaled time-to-eat-bad-guy.

The suspect vehicle accelerated. This guy wasn't going to stop anytime soon. "King 93, he is continuing. I have a failure to yield."

"Copy that, King 93, failure to yield, eastbound on Shaw."

Deacon inhaled deeply, then exhaled slowly, in an attempt to slow his heart rate and level out the tone of his voice. He couldn't afford to sound panicked while using the radio during a pursuit. "King 93, I am in pursuit. Suspect is continuing eastbound on Shaw, speed is approximately seventy-five miles per hour. Traffic is moderate to heavy and there are no pedestrians. Suspect is wanted for a four-five-nine to a business and possibly for narcotics sales."

"Copy that, King 93. Four-five-nine commercial burglary and confirm narcotics sales?"

"If this is Alejandro Bautista driving, that is a big affirm."

"Copy that, 93."

"Can we get any air support?"

"Standby. The pad is advising negative on air support, King 93. All birds are down for fuel."

"Copy that," he said, biting back his growl.

CHAPTER 11

Deacon continued broadcasting the location of the pursuit, direction of travel, and updated traffic conditions to provide other officers the information they'd need to quickly end this ever-increasing high-speed pursuit. If they were lucky, they would prevent the suspect from hurting people or damaging property. If they weren't—

He could only hope someone was in the area to take over the broadcasting the information because, at this speed, he needed to focus on driving and not on talking. It was only a freakin' pursuit of a wanted felon, so where the hell was everyone?

"Lincoln 10, I am monitoring the pursuit, go get 'em 93."

Deacon glanced at the clock on the car's heads up display. Eighteen-thirty hours. Lincoln shift was now in service. Thank God for their supervisor, Sergeant Doug Swanson. Deacon had never worked for a better supervisor and loved working for him. It was just a shame the sergeant was stuck supervising the graveyard shift that had just gone into service. Deacon sure missed him on his shift.

He'd often told people that Doug was the kind of boss you'd march with into hell with to arrest Satan. You knew you would be Code Four with one in custody in about twenty minutes. Doug was known for being fair and a straight shooter. He'd have your back and give you the shirt off of his. But standby to standby, if you did something to violate his trust.

Pissed that no one else was nearby, Deacon swore repeatedly.

"King 93, from Lincoln 51."

"Go ahead."

"I was a lil' late to briefing, but that's good for you. I have got spikes set for ya just east at Shaw and Stanford Avenue."

"Copy that, 51. We're coming in hot and in the number two lane at the moment." Deacon's blood pressure slightly dropped knowing that Kevin Washington was in position to help with spikes. He was only three blocks away. It was up to those assholes ahead of him to cooperate and not turn off of Shaw.

"King 93?" The question in the dispatcher's voice raised the hair on the back of Deacon's neck. He felt like a cornered dog, unsure if he should fight his way out or whimper and hide. *Eighty miles per hour and still accelerating. Breathe deep. Breathe again.*

"Go ahead."

"King 93, confirming the vehicle you have is three-Boy-Henry-Robert-four-seven-six?"

"That's affirm on three-Boy-Henry-Robert-four-seven-six."

"Ten-four, that plate comes back ten-thirty-five-Victor on a ninety-four Chevy Blazer registered out of Dinuba, CA."

A stolen car. *Shit.* No wonder why the guy isn't going to stop. Burglary, dope, and pursuit of a stolen car? This would be a chase until they ran out of dirt, and then they would have to jump into the water.

He glanced in the mirror. "Well, buddy. This day's sure gotten a lot more interesting, hasn't it?"

Justice paused his raucous barking only long enough to

flash his wolf-like grin. A few seconds later, Deacon was ready to toss his partner out the back. Yes, he loved him. But his tirade had gotten so loud Dispatch was having trouble hearing Deacon broadcast information updates.

"Lincoln 51, King 93. Suspect now back in the number one lane. We're coming up on Stanford Avenue."

"Copy that, 93. I see you guys now."

The Blazer rocketed eastbound at ninety-five miles per hour and was heading directly into the trap. Washington had pulled onto the shoulder just shy of the intersection and stood behind a power pole on the sidewalk for cover. He tossed the spike strip into the number one lane and was ready to pull it across the road if the suspect spotted the strip and changed lanes to avoid the spikes. But—while the driver might not know it—at those speeds, an abrupt lane change would be as good as a spike. Deacon prayed that Washington would remember to pull the chain out of his way and save his vehicle.

Deacon glanced at his speedometer and swallowed hard. One hundred five. Having the dashed lines in the road go solid did nothing to calm his nerves. One thing did— knowing Washington was about to end the pursuit.

"Game on, asshole," Deacon hissed. Slowly applying the brakes, he backed off so he would be able to maneuver his vehicle to avoid the spikes. "No way am I spiking my car," he muttered through clenched teeth.

Time seemed to stop. The Blazer approached the intersection. Eastbound Shaw Avenue at Stanford had a large hill at its center. The incline was equivalent to an eight-percent grade. On weekends, teenagers hit this hill and, more often than not, bottomed out on the opposite side. Dozens of gouge marks marred the asphalt, courtesy of their undercarriages. Also, the intersection was busy as hell. Because of this, the city didn't bother resurfacing the road or leveling the hill.

Not that it mattered. From the Blazer's speeds, it was evident that the driver wasn't familiar with their location. Seconds later, it blew all four tires on the spike strip, yanking at least five of the spikes from the strip into each tire. Hollow, they immediately caused the air to hemorrhage from the tires.

The spikes were wrenched in time for Deacon's patrol car to narrowly avoid them. The barking tirade in the rear increased. Unable to hear himself think, he yelled, "If anyone says that driver's training last week was bullshit, you bite 'em for me, okay?" knowing it was futile. His boy was in hunt mode and ready for his opportunity to strike.

Deacon snickered as the Blazer's shredded tires tore off the rims. Strips of rubber skipped across the road. A split second later, he spotted Washington behind the pole.

The tire-less Blazer hit the hill at one hundred ten miles per hour. Deacon grinned as it did a great Dukes of Hazard impression. The vehicle soared through the air and cleared the remainder of the intersection. A pedestrian on the corner stared, mouth agape, and dropped to the ground as the Blazer's undercarriage cleared his head by inches. The truck slammed back down to Earth. The vehicle started to swerve, and the driver completely lost control.

Raw metal dug into the asphalt. Like on the Fourth of July, a brilliant array of sparks showered the air. While the driver wanted to continue at his previous speed, inertia and the grinding rims dictated otherwise. The sudden increase in friction from tire loss forced the rims to turn. The vehicle began to yaw. What remained of the steel rims carved deeper gouges into the street. In an instant, the Blazer arched, aimed for the shoulder, and slammed into a power pole a good seventy-five yards from Washington's position.

Deacon sneered as Blazer's rims spun in vain, trying to push the pole down. Physics was clearly not the driver's *forte*.

Deacon keyed his radio. "TC. TC. Suspect vehicle has collided with a power pole just east of Stanford Avenue. Start me an EMS Code Three!"

"Copy that, King 93, EMS responding Code Three."

Deacon slid to a stop behind the vehicle, in time to see the driver's side door burst open. The rims stopped spinning. Amazingly, the driver exited the vehicle unhurt. *Why am I not surprised? An innocent person in an accident gets cut and bleeds out. A criminal gets ejected from a car and bolts for the hills. Only thugs and drunk drivers escape unscathed.*

Deacon exploded from his car and thundered, "Police! Stop! Get on the—" At the sight of the driver, he stopped in the middle of his command. He'd been right—Alejandro Bautista—the SOB was a damned cockroach. They stared at each other for a moment, reminding Deacon of an old west standoff. Then Bautista smiled, and Deacon knew he'd recognized him from the busted UC OP two weeks ago.

At the sight of the business end of Deacon's Glock .40 caliber aimed at him, the gloating smile faded. Bautista turned and, with no discernable injury, took off.

Racing toward the crash, Washington broke the radio silence and bellowed, "Leg bail. Leg bail. Suspect fleeing eastbound on Shaw!"

Deacon reached down on his belt, hit the door pop, and let slip his dog of war. Justice closed the gap on Bautista in a heartbeat. Once again, time seemed to stop. Bautista looked over his shoulder as a three-inch canine narrowly missed his nose and sank into his left shoulder blade at twenty-five miles per hour. Deacon's land shark hit the man at full speed, the impact delivering the force of a small car.

Everything came to a screeching halt. Bautista screamed, "*Detener al perro del inferno!*" as Justice buried his teeth deep, piercing all the way to the bone.

Trotting after them, Deacon grinned at the gangbanger calling Justice a hellhound when his partner clamped down with his jaw. He watched Justice's grip tighten, preventing the bastard from fleeing.

Suddenly, Bautista crumpled, kissing the concrete at full speed. Justice rode him to the ground, as if he was in the money at the PBR.

They bounced and rolled for several yards as Bautista's mouth filled with blood. Several fragmented teeth ricocheted along the sidewalk. His nose bled freely.

Deacon watched as multiple impacts forced the dog's jaws to loosen. Bautista tore free and rolled a couple more feet. His partner recovered quickly and lunged for the fugitive, tearing into his calf and, again, holding him in place. Eyes bulging, Bautista found his voice with a blood-curdling scream.

Back in control, Justice held onto the bite with no needless thrashing. With the dog holding him to the ground, Bautista bawled like a baby. Every time he tried to push himself up, the K9 pushed him back onto his back with his rear paws. With each futile attempt to move, Justice's bite deepened, reminding Bautista why it was a bad idea to move.

Deacon, with Washington on his heels, sprinted up to them and gave the command to release. Justice rolled his eyes up at Deacon and growled in protest. "Justice, out!"

With a look that was one of disappointment and frustration, Justice released his prey. He trotted back to Deacon's left leg, face full of blood and flesh, barking and snarling at the prostrate suspect.

Deacon's gaze locked on what appeared to be a small, bloody chunk of meat with a partial tattoo on it lying beside Bautista's leg. Crap. Not good. Sure, Justice had done his job. But Deacon knew that explaining that injury wasn't going to be filled with laughs and giggles—at least not publically.

He watched Washington do a double check, ensuring he was clear of Justice's teeth.

"I'll cuff," he said.

Deacon didn't envy him, not with that injury, as he keyed up his mic. "King 93, we are Code Four with one in custody."

"Copy that. King 93, Code Four with one."

CHAPTER 12

Jessica had tried to keep up with the pursuit. But she couldn't. When she came upon on the scene of the accident, she put her brakes to work. Her car slid to a stop, perpendicular to Shaw Avenue. Shoving open her door, she was rewarded with the sight of a police K9 getting down to work. She smiled, which was rare as of late, knowing that the ass who had stolen from her was getting what he deserved. Served the asshole right.

Within seconds, the smile disappeared. She spotted the backside of the woman heading for a nearby neighborhood at a fast clip.

With the police tied up with the injured gangbanger, they hadn't seen her. If she made into there, she'd disappear and they would never find her. And to Jessica, that was unacceptable.

Spinning from the accident site, she raced after the escaping thief, screaming, "Your thieving ass is kicked, bitch, stop!" The crook increased her speed. Bad idea, Jessica thought. She hadn't been a champion in the four-by-one-hundred and the fifteen-hundred meters for nothing. So what if it had been years ago?

လ.ૐ.ઉ

Deacon turned toward a woman yelling and saw the civilian hot on the heels of the suspect female. Damn. Talk about sloppy. He had been so focused on Bautista taking a leg bail—leg bail—he loved that term. So many crooks tried to make bail by using their legs. *Ah, the joys of job security.*

His eyes widened as the screamer raced after the fleeing suspect into the nearby neighborhood on Stanford Avenue. Damn, must be the store's manager, and she was one seriously pissed-off lady. Securing Justice to his lead, he took-off after them, barking into his lapel mic. "King 93! One in custody with 51. Suspect two has leg bail, on Stanford from Shaw. Units be advised, a civilian female's chasing after her."

"Copy that, 93. One in custody with 51. Female suspect on Stanford from Shaw. Confirm the civilian's description." He vaulted over a boulder in a front yard as he put out the civilian's physical description and her clothing so assisting units wouldn't take her for the suspect. He'd have to be careful with this one. The last thing he needed was his dog taking down the wrong female.

Thank God, I sucked it up in the gym. He gained on them as they continued south on Stanford. "Stop. Stand down," he shouted at the civilian. Did she stop? No. She poured on more speed. *Damn, she's fast.*

He figured she must have thought he meant the suspect since she was also yelling, "Yeah, bitch, stop!"

Deacon continued broadcasting updates as they ran into an all too familiar yard. "Ah, shit," he gasped, his eyes latching onto the bright cherry, lacquered shutters like a moth to a flame. God help him when old Mrs. Johnson called this one in. As he and Justice raced to the side gate, hoping to cut them off, he prayed Mrs. Johnson stayed inside, behind locked doors.

Reaching the corner of Mrs. Johnson's house, the female suspect plowed into one of the pink flamingos, knocking it to the ground. She stumbled and quickly recovered. The civilian was right behind her. If he'd had excess energy, he would have shaken his head at the how the store clerk hadn't only kept up but was nipping at her heels. Deacon pulled on his reserves. The safest location to take down the female would be the backyard.

೭ⴰꙄⴰꙄ

Jessica's legs burned. Her throat felt like sandpaper. Her breathing was labored. Refusing to be left behind, she snarled as the woman jumped the fence into the backyard and landed lightly on all fours like a cat. A second later, Jessica crashed into the fence. Rubbing her chest, she backed up. Eyes narrowed, she studied the fence, then grinned.

Energized, Jessica lowered herself into a racing stance, took-off as if from a sprinter's block, and, using the giant rock near it as a quasi-trampoline, soared over the fence. For a split second she thought she had been blessed with her target breaking her fall. No such luck. Her elbow slammed into the woman's jaw. Spinning from the collision caused both of them to land in a pile-up.

The woman landed face down.

Upon landing, Jessica's knee rolled, her weight compressing it. She pitched forward, her right knee hitting the concrete, followed by her head striking it like a hammer on an anvil. Dazed, stunned, and hurting, she heard a high-pitched scream shattering the silence. It took a second before she realized she'd been the one yowling.

Lightning sparked throughout her body. She shook her head, trying to clear it. *Damn it, Jess, get up! Pain's God's way of telling you you're still alive. So if you want to stay that way, move it!* She tried to stand, praying her knee wouldn't fail her again. It buckled and she fell to the ground. Unless the cop following them got there, she was screwed. As reality set in, anger left her. Scowling, she stared up at her adversary. What she saw filled her with panic and despair.

Fists clenched, the woman let loose a primal roar toward the sky. Blood and foam mixed on her lips, adding to her feral expression.

Jessica stared at the bulging veins in the crazy woman's neck and temple and gulped. Then the mad woman's eyes bugged as they flicked over the yard. At her cackle, Jessica followed the woman's gaze to a hammer lying atop some lattice stacked against the fence.

With terror escalating, she crab-walked, scuttling backward by pushing with her hands and her one good foot. Her heart sank. She had trapped herself in a corner of the fence line. As she watched the woman bend over and grasp the hammer, turn, and face her with a reptilian grin, Jessica hunted to find something, anything to defend herself with. There had to be something. Her hand landed on a soft pile of green, fuzzy projectiles.

A hammer versus tennis balls. I'm going to die.

തരുതു

Weapon drawn, Deacon cut across the rear corner of the backyard. He pied the corner in a wide arc, swinging out from behind cover like a pendulum. Suddenly, Justice pulled. Instantly, Deacon realized he'd scented the women they'd been chasing.

The dog's large shoulders strained as he fought the leash wrapped around Deacon's left wrist. The safety lead was designed to prevent an accidental release of the K9. It was basically a slip knot around his wrist, and made them nearly inseparable.

At hard jerk from Justice, Deacon almost lost his balance and was forced to holster his weapon in order to control his partner. As they moved onto the grass, he struggled to pull Justice back. His slipping on the wet grass was all Justice needed to tip the scales. With a powerful lunge, the dog almost dislocated Deacon's shoulder.

Like a husky in the Iditarod Race seeing the finish line before him, Justice towed Deacon across the freshly watered grass, as if he were a sled, to the other end of the yard. Relief roared through Deacon that he had maintained his balance and realized that his left wrist and shoulder were not hurt.

They skidded to a stop. He spotted the suspect advancing on the civilian over twenty-five yards away. *Not even Justice can close that gap in time.*

The suspect held the hammer he had used earlier, and raised above her head.

Once again, time slowed. The civilian was trapped like a rat in a cage with nowhere to go. He reached for his weapon. At hearing the holster back strap release, Justice hit the deck. Deacon drew his Glock 22 in one smooth motion, aimed, and picked up his sights. He focused on the Tritium core at the end of his barrel, just like had trained from thousands of repetitions at the range. The front sight became clear as crystal. His target became blurry.

"Cain PD! Drop the hammer! Now!"

Her eyes flared at him, filled with hatred and rage.

"Fuck off."

She turned her attention back to the woman at her feet. With that twisted sneer on her face, she spat, "This has been fun, but now it is time to die, bitch!" She reared back with the hammer, reaching behind her head to her fullest extent.

He smoothly took the slack out of his trigger and pressed it. Then he fired the second shot—a standard response—at the center mass of the suspect before the first one had hit its target.

The initial shot struck the female in the lower portion of her left shoulder. She jerked forward toward her left side a millisecond after the hollow-point round ripped through her torso and out her back, followed by a spray of bright red blood.

The second round tore through her abdominal aorta and severed her spine. Her legs crumpled like over-cooked spaghetti and the suspect collapsed to the ground. Blood spewed from both holes with the last beats of her heart. A crimson puddle quickly grew, covering the concrete.

A scream turned into sobbing whimpers.

Deacon held his hand parallel to the ground. Justice remained down, resting his head on his paws. Securing his weapon, Deacon rushed to the civilian's side and crouched at an angle beside her, trying to block her view of the downed suspect.

She twisted and clung to him, shoulders heaving with her tears. He wrapped an arm around her and held her close. Strange how it felt right to hold her, someone he had never met, and a feeling he'd never experienced with another victim. Gradually, the adrenaline rush subsided. As it did, he reminded himself it was irrelevant if this woman seemed to fit him. He was in uniform and crouched beside a body he'd just shot. Awkwardly, he released her.

His gaze locked on hers. "Are you all right, miss?"

"I think so. My knee hurts. But other than that I'm okay."

"Good. Let's get the paramedics to check you out." He glanced at the dead female. "And her."

"I don't think they're going to be much help," she murmured.

Deacon took in the carnage. A hint of bile crawled up his throat. He knew he'd be seeing that image in his sleep for a long time. "Just sit tight. Everything will be all right." He watched her shake her head in denial, her stricken gaze glued in growing horror at the spreading pool of blood.

Ashen faced and hand to her lips, she whispered, "Trust me. I'm not going anywhere."

"What's your name?"

"Jessica. Jessica Grady. I'm the manager of Speaker City. The one that was robbed." She looked at his name plate. "And you are Officer Deacon?"

"Officer Daniel Deacon."

"Daniel," she murmured. "Nice name."

"Thanks." He keyed up his radio. "King 93. A suspect's down. Shots fired. EMS Code Three needed at 1245 Stanford Avenue. Start a supervisor and block off this street. Suspect is not conscious." He leaned over and cuffed the dead female. While it seemed to be a bit unnecessary, it was policy as was checking her vitals. "King 93. The suspect isn't breathing and doesn't have a pulse. I am starting CPR."

"Ten-four, King 93."

Head cocked at forty-five degrees, Justice stayed put with a look of "Really?"

Yeah, Deacon knew performing CPR was an exercise futility, but it was policy. With each chest compression, blood oozed from the holes in her back and chest. After a minute, he discontinued the *pro forma* CPR. The medics arrived a few minutes later and took control of the body.

Deacon winced at the sight of him and Jessica covered in blood. *What the hell?* With a mental shrug, he stood and helped Jessica stand. "Justice, heel."

With his partner at his left knee and the lead in his hand, Deacon wrapped his right arm around Jessica. He lifted her and they limped toward the ambulance out front. By the time they reached it, her limp was nearly gone.

Jessica sat on the floor of the ambulance, her feet resting comfortably on the rear bumper. Deacon secured Justice in the rear of his car and joined her. An EMT handed them the necessary towels and water to clean up.

As they scrubbed their faces, arms, and hands, Deacon took in the scene around him. When he'd needed one, he couldn't get a fill unit to save his life, even during a pursuit.

Funny how all that changed when it was an officer-involved shooting. Once Dispatch broadcasted an 11-99, cops from Cain, along with neighboring cities and counties, barreled in to assist.

It all but rained cops. Everyone found they were free to go staff a post when it meant hours of pay with no paper.

At least the guys on swing shift were predictable. Then

he winced at the smell of smoldering brakes of marked units closing on Stanford Avenue and Mrs. Johnson's home. Soon, crime scene tape would mummify her house. Ah, well, the bright yellow couldn't clash any worse than what she had.

Teeth clenched, Deacon pulled his gaze back to the swarming officers. He hated feeling impotent. But with the shooting, he was sidelined.

CHAPTER 13

A rriving at the shooting site, Washington found a morose Deacon seated on the rear bumper of one of the ambulance rigs, his head hanging and staring at his feet. The lights and strobes of various patrol cars were still flashing in the slowly fading light. *Thank God, someone had the brains to kill the damn sirens.*

Whether it was mundane or important, officers scurried about like ants, performing necessary tasks. Washington's gaze drifted back to Deacon. He was seated beside a civilian on the floor of an ambulance, their backs exposed to the open medical bay. They both looked emotionless. *Christ, they look like shit run over twice. They're a couple of damn zombies.*

The only sign of any physical injuries was born by the woman who merely had a neoprene brace on her knee. One glance told Washington, she was the woman whose life Deacon had saved.

Washington scanned the area, infuriated that none of their fellow officers were with them. Here was a woman who'd nearly lost her life. The only person consoling her was the cop who had been forced to take another life to save hers.

He'd known Deacon for years. The poor guy hadn't ever

been in a shooting, let alone killed anyone. He had to be going through hell.

Forcing a smile, Washington strode over to his friend and clapped a hand on his shoulder. "Hey, buddy."

Deacon shifted his blank stare from his feet to his long-time friend. "Hey."

"You did good back there, real good. You and the beast, both."

"Thanks." Deacon tilted his head toward the woman. "This is Jessica. She's the manager of the Speaker City that got hit."

"It's good to see you're okay, Jessica."

"Thanks." She eased free of Deacon's hand and stood. She stretched and tested her knee. It held although a dull throb remained. "If it's okay, I'd like to be alone for a while. I'm going to go take a short walk. I won't go far."

He stared up at her. It wasn't until she had pulled free that he'd realized their hands were clasped. For the first time since the ordeal began, he took a moment to truly *see* Jessica, not a woman whose description he'd catalogue in a report, but the real Jessica.

At a glance, he'd peg her at twenty-six. Her porcelain skin reminded him of a winter's frost at dawn in Squaw Valley. Almond-shaped, glacier-blue eyes set off by high, elegant cheekbones and a straight nose. His eyes drifted to her full, soft lips that begged a man to kiss her. He wished they'd met under better circumstances, because he bet when she smiled everyone around her did. They wouldn't be able to stop themselves.

He bit back the urge to grin. Angelic she might look, but that was no angel who had charged after the suspect. Realizing he'd been staring at her, he wrenched himself back to reality.

Hot or not, now was not the time for this. Yet unable to stop himself, he asked, "Are you okay, Jessica? Would you like me to come with you? I mean, you might feel safer with an officer at your side." *Me.*

Deacon mentally winced, refusing to look at Washington. He knew what he would see—eyes narrowed, a furrow between his brows, and his mouth hanging open. What the hell? Just seeing the concern on her face warmed him, and then her soft smile broke free, and he almost melted as he returned it.

"I'll be okay, tiger. I'm not going far," she said, the back of her fingers brushing his cheek.

"Okay. If you need anything, anything at all, I'll be right here."

"Good." Her eyes skipped over the growing crowd. "I just need some alone time, quiet, to process what happened."

"I understand." Boy, did he.

She turned and slowly limped her way toward the perimeter of the crime scene. Deacon couldn't pull his gaze off her. Licking his lips, he muttered, "God, she's got a great ass and legs up to her armpits."

Laugh booming, Washington slapped him on his back. "Damn, Deacon, even in the middle of an officer-involved shooting, you've still got game."

Ah, hell. Deacon slanted a glance at his comrade and tried to play it off. "What?"

Still chuckling, Washington clapped him on the shoulder. "I loved looking at her, too. She's a good choice, Double D."

Shaken, Deacon shot his buddy a scowl. "What the hell are you talking about?"

"Dude, you weren't just totally staring at her backside, which believe me I understand, but you even mumbled out loud she had a great one. Not that I blame you. That Jessica's dead sexy."

"Poor choice of words, yo."

"Point taken." He jerked his head toward the backyard. "Anyway, you did good today. Seriously. If you hadn't handled it correctly, Jessica would be dead."

"And without your handling of those spikes and pulling

the strip back, I would've blown my tires and not saved her."

"There is that." Washington's massive paw tightened on his shoulder. "Listen, man, be careful. I mean real careful out here, brother. From the looks of thing, Jessica's going to have a big part in this OIS for IA. So promise me that you'll wait 'till this blows over before going after her. The last thing you want to do is something stupid, like ask Miss Jessica out."

Deacon nodded. Damn, Washington was right on both points. Jessica's statement was also vital for the process he was about to endure. The last thing the state needed was for him to screw up the homicide investigation by asking out the witness.

A moment of vertigo swept over him. He fought to stay erect and focused on the flashing blue lights of an approaching unmarked unit followed by a black Suburban.

"You sure you're all right?" Washington asked.

"Yeah. Don't worry. I know the score, and there's nothing to worry about," Deacon said, sneaking glances at Jessica.

"So why am I worried?"

"Beats me."

Deacon nodded at the deputy coroner's arrival in his meat wagon. Two huge men wheeled a gurney out of the SUV and pushed it toward the backyard. He expected the few hours to go by the book and didn't anticipate any surprises. The coroner would pronounce the suspect dead at the scene, then take her back for the autopsy after the crime scene folks did their thing.

Twenty minutes later, one of the coroner's men returned out front. "I went through her pockets and found her license. Tell your sergeant that her name's Rachele Tuefel."

"Shit!" Deacon spat as Washington snarled, "Fuck!"

ᘓᘔᘓ

In accordance with policy, Deacon waited at the shooting site until the Crime Scene Investigation Unit appeared and assumed control from the detectives. He hoped Jack White got the callout as lead detective.

While Jack wouldn't cut him any favors because of their friendship, the detective also was fair, open, and honest.

Frustration ate at Deacon. Five minutes of adrenaline during a shooting would become hours of questions and growing weariness. If he hadn't answered the call, and then taken Rachele Tuefel down, he'd be one of the uniformed officers scurrying around like termites constructing a crime scene mound, marking off their territory. One from which he was now excluded. And Jessica would be dead.

Forty-five minutes later, Deacon still hadn't been allowed to tell anyone what had happened. Frustration continued to build while he watched three police chaplains escort a sobbing Mrs. Johnson from her home. Maybe the councilor they would provide for her could help stem her daily calls to the station for help. As they drove off, he wasn't surprised when he spotted Sergeant Swanson climb out of his vehicle. As shift supervisor, he would have been tasked with overseeing the scene and interviewing him prior to the arrival of the detectives.

Deacon was required to give him his public safety statement, the same one he'd give the detectives. The statement would include how many rounds he fired, in what direction, who was hit, if any suspects were outstanding, the approximate size of the scene, and who the witnesses were.

He wanted to tell the sergeant everything that happened, not just the damn safety statement. Deacon wasn't overly worried. It was a good shoot, a clean shoot. But that didn't change how he felt. And because Deacon trusted Sergeant Swanson, Deacon wanted to pour his guts out. *Needed* to tell him so bad his hands were shaking. Staring down at them, he tried to make them stop but couldn't, wondering if it was the stress or his adrenaline dump abating.

Maybe both. Who knew?

Swanson approached him. Unable to stop himself, Deacon started rattling off everything he'd done.

The sergeant raised his hand, silencing him. "Wait for Investigations. We all know what happened. But that way, you'll only have to tell us once. Trust me, Deacon, you don't want to go through this multiple times. The damned therapist will make you talk about it until you're ready to scream. When that happens, don't hold back. Until the doc clears you, you'll be on admin leave."

Deacon took a deep breath, knowing his mentor was right. With a nod, he shut his mouth. He didn't have to wait long. Since it was an OIS, officer-involved shooting, the entire Investigations Division had been called and would complete the investigation. Detective White approached to take his statement.

He gave Swanson and White his public safety statement. Surprise rippled through Deacon when he realized that, even as he relived Rachele Tuefel's collapse and bleeding out, he had retained his composure.

White shook his head and turned off his digital audio recorder. "Solve no crime till overtime, huh?"

"Ha, ha. You're a laugh a minute," Deacon said.

"Seriously, brother, you all right?"

"Yeah, I'm good. I swear to God, I had no choice. She was going to kill the civilian, Miss Grady, with the hammer. The thing was on the downswing when I shot her." Deacon wasn't sure whom he was trying to convince, White and Swanson or himself, because, for some reason, guilt ate at him.

❧❧❧

Returning to the back of the ambulance, Jessica frowned at the scene she saw. Daniel Deacon looked like he was being beaten. Not physically but verbally. And she knew how painful and demoralizing that would be.

Instantly, the fear she had experienced morphed into out-rage. How dare a detective and some cop with stripes on his sleeve grill Daniel, the hero who had single-handedly saved her life. Lips thinned, she listened to him insisting that he had no choice. He only shot the woman to save her. How dare these two jokers do nothing but silently stare at him as if he were a criminal. *Oh, hell, no, they aren't!*

Wrapped in a blanket, she yelled over to them. "Excuse me. Just what in the hell do you think you're doing?" All three of them turned to her and stared, mouths agape in si-lenced shock. "Why are you questioning the man who just saved my life like he's a damned criminal? He saved my life, for God's sake. I'm the victim here. Do you hear me? I am the damned victim! And no one's asked me a single question."

She glared at the two men, her gaze skimming them up and down in disgust.

The younger one held out his hand. "Miss Grady, please give me a second and—"

"No, damn it, I won't wait. Th—that bitch was going to kill me!" The reality of nearly having died almost leveled her. Fighting tears and failing, she continued, "I'm alive on-ly because of Daniel. H—he should get a freaking medal," she sobbed, clutching his wrist.

He angled toward her, tipped up her chin, and, using the tips of his fingers, wiped the tears from her face. "He's right. It's okay. They're not—"

"It's not okay. I—" Unable to continue, she wrapped her arms around him, her tears streaming across his badge. While he stroked her back, she sniffed and snuggled closer. If she could, she would have crawled inside him. Even sweat-soaked, he smelled great, he smelled of safety.

Deacon arched an eyebrow at his two friends. Jack gave him a tilt of the head and a wink. The sergeant's expression was less approving. Deacon's eyes flared at both of them in return. After a few minutes, Jessica regained her composure, allowing him to step back from her.

"Miss Grady, I'm Detective White. Please, listen for a sec. I know you want to tell us everything that happened, and you will. But because this is an officer-involved shooting, there's a special protocol we have to follow. We've interviewed Officer Deacon and will again. Please, trust me. I want to talk to you, but back at the station. This isn't the place for you to make or sign the statement this will require."

Deacon's gaze locked with hers. He squeezed her shoulders and nodded. "Detective White's right. Let's get you back to the station where it's calmer and you can give your statement there."

Biting her lower lip, she nodded. "Okay."

Deacon helped her toward the detective's car. They passed the coroner's black Suburban. He knew the exact moment she noticed the knuckle draggers zipping Rachele Tuefel into the last bag she'd ever own.

Jessica jerked free, bent, and vomited.

Deacon rushed back to the ambulance and grabbed a cloth. Returning to her, he rubbed her back. "White, you have water in your car?"

"Yeah. Back seat."

Deacon wiped her chin then wrapped an arm around her waist and walked her to White's unmarked car. "Just lean against it, I'll be right back." He grabbed the water and handed it to her.

"Thanks."

After she had filled her mouth, rinsed it, then spit it out, he handed her the cloth. "You're stronger than you think. You'll be fine."

Nodding, she paused a moment before getting in the car. She cleared her throat. "Daniel, my friends call me Jess."

Before he could respond, Washington joined them and flipped open his note pad. "I've confirmed D's ID on the dude Justice caught. I ran a Blue Check on him. You were right, D, his fingerprints confirmed that he is Alejandro Bautista. Plus, when I tossed the car, I found his ID card, but didn't find any dope or other personal property."

At the mention of personal property, the sergeant, White, and Deacon exchanged glances.

"Oh, Hell no! Don't do it. I'm beggin' you, don't make me sit on that piece of shit. Isn't there a jail officer coming on in a few? He can deal with going to the hospital with Bautista and booking him," Washington said in a wheedling voice.

White held his hands up, palm side up. "I wouldn't ask if we didn't need *you* there. If he doesn't lawyer up and makes any statements, we want them, Kevin. And you know a jail officer won't be able to pull it off."

"Thanks a lot, Jack. You're gonna owe me big time. You know how much I hate Cain Regional Medical Center. The place is a pit." Pivoting on his heel, Washington stalked back to his vehicle.

As he disappeared, they heard Jess's muffled snicker. "In spite of your best efforts to stroke his ego, he didn't look like a happy camper."

"Well, he *really* does *hate* the hospital," Deacon said with a smile.

"Too right," White agreed. "D, grab your car and meet me 10-19, okay?"

"No problem, brother. I'll follow you."

"Wait with your partner there. I still have to check on the scene real quick."

"Copy that."

CHAPTER 14

Ubel Tuefel couldn't believe that his beloved Rachele was dead. Dead because some stinking cop gunned her down. But now, seeing her photo flash onto his television, he did. Grabbing the remote off his desk with a shaking hand, he turned up the volume.

"...the officer, a seven-year veteran and K9 handler of the Cain Police Department, shot and killed an armed suspected burglar. Anonymous sources have told me that Mrs. Tuefel and her accomplice fled an attempted robbery of Speaker City in a stolen vehicle. The officer engaged them in the pursuit, which ended near Stanford and Shaw Avenues, where Tuefel fled onto Stanford Avenue. While the details are still sketchy, according to my sources, Mrs. Tuefel was swinging a hammer at a woman's head when the officer fired two shots killing her."

White knuckled fingers tightened around the remote. The thin, plastic case buckled under the pressure, cracking into several places. Body shaking, he stared at the screen and the house where Rachele died. He wanted the names of the officer and woman who had killer her. Now!

He poured himself a double shot of Tequila and downed it in one gulp, then took a second and third. Finally, a coldness settled throughout him. Fingers tapping on his desk, he stared at Rachele's photo on the screen. "*Ich schwöre, meine liebling, sie warden zahlen*," he vowed. Yes, they would pay, slowly, painfully. And when they finally died, it would feel as if he'd given them a gift.

The news camera panned onto the crashed Blazer. If that stupid Eastside gangbanger wasn't dead, he, along with his mother and daughter, would soon join the officer and woman and begging for death.

"I'm here with Mr. Jeffrey Coats, a witness," the reporter continued. "He was at the corner of Stanford and Shaw during the pursuit. Mr. Coats, would you please tell us what happened."

Wearing an "I'm with stupid" tee shirt, Mr. Coats nodded. "Yes, ma'am. Like I was telling you, I saw the whole thing. The Chevy was like haulin' ass and, oh wait, I can't say that, can I? Damn. Sorry about that. Anyways, one of them cops spiked the car and it crashed into the pole and I was, like, whoa! That's when it got, like, sick!"

Between one breath and the next, the man's excited expression at getting his fifteen minutes of fame disappeared was replaced by a faintly ill look. "The dude driving bailed from the Chevy and had this Mexican standoff with the cop. I was, like, oh damn, dude! Bad idea! The cop's got a dog. Then the dude tried to run, but the cop dog was faster. The cop dog, like, jumped and hit the guy like Ray Lewis. Man, was it loud. And it looked like it hurt. Like seriously. And that big-ass dog bit his ass, too, 'cuz there was blood everywhere. I was like, damn! Dude, that's gotta hurt like a bitch! Next thing I know, some girl went chasing after the other girl that took off from the car, and the cop took his dog and chased after them." He pointed to the residence where investigators were working. "They ran over there and I heard all the gun fire. It was intense, yo!"

As the reporter nodded at every word the fool said, Tuefel wanted to wipe the bitch's phony sad, understanding smile off her face—using Rachele's ivory-handled knife.

"Thank you for talking to us, Mr. Coats." As she turned

back to the camera, Tuefel threw the remote at the screen, shattering it and silencing her voice.

He lifted his phone, punched one, and growled, "Luis, get in here!"

The man pounded into the room and froze. He had seen, and survived, some frightening and savage things. But, in this moment, nothing scared him more than the look on his boss's face. He looked like a wild man who had lost his mind. Lips were pulled back in a sneer. His hair stood upright and looked like he'd tried to pull it out. With the spit at the corners of his mouth, he reminded Luis of Crazy Rachele in one of her moods. But what unnerved him most was the single tear running down the boss's cheek and knew the man was ready to crack.

"I don't care how you do it. I don't care who you have to kill to get it done. Bring Alejandro, his mama, and his daughter to my bunker, shackled. And get me the names of that cop and woman who are responsible for my Rachele's death." His fist hammered the desk so hard his monitor fell over, shards of glass raining down onto the carpet. "Once they join Alejandro and his family, they will learn the meaning of vengeance."

Luis gave a respectful nod and, never taking his eyes off the boss, started backing out of the office.

Tears washed Tuefel's face. He felt torn. On more than one occasion, she'd created problems for him. Where he planned, she acted, usually without thinking of the consequences. But, for all the volatility in their relationship, their passion and obsession for one another had never waned. Neither had their mutual love of killing and money.

The ringing of his burner phone snapped him back to the present. With a shaky hand, he reached out for it, paused, and made a fist. When it finally stopped, he exhaled, not realizing he'd held his breath. A second later, it began ringing again. Teeth gritted, he grabbed it, flicked his finger across the screen, and lifted it to his ear. "You on the burner I gave you and someplace secure right?"

"Yeah, and maybe. I'm in a back room."

"Next time, get out of the office. You're car or the 7-11. You have their names?"

"Come on, Tuefel, you can't go after a cop."

Was this junkie moron for real? "Like hell, I can't, and you owe me that much."

"I don't owe you shit. You're free because I've buried calls and evidence, how many times now?"

"And I have kept your pain silent. So who the fuck is he?" Tuefel snapped.

"The shooter's—"

"Hold on." Tuefel tucked the phone between his ear and shoulder. Fuck, he loathed appearing as if he wasn't at the top of his game. Grabbing a sheet of paper and pen, he said, "Go." At the deafening silence, Tuefel pitched the Daum crystal heron he'd bought on their honeymoon against the wall and watched it shatter. "What. Is. His. Name?" he asked, his voice icy calm.

"The shooter's Officer Daniel Deacon. K9. Works swing shift on Patrol. No prior military. A SWAT and EOD wannabe. Nothing special," the man said in a rush.

"See, that wasn't so hard, was it? Now, what in the hell's the name of the woman who caused my Rachele's death?"

"She's nobody. Jessica Grady, manager of Speaker City"

"Which one?"

"Southside, Marathon Avenue."

"Where're they now?"

"Headed into the station for questioning. They'll be there for a few hours. I can guarantee it'll be a grilling."

"Call me as soon as they're out. Oh, and check your ears. I hear them bleeding."

"Go to hell, Tuefel."

"After you." He disconnected the call and quickly dialed Luis.

"Yes, boss?"

"The officer is Daniel Deacon. The woman's Jessica Grady. They're at the police station. Use our sources to find out where they live and bring them here. If necessary, snatch the woman from the Southside Speaker City on Marathon. She's the manager."

"You got it, boss."

CHAPTER 15

Back rigid, lips thinned, mind and expression blank, Deacon strode beside his escort down the hallway to the Investigations Division main interview room. He'd done everything by the book, yet it didn't help. He'd taken a life. Hollowness filled him. A grim-faced officer motioned him into an interview room. As the door snicked shut behind them, a chill shot up Deacon's spine. Suddenly, he felt like a criminal.

He sat at a standard eight foot wooden table with folding legs and prepared to face his inquisitor, knowing their station's modern interrogation rooms were equipped with video surveillance systems. Every word he said would be filmed and examined, on display like a caged animal at the zoo. He struggled to slow his breathing. God, he hoped no one could see his heart racing like a Pontiac GTO revving its engine waiting for the flag to drop.

He studied the plain, unadorned room and its peeling, beige paint. Detectives often joked it was that color because the government got it at the greatest discount. Hiding his trembling hands beneath the table, he stared at the smoke detectors.

He'd watched interviews and interrogations take place in this room before. All his life he'd dreamed about being a cop. Not once had he envisioned himself from this side of the coin. If he could have laughed at the irony, he would have. Then he'd spotted the glowing red light he'd been oblivious to on one of the smoke detectors and chuckled. Anyone—himself included—armed with minimal powers of observation should have realized that no small room needed two smoke detectors.

The placement provided the investigators, and the administrators watching the interview, a full view of his face and reactions via CCTV, and juries loved video, especially confessions. The only drawback was you couldn't see the face of the interrogators, only the backs of their heads.

An officer involved shooting investigation process was simple enough, the agency with the jurisdiction over the location of the shooting was responsible. Then the investigator determined whether or not the shooting was justified.

In this instance, Deacon's agency played two roles—conducting the criminal investigation dealing with the Speaker City incident and ensuring an administrative departmental investigation was performed. The second one was why he would sit facing his longtime friend. This interview and subsequent investigation would establish if his actions were within the department's policy, but it really served an unspoken purpose—covering the department's ass against the attorneys circling like sharks in chum-filled water.

Last to join the party would be the district attorney's office.

However the cards fell, Deacon was in for a long night. He had shot and killed a woman. Yes, it was justified. He could he live with that. But he wondered if his career dreams had died with her. At a knock on the door, Deacon sighed. *And here we go. Time to see if the DA's Office has come to the dance.*

He had watched the first of the investigators assigned to the case enter the room. The first to enter was Jack White. Thank God, his department had assigned him. Having a friendly face on the other side of that table helped Deacon relax—a little.

Jack gave Deacon a slight nod.

Deacon inhaled deeply and focused on slowing his heart rate and lowering his blood pressure. The second investigator entered. Deacon's blood pressure shot right back up. *Shit.* The DDA, Matthew Gabardi. Too all outward appearances, Deacon knew he appeared calm and collected, yet his heart still raced like a car with its accelerator jammed wide open. *Why me?*

Gabardi had a reputation as an attorney who never filed anything. A buddding politician, he went to great lengths finding reasons to avoid filing charges against anything that wasn't gift wrapped with a bright red bow, save any case that dripped with media attention and controversy.

Deacon still remembered arresting a parolee in a stolen car who was on parole for stealing cars and then confessed on video with a, "Hell, yah, I stole that shit! It was fun. too!" He had even left his thumb print on the rearview mirror as if saying, "fuck you," to the cops. Yet when Gabardi reviewed the case, he had issued a No Complaint Filed (NCF) Inter-Agency Memorandum. His only comment, "No one checked to see if the suspect worked at Red Carpet Car Wash. If they had, that would have explained his thumb print on the mirror."

When Deacon had read the form, he'd blown a gasket. What really had pissed him off was the defense created by Gabardi, not that it was much of a defense given the video confession. In that moment, Deacon wondered whose side the prosecutor was on, the state's or the criminal's. Because from his research—which was looking at every case Gabardi had refused to file had or lost—Deacon had begun to seriously worry about the DA's office.

And now, knowing that someone who never filed was assigned to his high-profile officer-involved shooting had Deacon in a sweat because Gabardi also was the proud owner of another reputation—building a name for himself at the expense of everyone around him. He coveted the position of district attorney. To prove he was the better choice than the current DA, he gleefully stepped on the careers of officers and garnered great press doing so. No, this wasn't Gabardi's first rodeo at hanging an officer out to dry. That was something Deacon couldn't afford, not with Ubel Tuefel as the widower.

Gabardi sat. The chair groaned in protest at the man's three hundred pounds plopping onto it.

Deacon struggled to suppress his surprise the chair had held together. Knowing his future technically lay in the asshole's hands had helped him succeed. He took a deep breath and refocused, determined not to be one of the stepping stones in this man's march to the top.

Two hours into the questioning, it had become obvious Gabardi didn't have additional questions but did everything possible to continue the dog and pony show. While Jack had asked pertinent questions, all Gabardi did was reword them. The redundancy had gotten painful and ridiculous. After the third hour, Deacon no longer cared and from Gabardi's smirk, he knew. Jack's flint-eyed glare warned him to watch his mouth. Thirty minutes later, Deacon was done.

"What were you thinking when you shot the victim *Officer*?" Gabardi asked.

Deacon stiffened at the insult in the way he'd said officer. From the fury on Jack's face, he'd heard the same insult. "Last time I checked, Councilor, the lady who's head Mrs. Tuefel was going to beat in, *she* was the victim. I did what was necessary to prevent the death of an innocent. I'd appreciate it if you could keep the facts straight. The suspect I shot is not a victim. We officers are not in the business of shooting victims. This is the fourth time I've told you this in the past thirty minutes. No matter how many times or ways you ask this question, my answer isn't going to change."

Daggers of death flew at him from Gabardi's eyes. His face turned red and his hands balled up into fists. "You didn't answer the question, Officer."

Jack lowered his head in an attempt to muffle his laughter.

"Yes I did and, as I said, have for the past thirty minutes." Seeing the asshole's sanctimonious smile, Deacon's lips curved in a small one of his own. "Fine, one more time. Tuefel grinned at me, then this big-ass hammer was descending—fast—and all I thought was, 'Oh shit. She is going to beat the woman's head in and I can't get there in time.'"

"Can you tell me again why you chose to shoot her, *Officer*?"

"Really? Didn't you hear what I just said? Tuefel was going to hit the victim in the head with a hammer. It would have killed her. I was over twenty feet from them. What the hell did you expect me to do when she was yelling, 'Time to die, bitch!' The woman would've died if I hadn't shot. Would it have made it easier for you if I'd waited until she'd killed the woman before shooting?" Deacon slanted a glance at the smoke detector, then inhaled, counted to twenty, and exhaled. *Keep calm. Your future depends upon it. This asshole will not stop you.*

CHAPTER 16

Ignoring the deluge, Jessica stepped out onto the front steps of the police department and scanned for her car. Where was it? Detective White had said he'd have it driven here and parked in the visitor's area. That was why she'd given him her extra car key. Yet no matter how hard she stared, it wasn't there. *Son of a bitch!* She bet it had been forgotten and was still parked where she'd left it—at the scene.

Shoulders slumped, she turned back to the station. Much as she wanted to contact the detective or Daniel, she didn't dare. When she had caught a glimpse of him being ushered into the inquisition chamber, he'd looked as beat as she felt and Gabardi hadn't had a go at him yet.

If, as rumored, he actually ran for DA, she would take a leave of absence from work and work for his opponent. A tremor rippled through her at the memory of his accusations. Hateful, slimy man. No, *creature*. And she couldn't even call the man pond scum without insulting pond scum.

Fury riding her hard, she re-entered the *dry* lobby, paused, and read the police department badge embossed upon the lobby floor with its mission statement written below it. *We will strive to be the best.*

The officers she'd met today certainly exemplified the

statement. Too bad the same couldn't be said for the DA's office.

Sighing, she walked up to the person behind the window. "I've got a problem. I was the witness in the officer-involved shooting and brought here by Detective White. He said he'd arrange for an officer to drive my car from the crime scene to here. But I can't find it."

"Let me call Dispatch and check out what's happened." A few minutes later, the older officer returned. "Dispatch advised it's still on site."

"Could I get a ride to my car?" She didn't need to see his head shaking no. His glum expression said it all. But ever polite as trained by her mother, she let him tell her the cruel truth.

"I asked. Even reminded them Detective White had ordered it brought here so you'd have it after your interview. I got told that all on-duty patrol units are currently tied up on priority traffic. I can call a tow truck, but they'd take it to impound."

"I'll wait until a unit's free."

"Could be several hours. But if you want to wait, I'll have someone escort you to the lounge. There's coffee there, tastes like dirt, but it's warm."

"Thanks anyway. I'll call a friend." Her boiling anger was only surpassed by the utter shock at the swing from the excellent service earlier to the shit she was now hearing.

Grappling her cell phone, she called Brian's office. After ten rings, voicemail picked up. Frowning, she dialed the store and got a recording, "We're very sorry but due to an attempted robbery, the store will be closed until—"

Frustration riding her, she scrolled through her contacts, then started sniffling at finding only numbers for the store and corporate. How sad was that? She didn't have anyone to call for help. What had happened to her? When had her life become consumed by work? *What a life*, she thought, jamming her phone into her purse.

Misery gave way to the black depths of depression. Using her hands, she scrubbed her face dry and, gathering her tattered pride around her, walked out into the rain. As soon as she got home, she was reconnecting with her college pals.

As she slogged along the road, she tried to focus on good things. Only four came to mind. She couldn't die from being wet, make that sopping. She wasn't in heels or her best flats. She had stopped bleeding inventory. She had met Daniel.

 ⌒⌒⌒

Shoulders relaxed, Deacon leaned forward, his elbows on the table, his finger threaded. "Are we finished?" he asked in a calm, cool voice.

"Yes, you've said that. But I'll ask you again, was it necessary to kill her, *Officer*?"

With a blank stare, Deacon looked up at Gabardi, who'd having managed to lift his girth from his sagging chair and had begun pacing behind Jack's and his chairs. Deacon's eyes locked with Jack's. *Do something*, he silently begged. When he caught Jack glancing repeatedly to the smoke detector, Deacon settled. Everyone was watching and recognized what Gabardi was attempting to do. And if the bastard's boss didn't believe them, he just needed to watch the recorded interview.

Deacon sighed. Looked like he'd be buying White dinner for that reminder. "My intention wasn't to kill her. It was to stop her. I couldn't have done anything different. All of my training, all my practice at the range, prepared me for that moment. I had one chance to stop the suspect from killing the victim. I couldn't afford to throw my rounds downrange and potentially hit the civilian. I had to make my shot as I was trained or an innocent woman died. As I've said repeatedly, I had two choices, let the innocent victim die—or, at the very least, be severely brain damaged—and then shoot, killing Mrs. Tuefel as my training demanded. Or I could prevent the victim's death or injury by shooting Mrs. Tuefel as my training demanded. And should the suspect object to why she's ended up wherever it is she ended up, I suggest she take it up with the devil in charge."

Gabardi stopped and froze. For once, he was speechless. Even those watching the recording could have heard a pin drop.

Deacon saw his opportunity and threw his punch. "I wonder, Mr. Gabardi, if I were swinging a hammer at your head while yelling, 'Time to die, bastard, die,' would you want the responding officer to wait until the hammer had crushed in your skull before firing?"

At the look on Gabardi's face, Deacon bit back a smile.

Jack snapped shut his notebook. "Officer Deacon, as you are aware, officers on the Officer-Involved-Shooting Investigation Team have interviewed the victim, a Miss Jessica Grady. Her account of the events is exactly as you have stated them. Do you have anything else you would like to add?"

"No, sir."

"Very well. Also, she requested that I convey to you her gratitude for saving her life. When interviewed by the press, she praised your actions and those of the Cain PD."

That's two steak dinners I owe you now, brother.

White faced the prosecutor. "Mr. Gabardi do you have anything else to ask that's pertinent to this investigation?" With nothing but stunned silence from him, White sighed. "Then I believe we are finished with our end of things. With no further questions or any further need of you, Officer Deacon, you're excused and thank you. This is Detective Jack White, Case Number 15-08769. End of recording."

The CCTV recorder was switched off, killing the soft blue glow of the monitors in the adjacent room. Deacon kept eye contact with White. With a simple look, the message of thanks was clearly conveyed with a nod in return.

Gabardi gathered his papers and glared at Deacon. With

balled fists, he rested his knuckles on the table and leaned forward. Creaking in protest, the table bowed.

He didn't impress Deacon. But the table not collapsing did.

Gabardi sneered. "I guess we are done as well, Officer Deacon. We will forward our findings when we are finished with our investigation."

Deacon stood. "Thank you. Please be sure to send me a copy. By the way, I've noticed on occasion my name's been misspelled on subpoenas by the DA's office. First name's Daniel—D-A-N-I-E-L. Last name's Deacon—D-E-A-C-O-N. If you're going to try to make a name for yourself by standing on my neck, the least you can do is spell my name right."

☙❦❧

Free!

After what had seemed like an eon, Deacon stepped out into the night and paused to breathe in the sweet, cool air of freedom. Lifting his head to the sky, he savored the first drops from a slew of rain splashing onto his face.

It seemed that, while he'd felt incarcerated but was only being interrogated, the weather man pulled some strings. *Weatherman, 4,006. Deacon, 0.* His arms raised in supplication, he enjoyed the cleansing kiss of water washing away Gabardi's bullshit.

Deacon dropped his arms and, grinning, raked his fingers through his dripping, wet hair. With his personal *Shawshank Redemption* now behind him, he headed for his patrol car.

"Officer Deacon. A word please."

He stopped. *What now*? On a sigh, he turned then froze at the seeing the chief.

"Sir?"

"Cut the formality bullshit, Officer. I was in the observation room during your interview. Are you okay?"

"Yes, sir, I'm fine." Deacon shrugged. "I've been through worse."

"That may be true, but Gabardi's behavior was beyond the pale. I'll be giving his boss a call tomorrow about it and filing a formal complaint. I won't have my officers treated as criminals. Hell, make that worse than he treats criminals."

Deacon quashed his desire to grin like a fool. Nothing would likely come from either the call, or complaint. But the DA would be on notice, which meant Gabardi would have an uncomfortably long day.

"I appreciate that, sir."

The chief clapped a hand on Deacon's shoulder. "No problem. Just do me one favor next time you are in an OIS."

"Name it, Chief."

"Wait for a count of ten before you go off on a DDA. It's always a good idea to ensure the recorder's off first. You almost didn't make it this time. And being the asshole he is, it'd suck having to explain that away in court."

For the first time since the shoot, Deacon relaxed and laughed. "No kidding. Done. Thanks, Chief."

He received a grin in return. "You did good today," he said. "You saved a woman's life. Now, get out of here and go home.

"Will do."

 প্ঞেপ্ঞ

Tuefel grabbed the burner cell phone on its first ring. "Where are you?"

"My car. And before you ask, yes, I'm alone and using the burner phone."

"Good, good. You're learning. Is he being charged?"

"No, the shooting's been ruled justified."

Tuefel's reached out to the photo portrait of Rachele and his fingers caressed her lips. Had he remembered to kiss her and tell her he loved before she left? God, he prayed she knew she was his world.

"You there?"

"Yes, just had to take care of something," Tuefel said. "Where's he right now?"

"On his way home."

"The son of a bitch killed my wife," Tuefel growled as he fought the choking pain of her loss.

"Yeah, well he's been a thorn in my side his entire career. So we both have a dog in this fight. The woman is your bigger problem. Once she's out of the way, you might be able to go after Deacon. Knowing the city and its attorney's, they'll kick his ass off the force. Then it's open season."

"Where is she?"

His asset chuckled. "She's…Shit—"

Tuefel ignored the call's abrupt termination. If his asset got too sloppy, he'd have Luis take him out. Quietly. After an autopsy, the cops would never look his way.

Anticipation licked his veins as he slowly smiled. He'd target the woman at home or in the store. A robbery gone bad. If the crew was in the front of the store, Luis could grab the woman and escape out back unnoticed. Then they'd snatch the officer. Last but not least would be Alejandro and his family.

Oh, yes, they would pay…and pay…and pay…until there wasn't enough left of them to torture.

CHAPTER 17

Deacon heard a faint whimpering as he approached his patrol car. *Oh, shit. Not good.* Tied up answering questions for over three hours, he'd forgotten about Justice. He didn't need to hear his partner's anguish to know what had happened. Having left the windows of the unit cracked open, he'd caught a whiff of what lay waiting for him as he approached. A tsunami of foulness crashed over him and almost sent him to his knees. Gagging, he shoved his mouth and nose beneath his undershirt and, standing to the side of the door, hit his door pop.

Justice flew from the car like a Saturn-V rocket and sped for a nearby set of bushes. "Sorry, buddy." His partner had taken pity on him. He hadn't finished what he'd started. That meant it might not take several hours of scrubbing as it had last year.

Dread dogging his steps, Deacon eased his way to the open door. Thank God. It had stayed on the rubber mat. Grasping the edges, he yanked the mat from the rear of the car and threw it onto the grass. The mess landed among the plants. Rain began washing it. Rivulets of filth ran off into oblivion.

Damn it. He should have dropped Justice off at the kennel before coming in. He just hadn't been thinking and his partner had suffered as a result. Grimacing, Deacon opened the trunk and removed his trusty bottle of Orange 409. Nothing, not even the utter vileness that Justice produced, survived the power of Orange.

While he worked, Justice splashed in the puddles. With a shrug, Deacon accepted it as...well, justice for having neglected his partner. As he scoured the mat, the floodgates of heaven opened. Wind picked up. Water sliced in from the side, cutting to the bone.

Within ten minutes, Deacon and Justice were back in their respective places in the car that now smelled like an orange grove. Throwing the car into gear, he backed up out of the covered parking stall too fast and narrowly missed backing into the marked Dodge Ram 1500 behind him.

Sure, everyone knew the K9 cage was a bitch to see through, even more so with a giant shepherd in the way. Not that the driver of the Ram would accept that as an excuse. Rightly so, too. Deacon knew he hadn't looked. As such, he'd been oblivious to the vehicles around him until an air horn blasted the K9 unit and he'd almost jump out of his skin.

Lowering his side door window, he leaned out and craned his head out.

"Damn, Deacon, what the hell were you doing?"

"Oh, shit! I'm sorry, Dirks." Talk about getting a lucky break. He hated even considering how Dirks would have handled his remodeling the Ram.

"No problem. Just be grateful that *I* watch where you're going."

"And don't think I don't appreciate it, too. Thanks again." As soon as the truck cleared the area, Deacon pulled out and headed to the Fifth Street gate to go home. As he waited for the gate to retract, he remembered his introduction to the man who was to become one of the biggest influences in his career.

At the memory of their first meeting, a slow smiled played at the corners of his lips. He'd been attending his first briefing when the rear door to the back parking lot opened. The poorly oiled hinges on the doors had screeched in protest at supporting the weight of the massive oak door. Light flooded the room, silhouetting the biggest man Deacon had ever seen.

He had filled the entire doorway. At six-foot-eight and weighing in at a muscular three-twenty, he would have stood out anywhere. But in a police precinct briefing, with his freshly shaved bald head reflecting the light beaming down like a mirror and his handlebar mustache, he was unforgettable—a good ol' country boy. Instantly, Deacon recognized that this man had seen his fair share of rodeos on the street, and had won all of them.

A minute later, he plopped himself down in the empty chair next to Deacon and thrust out a bear-sized paw. "Dirks Hamilton. Pleased to meet ya and welcome aboard. Do me a favor, will ya? Don't do anything stupid like gettin' yourself killed. Oh, and close your damn mouth. You look like a dumbass with it lookin' like the Grand Canyon, son," he said, laughing. "Oh, sorry I'm late, Sarge."

Deacon sighed. God, he missed those innocent days when he was never tired or feeling abused. Closing his eyes, he forced himself to listen to the rain. He'd always loved the symphony it made, especially beating down on his car's metal roof. It melted away his stress. Even the stress of being interrogated.

Interrogated. Interrogated like a damn criminal because I did my job. Things sure have changed over the past decade. He needed to thank Jack. The man had leashed Gabardi and helped Deacon maintain his composure, ensuring he still had a job. Without him there, the conversation with the chief would have gone very differently.

Justice stood and rested his muzzle on Deacon's shoulder and the top of the seatback. Deacon rolled his head to his right and, reaching up, scratched the top of his partner's head.

Sometimes dogs just needed reassurance, and sometimes

people just needed to give it. It was free therapy for both of them.

Seeing that the gate had finally retracted, he lifted his foot off the brake and pulled forward. Within minutes, they would be home. At least, that was the plan. For some unexplainable reason, he found himself driving back to where his Hell began.

A few minutes later, Deacon questioned his sanity, struggling to see out his windshield as sheets of rain that made it almost impossible to see. But if the storm stayed true to normal patterns, it should blow itself out within fifteen minutes.

Wrong.

It strengthened. What had been a rainstorm, now felt like torrential downpour.

Fatigued and mentally exhausted, he admitted he couldn't risk driving in this weather. Squinting, he searched for a place to safely pull off and stop. He started to slow, and then frowned at a woman hobbling along the apron of the road. Her shoulders hunched, head down, she struggled against the slashing rain and wind in an attempt to limp down the street. Talk about failure. For every step forward, she made two backward. Lord help her, she had to be nuts.

Not that it mattered. Insane or not, he couldn't leave her out here alone. Not in this weather. Not with the way Californians drove when the roads were only damp, and right now they were near flood stage. If she didn't drown, then one of the city's crazy drivers, like Miss Car-Dancing, would run her over. And after today, he couldn't afford that on his conscience. Cleared or not, the shooting weighted on him and would give him years of nightmares.

Pulling back onto the road, he inched forward. Once he was even with her, he'd do his duty and see if she needed help. A second later, he froze at his first good view of her.

"What the *hell*?"

It was Jessica. He could never mistake her ass or long legs for anyone else's. So why hadn't someone taken her home? What had happened to SOP? Was he the only one who followed it?

For cripes sake, she was both a victim and witness. It had to be Gabardi's fault. White would never have allowed her to be out alone, especially in this weather and with Tuefel, no doubt, having declared war on everyone involved.

CHAPTER 18

Deacon charged out of his car. "God damn it, Jessica, what're you doing walking out here?"

"I love the rain. Why else would I be slogging through this mess?"

He recognized snarling sarcasm when he heard it. Okay, her eyes flashing fire hadn't hurt. "I—I—"

She shoved long, dripping strands of hair off her face. "Look, I'm headed for my car."

"What? Why? It's in the station visitor's parking lot."

She sloshed up to him. "Oh, really? I think not, Daniel. It's still where I pulled over and some unknown cop's riding around with my spare key," she said, jabbing his chest with her index finger on each word.

Deacon held her hand flat against his chest. "Something's wrong."

This smelled. Could Tuefel already be making his move? If so, he had someone working for him on the inside. That was the only explanation for this clusterfuck.

With a narrowed gaze, he scanned the area around them. While he didn't see anything or anyone, just as Justice's hackle rose when he scented danger, so too did the hairs on the back of Deacon's neck. Hyper alert, he wrapped an arm around her and rushed her to his car. "Get in, now."

She balked at being shoved into his car. "What's the matter?"

"I saw White hand your spare keys to one of the yahoos at the front desk. That you're out here alone—" He shrugged. "I'll contact White as soon as I know you're safe."

"I can walk. I'm almost there."

"I know. And it doesn't make sense, given we're both soaked, but the storm isn't letting up anytime soon. So let's get inside and I'll crank up the heat. At least you can get a little warm while I take you to your car. It's the least I can do."

Jessica shivered, readjusting her thoughts about being wet didn't hurt. "All right" she said with a sigh. "And, thank you."

Arm wrapped around her, Deacon helped her into the front passenger side door. "I hope you don't mind the smell of wet dog and orange."

"Orange?"

"You'll understand as soon as you're inside."

He flashed a wicked grin, and Jessica almost melted on spot. The man was more dangerous than rich, dark chocolate. Sitting on the seat, she swung her legs inside the car, ignoring the water slushing off her pants and onto the floor. Inhaling, she caught the scent of orange cleanser.

She watched as Daniel slid behind the steering wheel. He dumped a bunch of terrycloth towels on the divider between the seats.

"That's a lot to carry around with you."

Chuckling, he jerked his backward. "It pays to make like a boy scout and be prepared. Jessica, I'd like you to meet my partner, Justice."

"Oh, my," she murmured, her eyes glued to the four-legged behemoth whining at a high pitch. "Does he always do this?"

"Yup."

She flashed him a knowing grin. "Because sometimes there're accidents that need orange."

"Absolutely, and it's always my fault."

"Naturally. You're the human and control ingress and egress from the vehicle." Chuckling, she took several towels. After mopping up the puddle she'd made on the floor mat, she used another to wrap her hair in, and the third one went to patting her face and arms dry. Once he had the heat blasting, she toed off her shoes and stuck her bare feet under the vent.

"Yup." Deacon shoved the day's paperwork onto the corner of his dash which served as his "In" box. He noticed Jessica staring through the grate at Justice and braced himself for seeing pure, unadulterated fear as he usually did. Instead, curiosity and a small amount of fear plus open wonder flitted across her face. He hoped like hell she didn't play poker. The woman was an open book.

"Don't worry. He can't get through the cage. And as long as you don't attack me, he won't try to attack you. He may whine and bark a bit, though. Justice doesn't care for riders." He grimaced as soon as the words left his mouth. "I—I didn't mean it to sound like—"

Sighing, she flopped back in her seat. As she reached back to grab another towel, her left elbow slammed into metal. "What the—"

"Sorry about that. You must have hit the side of the shotgun. The assault rifle's locked beside it next to me. Don't worry. They're safely locked in the gun rack."

She tugged the remaining towels off the weapons and took her time inventorying the interior. Metal bars behind them along with a plastic shield covered the back of the passenger seat along with wire mesh. The weapons were set back between the bucket seats in a kind of well. No wonder she hadn't seen them. Between them was a small work station. The radio and scanner sat back near the rifles with Daniel's briefcase nearest the front.

"I don't want you to think that wonderful aroma we're

enjoying is the rubber mat beneath Justice. Usually, we don't have a problem. Trust me, I'm a good partner. But today, I was stuck in the station answering the Gabardi's questions, without a break. So when I finally got released, I discovered need had overtaken training."

"Good thing it was raining then," Jessica said, laughing. "God, it feels good to laugh."

Deacon found her voice, her scent, everything about her intoxicating. "Yeah, it does."

"I'm betting Justice forgetting his training doesn't embarrass you all that often."

"Only when he uses the head in front of a bunch of kindergarteners."

"What?"

Deacon filled her in on the events from earlier and was rewarded with more laughter. Feeling light-hearted for the first time in hours, he headed to the scene of the collision. Lifting his radio, he keyed up. "King 93." Silence. Deacon keyed up a second time. "King 93."

"King 93, go ahead."

"King 93, show me en route to Shaw and Stanford transporting one female. Mileage 76,103."

"Copy that King 93. Mileage 76,103. Your time is 2248."

"Ten-four." At Jessica's questioning look, Deacon shrugged. "Policy. Any time a male officer transports a female passenger, whether civilian or someone in custody, we're required to give Dispatch our mileage. That way, if a lady cries rape or God only knows what else, there's a record. It also makes IA's life easier. Between my call now and when we arrive, they're able to quickly compute our diving time and distance are consistent with the information provided."

"Right. It sucks, but I understand why you would need to do it."

"Yeah. We all protect ourselves because some cops abused their authority."

Deacon turned up the heater, hoping it helped dry her a

little more. Hot air billowed from the vents. Inhaling, he caught the faint, intoxicating scent of barely there perfume. Straightening out his cruiser, he reminded himself to pay attention to the road not her. Maybe if he turned on the radio, he wouldn't keep glancing her way.

Seconds later, he was proven wrong as Jessica began to drum her fingers on the window to the beat of the music on the radio. The smooth sound of *Separate Ways* began to fill the cab.

"I love this song. No one can sing like Steve Perry."

"No joke. Journey rocks. It's too bad they split up. They were an awesome band. I guess they all do at some point."

Justice began to whine and sway his head back and forth. Jessica's mouth gaped open. "Yo—your dog—is your dog singing?"

"Oh yeah, he does that. He loves Journey too. The only problem is he seems to think he sings better than Steve Perry."

Justice chuffed and reached through the grate to lick Jessica's ear. "You know I think he likes you," Deacon said. "It's rare that, when someone new sits in my vehicle, my dog takes a liking to them. He's proven to be a good judge of character."

"Well, I for one agree with him. I am pretty cool."

Deacon's chuckle turned into a deep belly laugh. As he happily distracted his passenger with more Justice stories, his alertness to his surroundings faded.

Suddenly, the storm's intensity increased, demanding his full attention. "Typical," he muttered.

"What's typical?"

"The rain. Forget showers. When it rains in California, it feels like a monsoon," he said as raindrops hit the car hood so hard they bounced off it. While his windshield wipers did their best, it was futile. Too much water, too fast made for driving blind. Thankfully, there weren't any cars or pedestrians. Smart. A shame he and Jessica weren't inside keeping their heads down like the rest of Cain.

Forced to stop for a red light, the evaporated moisture from their clothing and on Justice's fur fogged his windows to the point that he needed to turn the defroster from low to high.

When she said, "Officer, you might want to keep that thing on. You wouldn't want people thinking we were up doing something to fog all the windows," Deacon's face burned. Damn, he'd probably turned as red as the light he was trying to run.

Grinning, she patted his arm. "Relax, Daniel, I mean, Officer Deacon. I'm just joking."

The instant the light switched to green, Deacon floored the accelerator. Soon, his embarrassment forgotten, they returned to their small talk, which morphed into deeper discussion about family, religion, and sports.

Abruptly, Deacon stiffened. It felt like a typical first date conversation. *Seriously man. What are you doing? You know better. Stay away from her until the case is resolved. Gabardi's already gunning for you. Don't hand him the goods.*

He straightened and retreated behind his proper, professional demeanor. As soon as the shrink cleared him, he could see her on his days off.

And see her, he would. There was something about her that didn't allow him to tear himself away. He'd always been a sucker for blue eyes. But blue was too tame a word to describe them. They were a deep yet a soft blue, reminding him of the Caribbean. Every time he looked into them, he found himself oddly at peace. A feeling he hadn't experienced in a long time.

Jessica pointed out the window. "Watch out!" she screamed.

Deacon's gaze followed her finger. A cat walking in the street. He swerved, narrowly missing it. "Thanks, Jess. I'd hate to have run over the cat. They're a pain in the ass to pull one out of my tires." He grinned at her sputters then her snort.

"That's one way of looking at it. By the way, I like it when you call me Jess," she said with a twinkle in her eyes.

A smile nipped at his lips as he glanced in his rearview mirror and saw Justice, hackles raised, staring out the back window. Through sheeting rain, he spotted a black Chevy Malibu. Yes, it maintained a healthy distance behind them. He couldn't put his finger on why the hair on the back of his neck suddenly mirrored Justice's, but everything in him screamed stay alert. Something wasn't right.

Arriving at the intersection of Stanford and Shaw, he keyed his radio. "King 93, on scene. Copy mileage?"

"Go ahead."

"King 93, mileage 76,107."

"Copy that, King 93. 76,107 at 2254 hours."

"Well, Jess, here we are and…"

Her fist slammed into the glove box.

Deacon and Justice jumped.

"Shit! Where the hell's my car?!"

"They must have towed it."

"Why the hell would they do that?"

"When you took off after Rachele Tuefel, you left your car in the road. The responding officers who handled the crime scene and traffic collision probably towed it."

"But when I checked at the station, the officer told me it was still here and asked if I wanted it towed. I said, no."

Deacon's roiling stomach joined the raised hackles at the back of his neck. "I'll confirm it with Dispatch. But if it's in impound, we won't be able retrieve it until morning. It'll take that long to process the paperwork and get Detective White to sign-off on it so you aren't charged."

"We?" She paused a moment, a half-smile twitched the corners of her lips. "Do you always provide this much help to all the ladies, Daniel?"

"No," he croaked, then swallowed hard. "You don't ever stop, do you?"

"Nope, where'd be the fun if I did?"

"Right, fun. Let's get you home." As soon as Jessica

gave him her address, 6987 E. Blackburn, he updated Dispatch again and asked, "Was a car towed from Shaw?"

"King 93, affirmative, vehicle towed from Shaw at 2045 hours."

Deacon pulled out on Shaw and contacted White, quickly bringing him up to date. At Jessica's giggles, he realized he was driving in the wrong direction. At least she'd waited until he'd finished talking to Jack. With a grimace, Deacon made a U-turn.

"That's better, Officer."

Damn. She couldn't let it pass. They continued in the rain.

"Daniel, you mind if I ask you a question?"

"No. Shoot." *Poor choice of words there.*

"The woman who tried to kill me, you mentioned her name earlier. What did you say her name was?"

"Tuefel. The woman who tried to kill you was Rachele Tuefel. She was the wife of Ubel Tuefel."

"Tuefel? As in The Tuefel? The Krusnik?" Frowning, she sucked her lower lip between her teeth. "Great, just great. The wife of The Krusnik?"

Deacon's gaze flicked to his rearview mirror. Yup, the Chevy was still there, and Justice hadn't relaxed. *Stupid, Deacon, really stupid. Why in the hell didn't I check for it when I pulled over? I should've noticed it hadn't passed us. Because, moron, you couldn't keep your eyes off her.* "I see you've heard of him."

"It'd be hard not to. He's the lead story every time a jury acquits him for drug distribution or murder. And most recently, when Mr. Pond Scum Gabardi refused to indict him."

Drawing his gaze from the Chevy, he stole a glance at her. Silent worry assailed him. He'd make sure she was all right, even if he had to spend the rest of the night on guard duty. Seeing her stare out the window at the rain while gripping the side of his patrol car's mobile computer, he sighed. His hand clasped hers and gave it a quick squeeze. "Don't worry. You're going to be fine. If he's pissed off at anyone, it'll be me."

She gasped and stared at him. "Oh, my God, you're right."

"Like I said, don't worry. Tuefel's smart. He won't come after a cop. It isn't good business, and the man's all about business. Come on, let's get you home. But if you can, do me a favor. Stop giving me a hard time, okay?"

Grinning up at him, she winked. "We'll see. And thank you again for the help and the ride."

"My pleasure."

CHAPTER 19

Deacon parked beside her curbside mailbox and took in her house. Impressive. A creamed-colored colonial. Perfectly maintained Japanese Boxwood hedges flanked the main walk to the front door. Just as with his place, giant twigs with leaves pretended to be trees. Sure, someday they might grow big enough to be worth something. But for now, lack of shade was all too common in new subdivisions.

The shuttered windows were painted in what appeared to be a navy blue or black. Unfortunately, Deacon would have to wait for light to know for sure. He had a hard time telling the difference between them during the day, let alone on a rainy night. He knew from the size it was a three bedroom, two bath home and loved it immediately—not that he'd ever admit, even to himself, that he was slightly jealous.

"This is your house?"

"Yeah. I was really lucky. I bought it a couple of months after the market crashed and got it for a steal."

"I'll say. It's gorgeous."

"Thank you. I'm really happy with it."

Exiting the car, he walked around to the passenger door and opened it. As Jessica jumped out and bolted to the door, Deacon ran through his options. Technically, he was off duty and would be for several days. So walking her to the door shouldn't be a problem. But he was in uniform and knew it wasn't the time or place. Just as asking her out was taboo. "Can I call you sometime?" he blurted out.

As soon as the words left his mouth, he wished he could stuff them back down his throat. He could see the complaint rolling in now.

"I'm sorry. What did you say?"

He fought for self-control, then thought what the hell and raced up to the porch. Drenched but not caring, he stopped on the lower step. The now they stood at eye level. God, she was beautiful. Ignoring the drumming thunder, he pressed his lips against her ear. "I said, well, what I meant to say was—"

"Do you want my phone number? Because I'll happily give it to you, but only under one condition."

"What?"

"I don't date guys I don't know." She stuck out her right hand and he clasped it in his. "There, we've officially met," she said. "But, what with you're saving my life and all, you aren't an unknown, are you?"

Thrilled replaced shocked. He loved that her grip was firm and solid, not weak and insipid like so many women. More importantly, she wanted to see him again. "No, I guess I'm not."

He quickly scribbled her number in his notepad. Damn the rain. He should have known better than to use a pen. Ink smeared around water. He quickly returned the precious cargo back into his pocket, but not before taking a second to memorize it. With an awkward smile, he pulled out one of his cards, wrote down his cell number, and gave it to her. "Call me if you need anything or just want to talk." Seeing her clutch it to her chest, he relaxed and backed down the stairs to begin the dreary walk back to his patrol car.

"Oh, and Daniel?"

He trotted back to the porch. "Yes?"

"I just wanted to say, thank you. I don't think I can ever

thank you enough for saving my life." For the second time, she leaned forward and kissed his cheek. Then with a wave, she rushed inside.

As he slogged his way back to his vehicle, he spotted the Malibu parked down the street and paused. His gaze pinged between the car and Jessica's front door. Hearing Justice's snarling bark and clawing at the rear window, Deacon sprinted to his vehicle. He wanted nothing more than to grab the lead line and hit the door pop. Only one thing stopped him. If asked why he had taken that action, he didn't think claiming his gut was screaming at him would work as a good explanation. Neither would declaring that his partner was all but lunging out the car's back window. Not with Gabardi gunning for him.

The best he could do was check out the Chevy as drove by it and confirm it was empty. Hell, for all he knew, it was a neighbor's car. "Should've asked her about it before leaving."

Getting in his car, he snapped his fingers. Stiff-legged, as if against his will, Justice came to him. Scratching behind his ears, Deacon murmured, "After we've eaten, we can return and do a patrol." Justice shook his head and snorted. Snot landed on Deacon's face and uniform. "Yeah, I love you, too."

ഇരുഇ

Luis lay on his side and waited for the cop to leave. Once the car passed, he sat upright. He would wait as long as it would take. Everyone, including the boss, thought he was slow and nothing but a thug. Not true. He was just smart enough to hide his genius.

It always surprised him that the boss didn't see beneath the façade. After all, to be a successful hitman—he was one of the best and in much demand, not that Tuefel knew about his sideline—required: careful planning and the virtue of patience, patience being absolutely essential for an assassin.

It required time to learn the target's habits and patterns. Studying the mark increased the odds of a clean hit exponentially. Knowing your target inside and out was almost as critical as recognizing when to strike. They were two sides to the same coin. Now wasn't the time.

He'd take the woman first. The cop could wait. One click of the man's radio and an army of hurt would descend on Luis, which Tuefel and he wanted to avoid. He'd hunt the cop later, after Tuefel had Bautista and the dog was out of commission—permanently. Ah, *Dios*, he hated dogs, especially cop dogs.

As he stared at the woman's house, a waterfall dumped on his car and he shivered. Being from Baja, he knew the importance of water. There it arrived in soft showers, not the torrents of water pounding the Malibu's sheet metal roof, making it impossible to think.

Boredom was the greatest danger to his success. Right now, it stalked him like a lion in the Serengeti, with stealth. Luis bit his tongue. The sharp pain and copper taste of blood focused him, keeping the lion at bay. For now.

He pulled his blade free and held it in his fist. Rotating it in the soft glow of the distant street lamp, he admired the light glinting off its eight inches of steel. How many throats had it sliced? He ran a finger along its razor-sharp edge. He hadn't counted in years. The soul could handle only so much.

Sure, the boss had ordered Luis to bring her to him. But the man wasn't thinking straight. If he were, he'd realize it would alert the authorities when they returned to interview her again. And that was something neither of them needed. Not with the boss so…fragile. No, he'd understand. The cop and Bautista were the ones truly responsible and deserving of the boss's special attention. Better to have the woman die in what looked like an accident.

Confident the cop wouldn't return any time soon, Luis started working. He measured out roughly six feet of five-minutes-per-foot-time fuse. Thirty minutes should be more than enough. He'd be long gone.

After it blew, the place would be crawling with cops.

He slowly sliced through the fuse with a surgeon's precision. One had to be careful when the black powder core was exposed to the world for the first time. He set his knife aside and ran his fingers along the length of the fuse. Flexing it with the tender caress of a lover, he checked it for any breaks along its length.

Luis grabbed a blasting cap from his ammunition can and held it between his index finger and thumb. He marveled at the awesome potential of such a little thing. Pure, unadulterated power. His grip tightened around it as he slid it over the end of the fuse. Lifting a set of steel crimpers, he squeezed the base of the cap, creating an airtight seal, ensuring that the fuse would burn all the way into the base of the cap. Then he gently laid it and the fuse on the seat beside him.

Time for the explosive. He always felt goosey when dealing with Composition C 4, better known as C-4 or plastique. Sighing, he reached out, gently raised the one and a quarter pound block of plastic, and retrieved his knife, staring at it with reverence. Its malleability and durability enamored him. He appreciated, no relished, the awesome destructive force he wielded in his hand. He was a god. *With control over power such as this, no man is greater than me.*

Plunging his blade into the base of a block, he burrowed deeply into it. Reliable and incredibly powerful, the explosive would be sufficient to level the house. Hell, if he planted it carefully, it would likely destroy those nearby. Slowly withdrawing his knife, Luis sheathed it for later use.

Crumbly morsels of C-4 fell into his lap like destructive bits of blue cheese. Not as tasty but more pleasurable. Picking up each crumb, he gently pressed them back into the block. He paused a moment and examined his handiwork. Pleased with his gouge, he raised the fuse, and then slid the blasting cap into the explosive, completing the firing train.

Crushing the end of the C-4 around the base of the blasting cap, he created a rudimentary seal that hid the cap from the world in an explosive womb. With a few quick wraps of duct tape, he secured it and the fuse in place.

Luis snapped open his chrome lighter. The metallic clang of the lid echoed through the air. Sliding his thumb across the grinder, he sparked the fluid soaked wick. The Flame danced to life and gently kissed the end of the waterproof military-grade fuse. The powder ignited and would continue to burn even in the typhoon assaulting his car. Glancing in the mirror, he saw that the tiny, glowing light from the burning fuse revealed his face—one that was deceptively calm and quiet. Glee surged, but remained contained within him. The birth of an explosion had begun.

He stepped out of the car and slithered into the night. Like a wraith, he moved across the rain slick asphalt and approached the house. The smell of burning black powder wafted through the air. He suspected only he would notice. *Dios, I love the perfume of plastique.* Disappointment burned within him that he wouldn't be around for the show, the conflagration he'd given birth to. Strolling up the driveway with the C-4, dangling at his side, it only took a moment for him to find the sweet spot. He ambled over to the gas meter on the side of the garage and grinned. When the gas was finally shut-off, they'd find nothing but a crater.

Grinning, he wedged the bomb between the gas meter and the new "smart" electronic gauge. He paused and stared at the electric meter. The news was filled with pissed-off people complaining about the "smart" meters overcharging. Just wait until they heard about another leaking gas line.

Luis laughed. Hell, they'd probably cheer when they heard about this. He placed the block between two bolts. Threads chewed into the explosive's flesh as he tugged on the C-4 one final time. It didn't budge. Satisfied it was snug and secure, he entered the backyard through the gate. The fuse continued burning, slowly counting down each second until the fury of C-4 was unleashed.

CHAPTER 20

Jessica stepped into her utility room and stripped off her wet clothes. She peeled off her pants like a banana skin, tossed her sopping clothing into the washing machine, and turned it on. Within an hour, they would be clean and dried and she wouldn't have to worry about mildew. Naked, she ran upstairs to her room. After slipping on a dry thong and a bra, she rummaged through her dresser and pulled on a pair of sweat pants and a Stanford Cardinal sweatshirt. It was her favorite. It didn't matter how many times it was explained to her, but she couldn't wrap her brain around why the Stanford's mascot—the Cardinal—was a freaking tree.

Jessica strode into her master bathroom. It had the classic and regal feel she'd wanted when she'd remodeled. The rubbed-oil bronze faucets gave an elegant look to the pedestal sinks. The Italian tile was a light, creamy brown with an off-white grout that looked as if it was straight out of the Vatican. She'd finished it off with black and crimson towels with an embroidered gold Celtic cross.

Her counter was a beautiful graveyard of littered bottles of lotion, make-up, and French-milled soap. Her mother said it was a miracle she ever found anything. Vanilla Sugar hand soap was the current flavor of the month.

For company, so they wouldn't get lonely, her hair straighteners, brushes, and tweezers lay scattered around.

Jessica undid her hair, bent at the waist, and brushed it a hundred times, then flipped it back and repeated the process. Leaning over the sink, she cleansed her face, washing away the grime and stress of the day.

Finished, she wiped it with a single swipe of her hand and stared at her reflection. It revealed a woman she didn't recognize—scared and defeated. And that terrified her.

Jessica slid down onto the floor, trying to deal with all that had happened today. All she had wanted was to stop the thefts and save her job. Instead, her actions had led to a woman's death. A woman whose husband was a notorious killer. Drawing her knees up, she wrapped her arms around them. Burying her face, she sobbed the hard tears of a survivor, pouring out her fear and anger while grateful to be alive. She had endured a lifetimes worth of trauma in a matter of moments. She driven like a maniac, yet she'd survived. She had chased down a crazy-assed bitch and her old knee injury nearly killed her for her efforts. And, finally, she had narrowly avoided her skull being crushed only because a Daniel had taken terminal action—a man who stirred deep emotions in her that she hadn't felt in years.

With a shudder, she withdrew into herself, stood, and faced the mirror. *Daniel Deacon. It has a nice ring to it.*

At the memory of his caring gentleness, a smile curved her lips. She still couldn't believe how she had acted. Because of her shyness, most people thought her cold, aloof, and certainly not the type to flirt with a hunk. But she had. "Lordy, I hope he calls." Hopefully, her feelings weren't born out of her near death experience.

Cupping her hands, Jessica washed her face again, scrubbing away all evidence of her weeping. Absorbed by the fantasy she was spinning, she didn't hear the rear door to her living room being forced open.

⸙⸙⸙

Deacon grabbed his ringing cell out of its holder between the seats and flicked talk, turning-off the infernal ringer. Damn Washington and his jokes. It wasn't right to have changed the ringer tone while Gabardi tortured him just because he had to leave all electronic items outside the interrogation room. The last one he'd chosen had been bad, but this one—it was a man saying, "Ring. Ring. Ring. Ring. Ring. Ring," which got louder with each word. Five times, that's all it had taken, and the man was screaming the word.

Flicking it onto speaker, he snickered, remembering how it had driven Justice crazy on the way home. "Deacon, here."

"Deacon. It's Doug Swanson. I just got off the phone with Washington. He said Bautista was willing to talk, but to you only. I sent Andrews down to take a crack at him because I know he was looking for him from last night's BO-LO. Washington's saying there's no way Bautista will talk to anyone but you. I've called Andrews and told him to return to the station, after he strikes out, to help finish up with your OIS. Be warned, it's pissed him off something fierce. I know what you've dealt with today and, as far as the investigation goes, you're done with this case. But it'd be a big help, if you'd go to the hospital and see what he wants. I'll sign your OT slip. You just need to listen. Washington will slip you a recorder, then write up the statement."

Deacon couldn't believe his ears. *You've got to be shitting me. And I was so close. Another five minutes, I'd be home and be unreachable in the shower.* Stopping at a red light, he looked up at the roof and mouthed, "Why me?" He sighed. "If it were anyone but you, Doug, I'd tell you to go to hell," he said. "But for you, I'll do it." He rubbed the bridge of his nose. Tension and worry of the Chevy beat at him, making his eyes so tight they could have crushed walnuts. And if Justice felt the same hunger he did, then his stomach was using four letter words, too. "Can you call Washington and alert him to my arrival in—"

Deacon placed his right hand on the radio mic and

winced. Jessica's purse. After removing her key, it must have slipped back onto the floor and been forgotten. "Tell him I'll be there in a few. There's something I have to drop off first. It's on the way."

"No problem. But don't be too long."

"I won't."

He keyed up his mic. "King 93."

"King 93, go ahead."

"King 93, show me out on a detail. Show me back en route to 6987 E. Blackburn." He paused a moment. "My prior passenger left some of her property in my vehicle."

"Copy that King 93. Back en route to 6987 E. Blackburn."

⌾⌾⌾

Luis tried the door handle. The only sound when he pushed down on the handle was the gold chain on his wrist. Damn, locked. After trying this at countless homes and finding them unlocked, it came as a surprise that this one was locked. No matter. The French door was well made, but would break just as easily as turning the handle.

Luis threw his two hundred sixty pounds on the door's corner beside the jam. One shoulder check proved all he needed. With minimal sound, he entered low and fast. Crouching behind the couch, he waited for a count of five. When the woman didn't come running, he knew she hadn't heard. He rose and moved into the hallway he assumed led to the bedrooms.

He stopped beside the first door in a hallway and withdrew his knife from the sheath attached to his waistband. It was deadly, savage, and personal. Good thing since his preference was killing someone up close, and watching their surprise as he pushed the knife in and the life drained from their eyes.

It was the intimacy that excited him. Luis firmly believed it you took a person's life, you owed it them to meet their eyes.

He held the knife by the handle, its blade against his forearm in a reverse grip, allowing him the greatest range of movement and flexibility. Weapon at the ready, he entered the first room.

Seeing a large lump in the bed under the sheet, he slashed and stabbed at it. It was like cutting through a dense jungle as he swung the blade in sweeping arcs. Bedding and mattress floated in the air like snowflakes. Finally, he plunged the knife point down in a final killing blow.

He tore off the comforter, wanting to guarantee he'd gotten his target. He hadn't. Instead, he'd killed a large stuffed panda with multiple stabs in its eye. With the hilt of the weapon still in the bear, it looked like the damned thing was winking at him. Glancing at the nightstand, he choked back a laugh at seeing several stuffed animals huddled together in fear and horror.

Torn between frustration and humor, he finally settled on a snort. Finding the serrated blade snagged on the bear's brow, he growled, low and ugly like the dogs he hated, and gave a sharp tug, freeing it. The head severed. It rolled across the bed and over to the nightstand, striking one of its legs. He left the room and headless panda hemorrhaging stuffing.

Deciding the door at the end of the hall was his best bet, he strode down to it, paused, and listened. After several minutes, his eyes adjusted to the increasing darkness. He threw open the door and sauntered into the vacant office. He turned on the desk lamp and examined the room. It helped learning as much as possible about the person he planned to kill.

According to the California State University, Fresno diploma hanging on the wall, he'd found the right woman—Jessica Grady. Based on the numerous awards covering the walls, she was a track star and worked at Speaker City. As with the hallway walls, framed photos littered the large, cherry desk, leaving enough room on the side for a turned-off computer, whereas his was always on. Then again, the boss paid the utilities, he didn't.

Books, ranging from college texts to romances, lined the bookshelves. There were even a sprinkling of horror, suspense, military, and fantasy novels. He'd be damned. She'd read some of his favorite authors. Turning to leave, he spotted a bucket, similar to one used by a child to make sandcastles, on the edge of the desk full of Chapstick. "Interesting."

He reached into it and removed a cherry-flavored one. He could always use another one. After applying a generous amount to his lips, he stuck it in his pocket, turned off the lamp, and retraced his steps into the hall.

CHAPTER 21

Deacon pulled to a stop in front of Jessica's house. "King 93, 10-97."

"Copy that King 93, 10-97."

He glanced back at the Malibu still parked nearby. Suspicion took hold of him and he tapped the plate number in the computer. His eyes widened. "Oh, God, no!" A stolen vehicle. Heart hammering, he jumped from the car and tore up her front walk. He pounded on the door loud enough that the neighbor's lights turned on.

Silence answered.

He sprinted to the window adjacent to the front door. Her living room—neat, orderly, nothing out of place. The kitchen was connected by a small breakfast bar. On the other side of the kitchen was a hallway. Must be the entrance to the garage and the master bedroom.

His gaze returned to the front room. Where the hell was Jessica? He took another quick scan of the interior. His eyes narrowed on the back door.

A shattered door frame. Glass and wood splinters littering the floor.

His blood ran cold. How the hell had he missed it? More importantly, was Jessica still alive?

A critical incident was unfolding in front of his eyes and

he stood frozen—as useless as a preacher in a whore house. Snapping out of his shock, he keyed his radio. "King 93. A 459 in progress at 6987 E. Blackburn! Start me some units now and give me the air!" he ordered.

"Copy that King 93. George 51 and George 90 respond "Copy that King 93. George 51 and George 90 respond to 6987 E. Blackburn for a 459 in progress."

"George 51, en route."

"George 90, copy that. Already en route," Dirks said.

Deacon thanked God for who He had provided as back-up. He hit his door pop. Justice leapt out and joined him as he sprinted toward the backyard.

ℰ↷ℰ↷

Jessica opened the refrigerator door, removed a container of Chicken Feta Pasta, and headed for the microwave. She had taken two steps when she saw the destroyed door. She clasped a hand over her mouth and, catching the scream as it fought to escape, ducked behind the breakfast bar. Her knee barked at her but, thankfully, not too loudly. Whoever it was must have gone down the other hallway to the other rooms. Holding her breath, she strained to hear something, anything. At first, she swore the house was as quiet as a morgue. Then she heard heavy footsteps coming toward the living room from the other hallway.

She remained crouched, ready to run at the first hint of trouble, and peeked around the corner of the breakfast bar. A huge, muscle-bound man entered her living room from the hallway. The look on his face and knife in his hand told her all she needed to know. *Time to get outta Dodge without screaming my head off.*

She set the pasta on the floor and, in a squat, inched her way toward the garage. She couldn't return to her room. She'd be trapped without an escape route. Making it to the hallway unseen, she inhaled for the first time.

ⱥↄⱥↄ

Approaching the broken door, Deacon keyed his radio, "King 93 to responding units. The resident's inside. Rear door to the residence recently forced open. Upon arrival, enter through the side gate. Form up at the point of entry. I'll need one at the front door to lock it down." Pistol drawn, he reached the back door and saw the refrigerator light blink off. Jessica. Thank God, he'd gotten here in time. Before he could move, she disappeared.

He scanned the area. "Jess, are you all right?" Why didn't she answer him? He'd been sure he'd caught a glimpse of her before the refrigerator light winked out. Maybe she'd seen the intruder. "Jess, if you can't make it to the back door, stay put." Nothing. "King 93, No response from the residence. I'm standing by for my fill. Units, I need an ETA," he barked into his radio.

"King 93, George 51. I'm thirty seconds out."

"George 90, I'm pulling up now."

"Copy that." Deacon raised his voice. "This is a Cain Police Department K9 Unit. If you are in the residence, make yourself known. I am about to search the residence with a Police K9. Come out now, with your hands up. If you don't, the K9 will be released to take you down." Deafening silence rewarded his efforts. "King 93, K9 announcement was made. No response."

"Copy, King 93."

"King 93, 51. I'm on scene now."

"George 90 same."

"Ten-four, I'm at the rear."

Deacon searched the darkness for the intruder. At the far hall, he caught a brief flash of light glinting off metal.

Damn, he hoped it wasn't a weapon, because he'd hate to be hit while rescuing the future Mrs. Deacon.

ⱥↄⱥↄ

Hearing Daniel's voice, Jessica scurried back to the kitchen and peered around the corner. She saw the intruder creeping up on Daniel. She knew the corner between the kitchen and living room was a blind spot and Daniel wouldn't see the man approaching. For such a big man, the assailant was quieter than a church mouse.

Her eyes widened at the wide and long serrated knife. The blade caught a ray of light and gleamed in the darkness. She'd seen one like it as a teenager in the first store she'd ever worked. It had catered to hunters and fishermen. Serrations on one side and a fine edge on the other. A shiver rippled through her at memories of that savage knife.

Oh, boy, the man was an expert. She might now have weapons training, but she knew holding it by the handle with the blade pressed against his forearm meant only one thing. This man was a professional killer. *Shit! Shit! Shit!* Taking a deep breath then exhaling, she crept into the kitchen. Spotting her cast iron skillet, she'd never been so grateful for her procrastination in putting cleaned things away. In one fluid, silent motion, she grabbed it off the stove and, on sock-covered feet, tiptoed around the breakfast bar.

She inched up behind the monster. Handling the skillet as she would a softball bat, she wound up and swung for the fences.

CHAPTER 22

Dirks arrived first on scene. Brakes nearly on fire, he skidded to a stop inches behind Deacon's vehicle. The smell of melted rubber permeated the night air. With the flip of a switch, he killed his siren but left his overhead lights ablaze. Red and blue lights washing over his face, he bolted from his marked Dodge Ram 1500.

Robert Smith's unit barreled down the street and, at the last minute, screeched to a stop behind the Dodge. "Want me to take the front?"

"Yeah." Dirks raced for the backyard. Nearing the gate, he skidded to a halt in horror. "Smith, screw the front, get to the back and help Deacon."

Smith paused and crouched beside the Corporal. "What's going on, Dirks?"

Dirks pointed at the growing plume of blue-gray smoke by the gas meter. "Burning time-fuse. Deacon must've stepped right into a serious pile of shit, 'cause he's dropped us right into the meat grinder." His eyes narrowed on the device. "It's a whole, hot mess of Methyl-Ethyl-Kill-You. Get in there and help Deacon. I'll take care of this."

"You sure? I know you're an ace, but you're half of our bomb squad and we can't lose you, man. So hurry the fuck up, but don't get turned into pink mist, all right?"

"Always a joker. Now get the hell outta here. D's in there getting his ass kicked."

Dirks didn't waste time. He didn't have it to squander. Squaring his shoulders, he prepared himself to go toe-to-toe with a pissed off bomb.

ↄⅇↄ

Deacon caught a motion out of the corner of his eye. *Sonuvabitch. A fucking blind spot.* He spun toward the movement and spotted Jessica stealing up behind a large silhouette. Whatever she was holding was heavy and she was on an upswing with it. The massive man dropped low and turned toward her. Light glinted off a large knife. In a split second, Deacon saw only two choices and their result. If he called out, he'd startle her. She'd freeze and die.

Releasing Justice's lead, Deacon slammed into the man, interrupting the knife's uppercut motion.

They pitched forward and crashed onto the tile.

Jessica missed her target. Her skillet connected. Deacon's shoulder was forgotten as pain exploded in his head. Helpless, flat on his back, his vision blurred.

The man's knife slashed through the air.

Deacon felt a thin, sharp burn across his exposed shoulder. Heat and dampness began to run down his left arm beneath his patch on his uniform. Pain, followed by numbness, shot to his brain.

Justice lunged. The man pivoted. Justice flew past him and nosedived into the side of an oak china hutch. The dog's skull crashed through the wood leaving him dazed. The man raised the knife for a down thrust into Deacon's face. Flat on his back and half-blind from the blow to his head, Deacon instinctively wrapped his legs around the man's torso. Muscles tightening, Deacon yanked him closer, attempting to grab the knife before he got stabbed to death.

He grasped the right hand holding the blade. The man's grip was a vise, and Deacon couldn't strip the knife. He locked his elbows across his chest as his attacker pressed down. The bastard was too big and too strong. Arms shaking, Deacon could feel his elbows were about to buckle and knew if they did, he and Jessica were dead.

The gleaming knife point drew closer. Panic set in. Adrenal glands dumped adrenaline. Deacon pushed with every ounce of his being.

It was no use.

Hearing Justice's snarl, Deacon knew one seriously pissed-off dog was headed their way at twenty-five miles per hour. He just hoped his partner arrived in time. The knife's tip pierced his cheek. Before he took his next breath, the beast collided with the intruder, knocking him off balance. With a savage yell, Deacon pushed up with locked elbows. He forced the knife out of his face, released his legs, and slammed his knee into the man's groin.

On a long, low moan, air escaped his attacker like a punctured tire.

Deacon scrambled back. With the man's mouth open in a silent scream and looking as if his pain burned down through his soul, he didn't know what hurt the man worst—the savaging Justice was giving him or the nailing he'd taken to the balls. Deacon didn't care.

"Justice, come," he ordered.

A second later, Jessica cranked off a second stir-fry salvo square right on the ear. With that, the man's scream finally surfaced. Deacon shook his head at the too-high-pitched shriek followed by yelled threats.

Teeth drawn back in a growl, Justice charged forward, his teeth clamping on the attacker's left triceps, his bite crushing down the arm and dislocating the shoulder in one smooth motion. He thrashed back and forth, twisting the arm like a towel, rendering it useless. The suspect struggled to regain his footing.

Using the man's momentary incapacitation, Deacon wrenched his right wrist one hundred eighty degrees. He twisted the hand holding the knife in an arm-bar takedown.

With the attacker's attention focused on Justice and his mangled arm, the tug of war over his torso was short lived. Deacon ripped the man's shoulder down to the floor. The attacker's face struck the wood. Hard. The knife flew across the hardwood floor. Between Justice and Deacon, the fight ended as quickly as it had begun.

Swinging a leg over the man, Deacon rolled him onto his back and assumed a mounted position. He grasped him by the back of the hair, pulled his head back, and pounded his forehead onto the tile floor.

Hearing a satisfying crunch, Deacon watched as their attacker's world faded to black.

With him unconscious, Deacon called Justice off—again. The dog dropped the arm like an unwanted chew toy and, barking nonstop, returned to Deacon's left side. He tried to remove a set of handcuffs from his pouch. He failed. He couldn't even open the cuff case. His fine motor skills were shot. Fingers refused to obey.

As he struggled to control his mounting rage at his impotence, Smith arrived, dropping a knee onto the man's back. Deacon had never been happier to see that freshly shaved gleaming head. Looking at his hands, Deacon stammered, "I—I can't work m-my fingers. Can you—"

"Glad to help." Smith quickly cuffed the unconscious man with Deacon's cuffs and stepped back. "Holy shit, D. You all right, 'cause I gotta tell you, you don't look much better than him," he said, pointing at their secured intruder. "In fact, I'm not sure which of you is in worse shape."

With assistance on hand, the adrenaline pumping through Deacon tanked. Holding the towel Smith had tossed him against his shoulder, he ordered Justice into the kitchen with a down/stay command. Last thing he needed was his partner slicing his feet on splintered wood and broken glass.

Smith motioned to the perp. "You want the privilege?"

"Nah, you can have it."

"You have the right to remain silent. Anything you say won't be much, asshole. You got some serious fubar," Smith said, reading the man a politically incorrect version of his rights.

Deacon started to shake his head and immediately stopped. Too much pain. "*Lethal Weapon* meets *Tango and Cash*," he murmured, chuckling.

Smith laughed. "Good. But which one?"

Deacon rubbed his palm against his eye. He shook his head and the adrenaline rush abated. Fatigue set in and his mind slowly sharpened. "*Lethal Weapon Four*?" As his mind continued to clear from the fog of war, he remembered why he'd returned. "Jess!" When she didn't answer, he slowly turned his head and located her. Eyes squeezed shut, she sat with her back against the breakfast bar and knees curled up against her chest.

Deacon slowly pushed himself up off the floor. He stumbled to her. Kneeling, he cupped her face in his hands. "Jess, are you all right?"

"I—I'm fine. Wh—what the hell's going on?!"

"I don't know. Yet. What do you say we find out?"

She nodded vigorously. "Why are you here? Not that I'm not thrilled and elated you are, but I thought you were going home."

"Your purse. You left it on the floor of my car."

"I did?"

"It's still there." At her raised eyebrows, he quickly recounted his worries over the Malibu, running the plates, and taking action. By the time he finished, he knew from her color the shock had worn off.

"Thank goodness I forgot my damn purse and you followed your gut."

He dropped the towel and tucked strands of hair behind her ears. "A good cop always follows his instinct."

"Oh, my God, Daniel, you're injured." She gently brushed his cheek with the back of her fingers. He sat motionless and closed his eyes. She moved on to his shoulder and lifted the sleeve of his uniform. Her grimace spoke volumes. "Don't move. I'll be right back with my first aid stuff. But I'm warning you, your shoulder requires stitches." She traced the slice in his shoulder patch. "And it looks like you'll need a new uniform shirt."

As she scurried out of the room, Deacon admitted to himself she was right. While the bleeding wasn't heavy, he required stitches and probably a tetanus shot. He sat on the floor, his back to the same wall Jessica had used, and watched the flurry around him. Additional units poured into the backyard and cleared the remainder of the house. Smith patted down their prisoner for some identification.

Scowling, Smith stood. "He's got nothing. Not a damn thing, Deacon. Here's hoping we have better luck running his prints with the FBI and through CAFIS."

"Shit." Deacon smacked his forehead with his palm. "Forgot to tell you, he's the driver of the Malibu out front. I ran the plates. They came back as stolen. That's when I ran to the house and saw the break in and called for backup. I wonder who he'll be more afraid of, us or whoever sent him here."

"Yeah. It'll sure be interesting to see the fallout."

"My gut's screaming, Robert. I can't shake the feeling Ubel Tuefel's involved."

"What makes you say that?"

Deacon started to shrug then stopped as pain radiated out from his shoulder. Hunched over, he clutched his sliced shoulder. "This guy is good, really good. I'm lucky as all hell. After everything that happened today, I'm thinking this was a hit."

With Jessica's return, Deacon slowly shook his head. Smith nodded and ended all discussion on the possibility of their being targets. As she neared them, Deacon realized he hadn't seen Dirks. Yet Deacon knew he'd arrived. He struggled to his feet, still clutching his shoulder. "Hold up, Robert. Where's Dirks?"

"Be right back," Smith said. He raced out of the house only to return moments later. "Dirks ordered everyone out, now! And you're to get to the hospital and get stitched up."

Deacon grabbed Smith's arm, holding him in place. "What's going on?"

"That unnamed sonuvabitch planted a bomb, tying it into gas line of the house. Best Dirks can tell it's got less than ten minutes left."

Deacon forgot about his bleeding shoulder and grabbed Jessica's hand. "Justice, heel." With a sharp tug, he towed her from the house. Reaching the front yard, he saw cops knocking on doors and ordering everyone out of the neighborhood. "Get in," he said, shoving her into his car.

As soon as Justice was secured, he made a U-turn and headed down the street. Once at a safe distance, he stopped and leaned across the divide, his lips brushing hers. "I'll be back."

She clasped his hand. "Why aren't you going to the hospital?"

"I can help clear the area. Sit tight with Justice, please. I'll be back."

"You got it."

Deacon exited the car and started back toward the house. Justice immediately attacked the rear door, fighting so violently that the car shook back and forth. *Damn it. He is going to hurt himself if I leave him in there.* He hit the door pop and his partner exploded from the back. Justice flew to Deacon's side like a missile.

"Okay, buddy. Okay. You stay with me."

He received a growl in reply.

"King 93!"

His radio erupted. It was Swanson. "King 93! Answer your radio damn it!"

Deacon sighed. "King 93, a little busy over here. Go ahead."

"King 93, Lincoln 10. Confirm you are Code Four? I'm coming on scene now. EMS is still standing by."

"Affirm. I am Code Four with the civilian. Go ahead and send in EMS."

Dirks's voice boomed over the radio. "George 90. Tell

EMS and anyone else coming to this mess to standby. And give me the air. No radio traffic until I advise otherwise. The scene is not Code Four."

"Copy that, George 90."

Blood seeping between his fingers, Deacon spotted Smith and limped up to him. "What the hell's Dirks think he's doing?"

"Saving all of our asses."

CHAPTER 23

D irks knelt before the gas meter as if he were bowing to a god. He was—to the Roman god of war and violence, Mars—and bombs fit both categories.

Dirks sighed. *Praise the Lord, radio silence. I can finally concentrate.* He ignored the smoke in his face from the burning black powder that filled the air like incense. He pulled a flashlight off his belt and took inventory of the explosive's components. "Great. Comp C-4. Black powder time fuse. Depending on what the burn rate is we have about five minutes or so. If I am wrong and it goes, none of us will know it."

He flipped from his stomach onto his back and wiggled under the main as best as he could. Wedged below the gas line, mud squirted up from below his head, coating him. Looking up, he saw behind the bomb and groaned. "Are you kiddin' me, no counter measures. This guy must've been a freakin' amateur or in a hurry."

Moistening his dry lips, he drew his knife. The cold blue steel glinted in the light of the blazing powder. "Dude must've thought no one would find you, you little bastard." In spite of the downpour, the fuse continued shrinking.

Dirks gripped the block of C-4, his blade cutting through the fuse like a plane through a cloud. He sliced off over half of the remaining fuse, a half inch of virginal fuse remained embedded in the C-4. He eased the cap out and tossed it. It landed twenty-five feet from him in the soft, moist soil where it made a harmless home for itself. *Game over.*

Water and mud dripping off the end of his moustache, Dirks stood and held the severed, burning piece up to eye level, watching the fuse burn itself to death. "Good guys one, dipshit zero. You lose asshole." Grinning, he pressed the button on his lapel mic. "George 90."

"George 90, go ahead."

"George 90, explosive has been rendered safe. Restore the air. We are Code Four. Send in the medics."

"George 90, ten-four."

With the all clear, the scene erupted. Two ambulances roared up to the site. Medics spilled out of them. The personnel from one ambulance, stabilized the unknown man, loaded him onto a gurney, and prepared to transport him to the hospital.

The second crew hurried to Deacon's side. He raised a hand holding them off for a minute. "I've parked Jessica in my vehicle down the street. Robert can you drive them back here?" At his "Sure," Deacon tossed him the keys.

৩৩৩

Deacon promised the EMTs he'd get himself to the hospital. He would, too. Their patch job was just that, temporary. He eased out of the back of the ambulance and made his way toward the sergeant's shouting. *If Doug doesn't kill me, Jack will. First the OIS, and now an attempted homicide on Jessica, the almost-murder-victim of earlier today.*

Sighing, he tipped his face up and let the cool rain cleanse him. Initially, night air felt wonderful but gradually the chill bit deeply into his wounds.

With a shiver, he reached down and scratched Justice between the ears. With a woof, he nudged Deacon's leg, stay-

ing right on his heels. The dog wasn't letting him out of his
sight, and it was clear that no one was going to convince
him otherwise. Justice's sense of smell was a hundred thousand times better than a human's, and he'd scented Deacon
bleeding.

A short time later, Deacon found the watch commander
and on-call detective standing, soaked to the bone, beside
the door to his K9 unit. He took a moment to collect himself. *And here we go.* After a deep breath, he briefed Swanson and White on what had happened, all except the bomb.
Smith, Dirks, and he had agreed earlier to let Dirks handle
that debrief. As EOD, it was his job.

The sergeant clapped him on his good shoulder. "Well,
shit. At least, you're okay. Although, it looks like you are
going to the hospital now, regardless of the previous reason.
But since you're going down there, why don't you talk to
Bautista? I'm sure Washington will love to see you."

"Copy that, Sarge."

"Hey, Sarge, why don't you take off, too? I'll stay here
and take care of the scene. It's no big deal. I'll just add it to
the growing pile of crap on my desk tomorrow. Besides, it is
all related to today's earlier events, anyway." White grinned.
"That'll free you to go work on another unusual occurrence
report for the chief."

"You sure, because I can call someone else out for it?"
Swanson asked

"Affirmative. Trust me, it'll work." White's smile faded
to a frown. "I'm adding this incident to the previous one in
the report."

"You really think they're connected?"

"Yeah. D and the Grady had left the station. I arranged to
have Grady's car driven to the station. When she left, it
wasn't there. The front desk tells her it's still at the crime
scene. D finds her walking back to the scene. They arrive
and discover the vehicle's been towed to impound. D picks
up the intruder's car—" White pointed at the Chevy Malibu
being loaded onto a tow truck. "—that followed them from

the scene to here and then tries to kill them. So, yes, I think each incident is part of a whole."

Swanson nodded. "It's yours. However you want to play it, it's your mess now."

"Thanks."

Dirks walked up to the huddle and tossed Swanson a one and a quarter pound ball of death. "This damn thing's a whole hell of a lot bigger than any of you realize."

Swanson made the catch and stared at the C-4. It took a minute for him to recognize it. When he did, he was grateful he hadn't fumbled it. "Where in the hell did you find this?"

"That? Why, it was the wonderful little present that was left on Grady's gas meter by Mr. Numb Nuts. Nothing like a nasty-ass bomb covering your tracks in what looks like an accident. Dude used a time fuse. Crude, but effective. Gave himself enough time to finish the job inside. Military grade stuff. Guaranteed to burn through rain, snow, sleet and hail." He jerked his head at Swanson's hand. "You're holding enough C-4 that, if it blew the underground gas main, it would've have leveled her house along with half the block."

Dirks snorted. "Shit, Deacon, you sure can pick 'em. Serious as a heart attack, Mister, you've seriously pissed off somebody."

Deacon understood the full gravity of the situation. He had since he'd learned who he had shot. He also recognized that if he hadn't returned, Jessica would by lying in a pool of blood. And if Dirks hadn't discovered the bomb, they wouldn't be having this conversation. He looked at White, but answered Dirks, "Earlier today, I killed Ubel Tuefel's wife."

Dirks whistled through his teeth. After a moment when no one spoke, Dirks said, "All things considered, that's the first thing about this mess that actually makes sense."

Deacon applied pressure to his oozing shoulder. "Minus me getting patched up, what do we do now?"

Dirks recovered the C-4 from Swanson. "Well, after photographing the hell outta it, I'm taking this bad boy to the range and making it go away. Otherwise, good luck to you guys. You're gonna need it. It's a helluva mess. Don't forget to call me if you need anything, especially if you require something shot or blown up."

White clapped him on the shoulder. "I'll catch up with you later, big guy."

"Thanks again, Dirks," Deacon said, then turned to Swanson and White. "Do we have anyone free who can drive me to the hospital, and then home? Between dealing with Bautista and getting patched up, I'm falling down. They'll also need a lift from my house."

Swanson looked around and spotted Smith exiting Jessica's backyard. "Robert! Get over here."

"What's up, Sarge?"

"I need you to follow the caravan in Deacon's vehicle. You're both to follow behind that shithead's ambulance. You stay right on his ass. No one gets in between you and that ambulance, period."

"No problem, Sarge." Smith placed his hand on the back of Deacon's good shoulder and guided him to the back of the ambulance. "Come on, brother. First things first. Right now you need to get looked at, and that means the hospital. Justice and I will follow."

EMS personnel tried to convince Deacon to sit on the gurney so they could wheel him to their vehicle. He refused and insisted upon loading Justice into his car first. With the pooch calm and safely tucked away, Smith and he returned to the ambulance. Climbing into the back of the ambulance, Deacon collapsed on the gurney and awaited transport to the hospital.

CHAPTER 24

Robert Smith slid behind the wheel of Deacon's marked unit, only to have Justice greet him with a barking tirade full of spit. "Nice to see you, too." He pulled forward and stopped beside Jessica's residence.

"Thank you for everything. Keep an eye on Daniel for me, okay?"

"No problem, miss. He'll be in good hands."

She shut the door and hurried into her house.

Robert took a moment to familiarize himself with the vehicle's configuration as Justice continued voicing his displeasure at Smith for moving his partner's car.

He wrinkled his nose at his surroundings. Deacon apparently shuffled stuff around to provide room for the girl, leaving the passenger compartment a complete disaster. Thankfully, it wasn't his vehicle or responsibility to clean the mess. Starting the vehicle, he reached across the center console to stack the paperwork.

Justice loudly explained to Smith that he was to leave everything the way he found it. "Easy, Justice. Easy, buddy. I'm just picking-up some stuff. Calm down. Your dad's going to be back in few, and he'll kill me if you chip a tooth from biting the fucking cage."

Show no fear, he ordered himself. Yeah, right, easier said than done with Justice's lips peeled back in a snarl. "Quit bathing my neck in your spit, stupid. I thought you liked me." He rearranged the mountain of paperwork that fallen off the dash and onto the passenger seat. Cripes, it was an entire day's worth of work. After spending several minutes to tidy up, he hit his forehead with his palm. "Dumbass, why'd you clean it up?" Because they were friends and Deacon's day had been hell.

When he started to pull away from the curb, he caught a glimpse of a distant flashing red light in the rearview mirror. Glancing over his shoulder, he discovered both ambulances were no longer on scene. "Shit! The fucking ambulances took off without me. God help us all if there's a problem. There won't be enough to bury when Swanson gets finished." His fingers tightened on the steering wheel, and Smith shoved the gearshift into drive. He floored the accelerator.

Justice slid on his mat, slammed into the back of the car, and growled from deep within his chest.

"Sorry, buddy." Reaching the main thoroughfare, he pushed his speed to seventy-five. Water blasted out from the channels created by the high performance tires of the patrol car. Hitting an intersection, he hydroplaned and drifted around the corner.

Justice slid again. His head bounced off the cage protecting the door window.

This time, Smith received a deeper growl and snarl.

"Shit. Sorry, dude. Don't eat me, okay?" Glancing in the review mirror, he saw eyes that made no promises.

Tires chirped when they found traction. He accelerated. Within seconds, he closed on the ambulance convoy. The flashing red lights and wails from the medical transports beckoned to him like a siren's call.

A blue Chevy Cobalt pulled out onto the street. The driver swerved directly in front of Smith's flashing blue and red lighted, siren-blasting missile.

He pounded the horn. Its blaring joined that of the siren.

With the Cobalt straddling the lanes of traffic, he realized the driver was so panicked, she couldn't make a decision. Fury nearly over-road years of training. Seeing the eastbound lanes free, Smith ripped the wheel to his left and crossed into the lanes of oncoming traffic, narrowly missing the weaving Cobalt.

His tires fought to prevent a slide. They lost the battle. "No!" he screamed.

Justice yowled.

The patrol car began to spin. It careened toward a telephone pole, the driver's side door facing it. Smith cranked the wheel into its slide and his vehicle responded. Halting the spin, he slammed the pedal to the floor. The engine roared with a stampede of five hundred horses straining to be unleashed. The needle redlined. The black and white surged forward and roared back onto the correct side of the highway.

The driver of the Cobalt lost control. The vehicle spun twice. As it slid onto the shoulder, it slammed into an abandoned Honda with a screwdriver jammed into its ignition. The Cobalt flipped, coming to rest on its roof, proving once again two things can't occupy the same space at the same time.

"Ah, shit!" Smith slammed on the brakes. The car skidded to a stop. He bolted from it, ignoring the rain, and plowed forward. Reaching the driver's door of the Cobalt, he winced at the shattered windshield. One look told him the female driver was out cold.

He lifted his head and stole a glance at the ambulance in the distance, its flashing red lights growing smaller by the second. *Please, God, this can't be happening.* Having no choice, Smith reached through the broken glass and, doing his best to support her weight, crawled beneath her. He pressed his shoulder against hers to take the stress off the seatbelt.

Removing his pocket knife, he flipped open the seatbelt cutter. It sliced through the tough webbing as if it were a perfectly-aged-and-cooked porterhouse. He slowly lowered the limp teenager to the vehicle ceiling and immobilized her neck. Then crawling, he backed out, cutting his palms on the tiny shards of glass scattered about. Certain her back and neck were protected, he fought for calm, and keyed up his radio. "George 51. Injury TC. Shaw and Blackburn."

Dispatch replied, "George 51 can you repeat your last transmission?"

"There is an injury TC on Shaw west of Blackburn. One vehicle! Driver is down and need EMS now!"

"Copy that, George 51. Injury TC on Shaw west of Blackburn. We are rolling Fire and EMS to your location."

Smith pushed himself up and knelt on his right knee. He leaned forward and placed his fingers on her neck. Her breath brushed his hand. *Thank God.* He leaned into her vehicle. Retrieving her purse, he checked her ID. He keyed back up his radio. "George 51, copy that. She is unconscious, has a pulse, but labored breathing. Name: Sally Henderson. Age: eighteen. Keep them rolling, Code Three."

He looked back up the street. Deacon and the bomber were long gone. Still… "George 51, we need another unit to escort King 93 and his prisoner's ambulances. Get a unit rolling to intercept and escort now."

"Copy that, George 51. All units are on priority traffic and are ten-six. We will start with the next unit available."

"George 51, the prisoner is a bomber and suspected hitman. Suggest you break a unit from anything, since nothing else has this priority," he snapped. *Sweet Jesus, I hope nothing happens.*

CHAPTER 25

Luis came to but kept his eyes closed, his body relaxed as if still unconscious. It took all his willpower not to shudder in relief that his mind functioned. Control was critical. He used the steady drum of rain on the ambulance roof as a focus. Before taking action, he had to inventory his physical condition to see if it was possible. Only then, would he check-out his surroundings.

A heart monitor beeped with normal rhythm—heart unharmed. He wiggled his toes and twitched his legs as if coming around—extremities unharmed. *Shoulder's on fire, feels functional.* But pain shooting down to his hand could prove an impairment—workable but painful. Left hand cuffed to gurney—older gurney. No other restraints. Cuffed between two support rails. *Need a cuff key or to disassemble gurney.*

Slowly, he inched his fingers to the side—nut and bolt of gurney support rail reachable.

He honed in on the voices over a dual band radio—medical traffic. Likely heading for the regional hospital.

He cracked his eyes open and he took in his immediate surroundings. Gurney in the center. Flanked by two males. One looked like an EMT, and the other a more highly trained paramedic. Luis almost smiled at the realization that they had no clue he was conscious. His one escape route was the rear door. He was too big to squeeze through the partition to the driver's seat.

The most dangerous time occurred when the EMT inserted an IV needle and opened the value on the hanging saline bag. *Don't move.* That he remained inert, as terrified of needles as he was, filled him with pride.

All that was left was to set the stage. He slowed his breathing to a deep and steady eight breaths per minute as the paramedic took his vitals. Pulling his stethoscope from his ears, the man dropped it around his neck and removed the blood pressure cuff from Luis's arm. As he typed in the vitals on a table, he said, "You aren't going to believe these readings. Blood pressure's ninety-seven over fifty-six. Heart rate's fifty-four BPM. If he's like this after being in a fight with a cop and K9, I'd hate to see him when he'd undamaged."

Eyes closed, Luis fought a grin and remained motionless, paying attention to their conversation.

"You're shitting, right? No way those figures are correct. His shoulder was dislocated. A cast iron skillet beaned his head, and the biggest freaking German Shepard I've ever seen ripped his triceps a new one. He wasn't just in a fight, he's the proud owner of an old fashioned ass whoopin'," the EMT said, disbelief dripping from every word.

"I know. That dog really chewed him up. I think he's gonna need some surgery. Stitches for sure. Hell, he might even have a brain bleed. A cast iron skillet packs a wallop. I'm surprised his skull isn't caved in. I'm betting when he regains consciousness, he's gonna wish he hadn't."

Actually I am glad that I did. Eyes still closed, Luis maintained his rate of breathing, keeping his heart rate and blood pressure low. His low vitals meant they wouldn't watch too closely, providing him the time to unscrew the gurney arm. Within seconds, he realized it was going to take a while, possibly longer than he had.

After several minutes, the paramedic broke the silence.

"This is crazy. His vitals rival that of Olympians. It doesn't make any sense. Minus the bleeding holes the dog made, I'd say he was in excellent health."

"He's in great shape. Hell, he's Superman."

"I'm tellin' ya, I've only read about vitals like this showing up with yoga masters and Zen Buddhist monks."

Just a few more twists.

The damned ambulance was weaving its way through traffic. *Fuck!* Who would have believed the roads weren't clear at this time of night, and in a storm. Luis worried that, if the clown didn't slow down, he'd die in fiery crash.

Luis ignored the medics debating which of their teams was more likely to make it to the Super Bowl as he continued to work the nut on the gurney arm. He only needed a few more minutes. He shot a slit-eyed glance at the medics, gauging the level of their inattention.

A smile twitched the corners of Luis's lips as the nut dropped into his hand, and then just as quickly cleared his expression. He palmed the bolt, nut, and washer and slid them under the sheet. *Nice and easy. There we go.* He rotated his wrist and slid the support bar off the frame of the gurney.

Gripping the curved handrail in his bear-paw hand, he rose, safe in the knowledge they were still inattentive. He twirled the steel bar, and, using the handcuff chain like a nunchuck, slammed it against the back of the paramedic's skull. His reward was a gut-wrenching crunch that sounded like a fist diving for a handful of tortilla chips. Bits of bone drenched in blood showered the EMT. Bathed in crimson fluid, the EMT faced Luis.

"What the—" A sliver arc sliced through the open air of the ambulance. The EMT's nose vanished, the cartilage driven upward. His head smashed into the wall of the ambulance's rear passenger compartment. His body slid to the floor and landed in a crumpled heap.

Unnoticed by the driver up in the cab, Luis rummaged through the medical supplies. *Syringes. Cleaning supplies.*

IV bags. Ahh, there you are. He opened the compartment door and grabbed bandages with gauze. Holding the IV needle close to the base, he gently pulled. It came free in one smooth movement. He glanced at the two dead men. At least they were trained to properly insert an IV.

Luis applied the bandage to the IV site. Then using his teeth to hold the end of the gauze, he wrapped it twice with the gauze to keep it in place. The blood dripping down to his wrist immediately stopped. Crude, but it would work for now.

Gathering his things, Luis eased his shirt over his damaged shoulder and arm. He quickly tightened his shoelaces. Ready, he balled his hand into a fist and banged on the back of the passenger compartment. Maybe he should have hit it with a lighter touch. The damned metal had barely survived. The ambulance came to a sudden stop.

Luis turned and drew back his foot. With one kick, the locking mechanism of the rear door disintegrated into dozens of metal shards. Steel splinters blasted onto the street. As the ruined ambulance back doors fell open, Luis disappeared into the loving embrace of the rain-soaked shadows of the night.

CHAPTER 26

Given the weather, Deacon couldn't believe their speed. They should arrive within five minutes, he thought glaring out the rear door window at the prisoner's ambulance. At the intersection of Blackstone and Tulare, they caught a red light. Unable to change the signal, Deacon's ambulance slowed for the intersection. Once all oncoming traffic stopped, they proceeded through.

Strapped to a gurney, Deacon watched helplessly as the second transport slammed to a stop in the middle of the intersection. The rear door seemed to explode and his prisoner leapt out of the second ambulance, a gurney arm handcuffed to his hand.

"What the hell?" To Deacon's horror, no marked unit followed their ambulances. He keyed the mic on his lapel. "King 93! Leg bail! Leg bail! Smith, where are you? Tell me you have him."

There was no response on the radio. No Smith. No Justice. And this damn ambulance was a death trap for his radio. Furious, Deacon beat on the wall to get the attention of the paramedic and EMT driving the ambulance. "Stop! Stop damn it!"

No response from the cab. Defeated, Deacon stared out the window as the second transport disappeared from view.

A sense of helplessness assailed him. Then at the thought of Jessica alone and unprotected, terror raised its ugly head.

His radio crackled to life. "King 93, did you have traffic?"

He nearly tore his lapel mic free from its cord. "Yes! The HMA who stabbed me just leg bailed out of the second ambulance. I no longer have a visual, but he was last seen running eastbound on Tulare. Suspect was wearing a black pants and sweater. He was running with a gurney arm bar handcuffed to his arm."

"Copy that King 93. Confirm he has a gurney and is what?"

"Affirmative, he had a gurney arm bar handcuffed to him. Whoever rolls has to look for an HMA with a big piece of steel handcuffed to his arm. Notify all outlying agencies! Get air support. This man's wanted for attempted murder of an officer and setting a bomb. Get someone over here now."

"Copy, King 93. Will notify allied agencies and have units head that way as soon as they become available."

Controlling his outrage, Deacon tapped his mic again. "King 93 demands units respond immediately to the leg bail. Now. No other traffic takes priority over the leg bail of this prisoner."

This time, the lack of a reply didn't shock him. It got him remembering—Jessica's car had been moved. His escaped prisoner knew where she lived. Deacon also suspected his address was known. Someone in a position of power or control of the system was helping the asshole, and probably Tuefel, too.

His ambulance didn't slow at leaving behind the second ambulance. Ten minutes later, it stopped at the ER entrance of Cain Regional Medical Center. When the doors opened, the medics discovered Deacon's mood not only hadn't improved, it had soured.

In a rush, the medics dropped his gurney out the back of the ambulance. The impact from the landing reopened his wound. It roared into an agonizing pain. "Argh. Hey take it easy." Sighing, Deacon dropped his head onto the pillow.

"Hey, there, D, imagine seeing you here like this," Washington boomed.

Deacon opened his eyes and groaned as they dumped him in Trauma Room One. "How thoughtful, they wheeled me here so we can all be together." His gaze skimmed over Washington and Bautista.

Deacon ignored the scowling medics who placed the head of his gurney against the wall, facing Bautista. Their eyes locked, and Washington wisely remained silent.

"So how's the back?" Deacon asked.

"Feels like shit."

"My dog has the effect on people—"

"Jesus, D, what the hell happened to you?" Washington interrupted.

"Some big ass guy crashed into a lady's house, tried to kill the two of us. He met my partner, too. Oh, in case you haven't placed her yet, the lady is the one who chased down Rachele Tuefel—who is…drum roll…now dead. I'm thinking Ubel Tuefel's a touch upset with her and me." He flashed his shark smile at Bautista. "You, too."

Bautista returned his smile with a tight, thin-lipped one. "People tend to die when you are around, Officer."

Deacon wished Bautista were within an arm's reach. It would be so much more satisfying to pummel him rather than play word games.

By unspoken agreement, silence descended with the arrival of Deacon's nurse and surgeon. The nurse rolled a table filled with wrapped surgical instruments next to his injured shoulder. "Don't worry, Doctor Morgan here will get you patched up in no time," the nurse said, grabbing a pair of scissors.

"Wait. It unbuttons. I'll take the uniform and undershirt off. Just help me sit up, okay." He knew his behavior appeared ridiculous, since both shirts were ruined. But he didn't care. It was both evidence and his red badge of courage. "Sorry about barking at you."

She chuckled. "No worries. Have you been given any pain medication?"

"Don't want any." After removing both shirts, he handed them to Washington. "Bag it. The DA will want it for the trial." If there ever was one. After ensuring his sidearm was secure, he allowed the nurse to help him lie back on the bed. "Hey, Kevin, you have a sweatshirt of something in your car that I can borrow?"

"Sure thing, be right back." Washington tapped Bautista. "Stay put and don't cause any trouble."

As the nurse scrubbed Deacon's wound with a betadine solution, he stared at Bautista. Washington returned with a sweatshirt. Deacon's gaze didn't waver when the doctor entered and injected a couple of local numbing agents. They worked fast. The brilliant pain was short lived.

"I'll be using dissolving sutures on inside. But you'll need to come back or see your own doctor to the move the external staples."

"Will do, Doc." Seeing Bautista's face pale, Deacon winked, but stayed silent as did the other two. The moment the medical staff left, he grinned. "I forgot the best part, Justice and I kicked his ass. Of course, Justice's contribution was to try to amputate his arm using just his teeth."

Bautista vomited.

Washington flashed him a shit-eating grin. "Seriously? Nice."

Deacon returned it. "Yeah, seriously. I think he popped the shoulder like a zit."

"Hell, yeah. God, I love that dog."

"Me, too. But there's a problem. Dude had no ID. Not that it matters. Between what's gone down over the last twelve hours, Tuefel's got to be behind the thwarted hit. No way this s a coincidence."

Tapping the mic of his radio, Washington leaned forward. "God blasted, I haven't heard a word. It's fucking impossible to get reception in this concrete jungle."

Deacon glanced at the readings of blood pressure and

heart rate monitor. Both displayed his mounting outrage. "Without his prints, we'll never find out who he was."

"Didn't someone use the Blue Check?"

"Slipped through the cracks. Too busy evac'ing the neighborhood and defusing the bomb." Deacon's head rolled to the side. He stared at the blip of his heart. "Something tells me he'll return and try to finish the job.

"That is why I asked to talk to you, *Officer.*"

Deacon mentally winced at the insult, and wondered if Bautista and Gabardi took the same elocution lessons. Deacon slanted the little turd a glance and saw his gaze hadn't budged an inch. "Excuse me, were you talking to me?"

"I knew he'd pay you a visit and I know who he is."

Deacon's brows rose. "Really?" he asked in a neutral tone, and then coughed twice. His gaze drifted to Washington seated on the other side of Bautista.

Yawning, Washington leaned back in his chair, seemingly disinterested, and pushed a small button on a digital audio recorder in the chest pocket of his vest.

CHAPTER 27

I'm all ears, Alejandro," Deacon snarled.

The man smiled. "It's Bautista to you, Officer. Only my *mamacita* and the boss call me Alejandro."

"You wanted to talk to me? Well, I'm here, so talk."

"Yeah, you're here, all right."

At his taunting, fatigue almost defeated Deacon's ability to maintain a blank façade. He inhaled, held it for the count of three, then slowly released it. Then he repeated the action another two times before speaking. "It's been a long day. I'm tired and in pain and ready to head home with my dog. So if you have anything to say, get on with it."

"Because of our two…memorable…meetings—" Bautista paused, a smile tweaking the corners his mouth. "—I can tell what kind of man you are."

Deacon struggled to maintain his poker face at how well the man spoke, but he failed. He had expected the usual F-bomb every other word. Definitely, not the average gang-banger.

And didn't that just chap his ass?

Nothing like learning you aren't above stereotyping. All it takes are stupid facial gang tattoos, and I to fall prey to making false assumptions, and that is very dangerous when dealing with a smart, crafty, and well-educated Bautista.

"And what kind of man am I?"

"The kind who doesn't give his word often, but when he does, he keeps it."

With those few words, Deacon's mouth rivaled the Sahara. Could this man really know his core by just looking at him a couple times? Not a chance in hell. Lucky guess. Not that it mattered. Deacon would play this by the book and get what they needed. "You've made that judgment based upon what? See me three times, counting now, and the first two lasted only for few minutes? I'm really impressed and interested in how you came to that decision."

"Your eyes. I saw them in the tunnel and then again yesterday when you took me down, and finally now. Also, my boys have said you're known to be honest. I understand you can't cut me a deal. So I'm screwed and, without a deal, if I'm lucky, I'll be back in the joint. If the DA gives me a deal, I'll tell you everything I know. But first, I want your promise that you'll protect my *mamacita* and daughter. She's only three. You have to send someone to get them ASAP and hide them good. If you don't, any deal that's offered is worthless to me. Call the DA and get me my deal. Tonight. I want immunity, protection, the works, including the removal of all my tattoos. Help me, and you'll get the real prize, not the brass ring, but the golden one. But I won't talk until *Mamacita* gives me the code saying they're safe."

Deacon knew Bautista had been around the block a couple times. But if his first demand was guaranteeing his family's safety, then he was not only scared shitless, but had good reason to be. "Why should I believe anything you have to say?"

"After yesterday's takedown, I'm a dead man. I've pissed-off the wrong guy. But if I help you, maybe, just maybe my family and I will stay alive. If you and the DA refuse, I might as well eat your gun now."

Deacon sat up. Jamming his pillow against the headboard, he leaned back and studied the gangbanger's eyes. Normal skepticism flared, and just as quickly died a fiery death. It wasn't unusual for someone, trying to stay out of prison, to deal. However, it was extraordinarily rare that protecting the mother and daughter was the most important part of the deal. *Interesting*. He suspected Bautista figured he was a dead man even with the deal. But his family's death because his actions? He couldn't have *that* staining his soul. On the other hand, without his info, they had nothing. No name for the asshole with the knife. No name of who he worked for. It was only a matter of time before there was another attempt, which might be successful. Deacon didn't believe blind luck would strike a second time.

While his gut shouted that Tuefel was at the heart of everything, from the meth taken during the botched OP to the last night's attempt on Jessica's life, they had nothing, could prove nothing. The bastard would be walking free, waiting to take his revenge at a time of his choosing.

His mind weighted and processed the potential outcomes—positive and negative—with the speed of a computer and, like the machine, arrived at the only logical conclusion. "You have my word. As of this moment, everything said is on the record and recorded."

Ignoring Washington's shock, Deacon held out his hand for the recorder. When it was slapped into his palm, he nodded. "Kevin, I can't do this without you. Can you get us moved to the lockdown part of the hospital and have armed security on the wing. Second, call White. Give him a heads up on what's going down. Have him move Bautista's family to a safe house, put a guard on Jessica, and meet us here. Third, get hold of the DA—not Gabardi, but the DA. Explain the situation. Tell him it is imperative he not speak with anyone about this. That we believe we've got a leak, and we need him here, prepared to make a deal."

Deacon knew he could be slapped down for overstepping his rank. Hell, he was acting as if he had command. He was an officer, not a corporal or sergeant or lieutenant or captain, and sure as hell not the chief. If this went toes up, he would be the one to suffer, no one else.

Even his friends would attend the lynching, just to save themselves, because they would've climbed out on the limb with him.

As soon as Washington disappeared, tension bled from Deacon's shoulders and lower back. "If your information's as valuable as you say, and it's worth it, I'll go up to bat for you with the DA, my sergeant, and Detective White. Talk, you don't have much time."

"I know your mystery man's name and who he works for. His boss and my supplier are one and the same. Ubel Tuefel."

Elation surged through Deacon. "The Krusnik?" At Bautista's sharp, quick nod, Deacon grinned. They finally had the bastard.

Hearing a sharp inhale from at the doorway, he pulled his weapon free and aimed at the person who had overheard them. "God damn it, Washington. Make some noise next time. I could've blown you away."

"Nah, you're too careful to shoot without checking first." Washington shook his head as if clearing it. "Now, excuse me, did he actual say he has the goods on the Krusnik?"

"Yeah, I did. Tuefel's my direct supplier, in addition to being the only supplier of meth for this region after he killed off all his competition."

"Is he strictly drugs," Deacon asked.

"Yes. But you can also tack on smuggling people into the country and mass murder to his long list of accolades."

Deacon licked his lips. Damn, he hoped like hell the feds didn't take Bautista out from under them. Although Deacon knew if Bautista could give them the goods on interstate trafficking and crime, the feds would grab him and grant his every wish. "That's great intel, but I have no hard details so talk away. What I don't understand is how you and I got into this mess."

"It started right after your narcs ripped me off. It was his dope and I quote, 'You owe me two hundred large. You have a month to pay.' That brings us up to yesterday. With his wife in tow and—let's just say if you think the big guy's good with a knife, you haven't seen anything until you've seen Rachele Tuefel work."

"So you were stealing 4K televisions to get fast cash."

"Yeah. Until that store manager caught us, it had worked like a charm. Those were the last ten sets I needed and I would've had the entire amount. Now with his wife dead, he's not only coming after you and that lady, Officer, he's gunning for me. He'll take my family and make me watch what he does to them before killing me."

"So you're willing to work with us to save your mother and daughter."

"Right. Once I have proof they're safe and my deal's signed, I spill everything. Your department and the DA will be heroes. By the way, you're right not to trust Gabardi. Don't have anything on him, but there've been times when some of my boys should've gone down and they didn't." With a raised brow, he shrugged.

"The lady he's after is the manager of the Speaker City you were robbing. Can you tell me now, even without a signed deal, the name of the big guy with the knife and C-4?"

"Really, C-4. Damn, the man's crazy. He goes by the name of Luis. No one knows his last name. Not even Tuefel. But you need to know two things. One, Luis is absolutely loyal to Tuefel. Two, the only thing Tuefel loved more than money was his wife. We're talking obsessive here. And if I heard right, Officer, you killed her."

Deacon pinched the bridge of his nose. "Well, that explains him wanting me, but not Jessica."

"The girl who chased us, right? Well, if she hadn't, his wife would be alive. I know it's irrational, but hey, the guy's a psychopath. I mean his picture's beside the definition. Not that Rachele was any better. She's single handedly responsible for the mass grave you'll find at his meth factory—once I give you its location."

"Mass grave?" Deacon and Washington asked simultaneously.

"Yeah. They're the illegals brought in to cook the meth. To paraphrase an old saying, loose lips tank profits and send the boss to Pelican Bay."

Bautista grabbed his water glass and drained it. "Killing his wife, Officer Deacon, puts you and pretty Jessica and me in same leaky boat. His wife died because of the debt I owed. Forget Tuefel ordered her to stay at my side, he'll see it as my fault. As for wanting you dead, you actually killed his beautiful wife. He wants pretty Jessica dead because, as I've said, if not for her chasing us, Rachele would be alive and warming his bed. What I don't get is that he sent Luis to kill us. I would've thought he'd want to do the job himself." He shrugged again. "Guess I can't be right all the time. But that leads me to another question. How did he get the pretty lady's name and address? You have a leak? Because if you do, my deal won't be worth spit."

His own suspicions coming out of Bautista's mouth, pissed Deacon off. It was one thing to wonder, another to hear the bastard cast doubt on the honesty of his family, his brothers and sisters. Hands fisted, his gaze skittered to Washington and then returned to Bautista and took in his expression—sadness, defeat, acceptance.

Jesus-H-Christ! Trusting one's fellow officers was the bedrock of their profession. Shaken, Deacon no longer knew who he could trust.

"In a way, Officer, we're partners. And I'm just guessing here, but your few stitches are courtesy of Luis's blade work."

Make that thirty-three internal stitches and twelve external staples. But who's counting? Not the putz in the next bed, that's for sure. "What do you know about this Luis? And where's Tuefel's operation based?"

"Ah, ah, not another word until my deal's signed. Okay, I'll give this much about Luis. He's a former *Zarato*, one of Mexico's Special Forces who went rogue and works as a mercenary for the drug cartels. He arrived in the US before the cartels went to war a couple of years ago."

"Why?"

"Why? Officer, don't you know? The States are where someone in his profession can make a lot of money. If I was a betting man, I'd wager he was a hitman long before working for Tuefel."

Deacon snorted. "Having experienced his expertise first hand, that isn't a bet, it's a guarantee." *I wonder if he's still taking private jobs. Jobs his boss knows nothing about.*

"Too true. Until recently, I thought he was nothing but a brainless, muscle-bound thug. Now...now I'm not so sure." Bautista's barely there smile vanished. "Don't make the mistake of believing Luis uses only a knife. He's also an expert with firearms and explosives." He poured himself more water and gulped it down. "A couple of weeks ago, some of my boys partied with him for the first time. He got drunk. Alone with Miguel, he bragged his most memorable kills were made unnoticed, in public. He loved being able to walk past his target, slide a blade between the ribs, puncturing the heart, and disappear into the crowd before the victim hit the pavement. Initially, I didn't believe Miguel. I mean, have you seen Luis's size. The guy's a huge bull of a man. Probably impossible to defeat in hand-to-hand."

Rubbing his shoulder, Deacon mumbled, "Tell me about it. So what made you a believer?"

"My boy turned up dead. Stabbed between the ribs, heart punctured. Bled out inside—almost nothing, no blood outside. Interesting, no?"

"Yeah, interesting." Cripes, Jessica and he had almost bought the farm. The more he learned about Luis, the more blessed he felt.

He yanked the bed sheet loose and used it to wipe his face. Tossing it aside, he noted Washington's concerned gaze. "We had him in custody, Kevin. And yes, I almost bought it in the process of arresting him. He had me pinned. I'm here because Justice ripped his arm good, then I nailed the balls, and Jessica, using a cast iron skillet, knocked him out cold."

"Is he here?" Bautista squeaked.

"No. He escaped thirty minutes ago. I was in the lead ambulance. Suddenly, the second ambulance stopped in the middle of an intersection and, through the rear door glass of my ambulance, I watched the bastard kick out the locked ambulance doors and escape with a gurney arm-rail cuffed to him."

Washington grunted. Bautista laughed. "Well, at least I'm not the only one who's had an encounter with your dog's teeth."

"Yeah. Too bad Justice didn't use Luis's leg as a rawhide chew instead of his arm."

"Think he's hurt bad enough, he'll seek medical help, D?" Washington asked.

Bautista shook his head. "Forget it, he'll take care of it himself. And don't waste time searching for him. Luis will go to ground at the meth lab. One that's impossible to find without my help. But don't worry, he'll find you when the time's right. Understand, Officer Deacon, to Luis I'm just work. You and pretty Jessica? You're personal."

CHAPTER 28

Deacon's gaze never stopped moving. He took in everyone around him and forced himself to admit he trusted no one. Not when his life was at stake. But, ever the optimist, he figured for now, in the lockdown section of the hospital, he and Bautista were safe. No way could Tuefel own the entire department.

His eyes flicked to the nameless US Attorney who recently joined the party. Arms folded across his chest, the man rested against the wall. His interest in the case set Deacon's teeth on edge.

It reminded Deacon of the time Justice had been lusting after Deacon's T-bone on the counter right before the damned dog had snitched it the moment he'd turned his back. He never did find the bone.

After that, he'd built the kennel and Justice enjoyed his meals—all his meals—outside. Deacon would lay even money his partner hadn't fully forgiven him for the banishment.

"Here." The Cain City DA handed a signed deal to Bautista, who scanned it as he had the fed's deal. "Remember, one lie and both the deals are off."

"Right," the US Attorney echoed. "I've got a couple special agents who will assist during the takedown."

"Just make sure you handle you're part of the deal. I want my mother and daughter Christina safe. Anything happens to me, they're still given a new life."

A US Marshal stepped forward. "It's already in the works. Three marshals are on their way to the safe house with them as we speak."

Deacon glanced at the FBI SAC, Special Agent in Charge, and waited for him to make his move. He didn't have to wait long.

"Where is his little operation?"

Bautista's chuckle was short and mean. "I've already told you, Fed, I'm only talking to Officer Deacon. You can wait outside."

"You just remember. If you don't deliver, all deals are off," the DA growled through clenched teeth.

His elbows on the table, Deacon tapped his fingers against the smile curling his lips. Bautista never ceased to amaze him. While they waited for the DA and his entourage of feds—no big surprise there—Deacon had learned that, but for being in the wrong place at the wrong time, Bautista would have finished his last year of law school and been a practicing attorney for a decade now.

Buying some meth and going to prison had destroyed his promising future. Maybe between having the tats removed and being given a new name, he'd have a shot at living the life he'd always planned.

The attorneys stormed off to file the paperwork and the feds made haste to get their people in place for witness protection for Bautista's family. Exhaling, Deacon raised his head and took in Bautista's laughing eyes.

"Where's Tuefel's hidden compound, and are you sure Luis will be there?" Deacon asked.

"Not so fast. Yes he will be there. From what you described of his wounds, he'll need some medical attention. Once he's tended them, he'll go after my family and your woman, Officer. We just have to get him before he gets there with our loved ones."

Every instinct Deacon had warned their window was short if not gone. "But it is likely he'd go the compound first to patch himself up?"

Bautista licked his lips. "Maybe. It depends—"

"On?"

"It depends upon how hurt he is and if he calls Tuefel. Luis isn't stupid, but so far he's been loyal. And Tuefel loved his crazy-killer wife. So he's got a hard-on for you, your Jessica, *me*, and my family."

Deacon agreed, but... "From what you've said, I'd say Tuefel won't touch them until we're there to suffer watching what he does to them, right?" At his nod, Deacon continued. "So if we get there first and our men surround it, then we'll have neutralized both of them. But to do that, we need to get there first. So where the hell is it?"

"Near Yosemite. Tuefel owns a large piece of property in the mountains above Oakhurst. The house is in the middle of it. His whole operation's run inside a natural cave near his house. That's the location of the lab where he cooks all the meth. The mass grave is in a ravine at the end of a tunnel. It's a perfect set-up. You can't see anything from the air. Shit, I couldn't even find it on *Google* maps, and I knew where to look."

"Christ, there're a ton of caves by Oakhurst that we know about and haven't explored." *And, I'm willing to bet, there's a lot we haven't discovered yet. It will take forever to search them all.* "Do you know the address? Can you see it on a map? Are there any landmarks nearby?"

Bautista exhaled harshly, exasperation clear in his face and tone as he shot back, "That's why I told you, Officer, you'd have to take me along. Last time I went, I passed the turn-off and I know where it is. It's really hidden. Without me to guide you, you'll never find it, not even with a map."

Not a chance in hell. Doug'll kill me before this Luis gets a chance. Then again, what other choice do any of us have? Deacon's gaze locked with Washington's. "Thoughts?"

"It's your call but it's worth a shot. I can't see this ending well for you unless we run with the ball and play some of-fense. Like the man said, this shit ain't gonna be over till *we* end it, or *he* ends it. We wait to be ambushed or we do what they'll never see coming or expect—bring the fight to them. I don't see it any other way."

Deacon closed his eyes and sighed. Why was it his choices always came down to satisfying his gut? He looked up at his buddy and nodded. "When you're right, you're right. I better call Doug, he can call the chief afterward." Pushing back from the table, he stood and felt briefly light-headed. He grabbed the back of his chair and braced himself. *Must've lost more blood than I thought. Or, it could be I haven't had but two hours sleep in the last forty-eight?*

The guard outside the room opened the door for the head of ER trauma. Deacon recognized him immediately. He was the same pretentious jerk, he had seen a number of times about the surgeries Justice performed on suspects. The man had a textbook case of short-man syndrome. He was all of five-foot-two and a buck forty soaking wet. But it was the obnoxious swagger that gave the strutting bald-headed man away. Asshole. Deacon had loathed him from the moment they met. It had only grown deeper with each encounter.

"Well, Officer Deacon, imagine my surprise when I heard you were the patient, not some poor soul who had the misfortune of meeting your partner. But I had to come and make sure the rumors were correct." The doctor lifted his chart and, with a smirk, scanned it. "It appears you'll live," he said between smacks of his gum.

"Yeah, how about that?"

He thrust him a prescription. "It's for Vicodin. Take one five-hundred-milligram pill every six hours for pain—"

Shaking his head, Deacon stepped back. "No pain meds, Doc. It's just a scratch."

Clearly pissed, the doctor handed the script to Washington. "The second is for Amoxicilin to fight a possible infection. See that he takes them. Staples are out in fourteen days."

As if he were in the military, the doctor pivoted on one heel and marched out. As he left, he grabbed the door and slammed it behind him.

"Be right back." Deacon stepped into the hall and in three steps clamped a heavy hand on the little man's shoulder.

The doctor jerked free and turned to face him. "How dare you manhandle me, Officer Deacon."

Deacon smiled as the doc tipped his neck back to meet his gaze. At six-foot-three and two-hundred-twenty-five, Deacon knew he could be intimidating, and he used every inch and pound to ensure it. He leaned down into the man's face, the tips of their noses almost touching. "I hope you enjoyed your little power play. But we both know you don't give a rat's ass over my treatment or the patient brought in courtesy of my partner. You just wanted a look and see at who was in there. I promise you, that if you say one word about who or what you saw in there, I will—and everyone in that room will—make it our life's work to ensure that you're locked away in some dark hole and never see the light of day again. Obstruction is a bitch. Do we understand each other?"

"No, no problem, Officer. I swear, not a word," the doctor said, almost sobbing the last two words.

Deacon released the doctor. "I hope so. See you around, Doc." Returning to the room, Deacon grabbed the two scripts from Washington and tore the Vicodin one into small pieces. As he tossed it into the trash, the door cracked open and the guard said Smith was waiting in the hall.

With Washington in tow, Deacon felt his paranoia raise its ugly head. He didn't like how he felt. "Where the hell were you?"

"Sorry about that. It wouldn't have happened if the ambulance drivers had waited until I got your car. I was within two thousand feet when a teenage driver of blue Cobalt seemed to panic at my lights and siren. Damned drought—drivers have forgotten how to drive in rain. It was bad enough she was going twenty below the limit, but she couldn't make up her mind which lane to drive in. She barely missed crashing into us, but did hit an empty Honda parked on the side of the road, flipped her vehicle, and was injured. She'll live—"

"Wait. Did you say a Chevy Cobalt?" At his nod, Deacon grimaced. "Her name didn't happen to be Sally Henderson was it?"

"Yes, it was. How'd you know?"

Deacon sighed. It was his fault. He should have listened to his gut and cited her. "She was the one I pulled over the other day for car-dancing. She going to make it?"

"I think so. The medics took a while. By the time I'd checked for a pulse, I heard you over the radio that that guy up and vanished like a fart in the wind. I'm really sorry, brother."

Deacon smiled. "Not your fault. Give me a second," he said, searching for that last phrase in his movie memory bank. "*Shawshank Redemption.*"

Smith laughed. "I love it, man. One of these days, one of us will stump the other. Seriously, though, sorry we lost him."

"Again, it's not your fault. You had to stop and help. He's gone now. Never forget, even if he gets away, Justice was served." Deacon joined Smith and Washington in laughing. For some unexplainable reason, that line never got old with the guys.

"Anyway, I left your car in the side lot," Smith said, tossing the car keys to Deacon.

"Which lot?"

"North. This place is jumpin' tonight. There wasn't an empty space in the law enforcement parking. What the hell's going on?"

"Besides this hot mess? I have no idea. I've been stuck with Bautista since I arrived. Thanks again, man. Oh, how's the boy?"

"He wasn't too happy with me driving and not you. He

told me about it the entire ride here. Jeeze, he's a loud one."

"That sounds right. Sorry about that."

Smith rubbed his right ear. "Huh? What? Don't worry about it. You all right?"

Deacon rotated his shoulder in a circular motion. The wound talked to him but didn't scream. Good thing, too. With everything that was coming down, he couldn't take anything that dulled his ability to make a snap decision or slowed his reaction time. Sighing, his raked his fingers through his hair. His head throbbed a bit but was barely noticeable. "I'll live. Just adds to the scars I've got cooking."

"Want me to hang tight a bit until you're officially discharged."

"No. I'll be all right. This Bautista—" Deacon shrugged. "I've gotta stick around. I know I'm being played, but—"

"Got it."

"Smith, thanks again for taking care of Justice and bringing me my ride."

CHAPTER 29

After twenty-five minutes of searching for his cruiser, Deacon prayed Smith had let Justice out for a brief pit stop before taking off to find him. As he approached the back door, he heard an all too familiar scratching. "Ah, damn, not twice in twenty-four hours." Too bad he hadn't bought stock in the Orange manufacturer his first week with Justice. If he had, he could retire early. With resignation nipping at his heels, he opened the back door.

As Justice leapt from the vehicle, a foul odor detonated in Deacon's face. While the dog raced to a group of shrubs and squatted, Deacon started to remove the mat, then stopped. "Hot damn, it was gas." After a few minutes, Justice returned, almost prancing. All was right in his world. Grinning, Deacon scratched behind his ears. "You did real good, buddy. Thanks." Once he'd loaded his partner in the back, they went in search of food.

Unable to decide what he wanted, Deacon traveled up Blackstone. He had just turned east down Shaw when Justice growled low and deep. Glancing into his rearview mirror, Deacon spotted Justice glaring at him. "Sorry buddy, I forgot."

Tradition dictated a corndog for each bite. Since Justice had two in one day and hadn't received his reward, the dog was expressing his displeasure. "When you're right, you're right. God knows I could use a chili lover's meal. Onward to Der, dude."

He smirked at the sight of his partner with his nose stuck out a partially lowered window. From the way his tongue was hanging out and to the side, he was enjoying every minute of the thousands of smells bombarding him.

Wonder if there's such a thing as doggie sensory overload.

Unable to postpone it any longer, Deacon grabbed his phone. No sooner had he punched his speed dial for Swanson, then a driver shot him an outraged scowl. "Newsflash, lady, there's an exemption for law enforcement. It isn't illegal for us to call while driving if it's related to work. God, I need to get a life," he muttered as the call connected.

"What's up, Deacon?"

Pulling into the congested drive-through lane, Deacon quickly briefed the sergeant. "Part of the deal is my involvement. Bautista—"

"Absolutely not! There is no way in hell you're going to Tuefel's place. Are you stupid or high? What did they give you at the hospital? Did you forget you were knifed and in a shooting and killed the man's wife? You got shit for brains? Because I think you do."

One thing about Swanson, you never were in doubt of his reactions to anything he perceived as putting his cops in unwarranted danger. "Um, Sarge—"

"Hold on a sec while I try to figure out what to do with an officer who's lost his damned mind."

Deacon grimaced. It was up to him to get the go ahead. If he didn't, they'd lose Bautista and Tuefel. Which meant one thing—Jessica and he were "dead people walking." "Sarge, it's already a done deal. Both the DA's office and US Attorney's signed the paperwork."

"They what?" he roared.

"Just hear me out. If we don't take Tuefel down, Jessica Grady's and my lives are over. Bautista won't be the only one needing protection. The two of us will, too—preferably in a foreign country, high in the mountains so I'll be able to spot anyone approaching."

"And that's why you want to go on this turkey shoot?"

"Not entirely. Tuefel needs to be taken down. Don't worry about me. It'll be the feds' show in the end. For now, I'm extra muscle and bullets and, for the lack of a better word, nothing more than a glorified bodyguard for Bautista."

The silence was crushing. After a couple of minutes, Deacon glanced at his phone. Yup, he still had a good connection.

Just as he was ready to buckle and talk first, he heard, "I'm going to regret this. I know it. Every time we have a joint OP with the feds and it goes toes up, we're the ones covered in crap. So what am I doing? Sending an injured shit-magnet up the hill in the middle of God's nowhere."

"Thanks, Sarge."

"Don't thank me. I'm only approving it because—ah, hell, D. I don't like it. It smells. So get your ass up there and back, before your new CI or I change our minds."

"Copy that. I'll keep you posted."

"If you don't, I'll kill you myself."

Grinning, Deacon said, "Thanks, Doug." As he quickly disconnected, he glanced to his right and groaned. Jessica's purse along with her wallet was still on the floorboard. "Shit." He had to return it, tonight.

He glanced at the clock on his dash. Double-oh-thirty. Much as his body craved food and sleep, he couldn't leave her stranded. Without her ID, impound wouldn't return her car. Seemed only Justice was getting a treat tonight. *Damn!* Looked like a PB and J for him when he got home.

An annoyed-sounding, tinny voice squeaked out from the speaker box, "Welcome to Der Wienerschnitzel. How can I help you?"

"Four corn dogs, please."

"Would you like to supersize them or have a combo meal?"

"No thanks. Just the four dogs," Deacon said as glob of slobber plopped onto his shoulder. "Damn it, Justice." He was a filthy mess. He plucked at his pants. They could stand up and walk under their own power.

He reminded himself, again, to get his ass to the cleaners on his next set of days off, whenever that happened, or be forced to wear his boots, a pair of jeans, and a *Kevlar* vest beneath his CPD sweatshirt. Between the CPD on both sides of the sweatshirt and his CPD hat, he *shouldn't* be mistaken for a perp.

Deacon dropped his K9 unit into drive, inched up to window one, and paid. At window two, he grabbed his order and, before he merged onto the street, he threw the first of the corndogs through the grate. Justice swallowed it whole. Some things never changed, he thought, tossing his partner the second one, then the third, which was immediately followed the fourth and last one.

Policy said Justice wasn't allowed to eat fast food. However, Deacon believed on a day like yesterday, the rules could not only be bent but shattered. Although within twenty-four hours, he'd be questioning that decision. From past experience, he knew policing the backyard for two days was guaranteed to necessitate his wearing a gasmask.

A short time later, he parked in front of Jessica's house. Her lights were on. Good. It looked like she was still up. Probably couldn't sleep with her back door busted out. If not for his injury, he'd fix it for her.

Retrieving her purse from the floor, he tucked the wallet inside and shoved the purse under his shirt to protect it from the rain. He got out of the car, popped the back door and released Justice. Together, they headed toward the front door. "Let's hope we get out of here before my stomach sounds like artillery shells going off."

Fifteen seconds later, the two of them were panting as he knocked. By the time she opened the door, his breathing was almost normal. "Hi."

"Daniel! Why aren't you in the hospital?"

He pointed to the padding sticking out from the top of Washington's loaner. "I was treated and am good to go. What with everything that's happened, we forgot this. Again." He pulled her purse free of his waistband and passed to her.

"Thank you, but it wasn't necessary. You should be home getting some sleep. You look like you've just experienced the lost weekend."

"I'll take off in minute. How's the door?"

"Forget the door. How's your—" She motioned to his stab wound.

With a wink, he rolled his shoulder. "I'll live."

She reached out, threaded her fingers with his, and yanked him inside. "How many stitches did it take?"

The concern in her face warmed him. It had been a long time since he'd had a woman care what happened to him. "Internal or external?" Seeing her eyes begin to water, he mentally castigated himself for being such a dumbass. "Sorry, bad form. Twelve external staples. Thirty-three internal stitches. Just a butterfly strip for the cheek. Trust me, it wasn't a big deal. Really, I'm fine."

She towed him with her into the dining room and pushed him onto a chair. "Have you eaten?"

"No, not yet. I'm gonna grab something when I get home then hit the rack. I've got an undercover OP I'm part of later this morning."

"Would you like some pasta? It's my own recipe."

Gratitude surged up so fast he couldn't smother his groan of delight. "I'd love some. Thanks a million." He watched as she blinked rapidly trying to stem another round of threatening tears.

"I'll be right back." She rushed into the kitchen, picked up a container he had seen earlier, and plopped it into the microwave. "It'll be ready in three minutes. If you're as hungry as I am, you're ready to eat your own leg."

"Pretty close." He sniffed. "It smells wonderful."

A few minutes later, she set a heaping plate of Chicken

Feta Pasta in front of him. At the first bite, he moaned. "God, this is good," he said between mouthfuls.

Neither one spoke again as they woofed down the meal. When he finished, he motioned to her door, shoved into place and hanging lopsided. "I'm guessing the officers who did that weren't carpenters."

"Not even close. There's more galvanized steel than wood in it," she said, chuckling. A second later, her gaze saddened. "I'm thrilled we met, but I'm also worried. In less than a day, you've saved my life twice. It's tears me apart knowing you've been injured because of me." She dropped her eyes to her soda. "I'm so sorry that man stabbed you. He wouldn't have if not for me."

Deacon hated the way her face reddened and shame marred her expression. "It's not your fault. And I'm okay. This—" He touched his padded wound. "—is not my first injury since I joined the force, and it probably won't be my last."

He clasped her chin between two fingers and tipped it up toward him. "For you, I'd do it again in a heartbeat." With his free hand, he wiped away the tears rolling down her cheeks.

"Do you know why that man was here? I know he wanted to kill me, but why? I haven't hurt or cheated anyone."

Deacon heard the wounded confusion in her voice and ached for her. Yes, because of yesterday's events, she had lost some of her innocence. But once she knew the full scope of what was going on, she would never be the same. All her illusions about life and people would be shattered. And it destroyed a piece him to have to be the one to do it. "Before I tell you what we've learned, it's critical you promise to keep it to yourself." At her vow, he licked his lips. "Also, do you have family or friends out of the area that can come here and take you to their home?"

"Yes. My parents. They live in Modesto. Why?"

"Good. Make the call. Once they're on the way, I'll bring you up to date."

He listened to her sobbing as she told her dad everything that had happened. After disconnecting, she washed her face in the kitchen and returned to the chair beside him.

"Why do you want me out of Cain?"

"Not just Cain, but the entire Central Valley."

"That man was here to kill me because of Rachele Tuefel, wasn't he?"

Staring at the table, Deacon picked at a fingernail. "Yes." He cleared his throat, struggling with how much to tell her. Exhaling, he began. "The thefts from your store and others have been going on for three weeks. The individual behind them recently lost five keys of dope in a undercover op. It's street value is unimportant, but he owed his supplier two hundred grand. That man gave him four weeks to come up with the money. If he doesn't—" Using his index finger, Deacon slashed across his neck.

"And the man who was in my house, what about him?"

"He was sent by the thief's boss to kill you and me, the drug dealing thief, and his family."

"If you hadn't come, I'd be dead—again."

Hearing her hyperventilating, he jumped up, ran to her side, and, standing behind her, cupped his hands around her mouth and nose. "Breathe." Once she had calmed, he returned to his chair. "On the way to the hospital, the man we fought with here in your house killed an EMT and paramedic then escaped out the back of his ambulance."

He took in her dumbstruck expression. It probably mirrored his as he'd watched it happen. Hunching over, he stared at his hands. Better that then seeing her worry-stricken face. Worse, he couldn't reassure her they were safe until Luis and Tuefel were in custody or dead. His personal preference was dead. Then they couldn't put a contract out on them.

"How bad is it, Daniel?"

"I won't lie to you. It's bad. That's why I want you stashed someplace secure. Right now, my trust level in everyone is very low. However, if everything works out, you should be able to return within a few days."

She clutched his hand in hers. "Daniel, are you going to be in danger?"

He shrugged. "Hopefully, no more than usual. I'm just along for the ride."

"Sure, you are. Can you tell me anything more?"

"Not much. It's classified and I've already said too much. But I felt it was imperative you understand what we, the two us, are up against. And I was worried if I didn't give you enough of the truth, you wouldn't leave. And if I don't know you're safe, I won't be fully focused on the op. Which—"

Nodding, she gave his hand a reassuring squeeze. "I understand."

"I wish—" He shook his head and glared at the broken door. "I'm so sorry you're getting a front row seat to the Daniel Deacon Shit-Magnet Show."

"I'm sorry, too. And, for the record, the show sucks and I want my money back."

Lifting his gaze, he met her laughing eyes. Within a split second, they both burst out in deep, rolling laughter. Hiccupping, Deacon wiped his face dry. "God, I needed that."

"We both did."

Ninety minutes later, Deacon carried her luggage into the living room and set it by the door. Turning, he pulled Jessica into a hug. Her head rested just below his chin. He loved how she fit him perfectly.

Sighing, he nuzzled her neck and inhaled the faint scent of soap and what he termed "all Jessica." God, what was about her that just doing this calmed him? As he went to release her, she pulled his head down to hers.

"Please kiss me, Daniel. I need to know I'm not alone in feeling this connection."

She grasped his head with both hands and kissed him. A car horn snapped them back to reality. Unable to let her go without leaving his mark, Deacon gently kissed her forehead.

After securing her home, he wrapped one arm around Jessica and held her suitcase in the other as they raced to her father's car with Justice pacing them.

After introductions were completed, Deacon seat-belted Jessica in and closed the door. As she disappeared, he cursed their situation, long and hard. At Justice's head bump against his thigh, he scratched behind his dog's ears.

His cell phone rang. He grabbed it and pressed talk before it woke the neighborhood. *Shit!* He'd meant to change the ring tone. He glanced at the caller ID and winced. Washington. Two minutes later his language would have embarrassed a trucker. "So much for going home and catching a few Justice. Looks like we've got to get back to the hospital. It's going to be a long night, buddy."

CHAPTER 30

L uis sprinted across Cain Avenue. Avoiding street lights, he slinked from shadow to shadow. Whenever the lights of a car neared his location, he froze against the side of buildings.

Drifting into an alleyway, he rummaged through several garbage cans, hunting for something to rid himself of the bloody gurney appendage. The third can was packed with the contents from a home office. Files, tax documents, and hundreds of pages of bank statements filled the can to the brim. He salvaged two staples and a paperclip from the identity theft gold mine.

Minutes later, he'd picked the lock on the cuffs and truly was a free man. He placed the cuffs and bedrail in a nearby blue recycle bin. Who ever said he wasn't green?

Luis sprinted to the end of the alley, rounded a corner, and nearly ran into police and fire personnel who had arrived in response to a multi-car pile-up. Several ambulances were parked near him. Whether to ferry the injured or serve as meat wagons, Luis didn't know or care. He just needed to get out of here and hole-up somewhere he could tend his injuries and then kill that cop and his lady love. Once he'd finished them off, he was heading home until things cooled off.

One last look, assured him he hadn't been seen. Fools. They were so busy, the one person the cops were hunting was about to make like an ebb tide and go out. Leaning against a tree, he pressed his hand against his shoulder. Pain flared through him like lightning. Fucking dog! But before he carried out his revenge, he had to set his dislocated shoulder, and stop the bleeding from the fucking dog bites. Then he'd finish what he started.

Teeth gritted, he decided to start with the easiest first. Crouching to minimize his profile, Luis grabbed a small branch lying near a sprinkler head and bit on it. A tiny bead of sap dripped onto his tongue, tasting faintly of maple syrup. He braced his shoulder against the trunk, wrapped one arm around it, and held it in a vice-like grip.

He eased the shoulder back then savagely slammed it into the trunk. Fiery pain sent him to his knees as it snapped back into its socket. The branch snapped in two. His chipped teeth clipped one another. He spit out a couple of fresh chunks of enamel. Luis took a long, slow, deep breath. He continued to breathe deeply. It channeled the pain and helped him focus. Once back in control of his body, he eased his shirt off, and tore it into strips. He wrapped his left arm with the improvised bandages, stemming the ooze of blood from the damned dog bites.

Confident it would hold long enough for him to get to the compound, he did one last recon and headed out of the center of the city.

Luis sprinted past several antique stores on a side street. At the tee intersection, he spotted a parking lot packed with cars, behind a row of bars across the street. He had his choice. It would be like picking fruit. They ranged from lowered Hondas with modified exhaust pipes to lifted four-wheel-drive trucks with "Don't Tread on Me" flags mounted on the tailgates of their beds. Either one would be too easily spotted. No, he needed something that let him blend with the traffic.

He kept low and moved quickly to the rear of the lot

where the lighting was poor. He sidled up to a gray Toyota and tried the door. It was locked. As he reared back to kick out the window, a car screeched to a halt, its high beams spotlighting him.

He spun and saw the driver of a BMW 700 sedan staring at him. Luis sneered at the man's deer in the headlights look. He sauntered over and opened the driver's door. *What a dumb shit. The car auto locks everything and this guy unlocked it?*

The man stared up at him over the top of his glasses which rested on the tip of his nose. "What do you want?"

Luis's fist delivered the reply in an upward motion, crushing and splintering cartilage. The man's head snapped back like a whip. A shard of what was once a nose ripped through flesh while the rest pierced his brain.

Using his one good arm and hand, Luis wrenched open the door, reached inside, and, jerking the man out of the car, tossed him into the grill guard of a nearby pick-up. The man's body momentarily hung up on the metal, then flopped to the ground like a puppet whose strings had been cut.

Luis reached inside and moved the seat back to its farthest position. Nursing his left arm, he slithered behind the steering wheel, adjusted the rearview mirror, and caught a glimpse of his face. Hell, he looked like he'd been through a war. No surprise, he had been. Oh, well, it could be worse. The fucking dog could have broken his leg and dislocated his hip. All things considered, he got off lucky.

He took a quick inventory of the vehicle. Empty, except for a large bag from Der Wienerschnitzel in the passenger seat. He sniffed, then looked inside it and found chili Mecca. Grinning, he settled the two chili dogs on the console and removed the wrappers. "*Gracias, a Dios.*" Famished, he inhaled the first in two bites and devoured the second in three. Having killed the contents of the bag, he threw the trash on the passenger floorboard. With a shrug, he shifted the car into drive and punched it. The tires broke traction, spewing smoke and water into the air.

Knowing full well the car would be reported stolen as soon as the driver's body was discovered, Luis pulled into the parking lot of a shopping center. Since he was driving a BMW, he searched for another one. He didn't care which model. After trolling through the parking lots of two shopping centers and the local mall, he spotted a 2007 Z4.

How about that? He parked and changed the license plates in under eight minutes. Not bad mainly using one hand and no tools other than a quarter.

Within minutes, he was back in the sedan on the freeway, secure he wouldn't have to dump the car for at least two or three days. Not a problem. In under thirty minutes, he would arrive at the compound. Once there, he'd treat his wounds, then if he left, he could use his own vehicle or, depending upon Tuefel's behavior, one of his.

Finally relaxed, Luis cruised north on the 41. No traffic, which was always good. He pressed the power button on the radio. Hearing Fort Minor sound off on a list of percentages, he reached out to crank up the volume.

The speakers blasted the beat loud enough it felt like his body had become a part of it. He bobbed his head to the rhythm of one of his favorite songs. Okay, he never took the time to see if what they were rapping about would add up to 100%. But then, he didn't care enough to do the math. He just wanted to rock out.

He set the cruise control and ran his hand over his left arm to his shoulder. The throbbing pain had begun to subside.

A second later, Usher came over the radio with "Oh My Gosh." With his shoulder thumping to the beat, Luis threw his head back and laughed as he smashed the pedal to the metal.

CHAPTER 31

Deacon strode toward Washington seated in a chair outside Bautista's hospital room in lockdown. He almost stopped mid-step at seeing Smith lounging against the wall facing Bautista's closed door.

"It's about time, yo. Where the hell have you been?" Washington asked.

Expression purposefully blank, Deacon returned Smith's nod. "I thought you went home, Rob."

"Did. I was just crawling into the sack when Swanson called and ordered me back here. Said you'd brief me."

Deacon took a shaky breath. "I talked to Swanson. Told him about the signed deal, that the man's only willing to work with me, and our part in it. You know, Kev, how I love sharing the credit."

"Gee thanks for including me, friend," Washington groused.

"My pleasure. Oh, you're gonna love this. He called me a 'shit-magnet.' He said we're to *only* have Bautista guide us to Tuefel's compound. Once we confirm the info is good, we're to get the hell out of there and let the feds, along with our guys, handle it."

Washington inspected him. "I don't believe it. He agreed and you're still alive."

"Yeah, I'm *sooo* lucky."

"This party just keeps getting better and better. Why the hell did you mention me? You've not only gotten us involved in treating Bautista with kid-gloves, but working with the feds. What the hell's wrong with you?"

"Can it, Kev. We both know that if we don't get this done now, it's only a matter of time before Jessica and I wake up dead. If we're lucky, it'll be swift. But something tells me Tuefel wants it slow and painful. I've gotta tell you two, I'd like to keep on breathing. And since we're friends, I figured you'd like me to continue sucking air. If so, we need to do this together."

Smith stared at them, his lips thinned. "What's the chief's take on this, D? I ask only because I'd like to keep my job."

"As far as I know, he has no clue. It's only a matter of time before he finds out, though. Trust me, your job's safe, Rob. We have a couple hours to come up with a game plan that gets the job done and us home alive. Let's get somewhere secure and talk."

"What about our deal-making charge?" Washington asked.

Deacon scanned the hallway for ease of ingress and egress. He'd never liked how open the area was or how busy the nurses were. So far, they hadn't lost anyone. But then, they had never a deal-maker like Bautista. Here was hoping Tuefel hadn't learned of the deal yet. "I'm thinking it's time we got Bautista discharged. What about you two?"

Smith laughed. "Let me rub my crystal ball real quick. Ah, yes, I see a bald-headed dick, who's been giving his nurses a ration, in your future."

Deacon sighed. "I'll be right back." Shit, just what his tired body didn't need—the little shit feeling like he held all the cards. Hell, he did. Reaching the nurses' station, Deacon rested his weary body against the counter. "Excuse me, ma'am?"

The nurse lifted her gaze and smiled. "It's good to see

you up and around, Officer. Now, how can I help you?"

"If Bautista's been medically cleared, we'd like to take him off your hands."

"You mean that asshole your dog bit? I had the pleasure of stapling and stitching up his wound when he wouldn't answer me. You'll appreciate this." She leaned a little closer and whispered, "Dumbass wouldn't answer me if he needed pain meds. So he didn't get any. Nice job on the bite, by the way."

"Thanks. It seems stupidity guarantees job security for both of us. Listen, I don't want create more work for you, but when you've got a moment, can you let me know when we can get him out of your hair?"

"No problem, sweetie. I'll be done here in a few. I have to go check on another patient and then I'll go pull asshole's chart. Meet me back here in say fifteen or twenty minutes?"

"Sure thing. And thank you. Oh, and I could use a copy of my discharge paperwork as well. My admin will want it."

"Okay. I'll grab that as well. See you in a few."

Deacon got lost and wandered for a bit. He found the elevators, grabbed the first one that opened its doors, and discovered it was not only going up, but some kid had punched the buttons for each floor.

Finally, he found Smith waiting outside the door. He pointed to his wristwatch and tapped it. "Glad you could join us."

"Shut up, Rob," Deacon snapped as they walked into the room and saw the nurse had beaten him back here. *Damn.*

"Excuse me, miss. Tell me you've got some good news?"

The nurse laughed. "Son, I appreciate the compliment, but I'm old enough to be your mom. Anyway, it would seem everyone's favorite person, his royal highness, cleared all of you over an hour ago."

Too bad Deacon hadn't known scaring the asshole so badly that he almost shit in his pants would gain him such fast action. If he had, Deacon would have taken action sooner. "That's great, thank you. Tell me something. Is that normal for him for him to sign crap and not tell you guys? If I pulled a stunt like signing a release order and not telling the person they were free to go, I'd get fired."

"Honey, we're lucky if we get a grunt. The only time he deigns to speak to us peons is when we intentionally push a gurney with a patient into his path and block it. We've got a pool going on how long before his head pops. You want in? It's five bucks." Deacon pulled out his wallet and handed her a Lincoln. "Put me down for one more than the highest bid."

As soon as she disappeared, Deacon helped Bautista stand. "Hands behind your back." He double-locked the cuffs to ensure they didn't get smaller. "Let's go."

As they headed toward the loading dock behind the cafeteria, a police officer from a different agency passed them with a less than cooperative prisoner. Although no gang expert, Deacon knew a *Sureno* gang member when he saw one. And this guy was a big one. Roughly six-foot-four and at least three hundred pounds, he looked like he ate rival Bulldogs for breakfast.

Deacon and his partners went on high alert. The situation held the potential to bypass bad and close in on catastrophic if either of the two rival gang members traded insults. Here was hoping Bautista stayed focused on what was in his best interests. Saving his family. Because Deacon was fairly certain he saw himself as "dead man walking."

He could see the letter he'd have to write explaining why there had been a rumble in the hospital hall. *Dear Chief, I regret to inform you my cuffed prisoner got his ass kicked because he's a freaking idiot who couldn't keep his mouth shut.* As they walked by each other without uttering a word, Deacon breathed easier. Thank God for small favors.

A short time later, the four of them exited the hospital via the back loading dock. Deacon gazed into the night the sky. Clear with a full moon. Yes, they needed the rain. But he hoped it stayed away until they had taken down Tuefel.

Deacon didn't relish being wet, cold, and exhausted all at the same time.

Then he noticed an army of clouds massing to the west. The Pineapple Express hadn't blown itself out. It was just regrouping for another frontal assault.

They crossed the vast parking lot and reached Smith's patrol car. "Sorry about the walk to your cars from here," Smith said.

"Don't worry about it Rob. It's safer for all of us to stick together with you parking here."

"Okay, ladies, remember. Since we're heading out of town, switch to C-Tac so we still have radio," Washington said.

Deacon opened Smith's rear passenger door. Hand on the back of Bautista's head, he shoved him inside then slammed shut the door. "Good call. Channel one won't reach all the way up there. If we're about to get into even more shit tonight, we have to be able to alert each other about it."

"I'd appreciate that, D. Especially since this is your mess and you are a walking, talking clusterfuck. With the way your luck is going, we all know how this will end up," Smith said.

"Not funny, yo," Deacon shot back.

"I'm not kidding, my brother."

"What about the search warrant?" Smith asked.

Deacon raised his shoulders and dropped them again. "It'll be interesting who acts first, us or the feds. Bet the sonuvabitches are able to get it sealed."

"You're right. You record everything the asshole said?" Smith jerked his head at the car.

Deacon snorted. "You know we did. It was all included in his deal, which he signed."

"When you guys are done with your little circle jerk, I'm ready to go," Bautista yelled.

No one said anything for several moments. Deacon sighed and broke the silence. "Time to check out this bastard's info. Let's get this done."

CHAPTER 32

In his study, Tuefel settled into the single red leather chair. The room nearly duplicated his office above. It even included a clone of his massive desk. Books lined three walls. The remaining wall boasted a window that showcased the same elegant view of the mountains.

There was one major difference. The oversized, fine red-leather wingback he sat in. His middle finger traced the rim of his sniffer half-filled with deep, amber-colored Cognac. He knew the image he presented in the flickering light of the fire. Lucifer seated on his throne in Hell. With heretofore unknown patience, he listened as his lieutenant stitched his wounds and reported the depth of his failure. Failure brought about by disobeying orders.

And Ubel Tuefel didn't tolerate either, the second being the worst. It smacked of betrayal. For Luis to *think* he could deny Tuefel his need for personal vengeance was an affront that couldn't be forgotten or forgiven. But now, he reminded himself, wasn't the time to take that irrevocable action. No, Luis would continue to live until after Tuefel had extracted every ounce of revenge his heart and soul demanded.

"Don't worry, sir. The cop won't be lucky next time. The woman and he will be dead before long."

Tuefel's hand momentarily tightened on his crystal sniffer. Forcing his fingers to loosen, he lifted it and swirled the liquid, inhaling the heady aromas of dried fig, raisins, vanilla, nutmeg, and cinnamon. Taking a taste, he swished it lightly over his palate, enjoying the taste of pastry flavors and dried fruits with a dry finish. Until today, he'd savored each sip and fell under the magic of his Louis Royer XO with Rachele at his side.

His eyes narrowed on Luis as the man poured himself a full whiskey glass of Tuefel's award-winning Cognac. *Philistine.*

"Hey, that is good."

Tuefel set his sniffer on one of Rachele's beloved French art deco chestnut-veneered side tables. Unlike his office upstairs, this room was their sanctuary. Surrounding him were memories of her. Once he'd avenged her death, he'd torch this place. Maybe then he wouldn't be haunted by the memories they engendered.

"I gave you explicit instructions to bring their asses here. It's my right and duty as Rachele's husband to make them pay. Not yours." Seeing Luis flinch and look away, Tuefel knew what he had seen. Eyes that reflected the truth—he was hollow inside, soulless. Tufel motioned to a wooden chair. "Turn it around so you're facing me, and sit." Once Luis sat, Tuefel stood, poured him a shot of *Casa de Corodés*, and handed it to him, knowing Luis loved real Tequila.

Tuefel looked into his sniffer and silently stared at the liquid. Finally confident he had himself under control, he raised his head. His gaze locked with Luis's. "Tell me, do you know why I'm known as the Krusnik? *Nein?*" he asked when Luis remained silent. "It originates from an old German and Austrian legend. A Krusnik is a vampire who feeds upon the blood of other vampires. Legend has it he does this to enable his strength to grow. His power increases exponentially with each feeding. He's careful in his choices, only selecting those worthy of adding to his abilities, then devours them. Gradually, his foes and allies are so weak he crushes them beneath his foot."

Tuefel rose and moved to the fireplace. Grasping the poker, he stoked the fire. Flames flared. He turned back to his henchman. "With my years in the *Kommando Spezialkräfte*, I made many contacts in this region."

The look of surprise on Luis's face said it all. Tuefel laughed. "What? You're wondering why German special forces would be in this area? That you have no clue is a testament to our training and skill and how poor our Mexican counterparts are. It's because of those damned cartels. They're some of the biggest purchasers of opium from those Taliban maggots. Didn't you wonder how or where they got all that 'Mexican Black Tar Heroin'? America isn't the only place they sell drugs. They expanded into Europe a long time ago. They've been shipping their product to the Fatherland for years. My team was assigned to assist the Americans take down the cartels. It was my team and I that gave your cartels many problems. After many interdictions and seeing the endless pallets of confiscated money, I decided to go into business for myself. Instead of wiping out the cartels, I took over."

Tuefel grasped poker again and shoved it into the fire. As one side of the iron turned a glowing red-orange, he slanted a look at Luis and slowly lifted his lip. Too bad he wasn't a real vampire. Then he could show some fang. "After each of the drug rip-offs, I killed the muscle. The key is to always leave the coward of the group alive. Then return him to his employer with one or two fewer limbs. So you see? My reputation is well-and-truly earned."

He rotated the poker and shoved the top side into the flame, thereby assuring both sides were equally hot. A log popped in the fire, shattering the silence. Tuefel turned toward him. For a brief moment, the poker, even to him, looked as if it were an extension of his body. Slowly, he advanced to where Luis sat and pointed the glowing end of the poker at him, its point at eye level, halting inches from his eyelashes. He knew Luis felt its heat and watched in satisfaction as the moisture of his eyes dried to cracking.

"I devoured those who opposed or disappointed me. I took that which was theirs and made it my own."

He stared at Luis who did a great imitation of a statue. No blinking. No moving. *Nichts*. Maybe, he finally understood whom he worked for.

"Luis you do good work. While this is the first time you disobeyed me, its result was a botched mission. *Aber*, you still have value. And I never dispose of things which have value."

With a tight smile, Tuefel stepped back, the hot poker at the ready but away from Luis's eye. "I believe we now have a new understanding. *Ya?*"

"Y—yes, sir."

"*Sehr gut*. Everyone is entitled to *one* off day. Today was yours. Bring all of them to me or it won't be only your eyes that suffer my wrath."

Taking in Luis's ashen face, Tuefel motioned toward the door. "*Raus*! Get out!"

Finally alone, he returned the tool to the stand, moved to the window, and stared at the mountains.

CHAPTER 33

Surprisingly, the trip to the compound took less than an hour. For some reason, Deacon had expected it to take longer. But what shocked him most was that Justice rode in silence. He didn't even sing to his favorite songs. It was as if he anticipated that the upcoming OP would be dangerous and was psyching himself up for it.

Deacon hated to admit it, but Bautista was correct. Yes, everyone knew the location of Tuefel's estate. It was set back off of Route 41 and covered by several hundred acres of densely wooded land. Perfect for a massive fire, especially under drought conditions. But his compound, now that was something else. Even with Bautista navigating from the rear of Smith's patrol car, they had missed the turn-off and had to backtrack.

The sonuvabitch had said it was a dirt road. "Dirt road my ass. Make that more of a curving, goat trail up the mountain."

Deacon's hands tightened on the steering wheel. He would have been worried under the best of conditions, but after the torrential downpour they'd just had, he was shaky, dry-mouthed, and sweating bullets. The loosened soil could give way any moment.

With his luck, as the second vehicle, the slide would

happen beneath *his* wheels. Ah, well, it would end his worries of Luis knifing him as he walked along a crowded street.

Over the radio, he heard Bautista croak, "Pull over now. The lab's just beyond these trees. If you go any farther, you'll be spotted."

"Jesus H Christ, will you chill? If you don't, you won't have to worry about Luis. You'll stroke out," Smith snapped over the open mic.

Deacon checked his cell phone. One flickering bar of service. "Biggest nationwide calling network, my ass."

Once he and Justice got out of the car, he backtracked along the crumbling trail, one arm in the air, until he had sufficient bars to make a call that wouldn't be dropped. He placed a call to Swanson and updated him with their status and location. "Washington wrapped yellow crime scene tape at the bottom of a tree beside the backwoods rutted lane Bautista calls a road. If you see the Tipsy Monkey liquor store, you're a quarter mile past the turn. Because of all the rain, the road's condition might not hold up under a lot of traffic."

Freezing in the chilly wind, Deacon began jogging in place. "I suggest everyone park behind the liquor store and hump it up to where we are. Oh, there's a fence with a lock on it across the dirt road. The key's under a pile of rubbish ten feet to the left of the gate. Tell them to slide their hand under the wire fence and fish around for the damned key."

"Why the hell didn't you leave it unlocked?"

"Bautista said you have five minutes after unlocking to relock or an alarm goes off."

"Got it. Heads up, White's getting your search warrant and will be up as soon as it's signed. I expect the feds to swoop in for the glory, but stay parked below to avoid getting their tits in a ringer if it hits the fan. Stay in touch."

"That'll be difficult. We don't have much reception up here. It's over three thousand feet and there aren't any towers nearby."

"You mean to tell me you three didn't get sat phones?"

Shit! It hadn't occurred to them. Deacon knew all three of them looked like the Keystone Cops. "We had Bautista with us and figured we had better get up here and get this done before this Luis returned for round two."

Swanson snorted. "Bullshit, but good save. White will bring several up with him. And if anything happens, book outta there and call."

"Yes, sir," he said to blank air. He stuffed the phone back in his pocket. "Justice, heel." He tapped his left leg. With Justice next to his left thigh, they trotted back to their observation position. It was damned chilly here in the middle of the night. Air seeped through his sweatshirt and vest.

With any luck, the storm would continue to hold off or bypass them completely. Even if it did, the wind lashed his skin as if he were naked. He breathed icy air through gritted teeth. Ah, well, at least it wasn't sweltering like the valley. Although, in another hour, he might feel differently.

"Justice, down, stay," he ordered upon reaching his vehicle. He slid inside, hit the dome lamp, and pressed a switch on the Code Three light bar assembly. The locks on the assault rifle and shotgun disengaged with a high-pitched click. Removing both of his long guns, he inspected them. His shotgun was topped off with five shells loaded into the magazine tube. The safety was off. No shell in the breech.

His AR-15 assault rifle had the department-mandated maximum of twenty-eight rounds. If they loaded the magazine with the full thirty the extended mag was capable of handling, the spring would be compressed too much and could result in a malfunction. Not what they wanted on an OP like this one. Satisfied his weapons were ready to deploy, Deacon opened the door of his cruiser and stepped out with his left foot. A quick survey of his surroundings confirmed his choice of weapon system. After securing the shotgun in the rack, he gripped the top of the door frame with one hand and pulled himself out while holding the rifle in his other. He glanced down at Justice, debating whether to take him along. A head tilt and squint-eyed glare warned Deacon he'd better think twice about leaving him behind. "Yeah, you're probably right. It will be safer for all of us, you included, if you're with me."

With the doors locked, he waited for Smith and Washington to join him, then popped the trunk so they could get additional gear. Smith slung his rifle over his chest. Washington loaded up extra pistol magazines. Still rummaging in his trunk, Deacon yelled over his shoulder. "Yo, Washington, grab our meat shield. We're gonna need him to get us through this crap and find the cook."

"Good point." Washington opened the car door and all but ripped Bautista from the back seat with one giant pull. "Hear that, sweet cheeks? You're gonna be our meat shield while you walk us through this hellhole and find the bad guys."

"What do you mean by meat shield?" Bautista asked, his gaze touching each of them.

Smith snickered. "Think about it. These places are notorious for booby traps and armed guards. So you walk us to the site, but you do it by walking ahead of us. If you try to lead us into any traps, you get to walk into them first."

Bautista hung his head and took a deep breath. "So I'm your booby trap and trip wire detector."

"You got it in one, genius." Washington clapped him on the back. "Relax. All you have to do is make sure not to step in shit and we'll all be fine. Then again, if you step in, or on, the wrong shit, it'll be all over quickly. Noisily, but quickly. So make sure you don't. We'd hate to lose time recovering the pieces."

Chuckling, Smith loaded a magazine into his AR-15. Turning, he grabbed a green canvas bag out of his trunk filled with a couple dozen high-capacity magazines for their two rifles. Like the AR, he slung it across his chest and tucked it against the opposite side.

Deacon slammed shut the trunk. "Glad to see you're bringing your bailout bag of fun."

"Damn straight, I'm bringing it. Overkill is underrated. You can never have too much ammo."

Deacon pulled back on the charging handle and released it like the pull starter on a lawnmower. When a round slammed into the breach of his rifle, he flipped on the safety. "Here's hoping we don't need it. With the way my luck's been going, we'll be throwing one hell of a party at the home of one of the biggest bad asses around. But you're absolutely right. You can never have too much ammo."

Deacon flipped his rifle across his back, pulled out a topographical map of the area, and smoothed it out on his car hood. "Bautista, get over here."

Hand clamped on his shoulder, Washington walked him over to where Smith held the map in place.

"What now?"

"Where's the cook? Point to it," Deacon ordered.

Squinting, Bautista poured over the map. "There. About an inch to the right of your finger."

Deacon calculated the best route and distance to their target. "It's in a cave, right?" At Bautista's nod, a stupid grin broke free.

"D? What is it?"

"That, gentlemen, is Tollhouse Cavern. And it resides in land owned and operated by the United States Forest Service. We don't need a warrant. Damn me, if the feds won't be drooling all over this."

Washington slapped Bautista on the back. "Hear that, numbnuts? We can legally walk right in there. We own that place."

Deacon quickly folded the map and stuck it into Smith's ammo bag. "Well, the federal government does. How much freedom have you had when here?"

"What do you mean?"

"I mean, how closely have you worked for Tuefel? Are—I mean, were—you able to go anywhere unsupervised?"

"Not really. Believe me, he trusts only two people—Luis

and his wife. And with his wife dead because of you, Officer Deacon, pretty Jessica, and me, we know what he wants with us."

Deacon's eyebrows rose. "Do you know your way around his set-up? Yes or no?"

"I had some leeway. Before Luis showed up, the Bulldogs worked as Tuefel's guards. When I saw him killing off everyone, I told him I knew people who could move the stuff. I survived because I made myself valuable. Something I no longer am."

Deacon looked into Bautista's eyes and saw something he didn't expect—remorse.

"Since I started selling for him, I haven't been unsupervised," Bautista continued. "The man's obsessed with his profits. He's watched me like a hawk, even when I chose which bricks I wanted off the pallets."

"That'll do. Since there's no expectation of privacy on public land, as long as we restrict ourselves to the cave, whatever's there is in plain sight. As for Tuefel's home, what's in the cave will help White get the warrant for the house."

Smith grinned. "Well, here's hoping the dope's where this fool claims it is. Gotta admit, I'd love to see the look on Tuefel's face when he learns his lab isn't on his property."

"He may be smart, but Tuefel's far from perfect," Deacon murmured.

"Again, your ass, not mine, yo," Washington added.

Deacon chuckled. "Better to be judged by twelve than carried by six."

Smith and Washington pounded fists. "Let's do this." Washington turned Bautista toward the path passing as a road. "Okay, is that road the fastest way to this cook?"

"No." Bautista nodded toward a thick, densely overgrown area beyond a riverbed, about fifteen feet from the roadway. "From here it's about a ten minute walk. There's a narrow path that way."

Deacon sighed deeply. In the dark, it looked like an impenetrable wall.

Washington laughed. "If it's through that crap in the dark, better make it twenty minutes."

Bautista grimaced. "There's a path fifteen feet in from that ditch."

"Why are we going that way? Isn't there an easier way?" Washington asked.

Bautista's jaw clenched. "Only if you want to get caught, and I don't. Do you think I'm stupid? Tuefel is paranoid. He has cameras and alarms all over the place. He knows the second someone nears the place. Doesn't matter if they're an innocent hiker or some asshole wanting to jack his stuff, they end up the same way. Dead. So we are going in through the backdoor," he growled through gritted teeth.

Deacon crossed his arms. He wasn't buying it. "How did you discover it?"

"When I first started working for him, he didn't want me anywhere near his lab. So I patrolled the perimeter until I found it. Don't even think Tuefel knows about it. Even then, I knew that this whole operation could go to shit, or I'd end up dead. As protection or payback, depending upon which one took place, I took photos of everything. Those, plus a notarized statement, are with my attorney in a sealed envelope. There's also notary stamp across the sealed flap. If I'm killed or disappear, he's to give it to the US Attorney. Satisfied?"

Smith let out a long whistle.

Washington gave Bautista's back a light shove. "Lead the way, Nancy."

CHAPTER 34

Deacon strode along a path barely wide enough to keep from getting snagged by the trees and brush. He had seen similar game trails throughout his life. The most recent he had seen were in the homes of cranksters who had carved walking paths to the TV, restroom and kitchen amongst their endless piles of crap.

The dense growth made it difficult to see where they were going. Deacon trudged forward. His partner's shoulder nudged him to the right and away from a washed out part of the path.

He grimaced at Washington's back. If he'd fallen down the hill and been injured, it would've been Washington's fault. His fingers were covering most of the beam of his flashlight. There wasn't enough light for Deacon and Smith behind him to clearly see the path ahead of them.

"Damn it, Kev, remove at least one finger from the flashlight. Without Justice, I could've just broken my neck."

"Suck it up, D. We don't have much time before dawn." His watch face brightened. "It's oh-four-fifty, sunrise in sixty-seven minutes.

"Well, shit," Deacon and Smith hissed.

They broke into a trot. Only a seasoned tracker could have heard their footfalls landing on the soft dirt and the temporary cessation of insects as they rushed past.

Bautista stopped abruptly. He twisted his hands, cuffed to his hip, and pointed. "There it is."

At the top of a knoll, they crouched in a huddle. Deacon scowled at the sight of trees and vegetation having been cleared. A small tent was set-up in the clearing's center. It almost looked like a crop circle. "How the hell did Forest Service miss this?"

"I thought we were going to some cave or something," Smith muttered.

Bautista stared at the tent. "No one should be working at this hour. The last of Krusnik's *employees* were recently terminally thanked for their services by Rachele. You'll find them along with others in the pit not far from here. Right now, the few he still employs are likely in Mexico rounding up a new crop of illegals to work the next cook. Tuefel's all about profit. By his reckoning, it's more cost effective and they're fewer people to rat you out."

Deacon stopped him. "You mean to tell me he has no guards down here?"

Bautista glared at him, a fire lit in his eyes. "Look, if there were guards, we would've already run into them. This place is a bunker that no one knows about. Plus, he has Luis. Also, Tuefel's murdered all of his competition a long time ago, including excess guards. So why guard it and draw unnecessary attention? It's just more people who can steal from him or inform on him, like I am right now."

Deacon understood and nodded. "All right then. Game faces, ladies. Time to do what we do."

They headed down the knoll, slowly, carefully. Deacon shook his head at Kev's choice of a shooting platform— Bautista's left shoulder. Poor bastard would be peppered with the hot brass clearing the ejector. Not fun when it went down the back of a shirt collar. They moved in a rear echelon formation, he and Smith covering them with their long guns.

"Smooth is fast boys," Washington reminded them.

They slowly approached the tent. With his left hand, Deacon pointed to Rob, his index and middle fingers extended, signaling for him to take that side and cover the opposing angle. He tapped his chest and repeated the motion for himself, indicating he'd cover the position on the right.

Smith nodded.

Washington positioned himself behind a tree and Bautista.

In unison, Deacon and Justice pied the entrance with Smith. The front flap of the two-man tent was tied open.

"Clear."

"Clear," Deacon said, his eyes widening at Washington smacking Bautista on the back of the head.

"So where's the cave? We better not've come out here to the middle of God's nowhere for a fucking tent. Double D, you've been had."

Smith nodded. "Agreed. With as much talk as there is about this guy, I figured it'd be more than this. Kev's right, D. We've been played. Let's dump this guy right here."

"Where the hell is this cave?" Washington demanded.

"It is right there. Look at the ground, Officer. You're the fucking *trained observer*."

Deacon knelt and rubbed his eyes. Fatigue gnawed at him like a starving hyena with a carcass. Every joint ached, especially his shoulder. For the first time, he admitted going on an OP this important without sleep was either stupid or a young man's game. Yet in this moment, twenty-eight years old felt ancient.

Sighing, Deacon dropped his hand from his face and draped it over his bent knee. After a minute, he opened his eyes. There was something in the dirt, shadows dancing in the moonlight. "What the hell?"

He shone his flashlight at an oblique angle and saw numerous shoe tracks entering and exiting the tent. He stood and secured his flashlight in its belt holster, pushing the flap back with the barrel of his rifle, he illuminated the inside with his barrel mounted tac light. His eyes narrowed on a pile of clothing dumped on top of a sleeping bag. With the rifle muzzle, he flipped the bag against the back of the tent.

"I'll be a sonuvabitch." If he hadn't been looking for it, he would have easily missed the metal-covered opening in the center of the tent.

It was simple, yet ingenious. A sleeping bag with some discarded clothing might seem rudimentary, but they were the perfect camouflage.

He crawled inside the tent and stared at an eight-by-four-foot plate. "It's here." On one knee, Deacon glanced back toward Bautista. "What'll we find down there?"

"Everything you are looking for."

Deacon swallowed hard. "Party time, ladies. Get in here, all of you. Justice, come."

With weapons secured and Justice hovering behind them as moral support and protection, Deacon pushed Bautista down between the other two officers. Seconds later, they shoved the heavy steel plate against the far side of the tent. Stale wind blasted out of the tunnel with a barely audible howl. Deacon aimed his rifle down the hole, the mounted light hitting a ladder that led down into the bowels of the Earth. Without taking his eyes off of the tunnel, he asked Bautista, "Who built the ladder, you?"

"No, Tuefel. But he doesn't know I've discovered it."

"You ever used it?

"No. If I'd been caught, I'd be dead." He bumped Deacon's shoulder. "I can't guarantee he hasn't wired the area."

"Gotcha, I'll keep an eye out for tripwires." Deacon continued staring into the black abyss. "Kev, will you stay here and keep an eye on him while Rob and I check this out?"

"Damn it, Deacon. Why do I have to stand out here with dingus? I had to sit there with his ass this whole afternoon."

Smith gave Washington a wink. "Because you two are so cute together."

Deacon groaned as Washington leveled a narrow-eyed glare at the smartass. Deacon would never say it, but the two sounded like an old married couple.

"Come on, Kev. Dive on the grenade, yo. After we clear it with the long guns, I'll trade you places so you can get down there and photo everything."

Washington threw his hands into the air. "All right, fine. But let me get him settled first."

Bautista sat crossed-legged on the sleeping bag. Justice crouched a few feet away, watching him.

Deacon took in Justice's bared fangs and Bautista's cringe. Damn, his partner was good. Seemed just the threat of feeling those teeth was sufficient incentive to remain motionless.

Washington joined Deacon by the ladder. "Want me to keep my light on you?"

Deacon nodded. "Yeah, keep the beam on the ladder until Smith and I are down." Boots and gloved hands on the outside of the ladder, Deacon slithered down it, never touching its rungs. Once on firm ground, he drew his rifle forward and turned on its tac light.

Its narrow beam lit directly in front of him, leaving him feeling vulnerable until Smith got down and covered their flank. In several places, roots from the now logged trees jutted from the dirt cracks in the stony walls. By Deacon's count, the shaft was roughly twenty feet long.

He stepped back so Smith could move forward. With their weapons extended, they entered cave and lit the lab with their tactical lights. Like swords, narrow beams sliced through the darkness.

Seeing no immediate threat, Deacon moved forward into the lab proper.

One quick look, told him Tuefel had done his geological homework. The ladder had been bored into the rear of the cave. Tollhouse Cavern measured roughly two hundred feet long and fifty feet wide. It was the perfect location for a methamphetamine lab.

He wouldn't have to worry about wandering idiots stumbling upon it. No law enforcement helicopter flybys. No chance of it being discovered, unless some hiker wandered upon them. Come to think of it, there had been some reported lost over the last few years. *Genius—until today.*

Stalactites and stalagmites covered the ceiling and floors. He couldn't ever remember which was which. Water running along the exposed rock explained the dampness. He focused on a ramp off to his right heading to the surface. It was more than wide enough to accommodate a vehicle the size of a quad or an ATV. Maybe even a Big Joe fork lift, which would be a big help in rapidly loading and offloading large shipments and getting them on their way.

Deacon took a closer look at the stacked boxes. "Get a load of the Sudaphed and Sudaphedrine tablets. Shit, they're so many they've spilled out all over the floor. Cover me." He moved closer. Removing his flashlight, he examined the packaging and shipping labels on the cases. "These came from pharmacies from all over the valley. How the hell did the auditors miss this?"

"Probably had his man highjack 'em. That's the feds' department."

"Right." Not far from the ramp were more than a dozen huge, round beakers. Deacon moved his light over them. "What do you think, ten gallons each?"

"At least."

Each sat in its individual metal basin. "Those resembled the heating devices we saw in a training video a few months ago. Shit, that's exactly what they are. Those basins are nothing more than Bunsen Burners. Make that Bunsen Burners on steroids with Honda generators providing the power."

The rubber tubing encircling each beaker's top edge fed into vents leading to the surface. Despite this intricate and sophisticated ventilation system, the place reeked of sweaty gym socks. Nasty ass gym socks, left to rot in a locker over summer.

Deacon knew that the gases produced could kill a man in seconds. If he were down here and those gases escaped, he'd be dead before he got to the tunnel, let alone stepped on the first rung of the ladder. So much for never using the info in that training vid. Interesting what you remembered when your next breath could kill you.

"I wonder how many died down here during the various stages of the cooking process."

"Don't know. But if our buddy above is to tellin' the truth, most died at the hands of Mr. Tuefel's dearly departed wife. Looks like to me like you did the world a favor offing the bitch."

"Right." Maybe he had, but Deacon knew his action would still haunt him. He crept into the center of the room. Crystalline powder and packaging materials littered the tables. Cellophane, plastic baggies, scales, knives, cash and various binders littered the tables. "Make sure Washington gets photos of the uncut stuff—" His light traced over the grayish yellow piles of crystalline meth, then moved on the white powder and finally to the meth bricks. "—the cut stuff, and what's ready for distribution. What do you think? Ten, eleven mil, once everything's cut and packaged?"

"At least. There're a minimum of two hundred bricks over there ready to go. The powder should make another couple hundred. From the op, we know they're a kilo each." Deacon hefted the bricks. He recognized the weight—two-point-two pounds. "Definitely a kilo." He tossed it back onto the pile, returned his attention to the table, and started snapping photos with his cellphone for the search warrant.

Smith approached Deacon and froze mid-stride. He turned his head toward the rear of the cave.

Deacon looked up and saw Smith ghost white and stiff as a board. "What is it?"

"Don't you smell that?"

Deacon inhaled long and deep. "Allergies have kicked up. Couldn't smell a shit-ton of dirty-ass meth if I fell in it. Why? What do you smell?"

Smith raised his rifle and jerked it back toward the ladder they'd used.

Deacon mirrored him as they crept toward it. At first, he

didn't smell anything. As they neared the ladder, the cave's wind direction shifted. Instead of coming just from the main cavern, it also entered through the opening above them and he caught his first whiff. It was an odor immediately recognizable—dead bodies. Once you had smelled decomp, you never forgot it. They followed their noses into a small side tunnel. It was narrow and barely wide enough for one man. Smith took the lead and Deacon covered their rear.

They followed the reek of death a couple of hundred feet to where the tunnel died, plummeting into the depths of a ravine. Bracing themselves, they aimed their tac lights into the void. The fetid odor of untold bodies in varying states of decomp punched him in the face, almost sending him to his knees and over the rim where he'd join Tuefel's victims.

"D, I think you're going to need a bigger boat."

"*Jaws.*"

"Yeah. And if the lab was a gold mine, the platinum is down there."

Deacon lowered his rifle and moved forward. He leaned out over the edge and shined his flashlight into the gully. A pile of decrepit bodies stared back up at him. There were dozens of victims. He could see numerous skeletons covered in frayed remnants of clothing and knew that they had been down there a very long time. There were others who still bore flesh and looked up at him with their empty eye sockets, begging for justice through their rotted gaping lips. He nearly threw up. "Holy shit."

Smith nodded. "You got that right. You believe this shit?"

Deacon shook his head and regained his composure. "Let's get the hell out of here and call Swanson. We're gonna need SWAT, the feds, search warrants out our asses, and every available body we have to pull this off and haul all of this crap out of here."

Smith nodded. "You've got that right. Let's go."

"Just need one thing before we go, though." Deacon pulled his cell phone out of his pocket.

"Dude, your fancy ass phone isn't getting' reception down here."

"I know. This is for the exhibits the judge will look at when approving the search warrant. Because something tells me that, in this case, a picture is worth a thousand words. Now shine your light over there." As he already had in the lab, Deacon began photographing the body dump, knowing the photos could be mistaken for those taken at Auschwitz.

CHAPTER 35

Luis finished changing the dressing protecting the sutures in his left arm. "Fucking, dog." He'd kill the animal first and then enjoy himself as he slowly took apart the cop.

Holding his shoulder with his right hand, he rolled it in an arc. It hurt, but he'd lived through worse. As long as it worked, he'd be able to defend himself. Tuefel was a fool. He thought to scare him? Ha, not a chance.

Luis nee Carlos Mendez, better known as the *El Diablo* wasn't devoured by anyone. And certainly not by Tuefel of the soft, manicured-hands.

He showered in scalding hot water—the hotter the better. After drying off and dressing, he returned to his bedroom. He checked his go bag, ensuring it contained everything needed to start a new life. Multiple new IDs and passports, new—well, relatively new—bankbooks from throughout the world, along with a hundred thousand in US dollars and a second hundred thousand in Euros.

For now, he would behave as expected. He entered his private kitchen and opened the refrigerator. Nice. Tuefel's cook had left him a plate of four fresh roast beef sandwiches. No way had the two dogs he'd eaten earlier satisfied him.

His stomach roared at the smell of fresh, rare beef and a horseradish mayo spread. He took a bite and moaned, the mayo mix dripping down his chin. He took another bite and more oozed out. Ravenous, he enjoyed all four sandwiches.

Having satisfied one hunger, Luis returned to the refrigerator to take care of another one before heading out to fulfill his orders—exactly. He grabbed an imported stout beer. When he wanted a beer, the only one that would do was one that looked like dirty 10W-40 motor oil. The darker, the better.

To the side of the refrigerator was a bank of sixteen closed circuit TVs. He glanced at the screens embedded in the wall. They reminded him of a faceted eye of an insect. And he hated insects. He never trusted anything with more than two legs. He loathed only one thing more than insects, that fucking cop's dog.

Tuefel's pretty hands hadn't been so nice after he'd installed video cameras all over that covered the entire compound. Each of the video feeds dumped into the bank in the kitchen. State of the art and expensive as hell, the whole system had to have cost close to six figures.

One of the angles covered was the southern entrance to the lab hidden in a tent. Luis thought using a tent with a backpack in it and a sleeping bag as camouflage over the entrance was clever. Of course, it was his idea. Even asshole cranksters didn't usually go into someone's tent. And if they did, they were easily dealt with.

Taking a long, slow draw on the beer, his gaze returned to the monitors. Staring at the south entrance video feed, he swallowed hard at the silhouette seated on a rock near the tent. Luis rubbed his eyes. The size of the monitor made it difficult to determine what he was seeing. The dirt and water spots on the camera lens from the rain didn't help either. Unfortunately, no amount of money could account for Mother Nature.

His gut told him that something was wrong, and he had learned long ago to listen to it. It had saved his life more times than he could remember. Leaning close to the screen, he stared at the silhouette for several minutes. His eyes strained in search of movement or something to confirm his suspicions. But there was nothing. *Not a damned thing.*

Luis was about to write off the images as figments of his fatigued brain when he saw the red light begin flashing at the bottom right corner of the monitors and saw that the trembler inside the tunnel had been tripped. He threw the beer bottle across the room. It slammed against the tile wall and shattered in shower of sharp confetti.

Pivoting, Luis tore off for the armory.

One of his ancillary duties was to stock, clean, and lubricate all of Tuefel's weapons. He religiously performed this duty on the first of every month, and spent nearly two full days completing the task. He shoved his key into the well-oiled lock on the gun rack. Tumblers compressed. The lock disengaged.

He swung the protective support arm free on the rack and selected a Winchester .308 with an ATN Mars six-by-four night vision scope. He loved this gun. Zeroed for one hundred yards, whatever he aimed at, he hit. Depending upon how far he was from his prey, the target was usually dead before they ever heard the shot. He chose the H&K USP .45 for use in close quarter combat, should things go to shit. Chambering rounds in each weapon, he topped off their magazines, and threw on a tactical assault vest.

Before leaving, he grabbed three fully loaded magazines for each weapon and strapped them into the ammunition pouches. Secured with Velcro straps, the magazines would stay snug in their pouches until needed. He opened a cabinet, grasped several more magazines, and stuffed them into his pockets for good measure. Better to have and not need, than need and not have. Loaded to the teeth, he zipped up the front and, double checking his pouches, ensured all of them were full. He strapped his sheathed his knife to his leg. Adrenaline coursing through his veins, he sprinted out the back door and down the service road toward the lab.

CHAPTER 36

No, no, this isn't good. They've been down there way too long. Dude, we need to get out of here. Like right now."

Washington fought the urge to cold-cock the piss-ant. "Shut up before I shut you up. Your voice irritates the hell outta me."

"But—"

"They'll be back when they're finished. Then we'll get the hell outta here."

"You don't understand. He's gonna discover we're here, and then we're dead. We gotta go. You can return with a fucking army—which you'll need."

Washington squatted, his nose within inches of Bautista's. Their eyes locked like two bucks in battle. "Get this straight, this is what we do. We gather evidence. Then, and only then, do we kick some ass. It's easier that way. Of course, if you're volunteerin' for another ass whoopin' by runnin' out on us—" He nodded at Bautista's wounds. "—Justice'll enjoy taking a second piece of you as a souvenir."

At the sound of boots pounding up the ladder, both of them stared at the hole in silence. Seconds later, Washington knew it had gone to shit. It was written all over Deacon and White's faces.

"D? How bad is it? What'd you guys find down there?"

"We'll fill you in on the way back. But right now, we've gotta get the hell outta here," Deacon said. "Like, yesterday."

Washington moved behind Bautista and jerked him upright. "How do you want to handle this, leave in the same order we arrived?"

"Yeah," Deacon and Smith said.

"Right." Placing a hand on Bautista's shoulder, he pushed him through the tent flaps.

A round slammed into middle of the gangbanger's forehead. Shards of bone and brain matter sprayed across the inside of the tent. The back of his head became a canoe on a river of gray and red.

Bautista's lifeless corpse collapsed.

Washington dove to the left inside the tent.

As the sound of the shot rang out, a vortex of air blasted between Deacon and Smith. The second one exploded out the back of the tent. Canvas confetti sliced through the air.

Deacon grabbed Justice and hit the deck. "Sniper! Get down!"

"Fuck! No shit, Sherlock," Smith snarled from other side of the opening as another round ripped through the area his head had just occupied.

Justice bolted out the back of the tent and disappeared into the surrounding forest.

Deacon motioned them toward the now gapping back. "Let's follow Justice. I'll provide fire, while you two head for the trees. You return the favor for my ass once you're there."

Without a word, his two brothers in arms slipped out. Deacon nodded, giving them the go signal. As they hunkered down with weapons at the ready, he began firing his long rifle and they charged toward cover. Deacon split his gaze between targeting the area around a boulder and confirming his teammates were shielded by the undergrowth.

Hearing Smith's long rifle spitting fire and Washington's

pistol blasting away, Deacon booked for the safety of the trees. Within seconds, he slid beneath some bushes and low crawled through dense foliage. Satisfied he'd reached safety, he rose and sprinted to a cluster of redwoods, then whistled for his team to join him. As they did, a redwood took a round center mass. Sap poured out of the ghastly hole. If a target had hung on the tree, the hole would be right in the middle of the bulls-eye.

"Shit, he isn't just killing people, he's now murdering trees," Washington muttered.

Deacon glanced around, searching for Justice. "Let's flank him. I don't plan to lose my partner. He's out there alone, tracking the sonuvabitch, and will try to take him down without back-up. Let's split-up, I'll follow Justice's path and go left. You two go right." Hunched over, he tore down the game trail.

He ducked behind a tree near the edge of the trail. Splinters of wood, xylem, and phloem showered him as it took a bullet, followed by the sound of the round having been fired. He dropped to the ground, his stomach kissing the earth, and crawled through the thick shrubbery and trees. He'd nearly reached the crest of the hill without being shot at and lifted his head to check out the area. Staying low, he utilized the hill for cover and moved toward the sound of shots being fired.

The team joined him. Deacon tapped Washington's shoulder and motioned toward the crest of the hill ahead of them, then signaled that he and Smith would provide suppression fire. They'd follow standard practice—never move without someone covering your ass.

As Deacon got ready to move, a smile broke free. He had a fix on the trajectory of the bullet that assassinated the tree and signaled the others to fire north. In unison, he and Smith slung lead while Washington sprinted beyond the hill's peak under the blanket of their fire.

Deacon paused and scanned the horizon. He didn't see anyone. "It's probably Luis." He shook his head. "Sonuvabitch is using one helluva high-powered rifle. And if he's everything Bautista said, he'll have lots of ammo and other weapons. Seems the man believes in redundancy."

"Did Kev make it over the hill?"

"Yeah, your turn." Before Smith could move, another nearby tree exploded, followed by an echo. Deacon's eyes narrowed as he backtracked the direction of the round. He had to take down the shooter, fast. Otherwise, they were as good as dead.

"Did you catch the muzzle flash, D?"

"Negative. But it had to come from the north or east." Static then a soft whisper came over Deacon's radio.

"D, Washington. What's your 10-20?"

"He's got us pinned down in the trees. We haven't moved from our last location."

"Copy that. I'm okay, but I don't have a long gun. I don't know where the sonuvabitch is, do you? I'm stuck here. Can't put my melon over the hill to take a look without making one hell of a target."

"Standby, just one."

Deacon checked his duty belt. It didn't have much for a situation like this. He instinctually reached for his leash. Where the hell was Justice? He should have taken out the shooter by now or joined them. Unless—no, he refused to think that knife-wielding bastard had gutted Justice. As he fingered the leash, an idea hit him.

He drew out the leather strap and quickly tied a taut-line hitch around his flashlight. He flung the light over a neighboring branch and let out the slack, allowing it to dangle at about waist height. From where he sat, it was a short reach to turn on the light and he would be able to keep his hand behind the tree branch for cover. He'd have his hand behind the trunk before the shooter could fire off a round.

"Washington, Deacon here. I'm gonna give him a decoy. Keep your eyes peeled for his muzzle flash."

"Confirming. You want me to give a sniper a shot at my head?"

"I'll draw his fire. You track his shot and find out where the fuck he is."

"Copy that. You'd better know what the hell you're doing, D, 'cause I don't want Justice coming at me if anything happens to you."

"Neither do I." Deacon released the transmit button on his mic.

With his back against the trunk of a tree and his butt buried in the dirt, he created as small a target as humanly possible. He inched his arm along the branch and aimed the flashlight north. He waited twenty seconds then activated it.

He had his arm back at his side before two rounds slammed into the tree with thumps hard enough to rattle his teeth, and then the shots rang out.

"Deacon, Washington. He's approximately two hundred to two fifty yards to the north. There's a storage shed just south of the main building. The shots came from the only window on the south side of the building. Can you see it?"

"Negative. We can't see anything at the moment."

Smith keyed his radio. "Washington, Smith. I've got him in the shed. We're gonna have to leap frog outta here. But first we gotta take out the bastard."

Deacon took several combat breaths to lower his heart rate and clear his head. "Washington, Deacon. Smith will hammer the window and the wall below it." He faced Rob. "Don't you let me down or St. Peter and I'll kick your ass when we see you at the pearly gates."

His muscles tensed, standing behind the tree, he took a deep breath. "Ease out and get in position. Let me know when you're ready." Three minutes later, he got the call. "Three, two, one, covering fire."

Time all but stopped. Deacon listened for returning fire and watched Smith fire three quick rounds from his AR-15 from fifteen feet away. Under normal circumstances, at that distance he'd be deaf. Yet because of the adrenaline dumped into his veins, Smith's rifle shots sounded like popcorn in the microwave.

Deacon tugged his leash from the tree and scrambled up the path toward the top of the hill. He stopped about halfway and dove behind a large granite rock. He slid to a stop and looked like a major league ball player sliding head first into home. He'd just missed landing in the sticky sap of poison oak by inches. Seconds later, bits of rock and dirt flew into the air and into his mouth. The leaves swayed near his nose. He spit the coppery mix of blood and gravel onto them.

"Reload!"

Hearing Smith call for cover, Deacon aimed down his red dot sight and fired into what was left of the shed window frame. He fired slowly and smoothly, pouring a steady stream of fire into it, forcing the sniper to keep his head down. Empty shell casings bounced on the ground around him like a bucket of spilled change. As they pinged off the rock, they sounded like war-torn wind chimes. Thank God, Robert brought his bailout bag.

As Smith tore past him in a mad dash for the summit, Deacon heard the distinct sound of magazines clanking against one another on the ground. "Thanks for the extra mags, brother." He'd have to buy Rob several beers for that—if they got out of this one alive.

With the final shell expended, the bolt locked open. Smoke swirled out of the rifle's breach. "Reload!" Performing a speed load, he ejected the empty magazine and let gravity pull it to the ground. The spring vibrated with a sickening, empty twang. A small plume of dust curled from beneath the magazine as it settled into the soil amongst the hot brass.

Deacon tore a fresh mag from his belt and slammed it in the magazine well. He slapped the side of his rifle with an open palm. The bolt drove forward and scraped a bullet off of the top of the fresh magazine. The round slid into the chamber.

"Covering fire, move!" Smith screamed as he opened up.

Deacon grabbed the two loaded magazines Smith had

tossed to him. He had no idea where Smith was and couldn't expend the energy worrying about it. His focus was pouring rounds into that sniper.

He fired three rounds then grasped his rifle in a British carry across his body and booked it. His boot slipped on bare rock. A plume of dust, pebbles, and brass kicked up in the air. It took four strides to regain his traction. He heard Smith's cadence increase as more ammo pelted the shed.

"Move it, D!"

Deacon raced over the crest of the hill, assumed a braced-kneeling position behind a large tree, and covered the shed with his front sight. He focused on the red dot. Ignoring how the shed became blurry, he lit it up as Smith and he performed the dance one final time.

Smith bounded over the hill before Deacon was halfway through the current magazine. With his partners out of the sniper's reach, he tactically reloaded to conserve his unspent ammo. Jamming the partially consumed magazine in his left rear pant pocket, he slammed one of Smith's gifts into his rifle's magazine well, topping off his weapon.

Minutes later, he joined his buddies. Together, they sprinted down the trail in a zigzag. With Washington leading the way, Deacon covered his back and Smith acted as rear guard.

CHAPTER 37

Deacon rounded the corner. Their makeshift command post came into view. They hurried down to the cars. Shit, where was Justice? Deacon stopped at the trail mouth. He spun and started back up the trail. "Justice! Justice, come! Come, damn it!"

Washington, hands on his knees, gasping for air, yelled at him in between breaths, "Deacon, we got to move! We've gotta get out of here! He's gone!"

Deacon refused to hear him and fixated on finding his missing partner. No way was he leaving without him. "Justice!"

"God damn it, Deacon. We need to—"

A round sliced through the night, blew out the rear window of Washington's car, and then the front one.

Racing to the patrol cars, Deacon crashed to the ground and rolled. He came to a halt behind the rear tire of his K9 vehicle and pushed himself into a sitting position.

His back against the rear quarter-panel, he watched Washington and Smith eat dirt behind the engine block of their vehicle.

Deacon checked to ensure they were okay and keeping their heads down. "Where the hell's Justice? Either of you two see him?"

"No. You see the shooter, D?" Smith asked.

"Negative! How about you guys, you see anything? You okay?"

Washington punched the ground in frustration. "Negative on that, and we're all good."

"Stay down, the asshole's got to be scoped." Deacon inched over to the driver side door, taking extra care to stay behind the engine block. Nothing like an aluminum metal engine block for stopping rounds—unless they were armor piercing. The side mirror exploded over his head. Once again, time ground to a halt like a rusty wheel on a bicycle with no lube on the chain.

A triangular piece of glass flipped end over end. He could see the words "closer than" on the face of the mirror as the spinning piece came to rest beside his right boot. He picked up the shard. Holding it over his shoulder, barely above the surface of the hood, he used it to slowly scan the horizon. Nothing.

After a few minutes of blood draining from his arm, the moon peeked out from behind a bank of clouds. His arm was on fire, yet Deacon continued to scan. He caught a glint down the road toward the compound. Scope flare. He dropped the shard. "I've got you now, you sonuvabitch."

Deacon keyed up his radio, his voice so low his mic barely picked it up. "He's behind a big ass rock down the road from you. Not on the highway, but the service road. He's about two hundred fifty yards down on the right toward the compound, east side."

"Copy that," Smith said.

"You got any bright ideas?" Washington hissed over his radio.

Deacon thought for a second and swallowed hard. "Lay down fire when I tell you. I'll run west of the road and we'll get him in the crossfire."

"You may be bat-shit crazy, but the plan's insane enough it just might work. You better get small, dude. Get real small," Washington said.

Please God, let me get through this. Deacon keyed up his mic, "Okay, boys, bring the rain."

Seeing Smith aim over the top of the hood, Deacon broke from behind his car and sprinted west toward several large oaks.

Washington reached inside his vehicle. He hit the release on the car's light bar and the lock disengaged with a snick. He ripped the gun free from its prison and snagged the bailout bag from the floorboard. He scurried back to Smith and jammed a slug into the open breach.

Deacon slid behind one of the trees and stayed prone, figuring he was safe since he hadn't received fire. Readying his rifle, he eased up the base of the tree. At the roar of the shotgun, he nearly dropped his weapon. His eyes widened as a one-ounce piece of lead traveling at fourteen hundred feet-per-second smashed into the boulder their target was using for cover. The big rock exploded, giving birth to a litter of little rocks as the shotgun continued to belch flame in its pursuit of jackhammering the boulder apart.

Deacon forced himself to, once again, take several combat breaths to slow his heart rate. Now focused and calm, he peered around his tree and grinned at seeing *Luis* pinned down.

During the second salvo of hot lead, he watched Luis lying flat at the base of the disintegrating boulder with Washington turning it into Swiss cheese around him. Several fragmented rounds ricocheted and dug into the earth mere inches from him.

With each impact, a small fountain of soil jumped into the air. The man was prone on the ground, his hands over his head in a futile attempt to protect himself from being sliced to pieces by the flying granite.

Seconds later, Deacon's ear piece came to life. "Running dry on slugs. Switching to buckshot,"

Shit! At Washington's range, the buckshot was useless. The psychological effect might work for one, maybe two shots. But that would be it. This guy was a pro. The second that chips of rock stopped hitting him, he'd figure it out.

Smith's voice cut in and out over Deacon's radio between the blasts of the big gage. "D, I've still got some…"
Boom! "…but we're gettin' thin. Whatever you're plan-
nin'…" Boom! "…do it fast."

"Copy that. Slow your pace." With the asshole pinned
down, Deacon knew his opportunity was time-limited. He
wouldn't get another one, especially with Smith and Washington running out of ammo.

Deacon leaned around the tree and aimed down his sight.
A barrel the size of a cannon pointed right back at him. "Oh
shit."

Behind the man, Justice exploded from behind a bush.
He T-boned Luis's back. Canines sank into the base of the
man's skull. Deacon watched Luis's eyes bulge as Justice
clamped down. The dog gave a hard shake and Deacon
heard the man's neck snap like a twig.

Breathing a sigh of relief, he dropped his head onto the
butt stock of his rifle. *Too damned close.* "God I love that
dog." Looking up, his gaze met the burning one of his partner. Like a silent sentinel, Justice stood guard atop the motionless body, his bulging muscles having buried the man's
shoulders into the earth. Getting to his feet, Deacon looked
toward Washington and Smith. They stood behind Smith's
car, their weapons aimed at the body, the faint haze of
smoke from the muzzles of their rifle and shotgun swirled
around them.

Deacon keyed up his mic. "Guys, we're Code Four. Justice took care of it."

"Copy that. Confirm the sniper is 10-15?"

"Standby just one." If the man was faking it, they were
about to find out. Deacon ordered the dog to bite again. He
did as ordered. When he released Luis, he left several large
holes in the dead man's right bicep. Luis didn't move, utter
a sound, or bleed.

Deacon strode up to the body, his rifle trained on the
man's head. His earlier walk to Investigations was nothing

when compared to this endless one down the green mile. He halted a foot from the body and watched the pool of blood beneath Luis's head to see if it grew. It didn't. The man was dead. Hands trembling, he twisted them on the grip of the rifle trying to steady them.

After what seemed an eternity, Deacon moved the final twelve inches to his partner's side. Although they both knew Luis was dead, Justice hadn't moved a muscle. Deacon knelt beside the man and completed a pro forma check for a pulse.

Nothing.

He keyed up his radio. "Affirm. 10-15 and 11-44. It's over." He met his partner's gaze. The dog whined, then repeatedly licked Deacon's face. Grasping the dog's head, he lowered his until their foreheads touched and gently scratched behind two big fuzzy ears. "That's another one I owe you, buddy. Thank you," he murmured, stroking the red streaked muzzle.

He pushed himself upright and tapped his left thigh. His partner responded immediately and assumed the heel position—K9 shoulder to human left knee. Sighing, Deacon radioed to his two partners farther up the road. "Let's fall back down the road a bit so we're out of sight. As soon as we've got cell service, I'll call Swanson. He needs to send in the troops before Tuefel figures out what's been going on. If he's anywhere near here, he heard World War III start and now, with the silence, he'll be wondering who won. If Luis doesn't contact him, he'll book."

"Copy that, D. Meet us at the cars," Smith said.

Together, Deacon and Justice loped down the road to the patrol cars. "Everyone okay?"

Smith answered first, albeit a little too loudly. "Other than my ears still ringing, I think we're good. Bautista's had a bad day though."

Deacon smothered a chuckle at Washington's mournful expression as he took in the condition of his car.

"Ah shit, man! Look at the damage. And it was just issued to me! Deacon you owe me, man! Who the hell's gonna fix this?"

"Motor pool?"

"Ha, ha, ha. Very funny, asshole."

With the adrenaline dump ebbing, a wave of fatigue almost sent Deacon to his knees. He rubbed his eyes. Until he smelled it, he hadn't realized he'd smeared gun oil across his face and eyes, which were tearing from dirt and lack of sleep. "Guys, I know the cars should be left here for crime scene, but we need the cover. Since there's enough room to do a three-point turn, let's move our cars down to the other side of the bar and park near the highway. If we don't, it'll be a naked walk out of here."

Smith grinned. "Naked. I like naked. Why're we standing around? Let's just get the hell out of here."

Deacon pressed the button on his door pop. Before he could say a word, Justice leapt up into his den, made three circles, and, flopping onto the vehicle floor, rested his head on his front paws. Deacon quickly secured his long rifle in the weapon mount and crawled in behind the steering wheel.

CHAPTER 38

Deacon opened the menu in his phone to favorites and pressed on Swanson's photo.

The phone rang once. "Deacon, that you? Where the hell are you? You and the guys okay?"

"We are fine. But Bautista's dead—single shot through the forehead. Gotta tell ya, boss, that Luis was a helluva sniper."

"What do you mean was? Did you get him?"

"I didn't. Justice did."

"Not funny."

"Not joking."

Deacon quickly filled him in. "Oh, and boss, Bautista was right. Off by the back exit there's a mass grave. I'm not shittin' ya, Doug. The first thing I thought when I saw all those bodies in the fucking ravine was Auschwitz. I'll shoot you the pics as soon as we're finished here. But we need help. And we need it now."

"I'll handle circling the wagons. You get a hold of White and get him everything, and I mean everything, he needs for the warrants, and CC me."

"Copy that."

"And, D, keep your head down. You guys aren't out of the woods yet."

Deacon disconnected. As he brought up White's number, the car radio erupted with activity. Swanson worked fast. He'd scrambled air support from the helicopter pad at the airport.

Dispatchers called for aid from the sheriff's departments of the local and neighboring counties. Deputies from both counties flew up the hill going Code Three in order to shut down the highway from the north and the south. At that point, all ingress to and egress from Tuefel's compound would cease, except for law enforcement vehicles.

Swanson had unleashed the hounds. No one made shit happen as fast as that man.

With the radio belching endless updates, detailing the army mobilizing to their location, Deacon breathed a sigh of relief and pressed on White's photo. With this call, White would wake-up the Investigations Division.

"Talk to me, D. What the hell's happened?"

That's what Deacon liked about him. Straight to the point. No wasted time. He started to brief him about Bautista and the deal.

"Okay. Okay. Hold on. Are you guys okay?"

"Yeah, we're fine. I've called and briefed Swanson. He's got SWAT, Narcs, you detectives, CSI, everyone rolling this way."

"Hold on a sec. I've got to get to my office."

Deacon sighed. For a non-smoker and light drinker, the man didn't have good wind. Strange, too. Deacon would have thought that running after all those kids of his White would have better endurance. Guess he played too much fantasy football instead of real football.

Hearing his friend's grunt when he flopped into his chair, Deacon grinned. "You're outta shape, old man. It's time you joined me at the gym."

"Fuck-off, D. Start talkin'. Tell me everything that's happened from the beginning. Give me all the details you remember. I'm going to need them for the search warrant."

Deacon ran down the whole list of events at length.

When he got to the mass grave, White went silent, didn't say a word until Deacon had finished talking.

"D, this is too good to be true. We own his ass, his house, everything. There's no way he won't go down for this. Drugs, murder, crossing state lines and countries. Shit, we may have to fight Mexico for him. And we'll sure as hell be fightin' the feds for jurisdiction on this one."

"From your lips to God's ears. But I won't believe it until I hear the foreman say guilty on all counts."

"You guys just sit tight. I'll scratch out the search warrant. Then we'll kick this guy right in the ass. There isn't a judge on the planet who won't sign this search warrant."

"Copy that. I'll send you the photos I took of the lab and bodies. Add them as exhibits for the judge. And, White, thanks for the help."

"Don't thank me yet. From what you described to me, you guys deserve a Medal of Valor. That is, if the chief doesn't kill you before you can get it."

"No kidding."

"Seriously, stay frosty. Keep your mags topped off and your eyes peeled. Where there's one, there're two—"

"And where there're two, there're four." Deacon finished.

"Hey, D?"

"Yeah."

"You know this is all your fault right?"

"What? How the hell is it my fault?"

You called down the thunder, my brother. It was you who said nothing ever happens when the sun is up. This whole mess started yesterday. It may have taken over two weeks to catch up with you, but didn't you get ordered in for day-shift?"

"Not funny, yo. *So* not funny." Deacon snapped his phone shut and walked to the trunk of his patrol car. This was going to be a long day on top of an already exhausting twenty-four hours without sleep. He popped the trunk and broke out his emergency stash of Cliff Bars. God, he loved these things. They were the best tasting protein bars he had ever eaten.

He bit the edge of the wrapper and ripped it open. The damned bar had melted into a ball of protein mess. Served him right. He knew better than to store them near the radio equipment. Not that it mattered when he was beyond famished. He hadn't eaten a thing since Jessica's house. And aside from her Chicken Feta Pasta, food hadn't crossed his lips for over twelve hours.

Glancing at his watch, he winced. As he wolfed down his sorry excuse for breakfast, Deacon divided the remaining Cliff Bars and tossed two to each of his compatriots.

"Good ol' D. Always comin' through with the food," Washington mumbled between bites.

Smith echoed his thanks through and equally full mouth.

Snickering, Deacon rummaged through his gear and found the box of Milk Bones. These damn things looked better than what he had eaten. After grabbing the box of doggy treats, he shut the trunk.

Pivoting, he faced a dancing Justice. A moment later, he added singing for his treats to hopping and bouncing. Laughing, Deacon tossed him one at a time. "Jeeze, buddy, slow down." He flipped his partner the fourth and last one, then filled his water bowl and placed it on the ground beside the bumper.

Justice buried his face in his water bowl, lifted his head, and sneezed, then returned to lapping as if he hadn't had water since they'd left home yesterday morning.

Munching on his second peanut butter and chocolate chip bar, Deacon sat on the push bumper of his vehicle. His tongue hanging out the side of his mouth, Justice trotted to the end of the parking lot. He stopped by the highway, sniffing through leaf litter and squirrel turds.

Deacon's gaze drifted to Washington and Smith topping off their long guns. Wanting nothing more than to crawl into Justice's den and crash, Deacon forced himself not to act on his body's demand.

"What's up?" Smith asked.

"You heard everything."

"Yeah, but you look like shit. Hell, if you were on the *Walking Dead*, you wouldn't need any make up."

Washington hooted. "Good one, Rob." On a wink, he turned back to Smith and they returned to their debate about who had been farther up Shit Creek.

"Man, Kev, I've never seen you move so fast," Smith said, scanning the horizon, his weapon pointed in the direction of the compound.

"Adrenaline will do that to you."

"After today, I think we've had enough of that stuff to shave two or three years off of our life expectancy, don't you?"

Deacon laughed and nearly choked. He cleared his throat. "I think you're right, Rob. But something tells me Luis was the prologue, and we're about to have another load dumped into our veins."

Washington's head jerked toward him. "What makes you say that?"

"Call it a hunch."

Deacon walked to the front of the car, leaned against the car's hood, and split his attention between the road to the compound and the early morning sky. From the looks of it, the rain had finally run dry and wouldn't be returning anytime soon. *More's the pity.*

Even with dawn crawling its way west, true west still revealed stars not seen in the city. At this elevation, they blanketed the lightening sky. Its sheer beauty never ceased to amaze him or fill him with a sense of peace. He needed to get out of the city more often.

"So, what do we do now?" Smith asked.

Deacon stretched and yawned. "Nothing. We wait for the troops to arrive. Since we're neck deep in shit, our only job is to stay alive. Which may prove difficult. We're exhausted and our ammo's depleted. White's cranking out the search warrant for Tuefel's property as we talk. SWAT and every other cop in the county should arrive shortly to serve the warrant."

Washington frowned. "So, what're we supposed to do in the meantime?"

"I haven't slept in I don't know how long. I'm going to crank out for an hour or two. Wake me up when it's time to get my ass chewed."

Smith nodded. "No problem, D."

Deacon loaded Justice back up into the car, put his water bowl in the back, and refilled it to halfway. Between this bowl and previous two, the blood on his muzzle turned the water pink. When he'd finished, Deacon returned the metal bowl to the trunk. Slipping on his Gortex coat, he opened the passenger door, grabbed his rifle, and gathered all his remaining ammo.

He handed Washington the long gun and the magazines. "Make sure you get me up."

"No problem, yo. See you in an hour."

Deacon returned to his car to a snoring dog. With a snort, he curled into a ball beneath his coat.

ⵌⵌ

Tuefel stared at the ceiling over his bed and listened. The gunfire had ceased a good twenty minutes ago. Yet Luis hadn't returned. What little patience Tuefel had had vanished. Throwing off his comforter, he rolled out of bed and quickly dressed. Opening the safe behind Rachele's portrait, he gathered all his incriminating documents and bank books, then lit a fire and pitched them in it. He didn't need his bank records. He had an eidetic memory and knew to all his accounts—numbered and not.

Confident the cops couldn't recover any evidence from them, he took off for the armory. Once the door opened, he selected his favorite assault rifle, an M-4. Seething that all his plans for revenge might be for not, he made his way outside and headed toward the location he'd pegged as where the final shots had originated. He dashed down to his shed, the thirst for blood rising within him. Upon reaching it, he discovered a very recent remodel.

He knelt and inspected the bullet holes. Based on the angle of entry of the holes and gashes in the metal skin of the shed, he determined the trajectory of the bullets. He used that information to estimate the location of the shooters. They'd been at the lab, but not via the main entrance. *Scheiße!* The cops had used the escape tunnel. But how had they learned of it?

He knew Luis would have had them in a full retreat to the main road. He must have tried to flank them close to the highway. It was what Tuefel would have done if he were in a firefight such as this. Going with his gut, he tore down the service road. He swept his M-4 back and forth, looking for signs of his enforcer or dead cops.

It took another five minutes before he found Luis's body.

Standing over his employee's savaged remains, fury warred with disgust for supremacy. "I asked you to do one thing. Bring me a few people. Instead, you disobeyed my orders. And that is why you're dead, you worthless piece of *scheiße!*" He kicked Luis's face. The steel toe of his boot crushed the corpse's cheekbones. Then he repeated the action several times.

Finally, Tuefel stuck the barrel of the gun into Luis's mouth, breaking his front teeth, and pulled the trigger. The head contained enough pressure to muffle the sound before it exploded. Pieces from the top of the skull flew out like a rocket, landing twenty feet from the body.

He rarely, if ever, used multiple men at his compound. A handful at most, that was his rule. People always had a price. Someone always talked. All it took was the right amount of money or the right kind of pressure.

Today's' events had changed his perspective. The loss of his beloved wife and his forced reliance upon just one man now enraged him. *Dumb.* Never again, he swore. Staring at what was left of Luis's body, Tuefel recognized his mistake. Because Luis had seen his grief, he'd thought him weak. Big mistake. One he'd never make again. He should have sent several men, independent of one another. Better yet, he should've done the damned job himself.

As he pulled back his foot to kick the gaping hole in Luis's neck, he froze at the low and slow thumping of rotor blades. They were rapidly approaching from the southwest. The deep thump sound meant the copter had only two blades. He identified it immediately—a Huey.

He waited and stared at the sky. Darkness still prevailed, but there was a hint of dark purple and navy blue against the eastern horizon. It wouldn't be long before white and yellow appeared.

Within minutes, he spotted the blue and red flashing belly lights of the copter nearing. Suddenly, a spotlight cut a swath through the dawn sky as it swept from right to left. They couldn't possibly know he wasn't in the house. He was too skilled to have been picked up by surveillance. His specialty was to evade and kill. He was the hunter not the prey.

He chuckled at the electric eye searching for him as it climbed its way up the hillside. The damned cops would arrive in force soon. He'd use the time to prepare.

The Krusnik glanced at Luis and spit on the failure's corpse. He eased back into the redwoods and moved through them in a zigzag motion, running for tree to tree. *Groß Gott*, he'd made sure that the house maintained the protection afforded by the forest.

Time to execute his vengeance.

CHAPTER 39

Deacon swam back to consciousness as repeated shakes to his shoulder made him feel as if he were in a rowboat fighting high swells.

"Wake up. Shit, man, wake up!"

"I'm awake. And if you want to stay upright, stop pounding on me, Kev." Deacon shook off the demand he return to the arms of Morpheus. As if he wanted to return to the nightmare of seeing the back of Bautista's head blown out. Not happening. He forced his eyes open and glanced at his watch. Seven-fifteen. One hour. Better than nothing. He pushed himself upright. "What's up?"

"You've slept through a helicopter circling overhead for starters. Shit, dude, you worried us. It took five minutes for you to wake. No reaction, nada, zip, zero. I'm bettin' you wouldn't react if a dump truck plowed through your house."

"You're probably right. I've had, like, four hours sleep in the last forty-eight." He crawled out of his car. Even through an ocean of tears and gritty sand, his eyes burned as if he'd stared directly into the sun.

Yawning, he rubbed them, trying to extinguish the raging inferno. He retrieved his phone and checked it. He'd several missed calls, the most recent from White. He hit his speed dial.

White answered on the first ring. "Dude! Where have you been?"

"Asleep."

"Asleep?"

"Yeah. I've worked the last forty-four hours outta forty-eight, remember?"

"Yeah, I do. And I've been awake since the shift before your shooting yesterday, remember? The calvary arrived yet?"

Deacon stretched, trying to work out the stiffness. The vertebrae in his lower back sounded off like gunfire. "Not yet. Who's en route?"

"Everyone. For the last hour, you've had air support. Both counties and the highway patrol are rotating their birds to keep one up with FLIR at all times. If Tuefel didn't leave when the shooting started, it's too late now. Because there's no way he won't be seen."

"Perfect. You get the warrant signed?"

"Yup. Pavelski signed it."

Instantly awake, Deacon jerked upright. "Really? He the on-call?"

"Yeah."

"Wow, no kidding. Hang 'em Harry Pavelski. Nice work."

"You don't know the half of it. Between you and me, Pavelski has a history with Tuefel that goes way back. He basically told me to make this a black bag op."

Deacon whistled. "I'll be damned." *Dumbass must've done something to him or his family, for Pavelski to tell White to take the sonuvabitch out if possible.* "Where are you now?"

"I just hit the freeway. ETA fifteen minutes."

"Copy that."

"Keep your heads down. You guys are in enough shit as it is."

Deacon laughed. "You don't have to tell me twice. We're parked behind the Tipsy Monkey Bar."

"Why am I not surprised? Oh, don't drink anything. Just sit tight. I'll see you in a few."

"Will do." With a snicker, Deacon slipped his phone into his pants pocket.

From his seat on his push bumper, he watched as, over the next ten minutes, controlled chaos unfolded. He chuckled at the oxymoron. But what else could one call it?

Cops from every jurisdiction swarmed the area. And God help the civilians trying to get to work. Sure, they wouldn't be impacted by the patrol cars that now blocking the private road to Tuefel's compound. But the unsuspecting residents would be pissed-off at the added forty-minute commute as they detoured around five miles of blockaded highway.

He glanced at the department's mobile command vehicle parked behind the liquor store, utilizing it for cover. No one wanted to tell the feds the RV they'd bought, using a cool million of Homeland Security's money, had been shot to death. Seeing the combined store sign and vehicle placard, *Cain Police Department Tactical Command Monkey*, he snorted. No truer words were ever written.

He spotted the SWAT officers arriving for their briefing. They remained huddled next to the armored personnel carriers they'd use to provide both mobile and heavy cover for the operation. Much to Deacon's chagrin, while he nodded to them, none acknowledged his presence.

Deacon's gaze narrowed. While he hadn't seen the chief arrive, from the look on the faces of his staff as they exited the command vehicle and headed his way, the chief was in a foul temper.

Time to get Smith and Washington. No way was Deacon taking an ass kicking alone. He retrieved his rifle from Washington and secured the long gun in his vehicle. With a nod, the three of them marched toward the RV like lambs to the slaughter.

As they entered the vehicle, Smith, Washington, and he stayed rooted at the back of it. Deacon fought to maintain a blank expression, but it was hard. He felt like all that was missing was the blindfold as he stood before a firing squad. Which, given that the three of them had busted the case wide open, didn't make sense.

He winced as the chief paced the length the vehicle, a vein bulging from the side of his neck as he yelled at a volume Tuefel could probably hear. "What the fuck were you three thinking? Did you wake up and eat a big bowl of dumbass this morning? What the fuck is wrong with you? Son of a bitch! You're all lucky I don't kill you where you're standing."

Deacon watched as spit flew from the man's mouth as the volume increased. Between the tirade and pacing, the bus rocked, reminding him of Justice's famous performances.

He'd known this chief for years. Believing the man cared about his officers, he wrote-off the shouting as the man's need to vent.

Scowling, the chief faced them. "I'm glad you got that piece of shit. At least you got that right. And now, Jesus—" He raked a hand through his thinning hair. "—I can't believe I'm actually going to do this, but we need every fucking body we have for this op. So you three cover the woods around that fucking glade. You assholes are to stay as far away from that damn house as possible when the warrant's served." He paused a moment, breathing hard. Blood and anger drained from his face. He grasped the back of a chair. Sweat dripped off his brow.

Deacon watched as the man slowly regained his composure, but not his color. "Chief? Are you all right?"

"I'm fine. Get your asses out of my sight. Report to Christiansen and Peterson."

CHAPTER 40

Bringing up the rear, Deacon stepped out of the command RV, paused, and inhaled a deep breath of fresh air. "You two feel like heroes who've become whipping boys?"

At their short, tight nods, he sighed. If they looked like shit run over twice, he didn't want to know what they'd say about him. At least he had an excuse—no sleep and two shootings within twenty-four hours took its toll.

"Gents, over here. You too, Deacon," White yelled.

Deacon turned and saw him standing beside his F-150. Ignoring the joke, Deacon ambled toward him. Against the rising sun, the mountains were granite spires piercing the sky, unwavering and majestic in their silence. He took in another deep breath of the warm, clean air, relishing the smell of oaks and pines, and thanked God they'd survived Luis relatively unscathed. Straightening his shoulders, he headed for his waiting comrades.

White motioned him to a folding chair. "Have a seat. Christ, Deacon, you look like death warmed over."

Deacon collapsed onto one of the redwood chairs. "It's good to see you, too."

"I'm relieved you guys are all right. But you sure know how to step in it."

Deacon rubbed the back of his neck. "Tell us about it. At least the chief didn't shoot us."

"From the look on his face, I thought he was going to," Smith muttered.

White snorted. "That'd be true to form. Survive one mess after another only to have him kill you. Oh, and my wife said to thank you guys for the overtime. We're gonna be able to pay off her car this month."

Deacon pinched the bridge of his nose. "Glad to be of service."

Smith snorted. "I think I can speak for the three of us, if you're in need again with your finances, remind us to get in another shooting the next time you're the on-call."

"Believe me, Smith, you just called down the thunder solely because you said that. Ask Deacon. He'll tell you all about it. I won't have to remind you, numb nuts. And for the record, I don't care what anyone says, you guys did good today. Real good. This is going to put a huge dent into the drug trade around here, and, as a bonus, we're nailing this sonuvabitch right to the wall."

Deacon leaned forward. "Hey, White. You've checked on Jessica, haven't you?"

"Yeah. I called her on my way here. She said she's fine."

Swallowing hard, Deacon nodded. Damn, he hoped he didn't get weepy over this. Nah, he was just overtired with dry, teary eyes. "Good. Thanks."

"She'll be fine, D. That girl's nothing short of resilient. She's been through a hell of a lot over the last twenty-four hours, yet she's still smiling."

They all had been through a lot. Jaw clenched, Deacon stared off in the direction of the road. How was it possible that it had only been a few hours since they'd met, yet he missed her?

He shook his head. *God, don't let me become whipped.* He could handle anything but that.

"Who signed the warrant?" Smith asked.

White slanted at glance at Deacon. "You didn't tell?"

"Didn't have time. The chief called."

"Got it. Judge Harry Pavelski. Told me to kick ass and take no prisoners."

Laughing, Washington leaned back onto the bed of the truck. "I love it. God bless that guy."

"Agreed."

No sooner had the word passed out of Deacon's mouth, than a massive paw clapped down on his shoulder and pulled. The chair tipped backward. Teetering on the hind legs, he glanced up at the human mountain standing behind him.

"How's it going, Dirks."

Deacon nodded to the grizzly-sized man. Standing next to him was his friend, SWAT sniper Sergeant Jason Peterson. Both were dressed in their full SWAT gear. From what Deacon had heard, Peterson was easily the largest sniper in the state. In his ghillie suit, he also looked like a moving forest.

It didn't hurt that both men came from a long line of mountain-sized ancestors. His sniper rifle, a Barrett fifty caliber nicknamed the Judge looked like a BB gun slung across Peterson's back.

Dirks leaned over the bedcover of White's vehicle and bellowed, "I sure am glad to see you boys're still breathin' after that hot mess! How the hell are ya?"

Peterson walked over, picked Deacon up out of the chair, and gave him a bone-crushing hug.

Air shot out of his lungs like a missile. Finally, he fully understood the phrase bear hug. When the man released him, it was a long fall back to Earth.

Petersen cleared his throat. "White, gear up and get to the EOD truck."

"Copy that, Sarge. Dirks, you make a helluva road block. Get the hell outta my way—please."

Deacon groaned at their long-standing, good-natured sniping.

Snickering, Dirks moved to the side. As White passed, he

clapped him on the back, almost sending White to his knees. "Glad to oblige, son."

Grinning, Peterson turned toward them. "You three gear up, too. Meet over at the MRAP for briefing in fifteen. You're not done yet."

ഗൈ

Tuefel snickered, his gaze flicking between his security monitors and television. He suspected the cops had wanted to maintain a low profile and try to take him in a covert action. *Good luck with that, boys in blue*. He only played when it fit his agenda. Today, it did. He'd get his shot at Rachele's killer and his fucking dog.

His gaze homed in on the very man he hunted. With his hound at his side, it would be an easy twofer. Success depended upon getting off the property without the eyes in the sky spotting him. He focused on the media pressing up against a roadblock a half mile from his driveway. Not that their arrival had surprised him. Once he'd found Luis's body, he'd known time was short. Here was hoping, they hadn't discovered the back exit.

His eyes narrowed on the reporter who had gleefully announced the death of his beloved to the world. "After the cop and his dog, you'll be the first person I kill, bitch."

As he watched her lips moving, he decided even if he couldn't escape, he'd take her out. Maybe even make her his first target. Why try to escape? He didn't have Rachele. He picked up the remote and unmuted the TV.

"...we're live above Oakhurst at the scene of a tense standoff. SWAT from the Cain Police Department has surrounded the residence of Mr. Ubel Tuefel. Details are few. But the overwhelming manpower reminds me of the military during Desert Storm."

Tuefel's eyes widened at seeing his sealed office staring back at him. Frowning, he stood, walked over to the massive window, and flipped a switch, retracting the metal shutters. He waited to confirm the camera had zoomed in on him then, with a sneer, flipped them off. Seeing the reporter's open-mouthed gape, he smiled.

As he resealed the house behind its bullet-proof shutters, he heard the bitch stammer, "Oh! Well...um...it would seem Mr. Tuefel is clearly...um...not happy about the situation. We apologize for that. We will bring you more as this situation develops. This is Grace Munoz, Channel Five News."

Chuckling, he reentered his armory. "Stupid asses. They think I didn't see the SWAT team assembling. Maybe after I take out Grace Munoz, I ought to send Channel Five a thank you for showing me the location of everyone I plan to kill." He looked over his rifles. He knew the only way he could break through the perimeter and find his prey would be to blend in with the throng of idiots by the roadblock.

Stripping, he quickly changed out of casual dress clothing into what he wore when hiking and mountain climbing. Then he broke down his favorite sniper rifle and slipped it along with ammo-filled magazines into his backpack. He lifted his gaze to the racks of weapons and selected two H&K USP semi-auto pistols. Each was chambered to .45 caliber and packed one hell of a punch.

A corner of his lips ticked up. He had a lot of holes to make. And he'd always loved leaving big ones behind. With a shrug, he admitted a profiler would say it was his signature. Like he cared, only one thing consumed him—completing this final mission.

Tuefel did a press check on the slide of each weapon, ensuring they were topped off. "Good."

Both of them contained their maximum capacity of black talon hollow point rounds. Nasty little buggers. When they slammed into body armor, the pressure forced the hollow point round to fold back on itself, revealing several sharp claw-like points. These talons, like high-speed drills, ripped through body armor and shredded the body beneath it.

His triumph over these fools would be talked about for years. Gloating over the expected outcome, he stuffed his cargo pockets with extra magazines for each weapon and slid each weapon into their holsters. He shifted the holsters to the small of his back near each kidney and wedged their J-hooks under his belt, securing them in place beneath his pants, then pulled his shirt out enough so it folded over weapons. A quick glance in the mirror confirmed the hand-held cannons were hidden from the world.

Walking over to his safe, he dialed in the combination. The door glided open on well-oiled hinges. Inside the cool, dry shelter resided a steel case full of Mark-2 hand grenades resting upon ten one-and-a-quarter-pound blocks of C-4.

He loved the fragmentation caused by the pineapple shaped body. It was particularly wicked and would be more than enough to initiate the C-4. Grinning, he selected four grenades and carefully added them to the magazines in his cargo pockets.

If the assholes wanted to raid his house, they could go ahead, and when they did, they'd learn why he was so feared. He selected two blocks of the plastic explosives and an electric blasting cap for each. Gently placing the C-4 in his bag, he grasped the blasting gaps.

The cops could possibly dispose of the grenades when, make that if, they found them, because they wouldn't. The pathetic, overconfident, stupid sons of bitches wouldn't see it coming.

He ran a guitar string through the pins of the remaining grenades and rigged the almost-invisible string to the frame of the safe. If the police tried to remove the case, they would be in for one hell of a surprise.

From running his own tactical team, it was SOP to plan for a secondary breach point. This rear door in the kitchen would most likely be it, while his front door would be the primary. Even if they didn't breach the door, they'd be sure to clear the room. SWAT was nothing if not predictable.

He marched into the kitchen, pressed the blasting caps

into the C-4, and secured the plastic explosive inside one of his cabinets. After he dried his hands on the nearby towel, he strung the electric leads from each cap through a hole in the side of the cabinet and shunted the wires dangling freely in the air beside an infrared motion sensor.

Tuefel dragged a wooden chair to the doorframe and positioned it outside the room to prevent activating the IR with his body heat. As he reached for the sensor, he ignored the creaking chair. His fingers found the groove they were seeking. The rear cover snicked open. With a smirk, he removed a LED light bulb from the device and twisted the cap wires in its place.

The show for the news would be spectacular. With luck, he'd still be around to enjoy the show. Still smiling at the thought, he jogged down the stairs to his study. Then he took a hidden elevator to a side tunnel that lead to the rear escape.

CHAPTER 41

Deacon, along with Washington and Smith, joined the others at the briefing area. In the shadow of the Tipsy Monkey, he took in the true size of the army assembled to take out one man. A monster yes, but as Deacon stared up at the Mine Resistant Ambush Protected personnel carrier, he couldn't help but wonder if it was too much or not enough.

A few well-positioned snipers should be able to take care of the problem called Tuefel. Instead, they looked like they were ready to roll down the ISIS-controlled streets of Fallujah. He shook his head. Sure, protection against a man like Tuefel was critical. But Deacon knew that the media coverage of this event would serve to give a louder voice to the citizens who believed the police had become too militarized and, in the process, had lost their original focus and mission.

Deacon glanced at the chief standing next to the MRAP. His color still hadn't returned. And, with his hands on his hips, he looked like a ghost from the wild-west.

Goosebumps joined the hair on the back of Deacon's neck rising like Justice's hackles. With a shudder, he shook off the feeling someone had just walked over his grave and tried to refocus on the operation.

He scanned the throng of officers. Between SWAT, narcs, EOD, and the detectives, they looked like flood pressing against an earthen dam. Woe to anyone downstream. Everyone, himself included, wore their heavies—three layers of Kevlar on the chest as well as the back.

The gear was patterned after Marine digital camouflage. It also had Kevlar neck, shoulder, and groin protectors. While jokes about the groin protectors were frequent, especially by the press, their purpose was to protect the femoral artery. Cops had learned about these vulnerable locations the hard way—losing too many good officers.

"Okay, listen up!"

Peterson's roar startled Deacon, jerking him back to the present. The mob's murmuring and bullshitting continued. He wasn't surprised. It happened whenever a large group of cops was facing a major OP and hyped up on adrenaline.

"I said quiet! All of you shut the hell up! Someone turn off that damned engine."

The talking ceased. The vehicle died. Silence filled the parking lot. Deacon moved to the edge of the herd to get a better view.

"We're passing out aerial photos of the compound. Take a good look at them, ladies. Get familiar with your environment. Where the hell's Deacon?"

"Right here, Sarge."

"Get your ass up here."

With Justice at his side, he made his way to the front.

Peterson clapped him on the back. "Since this here is Officer Deacon's bar-b-que, why don't we let him fill us in on what he's been cookin' and why we're here at the ass crack of dawn?"

Deacon cleared his throat and gave the team the *Reader's Digest* version of the last twenty-four hours. With only a few minor interruptions, he'd almost finished the briefing when he grabbed a pen and drew a diagram on the dry erase board attached to the side of the command vehicle. He included Tuefel's residence, the cave, and the path to the tent.

He even included the Tipsy Monkey and added an arrow to show north. Peterson yanked the pen from his hand and commandeered his diagram.

Not knowing what to do or where to go, Deacon didn't move while Peterson labeled the locations for his various personnel. As boxes and lines appeared, Deacon bit back a snort. He'd be damned if it didn't look like something out of John Madden's playbook.

"Okay, ladies. Our search warrant covers everything and anything on the Tuefel property. Since public owned lands, federal and state, surround Tuefel's place, we have a large area to cover and the freedom to inspect every inch of it. Search for hidden panels, storage areas, and escape routes. Leave nothing untouched. Then go through it again and guarantee we missed nothing. With that said, no one, and I mean no one leaves until Tuefel's in our pocket. This is our best and only chance to get his shit out of here and lock him away for life.

"Matthew's perimeter team will deploy first and stick two to a location. We don't know how long we'll be out here. But I think it's a safe bet at least twenty-four hours, so make sure you've got plenty of water, food, and ammo."

He quickly paired everyone up and placed each one in forty-five degree intervals surrounding the compound. "My sniper teams will be positioned in these locations." He pointed to five points in the center of the map and all covered ingress and egress from the house. "Deacon, correct me if I'm wrong, but there's a hill here that will allow you to cover both the compound as well as the lab."

"That's correct, Sarge."

"Great. I want a sniper team covering the lab entrance and the other on the residence. Andrews and the rest will be riding in one of the two APCs. Half of the team will be in the CPD MRAP while the other half is in the county's Bearcat. Andrews, you will have the forty and a shit load of bangs. Bring extra gas. Dirks, load the robot into the MRAP. When I give the word, deploy it from the rear. Once we bang and gas the crap out of that place, remote the robot into the residence. Clear as much as possible before we make entry.

"White, you've got Team Three. Your boys will handle the lab. Post up on the main cave and…"

Deacon's gaze drifted over the assembled the crowd. Something had changed. He'd once been this eager for action. Not now. Not today. His bones ached. His gritty eyes burned. Acid crawled up his throat.

"…Deacon, since your crew knows how to get to the tent quickly, you, Smith, and Washington will hold the rear exit. Your only job—and don't even think about doing another damn thing—is to take down anyone attempting to escape via that back tunnel. Let White's team clear the lab. You've been in enough shit. Don't get into any more.

"Once this place is cleared, and we're all Code Four, double back and make sure you didn't miss anyone hiding. This will be slow and methodical since this place is going to be a searching nightmare. No one enters a room without a partner. Period. Remember, when we are done, this area will become a crime scene. Treat it as such.

"Make no mistake, Tuefel's a billy bad ass. This is as real as it gets. Earlier today, three of our guys were almost taken out by one of his. Treat everyone as armed and hostile until proven otherwise. If you spot an unknown holding something resembling a weapon, don't hesitate. Eliminate the threat."

Deacon focused on calm, controlled breathing and tried to ignore the antsy cops around him. Unlike them, his mortality sat heavy on his shoulders. Without Justice, he'd be dead. And Luis wasn't the Krusnik.

"Any questions?" Crickets broke the answering silence. "No? Good. Get your shit and brief back your assignments with your teams. Deacon, you and your crew meet with White's team and go over the layout of the lab. Dismissed."

෧෬෧

Deacon joined Washington, Smith, and the rest of White's team at the command vehicle. As he briefed the team on the layout and what they'd find, cold sweat coated him. He paused, his gaze on the drawing of the lab layout, then he glanced at White. "It isn't a good idea to bang the lab. There're glass beakers everywhere. Although they aren't in the middle of a cook, God knows what's in those damn things. One bang and you've got an inferno or some nasty shit's released that drops all of us."

"Good point. We'll gas the hell out of it, first. Once its saturated, we'll make our entry with our masks on." White pointed to the tent. "How big's the clearing?"

"Plus or minus twenty-five to thirty yards. Why?"

"There is plenty of room then. The three of you triangulate on the tent. Smith and Washington deploy with your rifles. Deacon, take your long gun with you. Cover the tent opening. You and your partner will handle the apprehensions."

Deacon nodded. He liked the plan. Three long guns. One hungry, pissed-off Shepherd. They'd own the fucking tent. "Copy that. After last night, we need to load up on ammo. You guys have the trailer up here?"

Standing on his toes, White craned his neck and looked over Deacon's shoulder. "It's behind the Monkey. Make sure you top-off all of your magazines. If you have room, stuff extra boxes in your pockets. Take as much as you can. You need anything else?"

Smith grinned. "Could I trouble you for a glass of warm milk? It helps me sleep."

"You could trouble me for a glass of shut the hell up! That was too easy, brother. Everyone knows that's from *Happy Gilmore*."

Deacon and Smith shared a laugh while Washington shook his head. "Really? Right now?"

"If you're set, I need Deacon to show me where the trail starts."

"Let's go." Deacon started back toward the main turn-off

for Tuefel's house, then stopped and pointed. "What you want is this sucker. And screw getting any of your big vehicles up it. It's a curvy, crumbling sonuvabitch, and we're lucky we made back alive. Just follow us up it. We'll break-off for the glade while you continue on to the lab."

"Sounds good."

Frowning, Deacon stared up the track. "By the time we're done up here, there may be someone else handling the OIS."

White pulled back on the charging handle and chambered a round into his rifle. "I hope you're wrong."

☙❧☙

Smith, Washington, and Deacon, with Justice at his side, joined White's team at the trail head and assumed their positions as they merged into the stick. Deacon and Justice took point. Smith and Washington covered the rear. Then each man tapped up, signaling he was ready. When the front of the stick was tapped, Deacon as point man knew the entire team was ready to deploy. Ten minutes later, he relocked the gate and pocketed the key.

"Why bother?" White asked.

Deacon grinned. "Don't want the alarm going off and tipping him off to where we are." A few minutes later, he stopped and pointed to the shell casings littering the area. "This is where Luis had us pinned down. You can see from the brass a partial outline of my vehicle." He pointed toward the trees. "Justice took down Luis by the big rock over there."

"Right. I see him now. Black boot?"

"Yeah." Like the rest of the men, Deacon's expression remained emotionless as he stared at the corpse. "The rest of the firefight was up the hill. It's off the trail the three of us take while you continue on to the lab."

"That's the trail that you'll take to get to the tent, right?"

"Affirm."

"But we don't take that trail, right?"

"Affirm. You'll continue up the road to the lab."

"Copy that. We'll try not to kick the casings all over, but can't swear it won't happen. After we have Tuefel's ass in irons, we'll do a full walkthrough."

"Any last minute advice?"

"Don't get yourself killed. Good luck, brother."

"You too." They clasped each other's forearms.

With a nod, White took off with his team.

Knees bent and weapons at the low ready, Deacon glided across the dirt, while Justice, with his profile low, looked like a shark with feet.

Deacon spotted tree that had saved his life and was amazed at the damage the sniper round had done. Its speed had left burn streaks as it punched through the bark. It had ripped through dozens of growth rings until it fragmented, leaving behind a jagged cone shaped wedge, the size of his fist, missing.

Staring at it, he swallowed hard. There but for the grace of God was his head. He glanced down at Justice and sighed. "I think the tree hugging hippies are going to be pissed."

Justice chuffed his agreement.

Reaching the crest of the hill, Deacon froze, remembering the firefight of a couple hours ago. He raised his left fist, signaling stop. Squatting, he parsed the glade, checking every bush and blade of high grass for movement in the still air. Nothing.

With the all clear sign, the three of them rose, nodded, and, using hand signals, headed for their appointed positions.

Reaching his position, Deacon gave Justice a hand command for a down/stay. Then he stretched out on his stomach beside his crouched partner, aimed his rifle, and trained the scope on the tent opening.

The remnants of Bautista's head filled his eyepiece.

While he couldn't see the inside of the tent, he remembered the blood, brain, and bits of bone covering it. Mouth drier than Death Valley in July, Deacon sighed, set aside his rifle, and rested his forehead on the back of his hand.

He knew the man's death wasn't his fault, and yet anger and regret consumed him for not having prevented it. Even Bautista had deserved better than that. With eyes closed, Deacon admitted to himself all three of them should have paid attention to the man's fears, instead of blowing them off. If they had, the man might still be alive.

Justice nudged him and whined. Deacon lifted his head off his hand with the gentle pressure of a wet nose. He reached over and gave a gentle scratch behind two very large ears. "I'm all right, but thanks, buddy. I'm just feeling sorry Bautista died and I'm the one who has to tell his family."

The dog gave a soft woof, licked Deacon's hand, and then returned his gaze back to the target.

Sighing again, Deacon steeled his nerves and resumed watching his target through the scope, searching for a shadow or moment within the tent. Moments later, the radio bud in his ear crackled, alerting him to incoming communication. With a grimace, he settled in to a probable day-long operation.

"Command post, Team 1. We are in position and standing by."

"Copy that, Team 1, in position."

"Command Post, Team 2. We are aboard both APCs. We are in position and standing by."

"Copy that, Team 2, in position."

White keyed up. "Command Post, Team 3. We are in position and standing by."

"Copy that Team 3, in position. All teams in position and standing by."

When the radio went silent, Deacon knew the incident commander was being briefed. Tension in the air kept the insects and birds silent. The only thing he heard were the helicopter's blades cutting through the air as it circled over-head.

Then his radio came to life,

"Deploy."

Deacon grimaced as Justice head-bumped his elbow. "Quiet. Stay," he hissed. Damned dog lived and breathed the mission. He just didn't get that theirs was to do nothing.

"Command Post, Peterson. We are in position and have eyes on the target."

"Looks like the snipers have reached their position," he murmured to his partner.

"Copy that, Peterson's team is in position with eyes on. Status?"

"All is quiet. Nothing is moving at either target."

"Copy that."

It took another fifteen minutes before Team One confirmed their two man teams had established an inner perimeter around the compound. During the wait, a siren blared in Deacon's mind.

Deacon's ear filled with a flurry of radio traffic. White announced that his team had reached their position at the cave's mouth. "Command Post, Team Three. We are in position."

"Copy that, Team Three, in position."

"Command Post, Team Two. Confirming the perimeter is set and all operators are in position."

"Affirm, Team Two. All operators are in position."

"Copy that, Command. Team Two is rolling out."

At Justice's whine, Deacon looked down at his friend and partner and brushed the back of his hand along the dog's muzzle. Justice whined again. "I know. Hold on to your butt, buddy. Here we go."

⋯⋯

Dirks climbed into the MRAP. Seated beside him was

the EOD robot, a Talon from Qinetiq. The Talon robot was small and versatile. At a hair over one hundred pounds, it was able to open most doors and had the option of firing a shoulder mounted canon.

Moments later, the engines of both vehicles roared to life. The tires' teeth gnashed and bit into the asphalt. The two APCs leapt forward, drove single file from the Monkey, turned onto the dirt road up to the compound, and paused for the rest of Team Two, which would fill both rigs to capacity.

Chad Andrews and Kirk Williams climbed into Dirks's APC and sat. He snorted as Andrews lovingly held the forty millimeter launcher, stroking the barrel as if it were a beloved puppy. But then what wasn't there to love. It was capable of launching less-than-lethal wooden dowels or tear gas.

The dowels were particularly nasty. They skipped really well on nearly any surface and were devastating to the shins. For today's op, Andrews loaded it with gas and he had brought a ton of it.

He laughed and shook his head when Williams began humming the *A-Team* theme song. It didn't take long before everyone in the rig had joined in. They rolled up the over a quarter mile long driveway, stopping at a large oval turnaround in front of the main door. The MRAP rumbled up to it.

The second APC circled the loop and took position on the far side. The driver parked in a way that would allow them to utilize the engine block as extra cover. The MRAP stopped short on the west side, also positioning its engine between the residence and the passenger compartment.

"Command Post, Team Two. We are in position."

"Copy that, Team Two. You are clear to make contact."

Andrews flipped on the loudspeaker switch. "Ubel Tuefel. This is the Cain Police Department. We have a search warrant for the property. Come out now. Keep your hands where we can see them."

"Andrews, Peterson. We heard your broadcast from here. Volume is good."

"Copy that." They made the announcement again which had the same results- nothing. "Hamilton, deploy the robot."

"Copy that."

"Command Post, Team Two. We are deploying the robot," Andrews said.

"Copy that, Team Two."

Dirks cracked the back door to the MRAP. He lowered the robot to the ground and quickly sealed the doors. He fired up the remote control box. The Talon came to life. Rubber treads dug into the dirt. Gears spun. Motors engaged. The Talon took off like a remote-controlled racecar on steroids.

Via the four cameras mounted on the chassis, he had a full three hundred sixty degree view. He reviewed each in turn. All appeared clear, and he piloted it to the large, deep set, flagstone front steps. Angling the tracks perpendicular to them, he powered the Talon forward. It slowly climbed each step.

In a matter of minutes, Dirks had the robot at the front door. He examined the entrance with the PTZ camera and saw massive double doors with three steel hinges bolted to each one. The place looked more like a citadel than a house. The hair on the back of his neck stood erect. "Something's hinky, boys."

"Getting one of your famous feelings," Andrew said with a snicker.

"Something like that." Dirks raised the elevator arm and lined up the shotgun at the deadbolt. His radio erupted "Command Post, Team Two. We have no response. Deploying gas."

"Copy that. Team Three prepare to move. Team One, hold your position. Snipers standby and provide cover for Team Two. Team Two, deploy gas."

The engines guzzled fuel. Dirks watched Andrews open the hatch covering a gun turret.

A second later, he fed the barrel of the forty millimeter launcher through the gun port. It spewed multiple cans of gas grenades through the windows, each leaving vapor trails in its wake.

After covering the front, the MRAP drove around the perimeter of the house, chucking smoking cans of pain and misery through every window it came across to laughter as Williams sang the opening lick from "Smoke on the Water."

Over the cacophony, Andrews yelled, "Dirks. Hit it!"

Dirks flipped the cover to the initiator. He turned the key and pushed down the red button. The Talon belched eight, nine millimeter rounds of buckshot at the lock and door handle at point blank range. They disintegrated. The door flew open and slammed into the wall, what remained of the inside handle embedded in the nearby sheetrock wall.

Dirks drove the remote into the main living room. Using all four of his cameras and his thermal viewer, he examined the room and confirmed that no one was in there. "Living-room clear."

Taking advantage of the impromptu cover, Dirks inspected the gas filled residence. As soon as he announced a room clear, he shifted to the next. "We are running out of rooms in this house. Where the hell is he?"

With the last five words, the upbeat mood sank.

"The last bedroom's clear. He's gotten out of the house," Dirks reported over his radio.

"Copy that. Sniper team, cover the roof line of the residence. Team Two, gas masks."

The doors opened and the entry team formed up on the porch. Multiple flash bangs flew through the air. Landing, they spun like bottles across the living room floor. Several stun grenades followed. Light, smoke, loud noise, and rubber pellets filled the room. Five officers from the second vehicle charged the front door. Rifles up, they slipped through the entrance and advanced into the living room, flowing past the furniture like a river around a rock. The point man stepped through the threshold of the kitchen.

The infrared electric eye awakened and completed the circuit.

The detonation leveled the kitchen. The blast pressure wave of displaced air rushed outward, carrying shrapnel with it. The first two men flew backward, their bodies shredded.

Shocked silence descended. A split second later, both vehicles emptied.

Dirks rushed to the side of his fallen comrades. After a quick check, he keyed his radio. "Two down. Three alive but critical. Need a medivac ASAP. House is booby-trapped. No one enters without EOD. Warn all teams."

ఌఌఌ

Keeping his weapon trained on the tent entrance, Deacon slanted a glance at his partner. One look told him Justice's nose had caught a scent. Tail stick-straight, the dog's ears were flat against his skull. His lip curled back into a feral snarl. At his low rumbling growl from deep in his chest, Deacon's skin crawled. "Justice! Down. Stay."

The dog dropped beside him, but his eyes remained glued on the tent opening.

A blast pressure wave crashed down on him, punching him into the dirt like a giant fist. A second later, the sound of the explosion reached him. With ringing in his ears, he wasn't sure he could believe the radio. "Two down. Three alive but critical—"

It didn't matter who it was that went down. Some of his brothers weren't ever going home. Deacon's eyes watered, and, like a ruptured dam, angry and guilt-filled tears flooded his cheeks. Beating his fist on the ground, he swore he wouldn't rest until he'd caught the sonuvabitch and brought him to justice.

ఌఌఌ

Dirks left the fallen with the medics and pointed to his team, along with the rest of vehicle two. "You guys are with me. Step where I step. Don't touch a damn thing unless ordered to. Shoot the bastard on sight. We don't want him cranking off anything else."

They entered the house single file, everyone following in his footsteps. He examined the remaining rooms from the doorway and, once he was sure they were clear, broke off two man teams to search the room. They methodically went through each room, closet, and space that could conceivably hide Tuefel.

Flash-bangs and stun grenades went off throughout the house, followed by shouts of, "Clear! Officer out!" and "Small room clear!"

Once the house was secured, Dirks barked into his radio, "Double back. Make sure no one is in here."

They swept through the house like a tornado. Dirks nodded to Andrews. They went down a hallway and stopped before the one door at the end. Together the two entered Tuefel's armory. Dirks scanned the room. Wall mounts for firearms ranging from pistols to rifles lined it. Several of them had gaps. "Looks like he's armed."

"Right."

Dirks turned to leave, then paused spotting a large, open safe. He zeroed on a metal case of grenades, took a step, and studied it, then glanced at Andrews. "No one enters the armory. There're missing grenades." The grenades worried him more than the gaps in the racks.

Something glinted in the light cascading throughout the damaged house. "Sonuvabitch."

"What?" Andrews asked.

"A case of grenades is sitting on a bed of C-4. And the bastard's run fishing line through all of the safety pins. That line's affixed to the door you're holding. Don't move that sucker an inch. Not if you want to walk outta here." Dirks slowly backed away from the safe.

"Fuck me!"

"No shit. Okay, slowly, and I mean slowly, lift your hand, and get outta here."

Following orders, Andrews retreated, stepping cautiously after Dirks.

Together, they eased out of the inner armory. Reaching the hallway, Dirks partially closed the outer door and keyed up his radio. "Command Post, Team Two. We've found another EOD problem. I'll handle it."

CHAPTER 42

He'd been right. The asshole cops were everywhere. *Scheiße*, they looked like an invading army. Hell, not even their eyes in the sky could find him, not with all these clowns pouring onto his property from every direction.

The shockwave from the detonation in his house rattled the cave. He snickered. From the sound of it, it must have been the kitchen. Once he'd finished his business here—taking out that fucking cop and his dog and the reporter—he'd clean up his final loose end, his informant. Chortling, Tuefel rubbed his hands. "The fool believes he's safe. He'll learn differently soon. He's so worried about surviving his war with cancer, he didn't remember that I'm the Krusnik for a reason." If he'd made one phone call, the man could have lived whatever time he had in peace. Now? Tuefel shrugged. Disloyalty demanded death.

"*Dummkofts.*" Tuefel closed the elevator door and jogged down the tunnel to the cave. He knelt on the cave floor near the vehicle ramp and tied a thin, monofilament fishing line to a support beam. Securing it, he tested it. Good. The knot wouldn't come apart. He laced it through a hook eye on the floor next to the cave mouth that he'd pounded into the wall months ago.

Like the *gut Pfadfinderen* of his youth, he believed in being prepared. *Ya*, okay he hadn't obeyed most of what they
taught. But that one, he'd always believed was critical to
one's survival.

Smiling, he slid the filament through the safeties of all
four grenades and secured it around another hook. The first
person opening the door would pull both safeties free and
the firing pins would slam home. The explosion would be
equal to the one in the kitchen. It would also bury the
gravesite.

Standing, he slipped his backpack on and secured it.
Time to execute his vengeance. With a sneer, he moved to
the rear ladder and scaled it. Reaching up, he grasped the
small handle on the metal covering and shoved it aside. As
he cleared the hole, he spotted Bautista. After confirming
the tent flap was shut, he inspected the corpse. The single
shot to the forehead had a small entry hole. The round's exit
had taken off half of the back of his skull. Brain matter,
blood, and bone littered the floor and stained the tent walls.

A tiny flare of regret for having blown off the top of
Luis's head flashed in his soul. Damn, there was nothing he
hated more than regretting his actions. Yet Luis had deserved better from him. The man could have gotten away
safely. Instead, he had stayed and tried to protect him, the
Krusnik, who had just threatened to take first his eyes, and
then his life.

He glared down at Bautista, his jaw clinched and teeth
grinding. His entire life, the only thing he'd held dear had
been destroyed because of this sorry piece of shit. Without
Rachele, his empire, his home, everything he had meant
nothing.

Kneeling beside Bautista's body, Tuefel hammered the
man's face until the bones were powder incased in pulp,
before systematically repeating the action over every inch of
his body. "*Dieses für meine Frau. Zurück zur Hölle von wo
Sie. Sie Stück Scheiße kam.*"

Finally satisfied he'd wiped the man's image from the

world, Tuefel kicked him into the cave below. A smile broke free as the body splattered like a dropped watermelon on the granite floor.

If he were retuning, he'd kick the body into the ravine. However since the cops were aware of both the bodies below and Bautista's death, Tuefel decided to leave it there. He'd soon be covered under several tons of stone. Because even if they didn't trip the traps he'd set, he'd wired the entire cave and tunnel with C-4 that he could trigger remotely.

After licking his fingers clean, he glanced at himself. "Fuck." No way could he mingle with the press looking like this. He unhooked his backpack and checked it over. Good. Clean. Stripping off the ruined clothing, he tossed them over body below and shrugged. Let the Krusnik's clothing, soaked in the traitor's blood, cover him.

With economical movements, Tuefel removed two packs of wipes, scrubbed himself clean, and dressed in clean clothing. He grabbed the sleeping bag and spread it out. Kneeling, he focused on centering himself.

The cops knew of the back escape route. That meant there had to be snipers covering it. He'd wait here until the cave entrance blew.

෴

"Everyone fall back to the MRAP! Now!" Dirks ordered. He glared at Andrews. "That means you, too. Stay clear until I contact you. No one goes back in."

"Copy that. Do whatever you need to do to make those damned things go away"

"Copy that." He piloted the robot to the back door of the MRAP, opened up his red EOD bag, and grabbed a block of C-4. Removing the explosive, he smashed the block as if it were silly putty into a longer and thinner sheet, wide enough to cover all the grenades and explosives.

He gently removed a blasting cap from his bag, attached

the cap to a nonelectric wire, and placed it into a cap protec-
tor. He flipped a switch. The claw of the robot opened and
he set the C-4 into its grip.

With the C-4 secured, he inserted the blasting cap into
the explosive, spun the robot around, and drove it back into
the residence. The spool of trunk line started to spin. Once
inside, he maneuvered the robot's arm and gently placed the
C-4 on top of the case of grenades.

He paused, exhaled harshly, and drove the robot out of
the residence. He pulled it back into the MRAP with him.
He checked his hands. Rock steady as always. Thank God.
He shot Andrews a thumbs up, then inserted a shotgun pri-
mer into his initiator and took the metal key off of his neck.

Satisfaction filled him. With a hint of a smile, he keyed
up his radio. "Command Post, Team Two. Prepare for another detonation."

"Copy that Team Two. Prepare for—what?"

"Fire in the hole! Fire in the hole! Fire in the hole!"
Dirks yelled as command barked in his ear.

The Aluminized HMX burned and hit the blasting cap at
just under seven thousand feet-per-second. The cap exploded setting off the C-4. The blast pressure cut through the
grenades and the safe as if they weren't there.

It continued through the armory, stopping only after it
had ripped throughout the house, tearing a massive hole
through the foundation, and into the earth below it.

CHAPTER 43

Deacon's teeth rattled with the blast of another explosion as a high-order gale flattened the clearing. Traveling through the ground, the accompanying shockwave shook him down to his bone's marrow. Around him, trees moved in a violent, deadly dance before they crashed into one another like an arboreal mosh pit.

His mouth went dry. *Oh please God, no more. Don't let that be more of my guys.*

A second later, he thought he saw movement in the tent. He adjusted his rifle and focused through its scope in time to spot Tuefel peek out of the tent with a reptilian sneer and then disappear inside. As Deacon adjusted his range, and missed his chance. Tuefel pushed aside the tent front flap. He had two pistols—one in each hand—as he sprinted, hunched over and zigzagging, toward White's position at the entrance of the lab. Deacon keyed his mic. "Smith, Washington, Deacon here. Tuefel's out! Two guns!"

Justice went nuts growling and barking. "Justice, down, stay!"

Before White responded, Washington and Smith opened up. Their target acquisition was a split second off. Sure, they obliterated the tent.

But they missed Tuefel.

Deacon knew where the man was headed—a rock ledge that overlooked the mouth of the cave. "Fuck," he muttered as pieces of trees and boulders blew apart around the man, and then he dropped out of sight.

Deacon barked into his radio, "White, Deacon here! You've got armed company headed your way!"

c∕ɔc∕ɔ

Tuefel raced to a rock ledge overlooking the cave entrance. He'd reached the ledge just as a SWAT team member entered his death trap. Hearing the safety pins spring free and the safeties disengage, he dropped onto his stomach. He covered his head and waited. A second later, there were four loud and distinctive clicks as each striker slammed into their primers.

"Shit! Retreat! Grenade! Fall back, damn it! Move! Move! Move!" one of the team screamed. A stick of men sprinted up the ramp and out of the lab.

Tuefel cocked his head, watched, and waited. Then the blast pressure wave hit, shoving the team's leader onto his back. No sooner had it passed over him then he pushed himself up and stood as the rest of the SWAT team staggered to their feet.

Even from his position, Tuefel heard a cop's voice over the radio's speaker. "—got company! Two guns coming your way! He's elevated! Rock ledge, rock ledge! Team Three get down!"

The team leader looked up at him.

Knowing he had sufficient cover, Tuefel squeezed the triggers and both guns started to flash. Several rounds struck the rear guard as he raced up the ramp, leading the retreat. As usual, they'd hit center mass.

Grinning, Tuefel watched the man pitch backward. The two officers behind him broke his fall. They tumbled to the ground in a tangled mess of weapons and fatigues. Still smiling, he continued firing on them even after their fall had taken them out of his the line of sight.

He scanned for the rest of the team. They thought they were protected by the massive stalactites and stalagmites of the cave. He knew better. For now, he'd play with them, let them think they were safe, wait for the cop and his dog. Then, when he was ready, he'd trigger the remote detonator. It was all in the timing.

He hit the magazine release of his guns. The empty mags dropped out of their wells and bounced on the hard pan. Pulling two full ones from his cargo pants pocket, he slammed the fresh mags into the hungry pistols. The slide releases disengaged and launched the slides back into battery with fresh ammo in each chamber.

Then he shucked off his backpack, reattached his guns at the small of his back, and removed his sniper rifle from the pack. He quickly assembled it, retrieved a full magazine, and smacked it into place. With his weapon ready, he slid on his pack and reattached it, snorting at the team leader's unceasing gunfire.

Rock splintered from the multiple impacts. Chips sprayed the area—downward, not up where he was located. The man was a fucking fool. Tuefel inhaled, feeling his heart rate soar. Until this moment, after ten years, he had forgotten how much he got off on this type of action.

A second later, Tuefel scowled as rounds pounded the granite within inches his feet. The fucking cop had adjusted his aim. Unwilling to commit suicide by cop, he dove for cover beyond the line of sight of the lab.

He heard a man, he assumed was the team leader, yell, "Evac that man, now! All of you fall back into the lab! Move it! Move now!"

Tuefel poked his head up and watched two officers drag their fallen comrade behind cover. As the leader continued to dump rounds, Tuefel sneered at the man's barked orders, "Stagger your shots. Conserve ammo. I don't want salvos. I want steady fire at that piece of shit."

Tuefel dropped to his belly as additional weapons—Glocks by the sound of it—joined the gunfire symphony. The slow, steady stream of bullets forced him to keep his head down. However, he wasn't trapped. Oh no, he was on the move.

He knew this land better than anyone, and he'd prove it. If the cops weren't scared, they were worried about their wounded and running out of ammo. Neither of which impacted him. As they continued to kill the rock from his last position, he chuckled at his pun. Their inattention gave him all the time he required to flank them.

Time for him to stay focused on his mission. His first priority: to take out the man rallying the team. Once he'd accomplished that, the rest of the team would be out of the fight.

With his ribs against the rock, he low crawled his way partially down the boulder-strewn hill. Making it unseen to a new position where he could utilize granite for cover, he pushed up onto his feet and darted east. When they once again attempted to escape the tunnel, he'd mow them down. His best chance of success was waiting until half the team was out. Then he'd trigger the explosives and pick them off one at a time.

CHAPTER 44

Deacon shook with rage. He prayed neither White's team nor his killed Tuefel. Deacon wanted the pleasure.

Suddenly gunfire ceased. Silence descended. Until that moment, Deacon had never understood how the lack of explosions and shots could be deafening. Now, he did and he didn't like the helplessness that came with it. Despair assailed him as he keyed up his radio. "White, Deacon! You copy? You guys all right?"

"Team Three, shots fired. Shots fired," White said.

"Copy that Team 3. Shots fired," command acknowledged.

Jaw clinched, Deacon asked, "Anyone hit?"

"One took two center mass hits. His armor held—barely. At present, we're all in one piece."

"Copy that, Team Three."

"Deacon, White. Thanks for the heads up. You guys see him?"

"Thank God, we didn't lose anyone. Give me a sec to check out my immediate area." Deacon ignored his pounding heart and burning eyes. Instead, he raised his rifle into position and studied the surrounding terrain through its scope. "Negative. He's somewhere between us. Watch your back. Peterson, this is Deacon. You guys see anything?"

"Negative. Our view's obstructed by dense foliage. Can't see a damn thing from here."

"Copy that," Deacon growled.

"Deacon, White. There's a large rock ledge by the cave entrance we used. He's up there somewhere. With him elevated, we're pinned down."

"Copy that. At the back of the lab, there's a ladder. Take it. It'll get you up to the tent we're covering. We can remain here and hold the ladder while you guys make it out."

"Negative. We'll hold here. If we give this up this location, he can flank us again."

"Copy that. Hold there. Smith and Washington will flank the entrance from the south. Justice and I'll move in from east and trap his ass. Hammer and anvil."

"Copy that. Watch for crossfire. Let us know where you're at so we don't shoot your asses."

"You don't have to tell me twice."

Smith and Washington remained behind cover. Washington kept his rifle aimed down the trail while Smith called up to Deacon. "Do we have to get down there and do something?"

"No. You guys follow him. Don't take the trail. Swing wide and to the south. Make sure he isn't waiting for you. Don't walk into an ambush."

"Copy that. What are you going to do?"

"We'll take the east. Hopefully, we'll catch *his* ass in a crossfire."

"Let's do it."

Deacon watched Washington and Smith sweep south of the trail and vanish into the foliage. Then, side-by-side, he and Justice raced into the forest.

സസെ

Tuefel slithered through the brush. He should have taken the name viper, not Krusnik. East of the cave, he slunk up the embankment. With his rifle pointed at the ground, he paused and surveyed the land below him. Cops were textbook. They were marshaling for a counterattack—where his last position was—and he'd detonate the explosives then pickoff those who had gotten out at his leisure. Then he'd kill that sonuvabitch and his dog.

Kneeling behind a rock, he braced his shooting platform on a tree stump overlooking the lab entrance. He had a clear view into the cave. He saw silhouettes of the cops grouped in a kill box. Screw waiting for some of them to leave the cave and become easy pickings.

Reverting to his former habits, he made a cross as the good Catholic he'd been. He licked his lips, inhaled, and slowly released his breath. A small smile playing at the corners of his lips, he aimed his rifle. With systematic precision, he unloaded.

ⱷⱾⱷⱾ

Hearing weapons fire and screams of agony, Deacon shoved all emotion into an imaginary black hole. Right now, it was the enemy, preventing cold, logical thinking. His brothers had only one chance. Nothing short of death could stop his partner when on a hunt. Especially when he scented adrenaline-saturated air. "Justice, bikesh!"

The dog lunged forward, dragging him through the woods. As they plowed through the foliage, branches groped and grasped at his sweatshirt. "That's a good boy. Good boy. Where is he?" He released the lead line, freeing Justice. "*Ta'vi.* Find the sonuvabitch."

Deacon watched his partner to the exclusion of all else. Nose low to the ground, he sniffed, seeking Tuefel's scent. Spittle sprayed out of his mouth. Legs spread wider than his body, his paws gripped earth and tore into the dirt and rock. *Justice has him and is going to take me right to him.*

Entering the clearing, Justice's head snapped up. He

bolted as Deacon, running full out, struggled to keep up. They rounded a bend. He saw Tuefel. His heart skipped a beat. From on high, Tuefel was taking out his friends.

Deacon raised his rifle and pressed the trigger. Nothing. Jam! He slung his rifle across his back, drew his sidearm, and glanced down at his expectant partner. Time to bring out the big guns—commands in Hebrew for pursue, attack, hold, go. "Justice, *radaph, charab, achez, alaz*." He watched his partner take off like a locked-on heat-seeking missile.

Tuefel set his rifle aside, reached into his pocket, and removed a black box with a metal switch.

A detonator. "Shit!" Deacon knew Justice wouldn't arrive in time. Raising his gun, he prayed it could travel the distance with accuracy. He locked on his target and pulled the trigger—too hard. His jerk on the trigger lowered his barrel. The bullet shot out.

Deacon's eyes widened. The bullet sliced through the man's left calf muscle. From here, it appeared the bone was shattered. As Tuefel stumbled, Justice streaked toward him. Tuefel managed to draw a pistol. Justice took a flying leap.

A single shot rang out.

"Justice!"

A whine sliced through the air, piercing Deacon's soul. He'd never heard a louder sound—surprising, considering he'd been firing his weapon. Yet for some reason, he'd expected the loudest sound he'd ever hear would be a bang when expecting a click or a click that should have been a bang. He was dead wrong.

The man tried to kick him. He missed. Justice tackled Tuefel at twenty-five miles per hour. His open maw clamped down on Tuefel's right calf. Inertia caused them to spin. Tuefel's pistol slid over the edge of the cliff. His black box landed at his feet.

Deacon watched their collapse to the ground. The sound of their impact was accompanied by the echo of a bone splintering and a blood-curdling scream.

Justice's head shook side-to-side.

Tuefel pitched forward. His jaw broke his fall. Teeth smashed together. He spit pieces of two of them onto the ground. During the fray, he'd severed his tongue. It landed with a wet plop beside him as he coughed, blood spraying out from his mouth.

Justice's teeth locked together and he chipped a molar on what remained of Tuefel's nearly severed shin. The dog whined, tightened his grip, and clamped down.

Tuefel's eyes bulged. His leg a prisoner, he rolled onto his side. Arm shaking, he reached for the detonator.

Deacon raced toward them. "No!"

Tuefel's fingers wrapped around the device.

Deacon fired again. His round drilled through Tuefel's left eye socket, the hollow point round expanding to three times its original size, pureeing Tuefel's brain, and then exploded out the back of his head.

Tuefel's limbs went limp. His arm dropped. His hands spasmed. The detonator tumbled harmlessly onto the ground.

CHAPTER 45

Deacon skidded to Justice's side. "Medic," he screamed. His fingers threaded through bloody fur and located the wound. Tuefel's bullet had entered his chest and exited through the left shoulder. Due to the heavy bleeding, Deacon knew it was life threatening. How Justice had hung on to that leg bewildered him.

While he continued hollering for help, Deacon begged God to save his friend. Struggling to slow the flow of blood, he ripped off his sweatshirt and applied pressure to the wound's gapping exit hole.

Justice howled, gnashed his teeth, and snapped at him. The chipped tooth sliced a shallow groove in Deacon's forearm. He ignored it, rejecting any thought of stopping the compression. Dark red blood saturated the shirt and oozed through his fingers. "Hang on, buddy. Please, hang on. You'll be okay, I swear." He lifted his head and shouted, "Damn it, where the hell's that medic?"

His team charged over to them. While Washington hand-cuffed Tuefel's bloody mess and secured the weapons, Smith keyed up his radio. "Command post, it's Smith. Tuefel's down. Confirmed 11-44. We need medics and officers ASAP. We have two officers down. One's in the lab. And Deacon's partner is bleeding to death above it."

"Copy that, Team Three. K9 officer down."

Deacon thanked God for Justice's refusal to let go. He was a true hero. Just as now he fought to live, he'd disregarded the pain and still maintained his crushing clamp on Tuefel's leg. "Justice, out." He'd just ordered the dog to release and was ignored. Nothing.

The dog's eyes stared up at Deacon. Defiance burned in them.

Shit. He'd forgotten to say "out" in Hebrew. "Justice, *shamat*!"

On a low, pain-filled growl, Justice snapped the leg off, held the lower half in his mouth, then spit it out, and coughed. Actually it sounded more like the hacking a cat made with a hairball.

"Right, I've got it. You're hurting and don't want me ordering you around. Tough. Live, you belligerent hound."

As White's team fanned out and secured the area around them, he and his medic raced up to Deacon and Justice. The medic spoke first. "He's not gonna bite us, is he? He's hurting and may not recognize I'm trying to help him. Wrestling with him will only injure him worse."

"Get your ass in gear and keep him alive until we reach the hospital, or you'll have worse than a dog bite to deal with," Deacon growled. Swallowing hard, he gently restrained Justice, holding his partner's head still with one hand while maintaining pressure on the wound with the other.

"You're going to be okay, buddy. You're going to be okay. Don't you fucking die on me." Deacon drew strength from the fact that the dog's gaze never left his. From the corner of his eye, he saw the medic flip open a butterfly knife. "What are you going to do?"

"Shave the fur off around the entrance and exit wounds. Can't treat what I can't see." After he gave the dog two locals for pain, he pitched the syringes into his case. "They should help somewhat. While it's designed for humans, it should work on canines."

He rummaged through his pack, removed a couple packages of antibiotic-and-coagulant-coated blood stoppers.

Deacon grabbed one, tore it open with his teeth, and tied
the straps down, plugging the exit hole in Justice's side. The
medic applied the other one on the entrance wound. With
the application of each bandage, Justice softly whimpered.

"That's about all I can do. Get him to a vet. Now."

"Will do." Deacon squatted, slipped both arms under his
partner, and, as he stood, lifted. He didn't feel a single
ounce of the shepherd's one hundred twenty pound weight.
"Don't worry, buddy. I've got you. Let's get you to the
doc." He walked as rapidly as possible without jostling Justice more than necessary. Washington and Smith led the
way and White covered their rear.

Deacon winced at Justice's labored and shallow breathing. He didn't know if the problem was from the painkillers
or from the blood loss. It didn't matter. Because Justice was
barely hanging on. Worse, with Deacon's adrenaline dump
tanking, Justice's weight had begun to tax what strength he
had left. He slipped and stumbled over the uneven ground.
Frightened he'd drop his friend, he loped down the trail to
their vehicles.

Between his gasps for air, Deacon said, "Smith, hit my
door pop." The rear passenger door slid open. With a slight
backward lean, Deacon power-walked to the car and, set-
tling Justice in the back seat as gently as he could, was rewarded with a faint and weak whine.

He tossed Smith the keys. As Smith slid behind the steering wheel, Deacon crawled into the back. His hands stroked
his partner's head and ears. "Go."

Smith flipped on the Code Three siren and punched it.
Smoke and burned rubber filled the air behind them.

With the backs of his fingers, Deacon brushed the dog's
muzzle. "Hold on, big guy. Just hold on. You're gonna make
it."

The rear of the car swerved. Dirt and gravel swirled like
a miniature tornado. Siren screaming, the patrol car rocket-

ed down the highway like a flashing red and blue missile.

"There's a clinic near the end of town on the right. Go, go, go."

Siren wailing, Smith accelerated. All eight cylinders of the engine roared.

Deacon leaned over Justice and watched in horror as his labored breathing weakened and slowed. "Come on, man. Drive!"

The car slewed into the parking lot of an old post office turned veterinary clinic in Oakhurst and hit a newspaper stand, crushing it. Deacon's head hit the ceiling. Justice banged into the cage with a heavy thud. The car skidded to a stop on the sidewalk before the front door and the siren died.

Deacon pushed his door pop. The hydraulic arm engaged. The door sprang open. He jumped out, landing in the flowerbed. He gently lifted Justice from the car. Blood-soaked bandages painted Deacon's hands crimson.

Smith sprinted to the entrance and held the door open.

Carrying Justice in his arms, Deacon hurtled through the door. Finding no one in the lobby, fear seized him. He could feel his partner's life pour out onto his hands.

"Someone help us!"

Wearing scrubs, an older man, with a stethoscope around his neck, raced through a pair of swinging doors with a younger woman at his heels. "Easy, son, we were just in the back. What happened to—"

"M—my pa—partner's b—been shot. H—handgun. Single gunshot, A through-and-through. Entered the chest. Exited the shoulder. H—he's lost a lot of blood. Please, help him."

"We have to get him into surgery. Now." The vet stretched out his arms, his palms open toward heaven.

Helpless, Deacon transferred his friend to the vet. Blood dripping onto the floor, Justice looked back at him. His hollow gaze lacked the fire Deacon always saw in the rearview mirror.

The nurse nodded to the vet and disappeared down the hallway first. Carrying Justice, the vet waddled up to the double doors and shouldered through them.

Powerless, Deacon could only watch through the doors' plastic windows as Justice was lowered onto an operating table. He heard muffled orders and saw instruments placed onto a medical tray with a metallic clang. Poorly oiled hinges squeaked as the doors swung back and forth until coming to rest.

Seeing his partner's eyes close and his chest stop moving, Deacon fell to his knees. Exhaustion assaulted him. Without adrenaline to sustain him, fear of losing Justice overwhelmed him. He finally broke down and sobbed into his bloodstained hands.

CHAPTER 46

"F or actions of heroism and bravery and going above and beyond the call of duty, I hereby bestow upon you the Cain Police Department's highest honor, the Medal of Valor."

With a gold medal hanging from each of their necks, Smith, Washington, White, and Deacon stood on the podium for their Kodak moment. Deacon lifted the medal—a gold star with a red, white, and blue ribbon. The California seal took center place. Above it were the words "Medal of Valor." Along the bottom of it was "Cain Police Department."

As he examined it, all he could think of was that, after Tuefel's takedown, two of theirs hadn't come home with them. Why the four of them had metals draped around their necks baffled him. He released the decorative noose, let it drop onto his chest, and turned his attention back to ceremony.

The chief stepped back and motioned to the four of them. The crowd stood, their clapping drowning out the functioning waterfall. And wasn't that a kick. The thing actually worked. After a moment, the chief moved forward again and shook each of their hands.

When he reached Deacon, he leaned in close and whispered, "You're the biggest shit magnet this place has ever seen."

"Thank you, sir."

"Don't ever pull another stunt like this, or you'll be cleaning up shit at the animal shelter until you retire."

"You got it."

From across the room, excited barking joined the applause and jerked Deacon back to the present. Grinning, he took in Justice's medal, which luckily covered the bald spot on his chest. Every time Deacon looked at him, he smiled. If not for the missing fur, no one could tell Justice had been shot. He was his old self, farting and playing and waiting excitedly for the next mission. Too bad about the stitches and bald spots since the rest of his coat was shiny and smooth. But as he told Justice whenever the dog saw his reflection and whined, it wasn't a big deal. Fur grew back.

At the conclusion of the ceremony, some of the well-wishers broke for cake and punch. However, a crowed swarmed around Justice, patting his head and telling him what a good boy he was. And the ham loved every minute of it. Smiling, Deacon knelt beside his partner for photos and slaps on the back. When he glanced up, he caught sight of a brunette ponytail moving through the throng. *No way it's her.* His heart lodged in his throat. He pushed his way through the crowd, dragging an upset and frustrated Justice behind him. Apparently, the dog wasn't finished being fawned over. God help him. His partner had turned into a prima donna. Before he made it through all the well-wishers, the ponytail turned toward the lobby and disappeared. Pulling free, he raced to the front of the station. It was empty.

If he'd actually seen Jessica, she was long gone now. He glanced down at Justice and scratched behind his ears. "Well, partner. What do you say about buying that new TV we've needed for a while?" At Justice's sneeze, Deacon chuckled. "You're absolutely right. We'll go tomorrow." It took a while for the barking and prancing to stop.

ೞೞೞ

There was something to be said for getting back in to a routine. Yeah, *it sucked.* Jessica stared morosely her litter-covered desk. For whatever reason, she couldn't concentrate like she once had, blocking out all thoughts of anything other than work in the name of her job.

, She found it strange that, confirming the extent of the company's merchandise losses didn't interest her the way it would have two weeks ago. That was BD—Before Daniel. Considering the life-threatening chaos she'd endured two weeks ago, the new normal was to be expected.

It was no surprise that taking part in a high-speed car chase, pursuing an insane killer, almost being murdered—twice—and kissing Daniel had shattered her perspective on life. BD, she'd be outraged over the condition of her still damaged house. BD, she'd be outraged impound hadn't returned her car until earlier today. BD, she'd be outraged and seeking a restraining order against the media still circling her house and store like the vultures they were.

Even with her new reality, she hadn't altered a damned thing or followed through with any of the promises she'd made herself in the big picture. If she truly wanted to grasp life by both hands, then why in the hell was she at work? She had so much vacation time she'd entered use-it-or-lose-it territory. Why hadn't she reconnected with her old friends? All she needed to do was dig up her old address book and let her fingers do the walking.

She realized she was sick of her own bullshit.

If the past couple of weeks had taught her nothing else, it was that life was short. It was meant to be lived with gusto not as a drudge. If she acted accordingly, her recent experiences could prove transformative. Assuming she was brave enough to follow through on the pledges she'd made as she trudged through the rain.

She decided that the first thing she should do was call a

contractor to fix her home. The insurance adjuster had already confirmed her policy covered the damage. Then she'd go to the beach. She'd always wanted to learn how to surf. She might even go to Hawaii or take a cruise. She had the money—and the time. She needed to review why she'd chosen this profession, working in retail. Yuck. The hours were terrible. The quarterly demand for ever-higher net profits was soul killing.

Decisions, decisions, decisions. "Fuck it, I'm taking a vacation. Maybe a week at a spa. That way I can reassess my future while receiving daily massages." How had she forgotten her love of being pampered—facials, manicures, pedicures, massages of every kind. A spa it was—and not for one week, but two.

Certitude filled her. Tension bled from her. Shoulders loosened and descended from brushing her earlobes. With a grin, Jessica tossed back the last of her latte and pitched the cup at the garbage can. It hit the rim, wobbled, and toppled in. "Yes, ten points," she said, spinning in her chair and jerking her raised fist down.

Sighing, she stared down the overdue final inventory. And here was yet another change. She'd gone from being OCD, with nothing out of place, to not caring about her paper-cluttered desk.

With a gusty exhale, she propped her elbows on the desk and rested her chin on her laced fingers. "Work or the beach. Work or the beach. Come on, Jessica, decide." Licking her lips, she forced herself to admit, that wasn't the real question. "Call Daniel or not. Call him and find out if he really meant that kiss. Come on, Jess, be brave. Be the balls-to-the-wall woman corporate thinks you are. What's the worst that can happen?" Her shoulders slumped. "He's found someone else to kiss. And wouldn't that bite?"

Sniffing, she remembered how he hadn't smiled or acknowledged her presence at the ceremony. Hell, where was the woman who'd chased a killer through the streets?

CHAPTER 47

With Justice at his side, Deacon approached store. The door's electronic infrared eye, sensing the break in its beam, retracted the automatic doors. Entering the store, Justice head-bumped his thigh. He glanced down at his friend and chuckled at the doggy grin—mouth open, tongue hanging off to the side with slobber dripping on the floor.

Deacon crouched in front of him and scratched behind his ears. "Yes, we're going to see her. Just be a good boy, okay?"

Justice's cold, wet nose touched his.

"Glad to see we're in agreement," he whispered. Smiling, he stood, squared his shoulders, and approached the customer service counter with his buddy beside him. After being ignored for a couple minutes, he cleared his throat.

The clerk's head jerked up. "Oh, I'm sorry. I knew someone had entered but when I checked, I didn't anyone."

"No problem. I was just reassuring my buddy."

Chomping her gum as if she were a cow chewing its cud, the clerk nodded and glanced over counter. "You're buddy's a dog?"

"Yes, he is. We're cops. Could you page—" Confusion settled upon him like a wet blanket. Damn, where did he know her from? Apprehension crawled up his throat like acid. Had he arrested her? Was she a potential threat to Jess? Then he recognized her. "You used to drive a Chevy Cobalt, didn't you?"

The clerk gasped and swallowed her gum, nearly choking on it. Her gaze narrowed as she studied him. "Yes, but I totaled it a couple of weeks ago. How did you—"

"Sally Henderson, right?" Her nod and nametag confirmed it. He grinned. "I'm the officer who pulled you over a couple weeks prior for speeding and rocking out. Later, I heard about your crash. Sorry about your car, but I'm relieved you're okay. According to the officer at the scene, it was touch-and-go for a while."

"Yeah. My folks said I'm lucky to be alive." Her face put a beet to shame. "It forced me to get a job."

"Forced you?"

"Yeah, after the wreck, they said, 'If you want another car, prove to us you've grown up and deserve one. Get a job. Save the money, and we might help out with the purchase of a used car.' Can you believe them? I mean it isn't as if they don't have the money. They bought me that Cobalt for my sixteenth birthday—new," she snapped.

Deacon struggled to maintain a bland expression. But it was hard. All he could think about was how self-absorbed and entitled that last statement was. It pissed him off in a hot minute. As he studied her, disgust swelled. Foolish, stupid, spoiled little girl. What had this generation become? Didn't she realize she was fortunate to have the parents she did? Shit, if she'd been his daughter, she'd be walking or taking the bus until she could buy a vehicle on her own. Maybe then she'd appreciate it and having survived an almost fatal accident.

Before he could think of a response, his partner lifted his right hind leg, bumped Deacon's left knee, and began scratching like mad at his neck. Each time his claw touched his badge, it clanged against his pinch collar, creating an instrumental cacophony.

"What—" Sally leaned over the counter and stared at Justice.

Deacon followed her horrified gaze. Yes, Justice's stitches stood out in stark relief against his skin. And to be fair, his buddy could fit perfectly into the post-apocalyptic world of *Mad Max* in both appearance and, sometimes, temperament. But so what? The damned dog was a cop and a hero with a medal to prove it.

Then Justice sneezed. His snot smacked her right in the chin and dribbled onto the counter. And if that hadn't been bad enough, his upper lip snagged behind a lower fang. The poor guy looked like he'd escaped Hell. Come to think of it, he had.

Sally's squeak was quickly followed by a shudder and backward jump. Several, interminable minutes of wide-eyed silence ensued. Finally, she seemed to shake herself out of her paralysis. Grabbing a cloth from under the counter, she wet it and scrubbed her chin. "Gross, now I'm gonna have to redo my make up." She shot a glance to the window overlooking the sales floor. "Maybe I can wait until my break." She paused and gave Deacon a glint-eyed glare. "I'm, sorry, sir, but pets aren't allowed in the store."

Deacon glanced at Justice, then lifted his head and winked. "Him? He's okay. We're also friends of Jessica Grady. Would you please let her know Daniel and Justice are here?"

"You don't understand. No animals are allowed in the store. I'm sorry, sir. But if you don't take him outside, I'll have to get the manager."

Jeeze, Louise, didn't the girl ever listen? Deacon knew he'd told her they were both cops and he'd pulled her over. Lord save them from her self-absorbed idiocy, because Deacon doubted anyone else could. He smirked. "Good. Go get her."

When Justice growled low and soft, Deacon suspected it would expedite whatever Sally did, be it phoning Jess or racing up to her office. When she bounded up the stairs two at a time, Deacon glanced up and sent a silent thanks heavenward. A second later, he and Justice bolted after her.

At the second floor landing, Sally jerked open Jess's door and ran inside.

Grinning, Deacon gave Justice a hand command to sit and stay. Chuckling at the direction their lives had taken, he glanced around the doorjamb and into the office and saw Jessica.

Her chin resting on laced fingers gave the initial impression of tranquility. Her steely-eyed glare at Sally destroyed that illusion. Here was hoping she was more forgiving and receptive to their visit.

"But why are you so angry? I've said I'm sorry for not knocking and barging in unannounced."

"I know, Sally. You've said sorry to me at least twice a day since I hired you. This is your last warning, don't do it again."

Deacon's brows arched at Sally's hands fisted at her side. He didn't want their visit to cost the girl her job. Then again, the silly twit never seemed to learn. Relaxing against the doorjamb, he settled in to watch an interesting show.

"I wouldn't have done it, if there wasn't a problem customer."

Head still propped up, Jess murmured, "Really, what is it this time? Did they request you spit out your gum? Or was it that you actually provide them with customer service and stop shooting the breeze with your friends on your cellphone?"

"No, none of those things, Ms. Grady. He brought a dog into the store and refuses to take it outside."

Deacon grinned at Jess's eye-roll and heavy sigh. "I'm too busy to deal with that at the moment. Let it slide. Besides, a purse dog do can't do any damage and it won't be the first time it's happened."

"That's just it, it isn't a purse dog. He says they're cops and it's the biggest, ugliest, damned German Shepherd I've ever seen."

Jess's head jerked up. "Did you say German Shepherd?"

"Yes. It's a giant shepherd and it slobbers, too. It has two big bald spots and, well, it looks like a zombie dog out of *The Walking Dead*. And when it growled at me, I just knew it was gonna rip my throat out. So I came up here to you for help," Sally muttered to the floor.

Deacon laughed. When Jess's gaze locked onto his, he winked. "Hey, beautiful, mind if we come in?"

"You're here. You've actually come," she whispered. Blinking rapidly, she slowly stood. "I'll handle this, Sally. Return to your register."

Deacon chuckled and Justice snorted as Sally flew past them. Before he could take a step toward her, Jess had rounded her desk and launched herself at him. Thankfully, he'd seen her coming and was prepared. Wrong.

Clasping her to him, he fought to remain upright as she wrapped her legs around his waist and smothered his face in kisses.

"It's good to see you, too, Jess."

"I thought you wouldn't call."

"Really? I vowed our kiss was the first of many, not the last, remember?"

With a sniffle, she tucked her head against his neck and nodded. "I've been so worried about you—and Justice. I heard at the ceremony about what Tuefel did to him."

"Justice and I are on the mend. But I've gotta tell you, I truly think kisses are the best medicine a guy can get."

Hearing his name twice proved too much for Justice. He stood and jumped from foot to foot. Jealous whines soon had them on their knees beside him, rubbing and scratching everywhere he desired.

Deacon watched Jess while her fingernails scored his dog's fur behind a pair of radar dish ears. When her eyes met Deacon's, he smiled. *There are the eyes I've missed.*

"Well, Officer Deacon. Officer Justice. To what do I owe the pleasure?"

"Well, we happen to be in the market for a new TV. Then

I remembered I knew the perfect person to ask. Is Brian around?"

She reached over and shoved his shoulder. "Hey! Not funny, *Officer*."

"Not joking, Miss Grady. I figured he would know which TV I should buy. The store would then get credit for the sale. You could put it off to the side and I'd pick it up later, if that's possible, and I hope it is. Because that means I can take you out to dinner right now. If memory serves, we never had a chance to finish what we'd started."

"That sounds like a great idea."

Deacon stood and shuffled his feet. He frowned. "I thought I saw you at the awards ceremony. Why didn't you stay? I tried to find you. I even went out into the parking lot, but you weren't there."

Once again, rapidly blinking water-filled eyes, she nodded. "With all your friends and colleagues congratulating you—" She shrugged. "I didn't want be a fifth wheel. You know, get in the way."

"You *are* and never will be in the way. All of those people preventing me from reaching you. Being with you."

She beamed up at him. "You drive a hard bargain, Officer. Dinner it is. But I have one condition."

Staring into her smiling face, his heart melted—again—and he suspected it would for years to come. "And what's the condition?"

She canted her head toward Justice. "He's a good boy and I love him to death, but he stays in the car."

With a groan, Justice flopped to the floor and rolled onto his back.

Deacon snickered. "Look at the drama king." His gaze met Jess's. Returning her smile, he grasped her outstretched hands and helped her to her feet. Holding her close, he nuzzled her neck and inhaled the intoxicating scent of perfume and Jess. He hadn't met a woman alive whose natural fragrance could top Jess's. "Granted. I thought we could go to the local steakhouse and relax over a couple of drinks, while we wait to be seated. Does steak, potatoes, and maybe some dessert sound good to you?"

"Absolutely."

"Promise me you won't do anything crazy like ordering a house salad with dressing on the side and extra croutons as your main course."

She clasped his hands and laced her fingers with his. "Officer, I swear to you, you don't have to worry. I'll have the filet, rare. And just so you understand, I never settle." She leaned into him. "Only the best satisfies me," she murmured against his lips.

About the Author

Dustin Dodd was born and raised in the heart of the Central Valley of California in Clovis. He graduated in four years from California State University, Fresno, with a Bachelor of Science in Criminology with an emphasis in Law Enforcement and a Bachelor of Science in Psychology. He also attended California State University, Long Beach, where he graduated with a Master's in Public Administration.

He has worked as a police officer in the Central Valley in a region with nearly seven hundred fifty thousand residents since 2001. The region is famous for its easy access to Yosemite National Park, the Fresno State Bulldogs, and its agriculture. He currently works as a police officer in the Napa Valley. He met his wife Jenny in 2002 while she was a manager of a well-known coffee chain.

He has served his community as a patrolman, K9 handler, DUI officer, high-technology computer forensic analyst, homicide detective, crime scene investigator, Explosive Ordnance Disposal bomb technician and explosive breacher for the SWAT Team. He is currently assigned to the Patrol Division.

Dustin made notes of the true events he investigated over the years. Many of the incidents he was involved in, from search warrants to bombings, are stranger than fiction ever could be. It was from his exploits as a K9 handler, Bomb

Squad technician, SWAT breacher, and detective that he crafted "Savage Justice," his first novel with several more on the way.

Dustin served on the street with his K9 partner Kota for over four years. Kota's original name was Justice but his name needed to be changed for training to a shorter name in order to effectively give him commands during critical incidents. Dustin still serves his community to this day.